An Imitation of Life

Laura Solomon

AN IMITATION OF LIFE

Celia Doom is a grotesque, a giantess with progeria, a syndrome that makes her body age at three times the normal rate. Her horrified mother left her, newly-born, on the nearest doorstep. Let's not feel sorry for Celia, though. She is in part responsible for the devastation of her home town, Provencia (although the earthquake was not her fault). And she has been saved from a pitiable life by the gift of a camera. With this she documents the everyday lives of the townspeople as they pick their way through the wreckage that she has, to some extent, caused. Celia's singular story is told as she prepares a narrative for her final retrospective photographic exhibition which will be shown at last in the capital. *An Imitation of Life* takes the reader into a bizarre world where the extraordinary characters are lively distortions of people we may know. Aside from cockroach-eating Celia, Uncle Ed can "disappear" himself as well as objects in his magic show. Her adoptive parents Barry and Lettie together run the Butchette, a building created from the remains of Barry's Butchery and Lettie's Laundrette after the earthquake. Her two strong-minded grandmothers – Grandma Lolly (who ran a sweet shop) and Grandma Stuff, the widow of a taxidermist – give moral support.

LAURA SOLOMON was Joint-Winner of the inaugural international Proverse Prize (2009) with her novella, *Instant Messages*, subsequently published by Proverse Hong Kong in 2010. Also published by Proverse are *Hilary and David* (an epistolary novel) (2011) and *The Shingle Bar Sea Monster and Other Stories* (2012). Of Solomon, Maggie Gee wrote, when Chair of the Royal Society of Literature, United Kingdom, "Witty, clear-edged, both lemon-sharp and seductive, Laura Solomon is a writer to watch." Solomon has published two novels in New Zealand, *Black Light* (1996) and *Nothing Lasting* (1997). Her short story collection *Alternative Medicine* was published in the UK in 2008. Her first poetry collection, *In Vitro*, was published in 2011 by Headworx (New Zealand). Her plays have been produced at the Wellington (New Zealand) Fringe Festival and the Edinburgh Festival Fringe (UK). Among other writing prizes, she has twice won a prize in the Bridport (UK) International Short Story Competition. Her short story, "Sprout", first published in the Bridport Anthology, 2004, and then by Flame Books in the UK, was translated into Czech by Olga Walló and appeared in *krásná* in the Czech Republic in 2011. Born in New Zealand, Solomon spent nine years in London before returning to New Zealand in 2007. She has an honours degree in English Literature (Victoria University, 1997) and a Master's degree in Computer Science (University of London, 2003).

An Imitation of Life

Laura Solomon

Proverse Hong Kong

An Imitation of Life.
By Laura Solomon.
Second revised, enlarged edition published in Hong Kong
by Proverse Hong Kong,
11 April 2013, under exclusive licence.
Copyright © Laura Solomon, 11 April 2013.
ISBN 978-988-19935-5-7
Alternate edition: 26 January 2019
ISBN: 978-988-8491-57-5
[1st edition published in the UK by Solidus, 2009.]

Page design by Proverse Hong Kong.
Cover design, Artist Hong Kong Company.
Cover image by, "Grand-Duc, Wikipedia,
http://en.wikipedia.org/wiki/User:Grand-Duc",
licensed under the Creative Commons Attribution-Share Alike 3.0
Unported_license.

British Library Cataloguing in Publication Data.
A catalogue record for the first Proverse Hong Kong edition
of this title is available from the British Library.

Preface

I really dislike this novel. I dislike how it exposes a conceit at the heart of first-person narratives. I dislike it for its honesty. Its realism. I dislike *An Imitation of Life* (no connection to the original 1933 Fannie Hurst novel and its screen and television adaptations) because it imitates life instead of imitating how novels imitate life.

My publishers at Proverse Hong Kong warned (tempted?) me with the following précis of *An Imitation of Life*: "It is odd." They also deemed the novel a "page turner." The blurbs culled from reviews and featured on the backs of Laura Solomon's other Proverse books promote the same assimilative promise. Solomon's *Instant Messages* (2009) is "a page turner." Vaughan Rapatahana, Solomon's Kiwi countryfellow, declares her novel *Hilary and David* (2011) "Well-written" and "Absolutely unputdownable."

Still, it was the epigrammatic caveat "It is odd" that continued to pique my curiosity. The reason for this resulted from a pregnant pause. Proverse is run by a splendid, erudite couple. One of them described *An Imitation of Life* as "odd" then looked to the other, brow-raised, as if willing the spouse, who had just stepped into the room, to concur. After several moments of visible cogitation, the partner diplomatically assented, "Yes, it *is* odd." The thoughtful, understated Beckettian exchange prompted me to figure *An Imitation of Life* might be as "mundane and magical," as "disappoint[ed]"and "drama[tic]," as replete with "foolishness" and "the fantastic" as Solomon's short story collection *The Shingle Bar Sea Monster* (Proverse 2012). Supplementing these postmodern tensions is that narration throughout Solomon's oeuvre shifts between what a character late in *An Imitation of Life* calls "first person narration and 'eye of God' narration." Like, say, Joyce Carol Oates and Jane Smiley, for instance, Solomon seems equally at home employing first- and third-person narrators. A novel in first person. A novel in third. Short stories in the former. Others in "eye of God." Yet *An Imitation of Life* alternates between both forms, including free indirect narration. Sometimes Solomon's narrator Celia Doom impossibly (wonderfully? indicatively? convolutedly?) speaks for her own characters in first-person – and sometimes in third.

OK. I've jumped ahead of myself. Let me back up. Let me review. I told you I dislike this novel because of its faithfulness to realism qua realism, not realism qua literary convention. I proceeded to inform you of how I was introduced to *An Imitation of Life*, in the service of writing a preface for it. Then I cryptically jumped to a quotation that appears "late" in the novel. Let me add context to the quoted fragment that threw my preface out of joint. A little longer, the selection reads "...you describe episodes you could not possibly have witnessed. You switch from first-person narration and 'eye of God' narration." The critical interlocution here is George's. He's the agent semi-provocateur responsible for collecting the unpublished photographic work of Celia Doom. Celia, the über problematical protagonist of the novel, is as famous for her black-and-white shots as she is for her physical monstrousness. She suffers from progeria, a rare condition tripling the speed of her organic clock. Celia's afflictions also include giantism, sociopathism, misanthropy, lipodystrophy, and dissociative identity disorder. A monster without a Dr Frankenstein, Celia is human. George visits Celia daily, fumbling in her "attic to ferret around in [her] past." His rummaging does not reveal the representations he covets; Celia keeps her most poignant pictures hidden elsewhere, hidden from readers, and from herself. But what George does discover is the manuscript we are in fact reading. (Celia, Jane Austen-like, secretly writes as George fumbles.) George thereby represents us: Celia's readership. He reads what we read.

George's other critiques of the manuscript we are reading encompass the belittling obloquies commonly levied at postmodernist fiction. "Bam, bam, bam. One event after another. Where's the sense of flow? Where's the continuity?" "These characters just pop up and disappear. Nothing is ever fully developed." "There are also problems of pace. Time does not tick evenly through your pages. Sometimes a day seems to drag on forever, and sometimes a year is gone within a paragraph." Celia's rejoinders – "My temporal scale is out of whack"; "I'm out of time" – fall on deaf ears. "It's an incomplete jigsaw," George bewails.

George the marplot is right.

But so is Celia the monster.

The name Celia Doom evokes the anagrammatic Leica R Zoom, her favorite camera and lens. Even so, Celia's preferred lens is cracked. The un-replaced lens evokes the limits of all views, of all mimetic reproduction. Pace the poststructuralist play championed by Jacques Derrida, all representation – memorial, pictorial, ceremonial, narrativistic – is always already fractured, fissured, disjointed.

My favorite sentence in *An Imitation of Life* recalls the romantic notions of the déclassé Ralph in Edith Wharton's 1913 novel *The Custom of the Country*. Whilst honeymooning with his social-climbing wife Undine in France, poet-manqué Ralph rests on the grass only to see words floating in the air around him. Words for Celia, however, are far less lepidopteron. Her words are not butterflies. They are bats: "…as if the words that want to be written have wings, they flap about this house like bats, not content to rest in the belfry, they fly through these rooms, tangling themselves in my hair." Celia's theatricalized Big House allusions, abetted by iterated foci on Mnemosyne, unreliability, reflexivity, and monstrosity, pay homage to the work of Irishman John

Banville, who also writes under the nom de guerre Benjamin Black. Banville is a virtuoso at uncovering modernist meaning and connection and closure within the incongruities and disconnections defining our open-ended late-capitalist postmodern condition. Banville's first-person male narrators, like Solomon's most recent female one, are always in the midst of writing. They write from secluded bird's-eye-view locales: eyries, attics, bolt-holes, belfries.

Solomon's latest novel crucially addresses two conceits most novelists who write in first-person formally ignore: i) first-person narrators are themselves writers, and, ii) first-person narrators writing first novels are flawed writers. Solomon's patent honesty to this realist fact is a comment on how first-person narratives tend not to ascribe to what TS Eliot popularized as the "objective correlative." Let me back up a few more centuries. Prince Hamlet instructs his First Player to "Suit the action to the word." Hamlet's injunction, in other words, directs his actor to match his emotions to the causes at hand. Three centuries later, TS Eliot declares the play *Hamlet* an "artistic failure" because Hamlet himself overacts. Eliot sees Hamlet as hypersensitive, as over*re*acting to his present circumstances. Nevertheless, we could accuse the critic of the selfsame emotional aggrandizement. Eliot was not known for his expressive restraint.

Celia suits her actions to her words. She admits "[her] life has mimicked a bad novel" as she struggles to relate this abbreviated life: "It still sounds wrong, it sounds as if I am hitting false notes. I am out of key." Novelists, first-time novelists maybe especially, hit "false notes." They *are* "out of key." They *are* "out of time." They are, Hamletically, "out of joint." But not always. Celia, after all, proffers a flock of pretty pearls, a small congregation of which I've collected here and reshuffled.

a black rainbow

an oafish high wire artist
haunted by squashed ghosts
shrinking inwards
a gigantic violet

next door to an apocalypse
other-worldly sidekick
reluctant dresser of the dead
unnamed blamed

last ludicrous twist
shuck of the shackles
mask crack

An Imitation of Life

crack like my camera lens

words fell in midair
fell to the ground in silence
the split second that split time
the end of my life sentence

(The aesthetically beautiful verses in this found poem share the stage with tellingly pre-edited, clichéd Whitmanesque bravura, including the clauses "My name is synonymous with death," "I was now the giver of names," and "I am the town pet".) Found poems, as critic Walter Benjamin conceived of them, compel readers to play participatory roles in the making of meaning. The mixing and matching of much-loved lines allows individual arrangers alternate entry points to interpretation. Solomon makes a virtue of this puzzle-breaking and making, this detection and intellection. The page-turning I performed while (re)reading this oddly accomplished novel found me splicing back and forth to wonderful effect, re-membering, re-making. An "incomplete jigsaw" puzzle? Indeed. And necessarily so.

I really dislike this novel because it does what first-person novels so seldom do: it honestly exposes its own textuality. Beyond emphasizing a litany of personal illnesses made analogous to social pathologies (progeria, giantism, schizophrenia; isolation, hysteria, murder), beyond exploring a host of literary genres (Grotesque, Gothic, Picaresque, *Bildungsroman*), beyond featuring a murmuration of maladied personae (a magician, a mortician, a whoremonger, a pornographer, a taxidermist, an imposter), Laura Solomon does that thing we dare not do. She does not speak for her first-person monster; she refuses to appropriate the voice of Celia Doom. Solomon lets this monster relate her own, flawed, realist, human-all-too-human story.

Dr Jason S Polley
Hong Kong Baptist University
Kowloon Tong
Hong Kong

Jason S Polley is author of *refrain* (Proverse, 2010), *cemetery miss you* (Proverse, 2011), and *Jane Smiley, Jonathan Franzen, Don DeLillo: Narratives of Everyday Justice* (New York: Peter Lang, 2011).

I

I was born too soon. Mine was not an easy birth. Nature failed to take its course. From my mother's womb I was untimely ripped, torn out of the darkness and thrust into the light. I was six weeks premature but I had no need for an incubator. I was gigantic, clocking in at a heaving twenty-one pounds six ounces. I was triple the size of your average bubba, a great flubbering lump of an infant, who lay screeching upon her mother's stomach, fists slamming down into her flesh, tiny nails clawing across her skin.

I was torn from the womb complete with fingernails, toenails, a healthy head of hair and a good set of gnashers. My canine teeth were abnormally large and hung down over my lower lip. My eyes were not blue like the eyes of other babies; the left one was pitch black, as if it had been sliced from night itself and the other was plain white, a burning sun. My hair was not red, nor black, nor brown, but devoid of colour, as if being born had given me such a fright that it had bleached each and every strand of pigment. I was the scariest baby this world had ever seen. My mother took one look at me and decided that this first hello would also be a last goodbye.

I was the baby left abandoned in the basket. Unlike Moses, I had no river, nor were there bull-rushes for me to nestle amongst. My mother did not bother to remove me from my hospital blanket; she was too scared to unwrap me. She wanted me out of her sight. I say basket; it was a box. Brown cardboard it was, with *Barbados Bananas* printed on the side in yellow ink. Exotic. There was nothing else in there with me: no note, no rattle, no dummy for me to suck. I had been left to my fate; a fate which would prove to be both terrible and great. It was not my lot to be mediocre.

This is the story of how I came to be, as it was told to me by Lettie, when she wanted to remind me that I did not belong to her, when she wanted to disown me. She would start with my humble beginnings and move on to the ruckus I had managed to create in her household.

"Had I not had such a good heart," she would say, "you really would have been lost. Barry wanted nothing to do with you. If it hadn't been for me..."

My arrival had turned Lettie's ordered life upside down. I had so terrified the family cat that it fled into the night the minute it laid eyes on me and was never seen again. The dog, Mutt, an enormous and savage Alsatian, made a run for the far corner of his kennel, where he sat whimpering for the next seven weeks, venturing out only twice a day for a brief scoff at the food bowl and a quick slurp of water before dashing for cover again.

I was a difficult feeder. There was no question of the breast, and I was too bad for the bottle, chewing angrily through several rubber teats, and, in one instance, gnawing away on the bottle itself, milk spilling everywhere, plastic falling out of my mouth in gnarled fragments. Lettie soon resorted to a length of rubber hose, one end of which she would hold in my mouth, while she poured milk down the other. And I, I did not choke as a normal baby would, but took down as much as I could and saved up this sustenance for later, timely, regurgitation.

I was not a sleeper. I howled all through the night – great, long, otherworldly screeches which ricocheted around the house ensuring that neither parent was granted a single wink of sleep. Everybody had always said that my adoptive mother was a woman who had a good head on her shoulders, but even she was driven out of her mind by this thing, this freak with a capital F. She had no idea what to do with me. She was unravelling, at a loose end. Barry didn't want to know. He was pretending that I was not there at all. I stretched the limit of Lettie's endurance far beyond breaking point. She took seven long weeks of me and then she shoved me away, out of sight from the world.

The basement was her solution. To the old girl's credit, she did her best. It was not a case of merely shoving me down there amongst the bricks and the cockroaches; before she shut me away, she indulged in a wee spot of home decorating. She painted the walls in bright primary colours; great splashes of blue, yellow and red washing across the cellar in an attempt at cheeriness. She hung mobiles from the ceiling and placed soft toys and cushions upon the floor. There was a sheepskin rug and baby powder. There were two small windows and a dusty sort of light. Please, don't think my adoptive mama cruel. She was at the end of her tether; she felt that she had no alternative.

I had no visitors to my basement home; the only soul I ever saw was Lettie, who felt it her duty to continue to pay her twice-daily visits. The same routine every time; Lettie, appearing tentatively at the top of the stairs with a torch, peering down into the dusky gloom in an attempt to discern my mood before venturing into the cellar with her hose and her jar of warm milk. When she thought I was calm enough, and providing that she was feeling game, she would come down and feed me as quickly as possible before sprinting back up the stairs and into the safety of the house. She was especially terrified of my fangs, those gigantic canine teeth, which had grown at an alarming rate and hung down over the edge of my lower lip like the tusks of a walrus. She knew I could bite; she had seen what I had done to those baby bottles and she did not care to meet the same fate as that shredded plastic. She never came near; she stood at a distance and poked the feeding tube into my open gob and tipped sustenance into the other end of the pipe. And Barry's words would drift down from above. *What the hell are we gonna do with her?*

After three weeks in the cellar, my feeding difficulties escalated. I would take down none of the milk and nothing of anything else either. To me, it was all abject. Lettie tried using artificial flavouring: banana, vanilla, chocolate, strawberry. I was not interested. She attempted other liquids: orange juice, Coca Cola, lemon barley water, ginger ale, coffee, beer. I grew pale and wan, sallow, my cheeks became cold hollows, my big limbs began to wither. Eventually she struck gold, or, rather, orange. She poured Fanta down the hose and I guzzled like a baby calf at the teat. Fanta was the answer. And it remained the only thing I would drink for the next month and a half. Lettie figured that it was better the orange fizz than nothing, although she was unable to fathom how I managed to extract sufficient nourishment not only to survive, but to enlarge, for at three months, I weighed a hefty thirty-three kilos. Lettie did not believe that I could live on Fanta for ever; all that sugar and food colouring could not be good for a young 'un. At the beginning of my fourth month she grew understandably concerned. I was glowing an unusual shade of orange. She had heard me fizzing in the night. If I would not take milk, then I should learn to take solids or else my death would surely be imminent, and she did not care to have such a weight on her shoulders.

So it was that, sometime near the beginning of my fourth month, Lettie came down the cellar stairs with a hose in one hand and a bowl of some very sloppy looking pumpkin mash in the other. What was she thinking? I would allow that orange slop nowhere near me, nor the mashed spud or mushy peas or rice she tried to feed me, night after night, as she grew increasingly more desperate. This was familiar territory; this was the milk revisited. Perhaps, she thought, she's taking exception to the hose, and she risked spoon-feeding me, only to have me chomp through the metal like it was butter, spit out the remnants of the spoon and then take to her wrist for good measure, leaving puncture wounds like a vampire's kiss. She was tearing her hair out; she had large bald patches and she was going grey, besides.

I, however, had a secret. Lettie had been right; a young babe cannot live by Fanta alone. Unbeknownst to my adoptive Ma, I had been snacking on the sly. And unbeknownst to me, she got down upon her knees one evening when it was still light and pushed her eye up to the keyhole set into the cellar door and bore witness to her over-sized daughter crawling across the basement floor, snatching up bugs and insects from the dirt and stuffing them into her gob. Oh shameful truth! I had been feasting on these beasties for a good six weeks, ever since first sampling a rather slow-moving spider, and my palate and digestive system had come to crave these fine insect friends. They knew I was their master. The bees did not sting me. The spiders knew they were beat and did not scuttle away at my approach, but gladly gave their lives that I might live. On the other side of the cellar door, Lettie was gripped by a savage repulsion. Sensing her presence, my face flung towards the door and her horror was intensified. House flies fell struggling from my lips. A spider's leg hung from one corner of my mouth. The insectivore was outed. My substantial size was due not only to freak genes, but also to the many thoracic snacks I had been enjoying on the side.

She knew what I needed. Her newfound maternal guilt overcame natural revulsion. She could not allow me to continue to fend solely for myself. She had to believe that she was caring for me; she wanted me to exhibit signs of a normal infant's dependence upon its mother, despite my obscene behaviour, despite what I was.

She was a good old mum, in her own way. She took to catching bugs in jars and bringing them to me, holding them out in extended arms. *For you.* The bounty was always varied, a mixed diet, as well-balanced as could be expected under the circumstances. At the local fishing shop she found what came to make up the bulk of my intake; worms and maggots, squirming annelids, writhing larvae. I took to these with a passion, shovelling great fistfuls into my gob, frenzied, while Lettie turned away in nausea and fear and Barry sank yet deeper into denial.

They often longed to be rid of me. Barry talked of me as if I were some cheap chattel they'd purchased by accident.

"Maybe we could do an exchange. Take her down the orphanage and play swapsies. Bring us home a little angel to take the place of this devil."

And, in his harsher moments, he'd comment, "Her mother should've thrown her in a sack with a few rocks and drowned her, like a kitten."

It was Barry who remembered that they had forgotten to name me. The two of them had been doing their best not to speak of me at all, but when they found themselves forced to address the issue of yours truly, they spoke in hushed whispers and called me 'her' or 'she' or 'it'.

"I guess it might be easier if we gave it a name," said Barry to his wife one evening, as the two of them sat watching *Wheel of Fortune* on the telly.

"Shit," said Lettie. "That had clean slipped my mind. But what name would suit her?"

They racked their brains. Barry suggested Myrtle or Murgatroid or Muriel. Lettie came up with Daisy or Petal or Rose, hoping that the name might alter me, praying that I might come to resemble my moniker. Barry thought Doreen or Noreen or Maureen. Lettie thought Crystal or Moonbeam or Heaven. Barry thought Hell.

Eventually, after long debate, they settled upon Celia. Neither pretty nor ugly, neither spectacular nor plain, it was an in-between kind of name that they hoped I would live up to. It was middle of the road.

*

Only later did they match my first name to my last and realise that they had made a terrible mistake in the naming of Celia Doom.

*

Their lives were very much affected by me. Lettie thought she must have committed some terrible sin in a past life to be now so burdened, and Barry became a sort of meat-hacking, speechless automaton, staggering silently through his days, lost somewhere inside himself. He would rise, dress, eat, head to his butcher's shop, hack meat, eat, hack more meat and then return home to eat and watch the telly. At midnight, he would slink quietly off to bed. He'd once been popular with the ladies, but now gone were his saucy comments and his sly ways; this was a new and much subdued Barry, worn down by his new daughter to the point where his only defence was to try to pretend that I did not exist. Lettie made more of an effort. "Nature versus nurture," she would say to her husband. "She's not to blame for whatever horrendous genes she inherited. It's up to us to provide her with love and support. We must try to make the best of this worst of situations."

I was the black cloud that had entered their formerly sunny sky, the guest who casts a dark spell upon the wedding party, the evil fairy who arrives, uninvited, to the christening. I was the devil's walking parody on all two footed things.

All in all, I was not exactly a gift from God.

II

George, who has taken to calling himself my agent, shuffles about upstairs, thinking he will unearth some gem which will make his name. He's hunting for photos for my retrospective. *Good luck to him*, I think, I've stashed the jewels elsewhere while he frustrates himself sifting through endless garbage. No doubt he is stumbling across my many mediocre snaps, no doubt he is finding kid's toys, old rusty tools and tins of dried up paint; all the debris that accumulates in an attic over the years. But he will not find anything great up there. Everything great is elsewhere.

What does he take me for? I ask myself. *Does he think I was born yesterday?*

I sit in my living-room, staring at the broken glass of the Grandfather clock, wondering when he will come bumbling down that ladder, clutching his bounty and looking at me in eager expectation of his eleven o'clock cuppa and biscuits. From this vantage point I can see the shards of glass that lie beneath the hands of the clock, which still tick-tocks even though its face was smashed years ago. The little hand is on the eleven and the big hand slowly creeps round towards the twelve and right on cue, just as the old thing starts to chime its melancholy hour, I hear his clumsy foot upon the stair and then his face appears in the doorframe, *Time for elevenses, then* and I rise from my chair to put the kettle on.

I spy on him from the kitchen. He looks so small – my house dwarfs him; everything here is extra large, specially designed so that my gigantic self may live here in ease, great high ceilings, wide rooms, an enormous sofa, even the kettle is larger than an ordinary jug; the cups are oversized, and so are the plates. He must feel tiny here, like a bug, and lumbering about in that vacuous attic, it is amazing he does not simply vanish into empty space, into nothingness. He stands awkwardly in one corner of the living-room, shifting his weight from one foot to the other and then back again, and in his right hand he holds a stack of photos which he will show to me in an attempt to jog my memory, hoping for a neat little narrative, a joke, a few words to fit the picture. Maybe I will oblige and maybe I will not. Today, I am feeling a little disgruntled. I 'forget' to put sugar in his cup because I know he likes it sweet and I lay only plain biscuits on the plate, because I know he fancies the chocolate ones. Smiling, I enter the room and he spins to face me.

"Biccy?"

He extends one greedy hand and then lets it fall to his side in disappointment at the absence of chocolate ones.

"No thanks."

He doesn't dare ask for what he wants; instead he takes his cuppa from the small tray I carry and leaves it to cool on the mantelpiece.

"I was wondering if I could ask you to take a look at these," he says, extending the small clutch of pictures towards me, his hands shaking, just a little.

I fix him with my one white eye; I impale him upon its glare. I say nothing; I am comfortable with the silence, but he isn't. He shifts back and forth on his feet, he twitches.

"Please?" he adds. "We just need a few words. I'm not even asking you for a title..."

Titles! I think. Don't talk to me about bloody titles. I never named anything. Somebody else always did my naming for me. They dreamt up a whole load of silly titles: "Cracks In Pavement: Provencia 3am," "City Scar With Pigeons," "Two Old Ladies Share Tea." I used to blush when I saw the dull names they'd given things, because I knew the world would think that these words had come from *my* tiny mind. The shame of other people's words being pushed into my mouth. Sometimes they did the sensible thing and left the placard beneath the picture blank.

He takes the top shot from the stack he holds and passes it across to me, that sickening, pleading look in his eyes. I look down at what he holds.

Oh, George, I think to myself. *Why the hell did you have to choose that one?*

I know instantly exactly what it is. It is one of my early ones, a shot of one of Jacob's explosions. It looks like something falling together, but it is something flying apart. A sharp pang stabs me in the chest, as if somebody has stuck me with a knife. I remember it well; it was the first thing we did together. The bridge. But more of Jacob later. There's a lot to explain.

After I have seen this one, I don't want to see the rest. Something in me has been triggered, some defence mechanism. I am a soldier, defending an old war wound. I turn cantankerous.

"I think you'd better go now," I say.

I am thinking, *if you know what's best for you sonny, you'll skarper quick smart, no need to tell you twice.*

"But I haven't drunk my tea yet," he says impudently, forgetting that I have nonchalantly weathered storms that would have polished him off in two seconds flat, forgetting who and what I am.

"Out!"

I extend one arm and point to the doorway and when he doesn't leave I rise from my chair, raise myself up to my full gargantuan height and I tower over him, like Goliath and he, knowing he has no rocks to fling, turns on his heels and heads for the door.

After he has gone, I sit munching the biscuits he didn't eat and listening to the clock tick its two-four beat, waiting for the chime at noon, which signifies that it is time for my lunch, which today will be six fried eggs and eight rashers of bacon, just a snack, my appetite's nothing like it used to be, things slow down when you're my age, metabolism can't take the tucker that it used to. And my age? In real time I am thirty-two, but in my time, on my own special temporal scale, I have just turned ninety-six. I am knocking at death's door. But today, when the hour rings out, I do not head for the kitchen; instead, I walk to the old Grandfather clock and put my arms around it and haul it to one side, revealing the hole in the wall which that bumbling idiot wouldn't find in a month of Sundays. Here lie the goodies; the shots I refuse to show, the snaps which would, were I to go back on that promise I made to myself long, long ago and put them up for sale, fetch a tidy little sum. I cannot look at them without shivering.

*

I was the freak who froze time. We were not in fashion then, when I started. At least, not on this side of the lens. Diane Arbus had done her thing, immortalised her misfits then topped herself, so there had been one of you who supposedly *felt* like one of us doing us, but there had never been one of us doing you. Not that I'm a big one for making such 'us and them' divisions, but sometimes it suits a girl to steal the mentality of the so-called oppressor. Nowadays, of course, lepers are all the rage, especially those who've made it big in the art world. Only those outside, it is supposed, are fit to pass comment on those locked in. I've looked

An Imitation of Life

from both sides, from outside and in and now hunch within my misanthropy like a conch inside its shell. My hunch is physical as well as psychological. Years of trying to fit into spaces which were not designed for me, years of ceilings which were too low and walls which were too close together have resulted in a permanent stoop and an unsightly bulge on my right shoulder, like a bung wing trying to sprout.

Opposite me is a mirror. I peer sleepily into it, and am still shocked by what I see, even after all these years. They have served me well, my ugly mug and my creepy eyes. My face has been a good disguise; it has granted me protection. And now I hide out in this house, an old elephant waiting to die. It is well known that I refuse to have my photograph taken; it is common knowledge that I am a recluse. These things work in my favour. Without these details, I would be bland, just another glory seeking snap-happy kid. My own myth swirls about me like a floating black cape. My phone rings red hot, I am in vogue. I ignore them when they come knocking; I ignore the phone calls and the letters which flop through the slot and fall upon the floor.

George was not different, just timely. His letter fell through the slot whilst I was experiencing one of my rare moments of weakness; I was feeling needy. It was pure vanity on my part, letting him in. It was the desire to look back, to make one last effort at heaving myself towards immortality. It was the effect of getting old. The body decays with the spirit trapped inside. Something in me still wants out.

His seductive words poured off the page like liquid honey. *National Modern, a selection of works, genuine Dooms.* And the clincher. *Retrospective.* A sign that not only did you arrive, many moons ago, but also that you stuck around. A chance to look back, to tell the untold story. A chance to tell the story to *them*, our rivals in the capital, who have at last deigned to grant me some decent exhibition space.

George is a local boy who fancies he has some big-shot connections. He must have been pulling some strings; I still can't quite believe that after all this time they have consented to holding a Doom exhibition in one of their major galleries. They're probably hoping I'll croak right before opening night and send ticket sales through the roof.

I know exactly what they want from me. They want a neat little commentary, they want a cute package, just so much angst, just so much trauma, just so much joy. They want a facsimile of my life for the people to ooh and aah over. And I intend to play the game.

Oh yes, I will say, *a narration by moi? I'm flattered, really. Next month? No problem.*

And I will smile the crocodile's grin.

I have time on my hands.

They want realism but my life will not be reduced to trite facts and amusing anecdotes. It will not be neatly stored away for later viewing by greedy eyes. They will get my version of the truth, which is all that will ever be known. Part fact, part fiction. Where necessary, I will take liberties. It's my prerogative to make things up as I see fit.

I am aware, as I write this, that my words will be chopped, edited, filtered. What I write will not be what you read. I am told that this story will appear in a brochure which will be on sale at the exhibition, price yet to be agreed upon, probably fifty cents. You will finger my life story with grubby hands; greasy mitts will leave fingerprints on the glossy printed paper. On top of this narrative which they hope to sell, I have been asked to pen a short sentence or two about each framed snap; words which might be placed beneath each and every picture that hangs upon the wall. Each day he places some 'discovery' he has unearthed before me, and over tea and biscuits I belch out a few begrudging words for him to hold onto. He scribbles them all down frantically, as if afraid they will fade into nothingness as I speak them, afraid he will forget. These short phrases do not bother me; I am not concerned about their accuracy. Most of the time I make them up.

To tell the truth, I couldn't care less about the words that will accompany the pictures; the snaps tell their own stories. But they do not tell mine. Mine will be there, in the brochure, laid out plain, for all the world to see. As clear as day, as clear as mud. What I am interested in is what is expected and what I will deliver and the gap between the two.

They think they're getting a neat three thousand word summary, nothing too disruptive, melancholy or unsettling. They think they're getting a whisper, but they're getting a fist in the face.

What they're getting is a hurricane.

What they're getting is an epic.

III

After six months in the cellar, I made up my mind to start behaving nicely and be a 'good little girl'. The bad guy act was starting to wear a little thin. It lacked punch. They had grown oblivious to my antics. Lettie didn't even blink when I lunged at her leg in an attempt to fang her, and Barry had so blotted me from his mind that it was just as if I had never even existed. Further, as much as it pains me to admit it, I was lonely – I longed for human contact, any contact.

The devil donned the angel's mask. It gave poor old Lettie such a fright she nearly fainted. On that night, as I teetered on the brink of my second year on earth, she appeared, as per usual, at the top of the stairs, nightgown wrapped tightly about her body in an attempt to keep out the otherworldly chill that I emitted. In her left hand she held a jar of mixed goodies; spiders, house-flies, ants. In her right hand she held the torch. The cellar was as quiet as death. There was no screeching. There were no howls. She thought, at first, that I must have been snatched, stolen, and she heaved a slightly guilty sigh of relief at the thought. Descending into the basement, she scanned the room with the beam of her torch and caught a glimpse of me lying there, on my back. I was not absent. I was silent and still. I had never been silent before. I had never been still. Her second conclusion, then, was that I must be dead, and confronted by that thought, another guilty sigh passed her lips, followed by a cry of disappointment as I began to kick my legs in the air in slow, circular motions, as if pedalling a bike.

"Celia?"

I fixed her with my steely gaze. I broke the silence; I cooed. She was highly confused, I could see it. And then, my *coup de grâce*, I smiled. A beamer, a beautiful grin, splitting my face from ear to ear. It was as though the sun had come out from behind a thundercloud. Lettie gasped and switched off the torch, plunging us both into blackness. In the darkness, she gathered her courage and flicked the beam back on again.

"Celia? Sweetheart?"

I giggled and waved. Waved? She could barely believe her eyes, but there I was; those were my teeth, my hands, that was my hair, and those were my hefty legs. It looked like me, it was the correct exterior, but the interior, the spirit inside, was so radically different from what it had been before that she came to the conclusion that I had been not body-snatched, but soul-snatched.

She came tentatively forward, unscrewing the lid of the jar as she advanced, placing what she had gathered before me, like an offering. Tiny creatures scuttled to and fro behind the glass. Under normal circumstances, those poor critters would not have stood a chance, they would not have lasted more than two seconds before being snatched and devoured by your humble narrator, but I was not the same wee tyke that I had been before. I was attempting transformation. I had turned over a new leaf. I was Being Good.

My eyes were on the spiders. Carefully, delicately, taking care not to smash the glass, I reached out and upended the open jar. *Go free little friends*, I hissed and chuckled happily to myself as the creatures that I had let loose ran for all four corners. Lettie eyed me sceptically. I kept a straight face. That night I took down pumpkin and peas and spuds from a spoon. The implement remained intact and so did my adoptive mother's forearms. I sipped milk from a little plastic cup. It seemed too good to be true, but I didn't bite once. Lettie reached out tentatively and stroked my head. Just once, but still, it was something. She called Barry to come and see, but he was busy watching the telly and he didn't believe her anyway.

*

Nobody could be sure of the exact day of my birth, nobody knew how old I was when I had been left on the doorstep, but Lettie, wanting to reward me for my good behaviour, picked an arbitrary date, five days before the day I had arrived on their doorstep, and named it Celia's birthday. The thirtieth of March became my day. My first birthday was celebrated with a small carrot cake in which was stuck a single blue candle, the flame of which lasted only an instant before it guttered and died, dripping wax into the cake. In the dim basement light, the cake was sliced and Lettie and I ate two pieces each, with me taking mine most politely from her hands, a perfect little lady, more like a well trained lass of twelve years than twelve months.

So perfect was my behaviour on that day that Lettie finally bent down and took me in her arms and, straining under my weight, carried me up and into the house to lay me down before her husband. He would not look. He'd just eaten his lunch and he wanted to keep it down. I had changed my nature but I had not changed my looks.

*

I have not yet told the truth about my face. I made the Elephant Man look like a supermodel. Barry, a butcher, a man used to seeing withered tongues, burst brains, twisted flesh and exploded intestines, vomited the first time he saw me and for the next five years of my life, he refused to look at me. He averted his eyes. Lettie forced herself to look, though it hurt her vision; it gave her headaches, migraines, to see me lying there. I possessed a mirror-shattering type of ugliness, too revolting for this world. I lived in Barry's house but he never saw me. I was the silent ghost that crept from room to room as he went about his business, I was the new Model Infant, doing only what I was told, never crying, always smiling, but he didn't want to know.

And the other parents, the real ones, did they ever think of me? They must have wondered, I suppose, what had happened to the baby they had abandoned, wondered what the future could possibly have in store for a monster like me. And when I thought of them I felt something harden inside my chest, as if my heart was turning to stone, or freezing and turning to ice. Or melting into nothingness, like the icy cold vacuum of outer space, as if my insides were made of snow and would disappear overnight, leaving me to awaken in the morning and find my heart gone, not a single trace of it left, just a puddle in the middle of me, like that left behind by the Wicked Witch of the West.

IV

The next day George is there, same time as the day before. Regular as clockwork, he is, doesn't miss a beat. I am ignoring him. Again. He is annoying me. Again. The false cheer, the heartiness, when really he is thinking, *grumpy old bag, who does she think she is, with that terrible attitude, most of the planet's never even heard of her so she might as well come down off her high horse.*

"Morning Celia," he shouts, as he traipses past my bedroom door, where I lie ruminating, and he's off, up into the attic where he scours the debris of my life like one of those losers who goes through the garbage bins of celebrities, desperate for that empty aerosol can, that old pair of undies, that discarded tube of toothpaste which must have once been touched by the golden hands of the famous. Hoping some of the glitter might rub off on them. He'll find no glitz up there; only more mediocre pictures and a few of my old fleecy-knit casuals. He thinks he should be given a few brownie points just because he can look me full in the face without cringing. I once had a reputation as the gorgon men cannot look upon for fear of instant death. He seems to make a point of gazing without flinching, as if proving himself. He can look me in the face, but he can't look me in the eye. Whenever I fix him with my colourless gaze he turns away.

I haul myself out of bed and my feet hit the floor with a slap, my old floral nightie billowing out around me. I catch a glimpse of myself in the mirror; my frizzy white hair stands up on end, black bags circle my eyes and my face hangs slack upon my bones, like folds of fabric. I waddle out into the living-room, plonk myself down in one of the old armchairs and listen to him banging about in the attic like a bull in a bloody china shop. After a spell, he ventures back down the stairs, clutching a fistful of snaps.

"Time for tea and bickies, then? Shall Polly put the kettle on?"

Is it just my imagination, or does he talk to me as if I am an imbecile? I know I'm a tired old tart, but there is, as they say, life in the old girl yet. My body may be fading but my mind is fine, not yet ravaged by Alzheimer's (touch wood), no solid facts such as my own name have gone scuttling from my memory.

I ignore him, but he is like a recurring nightmare; he won't go away. He has learnt not to wait for a response from me, he simply walks past me into the kitchen and switches on the jug, then I hear him reaching up into the kitchen cupboard for the biscuit tin and I think to myself that he'd better get me some chocolate ones or there'll be bloody trouble.

"Quite a bounty today," he cries out, and I am not sure whether he's talking about the biscuits or the photos or both. Not the biscuits, as it turns out, for he comes through with a couple of broken Shrewsbury biscuits on a chipped piece of china and I shun this pithy offering and take a large, loud slurp of tea, burning my mouth. He doesn't wait for my full attention, instead, he lays the morning's find upon the table; a couple of weary hookers flashing their suspenders, two toothless old codgers sitting on a park bench, an ice-cream vendor, a mangy looking dog. No landscapes; never was too keen on those. In my entire photographic career I think I snapped a sum total of one mountain, one beach and one sunset. And all of those were atrocious. Not my thing; not my style. In my life I established close relationships with no-one; in my art I was a people person. Nothing pleased me better than snapping a human unawares; it made me feel so stealthy, so sly, so powerful.

My mind, I pride myself, is as sharp as one of Barry's butcher's knives. I can remember taking every picture he lays before me. Staring at each one brings it all back, the luminosity when I peered through the lens with my white, right eye and then later, looking back at the world with my dark eye, the blackness, the endless night.

He is always very keen. He can't even wait for me to get half my cuppa down, he's already pestering me, asking, who were these guys on the bench and who did that dog belong to and who's that man with the vending van and in what year did I take that shot

"Strangers," I say. "Just a couple of old geezers and their mongrel."

Geezers and mongrel, he pens on a piece of yellow sticky paper and places it upon the back of the photo in question.

And then he brings out a picture of Ed.

"Who's this?" he asks and I am silent.

I am at a loss for words. Ed can be defined as many things, but also as nothing in particular. The man who although largely hidden from view, had such an impact on my life. The man who

25

hid his identity from me for the entirety of his life, the man who spun a golden world in my mind; a world to which I longed to belong, a world which never existed. In a way, there were three of him, the Ed I made up in my mind, Ed as he pretended to be and Ed as he actually was. But how could I tell that to this young intruder? I fix him with my beady stare. I can see that he still needs words. He won't rest till I give him a trite sentence or two.

"Ed was a very unusual man," I say. "*Highly* unusual."

Unusual guy he writes on another piece of paper, which he sticks to the back of the photo of Ed, before querying "What was so unusual about him, then?"

Which is when a book leaves its place on the shelf, goes flying across the room, smacks into the side of his head and falls to the floor.

"What the hell was that?" he yells.

"Sorry," I say, moving across to close the window. "Bit of a breeze today."

He looks sceptical. Jacob's shoulders are shaking with laughter. Jacob, my ghost, my shadow.

"Okay," he says, a little shaken. "How about the vendor, then. Who was that guy?"

"Just somebody selling ice cream," I reply. "Didn't know him from a bar of soap."

Ice-cream guy, he writes. *Stranger.*

We progress through his little stack this way, with my pithy explanations piling up. He is so persistent that there is no point in being silent, it's quicker and easier to give him what he wants, to make something up so I can get him out of my hair and get back to the real work, the penning of this 'brochure' they've asked for.

When he has what he wants he says, "Right then, best get back to it, I suppose," and traipses back up the ladder which leads to my voluminous attic. Jacob sits quietly in his corner, refusing to speak. He is angry at me for writing 'our' story.

"They'll think you're a fruit loop," he tells me, but we both know that 'they' have thought that for years anyway and so I have nothing to lose by backing up their hypotheses with some good solid evidence.

I switch off the telly, heave myself up from the lounge chair and lumber across the room to the gigantic desk at which I pen my poison tale. I sit down upon the enormous chair, which George calls 'the throne', as if it is a toilet. Thick black ink flows, like tar, from the nib of my calligraphic pen. This sheet of blank paper stares up at me like a white unblinking eye, like a landscape of snow. If I don't put black marks on it, it will devour me, swallow me whole, drag me down into its nothingness. I must write something, while the intruder bangs about upstairs. Before the box upon the doorstep, came the background; there was a time when I was not even so much as a twinkle in my absent father's eye, there was a time when I had not yet been brought into existence. There was a time when I was a cold white diamond shining in the night sky.

V

Fate brought them together and fate kept them apart. They were entrepreneurs, both of them, folk skilled in making a buck. *Barry's Butchery* was positioned directly adjacent to *Lettie's Laundrette*; his building was painted a deep shade of ocean blue, with a purple neon sign proclaiming *Best Cuts In Town* towering up from the roof, hers was painted a dusky pink, with *Best Wash Around,* in yellow neon, rising up into the sky. They were located in the heart of the city.

They married late; he had been written off as a bachelor, she as a spinster. Neither was unhappy being single. Lettie had a wide circle of friends with whom she could chat about everything from new types of spin-drier to the political situation in Cambodia and Barry had his mates, with whom he could discuss beer, football and women. He was known about the town as a ladies' man. He was not the marrying kind. He winked at you when he weighed your sausages and the gals were all agreed that there was something undeniably sensual in the way he slapped steaks and pork chops down upon the scales. He had his own little fan club; women who would gather outside the butchery and press their eyes to the glass just to see him slamming chunks of meat around. He'd sewn his wild oats. He had the notches in his belt.

Lettie, also, was not without her admirers. There were men who brought in underwear that was perfectly clean and still smelled of soap powder from the last wash just so they could have the chance to chat with Luscious Lettie for a minute or two; there were men who paid the extra for the folding service just to know that her hands had been on their knickers. And then there were the men who made sure their underwear was always well sullied, who liked the thought of young Lettie Major laying her pretty eyes upon their various stains.

They had more than this in common; there were coincidences which frightened them. Lettie had begun work in the laundry business at the age of eighteen, employed under Dirty Debs, who had a reputation for returning your washing in a worse state than it had been in when you dropped it off; Barry had been apprenticed to Bloody Bill on the day after his eighteenth birthday and when Bill had retired, two years later, Barry had bought the butchery for a song, and turned the business around, so that profits soared.

When Debs went in for a triple by-pass and never made it back from the hospital, Lettie found that the laundry had been bequeathed to her in Debs' will and she set about to make it the best damned place to get your washing done in the entire country.

For years they did not meet. They drank at the same pubs, ate lunch at the same café, walked down the same street each morning and at night walked back down that same street again, and yet they never exchanged a single word. Lettie bought her meat at the supermarket and Barry did his own laundry at home. Often, in the evening, one would walk past the other, see the key turning in the lock, signifying the end of the day, and both would wonder where the other was going and who with and what to do. Nil communication. The thought of actually speaking turned legs and mouths to stone, the words failed in midair and fell to the ground in silence. If it had not been for the earthquake, this sorry state of affairs would've continued to the grave.

*

The day was a Saturday and both were working; Barry in his bloodied apron and black leather boots, Lettie in the starched white overalls she always wore in the laundry. They should've known that something was up when they saw a fleet of alley cats run meowing down the street; they ought to have suspected that tremors were on the way when they bore witness to a stream of stray dogs streaking across the road in a motley coloured pack. They were oblivious, each engrossed in his or her own universe; Barry flirting with the housewives who'd popped in for a little something special for the evening's dinner and Lettie pressing some of the many business shirts that would be picked up that afternoon to be hung in wardrobes citywide – Monday morning's arsenal. As Lettie flicked the iron from warm to hot, as Barry lifted a fresh piece of cow from its plastic tray, the ground gave its first preliminary shudder; a test quake. Both looked up from their work, Lettie thinking a truck must've rattled by, Barry blaming the folks upstairs, with their three young children who did make an awful racket. And each thought nothing more of it.

But the earth was angry. It did not like to be ignored. It shook again, this time more violently. In the laundry, a pile of clean clothes fell from table to floor, in the butchery, three pigs heads slid off the shelf. It occurred to neither Barry nor Lettie that this might be the beginning of a quake. Such tremors were unheard of

29

in their city; they lived as far from their country's main fault line as it was possible to get without falling into the ocean. They'd seen no educational videos, heard no "please head for the doorframe do not go outside under any circumstances" warnings on the radio. This was outside their realm of experience. Barry had once seen earthquake footage on the telly, but had refused to believe what he'd seen; it was fabrication, he said, those collapsing buildings were a Hollywood set, those fissures in the earth were painted on. Lettie did not watch TV, choosing instead to spend most evenings reading and re-reading the children's classics she'd taken with her when she'd left the family home, and confronted by this second tremor, the first thought that entered her mind was that some giant had escaped the confines of his castle and was rampaging unheeded through the city.

The tremors worsened. At Lettie's, the washing machines and dryers began to move and shake as if possessed by a poltergeist; at Barry's, pig carcasses began to sway back and forth on their hooks. Lettie gulped. Barry broke out into a nervous sweat. There was a pause, a hiatus in the shaking. They dared not think that it might be over; they dared not think at all. A low keening moan filled the air; a dreadful wailing. Outside, the birds were going stir-crazy, flying in sick and pointless circles, hearts and wings beating double-time. Twelve pigeons fell from the sky as if some demented mafioso was sending a message. Death hung in the air like a black rainbow. Barry was doing his best to stand tall and be a man; he clung to one of his hung pigs as the room swayed, using the carcass for balance. Fear was rising in his throat, a nameless terror. He would be trapped in here, something would fall; the room would collapse and he would be squashed like a bug, mushed. Lettie was keeping her cool. As the ironing board scooted about the floor like a mad thing on wheels, as the doors to the spin dryers banged open and shut, she calmly kept on with her ironing, following the board about the room and pressing collars and sleeves as best she could.

At precisely the same moment in time as Lettie's ironing board collapsed, the pig which Barry had been clutching fell from its hook. These events served as a precursor to the next thought, which was to enter both minds instantaneously; *outside*. Indoors was no longer a safe place to be; the threat was now inside with them and was a beast with yellow reptilian eyes and claws and bad breath.

They stepped through their respective doorways like two puppets controlled by a single master. They turned their heads; Lettie to the left and Barry to the right. Eyes locked; freeze frame. They might have kissed, had it not been for what came next. Lettie saw it first, it was heading down the street, travelling towards them slow, languid, taking its terrible time, a gigantic wave, which paused for nothing and no-one, but rippled houses and concrete as if they were made of nothing more than sheer flimsy fabric. The world was being reduced to rubble. Barry was looking the other way. The ground beneath their feet buckled and heaved. Between them there opened a divide, a bottomless abyss, like the mouth of hell.

Barry tried to move but his knees were locked, his feet glued to the pavement. Shock had severed the connection between mind and body, so that although the thought *run Barry run* played repeatedly through his mind, no message reached his legs. It took Lettie to break the spell. She turned her head and looked over her shoulder. The only piece of either building left standing was the doorframe.

"Go stand under that," she instructed, pointing towards all that remained of Barry's Butchery. "Move, pronto!"

He did as he was told; she followed suit and took shelter under what was left of her laundrette. Hanging onto her own doorway, she watched the gigantic ripple pass away from them, reach the end of their street and then simply melt down into the earth. She looked at Barry in astonishment and he looked back at her, and there, beneath their respective doorways, they fell deeply and irrevocably in love.

*

Everybody else in the street was either dead or dying. From deep within the cracks which had opened in the earth, they heard the cries of those who had not been as fortunate as they. From beneath collapsed buildings they heard human yelps, cries for assistance, pleas for aid. They turned a deaf ear. They told themselves that they were powerless to help. They stared at one another and trembled with love and fear. The rescuers who found them an hour later thought that they owed their lives to the doorframes, but they didn't. They owed their existence to selfishness and luck.

Theirs was the only road affected, there was not a single other street in the city that had been touched by the quake.

"It was God's will," Lettie told Barry later. "He knew this was the only way to bring us together."

And Barry had thought to himself that it must be a cruel and callous God who would so carelessly sacrifice lives simply for the sake of a trivial love between a butcher and a laundry girl. Sometimes, late at night, he would think that maybe he should have acted differently, perhaps he ought to have summoned the courage and ventured away from the weird little sanctuary that was his doorframe and done what he could to offer the dying, if not some assistance, then at least some comfort. It was on nights like these that he would reach for his cigar and his bottle of Scotch and sit up and watch the hands of the clock ticking round past midnight and sliding into the early hours of the morning and think about what might have been, had he stepped out onto that different track, jumped aboard that other train and given freely of his help. Lettie paid not a second thought to the dead.

"There was nothing we could've done," she would declare. "We were too busy saving ourselves to have any time to reach out to them. Besides, we were powerless. If we'd had a length of rope, sure, we could've chucked that down one of those crevasses, hauled someone back to the surface of the earth. If we'd had a spare crane or two at our disposal then maybe we could've pulled aside the rubble and freed some trapped souls. We had nothing but our wits and our doorframes and we couldn't leave those."

Barry did not share everything with Lettie. There were parts of himself he kept secret. He did not tell her about the nightmares in which he had taken the place of all those not saved, in which various versions of himself were scattered down the street; beneath bricks, under wood, buried in iron, or lost, forever, deep inside the earth.

*

The courtship was brief; the honeymoon largely blissful. They found themselves upon a deserted isle which was so paradisial it was hard to believe that it was real. They ate fish and fruit and coconuts and smothered each others' bodies in suntan lotion and beer. There was however, one small problem in paradise. Lettie discovered that Barry's mind wasn't the only thing affected by the quake. Vital parts of him now failed to respond. Theirs was to be an unconsummated marriage. Lettie was disappointed, but understanding. She hugged her husband as her dreams of producing a large brood of children went up in smoke.

They kept their spirits up; generous insurance payouts had ensured that, in their absence, both butchery and laundrette were being rebuilt and the happy couple relaxed and enjoyed their time in the sun, reassured by the knowledge that they would return to buildings which were both different and the same as they had been before. Lettie was looking forward to ten brand new washers and five spin-dryers. Barry had ordered marble counters for chopping and hacking upon and as he lay bronzing himself, he dreamt of the satisfying sound of lumps of flesh slamming down against this new surface; not meat against metal, but meat against stone, a sold hearty thwack, the mere contemplation of which sent shivers flooding down his spine.

Upon returning home, they discovered that all had not gone exactly as hoped. Theirs was the only building on the ruined street; nobody else had rebuilt, everybody else was dead and those who had inherited the land in this road were still in shock at the sudden and unexpected loss of friends and relatives and had not even considered what use they were to make of their inheritance. The city council had made no repairs; the road buckled like the back of a snake, like a stormy ocean; huge crevasses still gaped. Makeshift bridges had been built across the gaps in order that the construction workers employed by the newlyweds could go about their business. The heavier supplies had been flown in by chopper.

The master builder had chosen to re-interpret the original building plans along what he called 'more contemporary lines'. An architect had been sub-contracted and it was this man (whom Barry was to hold responsible for the balls-up to his dying day) who was called in to hand them the keys and take them on a tour of this new place that had been created. The newlyweds had stood anxiously in the street while he fumbled for the correct key, which, when found, he held high in the air in victory.

"Ta-da! Welcome to your new work environment."

Barry and Lettie stared in shock. There was only one door. There was only one goddamned building. The architect, whose name was Kyle, pushed the door back on its hinge and Barry and Lettie found themselves peering in at a cavernous space which seemed to have no ceiling, no sides, no far wall.

"It's all about space and light," the architect was saying. "A clean, clear workspace will equal a clean, clear mind."

Everything was white, not a quiet and obedient kind of white, but the sort of white that moves in through the eyeballs and dazzles the brain. Barry was looking for his marble slabs and squinting.

"What the hell is this? Where are the hooks? The marble chopping blocks? The drawers for cleavers? The display counter? This place was meant to be fit to move into straight away. But this, this is just....an emptiness."

Kyle was not phased.

"And that, my friend, is the beauty of it."

"This is one building. We can't combine."

"Why not? Think of the novelty. Larry and Betty's Butchette."

"Butchette? Whoever heard of a Butchette? Anyway, we're Barry and Lettie, not Larry and Betty.

"Think about it Larry, I mean Barry. Maybe they come to see you and you hand them a steak and they accidentally spill a bit of blood on their clothing. No problem. No need even to leave the building. Just walk across to the other side of the room and let Lettie fix you up. Just think. They go to Lettie to pick up the laundry, she says, *you sure you got enough meat to see you through the week?* and then they remember the steak, or a lamb roast, or some blood pudding and she sends them straight to you. You can create a lot of extra business if you're cunning."

He tapped the side of his head with a forefinger. "Now that, Tiger, is what we call smart thinking."

"Where are my machines?" asked Lettie.

"All in good time, my dear, all in good time."

He was smug, sly. He extended a finger and flicked a switch and the wall to their left began moving slowly upwards. Lettie screamed. Barry was filled with an intense and violent hatred.

"It's just hydraulics. No need to worry."

The wall continued moving. Lettie was clinging to her husband's arm.

"Your machines, my dear."

She barely believed her eyes. They were machines without outsides. Everything stood exposed; wires, pipes, the works. You would be able to see the damned things in action. Those machines were naked. She didn't want to see them working, didn't want to know their dark secrets. She'd always liked the mystery of it, the magic; shove in the clothes, add a bit of powder, push a button and the garments fell out clean. Put the wet clothes in another machine, push another button and they came out dry. At the sight of all those insides, she felt angry, cheated.

"What are those bloody things," asked Barry. "Didn't they get time to put covers on them? They'll fall apart in two seconds flat, they will."

Kyle-the-architect was chuckling softly to himself.

"See-through covers, son. Perspex."

He reached out and tapped two fingers on the invisible skin of one of the machines. "Funky, huh?"

Funky, huh? Who was this guy and what had he done to their dreams? Stomped on them, that was what, built over them with his own stupid vision of the way things should be, when they were the ones who had to work in the bloody place.

"Listen buddy, if this is your idea of a joke then your sense of humour is pretty damned sick. We wanted to come home to what we had before and what we've got is this spaceship here."

Kyle's mouth dropped open in mock-offence. "This is cutting edge stuff. Open-plan. Form follows function."

"This ain't no swanky foreign saloon," protested Barry. "This is supposed to be two separate buildings, clearly defined territory; a butchery and a laundrette. And where's my marble?"

"Your marble will be arriving tomorrow, darling. This whole thing is beginning to get boring."

Darling?

Barry's head grew hot.

"The people of this city don't want their pork chops mixed up with their knickers. They don't want mince all over their Sunday suits. They want separation. Order. They don't want change. They want everything to stay as it was. Who are you to come in here and start making alterations?"

"Oh, get with the programme. They'll take whatever you give them. And if you're worried about the walls…"

From out of nowhere he produced some gold-coloured thick paper screens covered in intricate patterns, which he proceeded to erect, dividing the room in two.

"These are byobu," he said. "Everyone's going Asian these days. Which reminds me, if these bare white floors get a little too much, there's a stack of tatami mats in one of the cupboards over there."

That was when Barry lunged at him. It was something Lettie had never before witnessed; his angry face was not a face she'd yet seen. It was hard to believe that it was her husband down there on the floor, with the architect in a stranglehold. It could not be her Barry that was slamming his fists into little Kyle's face. She couldn't see her man there anymore; it was as if he had vacated his body and somebody else had moved in. She stood watching as if paralysed. Her stomach felt tight, knotted, filled with nausea. Somebody else's voice was speaking, somebody else's words were coming out through her mouth.

"Stop it, please, stop. He's not moving any more."

The violence stopped as abruptly as it had began. Barry came back to himself, as if suddenly waking up from a long slumber in which he had dreamt he was somebody else.

"Lost the plot," he kept muttering to himself. "Lost the bloody plot."

Lettie began slapping the face of the architect who lay unmoving upon the Butchette floor.

Barry was not, thankfully, a murderer. Kyle began to move, to groan. His left foot twitched uncontrollably. He was, unmistakably, alive. He rose groggily to his feet and staggered out the door. The incident was over. But Lettie had seen a new side to her husband, and her idea of who he was would be forever altered.

*

They did their best to carry on as they had been before. They priced up the cost of adding an interior wall and presented this to the insurance company who laughed in their faces. They had not the cash to fork out for the wall on their own, and so, for the time being, they stuck with what Lettie called "those Jap things" and what Barry called "the flimsy screens". Both were too scared to use the hydraulic wall which had initially kept Lettie's machines out of sight; neither trusted such silly gadgetry. This wall remained permanently raised. Lettie threw stretches of cloth over the machines in order to hide their secrets and Barry hung hooks from the ceiling and knocked up a display counter from some old bits of fibreboard he'd had lying about at home. They reinforced the road's bridges with steel and wrote angry letters to the council about the long delays in repairing the street.

"But nobody else wants to build there," they were told, in the infrequent and impolite replies that they received. "That road is haunted by squashed ghosts and the fallen. We're not spending a million dollars repairing a street that's only going to be used by two people."

The Butchette's electricity and water supply were connected to one of the streets which ran parallel and there were frequent problems. The power would go out mid-wash, the water would splutter, gush and cease, just as Barry was sluicing out his section of the Butchette, or just as Lettie's machines were entering their rinse cycle.

Barry's marble arrived the day after they opened up shop. He heard the blades of a chopper whirring overheard like some unholy locust and he ran outside to see huge pink slabs being lowered slowly to the ground. Lettie was close behind him and she drew in her breath when she saw what was arriving from the heavens. She ran towards the marble, with Barry yelling at her to be careful. She reached out her hands and guided the stone on its path to the ground. It was beautiful, an unusual shade of dull pink, flecked with gold and run through with red swirls.

"Nature never made marble like that," scoffed Barry. "That's been made by man, that has. Manufactured in some factory. I wanted my rock to come straight from the hillside, not tampered with and altered and dyed. Piece of bloody shit, that's what that is."

He was a hard man to please.

"Too good for meat," said Lettie, and commandeered the gorgeous stone as her folding table.

Barry ordered a stainless steel counter like the one he'd had before the quake.

Business was slow. Folks were scared of the gaps in the road, frightened of the sleeping earth, which might wake, grumbling, and swallow them whole. Trust had to be regained; custom had to be coaxed. Hoping to provide added incentive, Lettie set up a café bar in one corner and the Butchette became something of a local hang-out, popular with the many artistic types who were so rife in Provencia in those days. People would sit for hours over a liqueur coffee, musing to themselves, chatting with friends, the vegetarians amongst them shooting disapproving looks in the direction of Barry who would be busying himself chopping up cows and muttering about ponsy bloody good-for-nothings wouldn't know an honest day's work if it jumped up and hit them over the head. At first, Lettie would serve the drinks herself, racing back and forth between her washing machines and the flash new espresso machine that had been ordered from the capital. Later, when business began to pick up they employed a couple of locals to do the work. They spent a good deal of cash on advertising and at the end of the day, they charmed back customers on the strength of novelty value and quality service. They fought the chaos until the world was orderly and calm.

*

It wasn't until some time after they had settled into life at the Butchette that Barry and Lettie began to discuss their respective backgrounds, and when they did compare notes, they were surprised and delighted to discover further similarities between the lives they had led to date. Both were born and bred Provencians, both were from the South side of the river, both had rebelled against the family profession and struck out alone, preferring to pen their own script rather than following the lines that the family had tried to write for them.

Lettie had been born just after the end of the war, on 29 January 1946, to William and Beatrice Major, proud owners of Major's Sweet Shop. She'd grown up surrounded by jars of lollies: jelly babies, gummy bears, liquorice whirls, chewy milk bottles, fizzing sherbet, raspberry drops. Beatrice Major was a chain-smoker; her hands and teeth were stained yellow with nicotine and she was never seen without a cigarette in her mouth. She kept a bottle of gin down under the counter, from which she took intermittent swigs during the course of the day. She was forever dipping her grubby hands into the lolly jars, munching sweeties, licking her fingers and then diving into another jar for more candy. These were the same hands that fished you out *your* lollies, whenever you dared to enter Major's Sweet Shop, the same sticky hands that grabbed at your change and struck at the cash register. Mrs Major saw no need for tongs. Some said that the back of the shop, where Beatrice stored the big bags of sweets from which the jars were filled, was infested with rats, and that Beatrice paid off the local health inspector in order that he give her store a clean bill of health after each annual inspection. Lettie's mother had something of a reputation as the town witch and the kids who came to her store did so only because hers was the only sweet shop for miles. Nobody ever stole from Beatrice Major. They paid their money, took their sweeties and ran.

Lettie's father, William, was a solemn, silent man, responsible for stock-taking, keeping the books and generally ensuring that the store remained up and running while his wife stood out front and served. His weak heart had ensured that he'd successfully avoided being drafted during the war. Lettie was her father's daughter; she was a shy child, happier to sit on her father's knee and watch as he added up the monthly budget than to stand out the front of the store and bear witness to the terrified children lingering outside, trying to summon the courage to enter. She was a well behaved little girl; she did whatever she was told whenever she was told. *Too* good, some said, nobody can be *that* good *all* the time. She'd shame the devil, they said. But Lettie was not good because she thought she should be, she was not sweet through fear of reprimand, she was *innately* good; naughtiness just didn't appeal to her.

Her brother, Edward, had been born three years to the day after his sister, and their mother would sometimes comment that all Lettie's badness must have been saved up, to lie in wait for Ed. He was as bratty as his sister was virtuous, as tainted as Lettie was pure. He hid slugs and snails in the lolly jars, he pressed his bare bum to the inside of the shop window, causing the kids outside to turn away in disgust, he punched his sister repeatedly in the arm, he ran wild through the streets of Provencia, causing havoc wherever he went. He showed an unhealthy interest in the dissection of various members of the animal kingdom; he secured himself a scalpel from God knows where and could often be seen slicing open some sparrow, goldfish or small lizard in order to inspect its anatomy and had once, much to Lettie's disgust, been discovered mucking about with the entrails of the neighbour's cat, Tiddles. He was a compulsive liar, always fibbing and making up silly stories with which to entertain the other kids. He was a bright child, far quicker than his placid sister; he might have been given the wickedness, but he'd also got the brains. His parents tried to chalk his bad behaviour up to superior intellect and boredom and paid many a visit to the local school in order to try to have Ed placed on some special advanced education programme, but they were told that the school had not the time nor the money to dedicate to its biggest brat simply because his parents believed he needed 'extending'.

It was assumed that Lettie would take over the running of the sweet shop; nobody was placing their money on Ed, whom everybody thought was likely to leave home at fifteen and turn to a life of deviance and crime. When he stayed on at high school, passed all his final exams with flying colours, despite the fact that he'd been to a sum total of twenty-five hours of lessons all year, his parents were pleasantly surprised and rewarded him by offering to buy him a gift of his choosing under two hundred dollars. When he said he wanted a microscope, a stethoscope and a mortar and pestle they were a little confused. When he announced that he had applied for, and been accepted into, the nearest medical school they were speechless, though not as stunned as they were when he came home with straight As at the end of his first year.

It was Lettie who now became the family disappointment. The so-called 'good girl' of the family was displaying a latent rebellious streak and was refusing to follow in her mother's footsteps, but was talking instead about playing renegade and heading down the road to take up a position that was on offer at Debs' Laundrette. Nobody thought she would go through with it, but when her eighteenth birthday rolled around, she upped and left, found her own one bedroom flat and started working regular shifts for Debs. Her father cried for a week and her mother, hard old Beatrice, declared that her daughter had broken her heart.

It was a heart soon mended.

"You do what you have to do," she said to her daughter, magnanimously, a week after Lettie had left home. "Don't let me run your life. And don't worry about your father's tears. They'll soon dry up."

They did indeed dry up, for six weeks after Lettie had left home, the old man died, not as a result of the bung heart, as everybody had expected, but as the result of a stray blood clot travelling up his body and lodging itself in his brain. And his guilt-ridden renegade daughter mistakenly imagined that it was she who had caused her father's death, for no matter how many times she was told that his death had been caused by the blood clot, she still believed that her old man had died of shock and no matter how many times her witchy old heart-of-gold mother tried to reassure her that it was not her fault, young Lettie continued to blame herself.

*

Barry had been born exactly one month after his wife. He was the son of Thomas and Dawn Doom, owners of *Doom's Bird and Beast Preservers*, the one and only place to get your dead animals immortalised in the whole of Provencia. He was an only child; there was no room for more than one offspring in the Doom house, for it was filled to overflowing with stuffed and mounted squirrels, foxes, ferrets, weasels and stoats, as well as numerous species of bird and fish. Deer heads hung on nearly every wall and in one corner of the living-room sat the Doom pride and joy, an enormous brown bear that Thomas had had shipped over from the States. In the master bedroom were two stuffed hyenas, one either side of the bed.

Barry's father had returned home from the war a hero. To Barry, it was as if some stranger had come waltzing into his life and said '*I am your father*', for he had no memories of his Dad from the years before the war, only the fiction his mother had told him (*Your Dad's away fighting for God and country*) and the photographs she'd shown him of their wedding day. Barry felt uneasy around this 'hero', felt that his father didn't quite belong here. It was as if this man, this 'Dad' was trying to fit back into the shoes he had worn before he'd left to fight on foreign shores, and failed to realise that his feet had grown six inches in the time that he'd been away. Or else, that his shoes had shrunk.

His mother said his father was lucky to be alive. His father said that his mother 'kept a good house' and that she was also of 'invaluable assistance' to him in his taxidermist's studio, where she would hand him his implements as they were needed, like a nurse at a surgeon's side. The young Barry Doom had a remarkable array of stuffed toys at his disposal; he grew up surrounded by many fine animal friends, to whom he gave both names and personalities; shy Sally the squirrel, cunning Felix the fox, callous Kylie the crow. It was a game he indulged in until adolescence, when he became ashamed of the habit, and instead began mocking both the animals themselves and his father's chosen profession. Behind his Dad's back, he made jokes at the old man's expense, loudly declaring his intentions to become something sensible and non-creepy; an electrician, a plumber, a carpenter. Or a butcher; a man of meat.

His father had other ideas in mind. It had never occurred to him that his son would not choose the taxidermist's trade; he was simply waiting till the boy came of age, and then he would impart to him the appropriate knowledge and tricks. On Barry's thirteenth birthday, his Dad pulled him to one side.

"Come on, son," he said, winking at him. "I'll show you how to stuff a bird."

Barry followed his father out to what had once been the garden shed and was now his Dad's studio.

"We won't be needing your mother, today," said his father. "You can take over her role and hand me the tools that I need."

Upon a battered old table in the garden shed sat two black crows. Thomas picked one up and buried his face in the feathers. Barry winced.

"Okay, boy," said Thomas. "Here's how it's done. Pass me that scalpel and those forceps, would you?"

Barry did as he was told. His father treated him to a running commentary.

"Place the bird on its back and separate the feathers over the abdomen. Slice the old bugger right down the middle, then yank the skin away from the abdominal wall. Like so."

He demonstrated.

"Then you just peel the skin away, easy see, and you remove the eyes with the forceps, like this."

He plucked out the crow's eyeballs and flung them into a nearby bucket filled with discarded pieces of animal.

"Now it's simply a matter of removing the brain and muscles and skinning out the tail."

The old man's hands were swift, sure, and steady.

"Here, run some warm water in that bucket over there, would you, and add a squirt of detergent. Right. Soak the skin in detergent for two or three minutes, rinse, and dry it with a hair-dryer."

Another boy might have been repulsed by the ritual, but Barry was simply bored. All that fart-assing about, all that precision work, didn't appeal to him at all. Barry was developing into a big lad, sturdy, and he struggled to imagine himself twaddling about in a shed like this one all day, slicing and peeling and rinsing.

"Now then," Thomas continued. "It's time to make an artificial body. Take a handful of wood-wool, roll it into a ball and bind it with thread. Shape it as best you can."

Barry's father's hands quickly fashioned the body of the crow.

"Get drying that crow skin, Barry. We're gonna be needing it soon."

Barry dutifully plucked the dripping skin from the bucket, plugged in the hairdryer that lay on the floor and stood blow-drying the skin and feathers.

"Fashion yourself a neck from galvanised wire, then push the wire through the length of the body. Hurry up Barry, we need that skin."

Barry dried the thing as fast as he could, and handed it to his father.

"Turn the head inside out so that the skull is exposed. Fill out the skull with cotton wool and the cranium with clay. Stick the skin onto the dummy, then wire the wings from the outside. Position your bird on a suitable piece of wood and voilà! Bob's your uncle but for a few finishing touches."

He paused to admire his handiwork.

"Pass me the kapok, Barry. It's on that bench over there. Feed in the kapok through the eyes to fill in any unwanted spaces near the ears, eyes and throat. Place a piece of cotton wool in each eye and arrange the eyelids around it. Don't forget to tie up the beak. Give your bird a bit of a preen."

He arranged the crow's feathers, smoothing down any which stuck out at unsightly angles. The blank cotton wool eyes of the bird stared out at Barry like the blind eyes of a statue.

"Barry, pay attention! Get me that box of eyes over there, would you?"

Barry reached for the box of small glass globes.

"Now, it's best to paint the glass eyes yourself, for extra authenticity, but if you're a busy bastard like me you've not always got the time, which is why I buy these ones, pre-painted, see."

He held one up for Barry's inspection. Its yellow iris gleamed.

"Now remove the cotton wool from each eye, place in a small dab of clay and then position the glass eye. Like so. Get me those paints from over there, boy."

Barry obeyed his Dad

"All that's left now is to colour the damned thing in. It's best to use oil paints, which is what you'll find I've got here. The legs, the beak and the eyelids must all be painted, because time will discolour them."

His father's expert hand applied the swift strokes.

"And that's us done, son. Whaddaya think?"

"So fiddly," thought Barry. A lifetime of this would be a lifetime in hell.

"Happy Birthday," said his Dad, pressing the crow into Barry's arms. "From me to you, kid."

Barry put the finished crow down on the table.

"Birds are the easiest, eh? It's the fish that you'll struggle with, when the time comes. Lot trickier. But you'll get there, with a good lashing of patience and a great big dollop of perseverance."

Barry thought he'd rather slit his wrists.

"Why don't you have a go, son," said his Dad, throwing him the second crow. "Don't worry if you make a bit of a hash of your first one. You'll soon get the hang of it."

Barry stared down at the unstuffed crow, at its dumb dead eyes, its slick black feathers and its sharp orange beak and knew then, in that instant, beyond a shadow of a doubt, that he wanted to be a butcher. He hated the thought of this pansying about, fiddling and faddling, just to make some dumb dead animal appear lifelike. Meat was easy. Meat was for clumsy men like himself. Meat was solid and dependable. Meat was good. People would always need a butcher; butchers were indispensable, unlike taxidermists. Stuffed and mounted animals could fall out of fashion and what would happen to you then? You'd be shafted. Stuffed. Demand for his Dad's work was falling already, though the stubborn old codger would never admit it, just kept on working at his usual steady rate, hence the extra numbers of dead animals that had been cluttering up the house of late. You could hardly say taxidermy was a boom industry now, could you? If his Dad wasn't careful he'd be left with the work he did for the Provencia Museum and that would be it. The art of taxidermy, if you could call it an art, had had its heyday.

He pretended for five years. For five years he was taken down to the garden shed each Saturday, giving up valuable hours that he would much rather have spent kicking a football round with his mates, and he watched and learnt as his Dad imparted fatherly wisdom. He hated himself for not having the guts to stand up to his old man, hated himself for not being his own person, for not saying, '*Look, taxidermy's just not for me.*' He had his reasons for pretending. His mum, Beatrice, had taken him to one side and whispered in his ear that his father's health was failing.

"Heart problems," she said, "be careful with him, Barry. Don't give him any sudden shocks."

*

But he had to break the news sometime. He wasn't going to spend his whole life living a lie. Two days before his eighteenth birthday, Barry Doom announced his plans to leave home and go work for Bloody Bill at the local butchery. This announcement was greeted with silence. Then tears from his mother and slightly hysterical laughter from his father, who emitted a cackle not unlike the noise those two hyenas that stood in the Doom master-bedroom must have made when still alive. They didn't think he was really going to leave, but true to his word, he packed his bags and he upped and left and Barry's father was felled by a heart-attack two weeks later, on exactly the same day that Lettie's Dad had died of his rogue blood clot. (Yet another of those terrifying coincidences that made Barry and Lettie believe that their love was Meant To Be.)

*

Left behind, after the deaths of these fathers, were two guilty kids and two middle-aged widows, whom I eventually came to know by the affectionate titles of Grandma Lolly and Grandma Stuff.

Barry was as relieved to knuckle under and get hacking at Bloody Bill's as Lettie was to be let loose in the laundrette. For both of them, the move away from home, the rejection of the career path they ought to have chosen spelt freedom, and their union, their marriage, did not seem like a bind, or a noose, but a chance to combine the gull's wings they had discovered and experience greater liberty, to become a sort of married albatross, soaring high on the hard-won success of the Butchette.

And I, Celia Doom, was the hiccup, the girl who threw a spanner in the works.

VI

My hand cramps as it grips the pen. Pain shoots up my lower arm, like the roots of a gnarled tree. Sometimes I think I shouldn't bother setting this down; sometimes I think I should just go back to watching the telly. It's a lot less dangerous than this dive into memory, a lot less frightening than the gaps into which I fall when there are no words there to be written. Next door, the hippies are creating a right ruckus, munching those green cookies of theirs, singing those terrible old songs from the sixties, banging those ridiculous drums, their lank hair long and greasy. Can't tell whether they're boys or girls or neither or both. Don't they know they're four decades too late? And they say that I'm untimely.

George comes bumbling down that ladder again, and for once I feel almost relieved, he will provide a distraction, he will shove more memories in front of me. Even making his lunch will be a welcome chore. Something to do. I press "play" on the remote and the telly flicks into life though no sound comes out, I must have hit the mute button by accident, when the thing was switched off. Miniature people move across the screen, their mouths opening and closing like fish in a bowl, their tiny soap opera dramas played out, their words obedient to every line that has been scripted.

I don't ask him what he wants for his lunch, he'll get whatever I dish up, which will probably be bacon and eggs, as it is almost every other lunchtime. He has cobwebs and dust in his hair, the attic hasn't been given a good clean-out during the entire time I've lived in this house, but I don't tell him about the webs; let him walk through the streets looking a fright, let him attract the sorts of stares that were once aimed in my direction, let his wife pick them out of his hair when he arrives home. He is clutching his usual little stash, they want over three hundred photos for this exhibition and, where possible, they also want the negatives, though many of those have been lost. I leave him in front of the silent television and wander into the kitchen where I throw a slab of lard into the frying pan, following this with eight eggs and an entire pack of bacon. When it is done I serve it up on two of my enormous plates and walk back into the living-room and when I look across at him I get such a fright that I drop both plates and our lunch falls to the floor, a smeared mess of white and yellow, run through with cured flesh. He is not watching TV; he is standing at my desk, he is rifling through my notes.

"What the hell do you think you're doing?" I boom at him, my anger fuelled by the terror I feel at the sight of him laying his beady eyes upon my words.

He is not fazed. He is growing immune to my tantrums. This is the problem with frequent anger; those on the receiving end of your wrath simply tune you out. You lack surprise value.

"Is this for your brochure?" he asks.

"Mind your own bloody business," I snap.

"This stuff isn't real," he says, holding up a page of mine by the corner. "I don't believe you. You're making it up. These are tall stories. This 'Butchette' you write about. That never existed. The cracked road, the bridges. These are shaggy dog stories. You're a fibber."

"These words are not for your eyes," I say, attempting to snatch the paper from his hands. "What do you know about whether it's true or not? Who are you to dispute what I say?"

"No-one's going to believe you," he says smugly.

"I don't care," I say, grumpily, standing in the dropped eggs, mushing them into the carpet. "It's my brochure. What I say goes."

"And all that stuff about the Dooms and the Majors. How could you possibly know all that?"

"I was told," I say. "Lettie used to tell me stories."

He sniggers.

"And it looks too long already," he says. "They'll not take anything over three thousand words, you know."

He doesn't know when to shut his trap.

"It'll be as long or as short as I make it," I say and then I stomp to the hall cupboard and pull out my enormous vacuum cleaner, three times the size of your average Hoover, and I suction up what I can of our lunch and then I am even grouchier than normal as I have low blood sugar levels, which always results in a bad mood. The vacuum swallows the lunch in a single gulp, leaving only a tell-tale yellow smear upon the carpet, a stain which I ignore. I am in no mood to go through his latest bounty now, but the sooner I speak, the sooner he will be out of my hair, back up into the attic to ferret around in my past.

"Are you sure you don't want me to make you something else?" he says, looking down at the remains of the egg.

"No I don't," I snap. "Just get on with it. Let's get this over and done with."

Another seven photos, nothing too eye-catching, meat and potatoes shots of the sort which Arty and Angie sold to magazines, keeping the cash for themselves. The first made the cover of *Photography Today* though I don't know why, because it is overexposed and slightly out of focus and the subject wasn't even very interesting; a human statue, dime a bloody dozen they used to be, men and women swathed in white bandages and done over in paint, standing just as still as inertia itself and at first you think this person is made of stone, until you look again, or they blink, or twitch a little finger by accident. Which does not happen in a photograph, of course; in a photo humans are always frozen and so it takes a good deal of close examination to determine whether the person who made the cover of this magazine is real or fake and, in a way, impossible to come to any final verdict on the matter, unless you know the truth. They paid me a thousand bucks for this, which was a fortune at the time. Not that I ever saw any of the cash.

I give George a couple of trite sentences to go with the photo and we progress onto the next shots, more early ones; a small Indian girl in a pair of brightly covered overalls clutching a clockwork monkey, a fat businessman eating a hamburger outside McDonalds, some kids dressed up for Halloween, one disguised as an angel, another as a ghoul, a third as a wicked elf. More early ones; the snaps in the attic are layered like sediment in reverse; the most recent sit at the bottom, upon the floorboards, on top of those sit the snaps I took in my middle age, and floating on the surface are the pics from my young years, when I was still in the process of mastering my art. Some of these are blurred, some badly developed, others just plain embarrassing. About one shot in a hundred shows promise; it was the promise that I clung to, like a drowning woman clinging to a life-raft.

But now the job is over for another day; it's back to the attic for George and back to the drawing board for me. As I sit myself down at my desk, Jacob breaks his vow of silence for the first time in days.

"What the hell did you choose that moron for?" he huffs. "Surely there were plenty of other morons you could've picked."

"Hey," I say. "Give it up. He offered his services and I took it upon myself to accept graciously. Time was ticking. I'm not as young as I used to be. Not as young as everybody else my age."

He picks at the hole in his side with one gnarled finger.

"He's an idiot," he says. "You deserve better."

"I'm flattered."

"The captions won't speak for these photos," he says. "The photos speak for themselves."

"But who's speaking for me?" I ask.

"You're in those photos," he said. "In a way, they're all about you."

"Rubbish," I say. "They were nothing to do with me at all."

Jacob is quiet again for a while, and I wonder if he will vanish, again. He comes and goes as he pleases. Some days he is a permanent presence and at other times he is elsewhere, not bothering to bother me. Where does he go when he is not here? He is in another realm, lingering, watching, unseen. He melts through windows, goes walking through walls. The dead know how to entertain themselves, you know. Today he does not disappear. He stays, and starts to laugh; his severed neck twitches.

"Imagine the shock," he says. "If he looked behind the clock. A hidden history, just sitting there waiting."

"Those things are not for his eyes," I say. "He'd never think to look there. Not in a million years. And he wouldn't believe his eyes if he did. He doesn't believe anything."

George wants a history which is 'the truth', but of course there is no such thing. It all depends on who is doing the talking and in this case the speaker is me, you have only my version of events. If you can find somebody who will speak of my life from another angle, then I suggest you listen to them and not to me. Until then, you're stuck with my words. Tough luck.

VII

Provencia. We used to be a city, but now we're not even a town, three thousand three hundred and thirty-three of us at the last count, though I don't know why they bothered to include the final three when they published the census results, perhaps they were trying to make the rest of us feel less alone. Bear this in mind; those census results took the transient population into account and even then I think they fiddled the results. They put the permanent head-count down as two thousand five hundred, but my guess is that the true figure is nearer to the fifteen hundred mark. They thought we were in need of a morale boost; they're trying to convince the last of us to continue clinging to the wreckage, rather than abandoning ship and heading West like everybody else. We are the dark shadow that looms beneath the wing of the country's thriving capital, we are its inverse, the price that has to be paid for its success. The capital has a name, incidentally, but we Provencians refuse to speak it. A petty retribution, as if by not deigning to say its name we rob it of some of the all-reaching power it exerts over us. I guess you could say we have a bee in our bonnet.

*

'Provencia. It's All Right Here', say the signs on the freeway leading towards what was once the city centre and it's true, we're not lacking anything. We've got shopping malls, hydro-slides, churches for the religiously inclined, public libraries, a couple of museums, public gardens, public schools, private schools, swimming pools. And all of these stand empty. There is a river, which runs right through the centre of the city, splitting it in two like a peach. The river used to divide the haves from the have-nots, the nots to the South and the haves, which included the business district, to the North, though I'm over-simplifying, of course; there were enclaves of have-nots in amongst the haves, there were venturous haves among the nots.

The family home sits to the North, but only just; we're five minutes walk from the river, I used to go down there and admire the high tide mark, a line of garbage and glass, old fag butts, broken bottles, empty cans, plastic bags. Flotsam and jetsam. Seashells are overrated. The Opal, our river's called, a prophetic touch from the coloniser who dreamt up that moniker; the pulp and paper mill sees fit to pump gallons of oily effluvium downstream every day, what birds there are left hop sadly about with their feathers slicked down to their bodies as if with black Brylcreem pomade, damaged, flight no longer a possibility. Bereft gulls squawk along the shoreline. The greenies have done their protesting; done the placards and the petitions. They gave up, turned their backs, upped and left like most of the rest of the city. No doubt they were thinking *this place is beyond saving. Our energies are wasted here* and went off to rescue some beached whales or other worthy animals, leaving we wretched Provencians to destroy what's left of our environment and ourselves with it. The hippies next door sometimes head out there and sing a few half-hearted protest songs, but no attention is paid.

We are nowhere near the sea; the nearest ocean is three hundred miles away. We border, to the east, a desert, to the west, a mountain range. As a region, it's fairly geographically diverse. Oh, one more minor thing to mention; these days our city lacks a centre, there is, quite simply, nothing there. But this is a tale of the past, so let's talk 'then' and not 'now'. Let me say 'was' rather than 'is'.

Let's zap back thirty-two years, to Provencia as it used to be. In those days the population was more than a hundred times the size it is now; we've suffered quite a fall. It was a well-planned city; it did not sprout haphazardly, a few buildings here, another few popping up somewhere else. No, everything about Provencia was planned. This city was made from a blueprint. Fat men in suits sat around a wooden table for hours debating the layout, the plan, and that plan was obeyed to the letter. No imagination went into the naming of our roads; this was a place where the streets were named with numbers. Two ring roads circled the city, from those you could take any number of roads inwards towards the centre, passing through the suburbs till you reached it, the thumping heart of the place, the CBD. Each suburb was its own little self-sufficient unit and yet the suburbs also seemed to work together, they synthesised, culminating in the glorious whole that was Provencia. Or the glorious hole, depending on who you were talking to. And whether you were speaking past or present. But back then, in the very heart of this city, bang smack in the heart of this hole, was the CBD and right in the middle of the CBD was the

'Butchette' as the architect had coined it. It was a cozy little cocoon, its own neatly encased little world.

*

Barry and Lettie didn't live at the Butchette; they owned a tidy little three-bedroom bungalow. They had worked hard to afford their first home, they'd saved their pennies, foregone holidays, lived on vegetables they picked up for a song from the market down the road and cheap cuts of meat that Barry said he couldn't give away. Three years after the Butchette had opened its doors they had a decent deposit to put down on a place and after much snooping around the suburbs with various unscrupulous real-estate agents, they stumbled across Third Street, a lovely tree-lined road in one of the quieter suburbs and the house that happened to tickle their fancy was Number Thirty-Three. It was a wooden bungalow, 1920s style, on a quarter-acre section graced with plum trees, a grape vine, an enormous fig tree, hydrangea bushes, gladioli, rose bushes, a sizeable vegetable patch and more snails than a French restaurant. Their glutinous bodies slid down the cracked pathways, leaving snotty little trails of slime behind them, their brittle shells no protection against the imminent descent of Celia, who, on those rare occasions when she was let loose in the backyard, was fond of scoffing them whole. (They put a wire out there for me eventually, and once every couple of months they would strap me into a harness, hook me onto the line and let me run up and down like a goat, or a pet sheep, taking in the sun.)

The house itself was roomy, open, with big bay windows in the bedrooms and the living-room, and panels of stained glass set into the walls at random intervals. The bathroom was lined with tiles imprinted with blue and yellow fish, an enormous medicine cabinet and two mirrors positioned opposite one another, so that to stare into either one of them was to see yourself reflected infinitely, down an endless tunnel of mirrors. The master bedroom had a beautiful set of French doors which opened out onto a patio, upon which my adoptive parents held many a barbeque in the long summer months. Until I came along and everything changed.

Three months after the house had been purchased, I had arrived, snuggled inside my banana box, and was fairly swiftly shunted into the cellar. I was never given a room of my own. There were empty rooms upstairs I could've inhabited, but Barry wasn't having a bone of it.

"She's not living on the same floor as me," he said. "She might come and bite me in the middle of the night."

Above my head were the stained-glass windows, the velvet drapes, the beautiful bay windows which caught the sun, the open rooms, the light. Mine was an infancy lived underground.

Once I had proven to Lettie that I was worthy not only of leaving the basement, but also of leaving the house, I was driven to work with my adoptive parents every day, carried across the bridges in their street and placed in a makeshift pen in one quiet corner of the Butchette, on Lettie's side of the byobu, where I amused myself by playing with my own little menagerie; the many stuffed toy animals that Lettie had bought for me in the hope that these would keep me happy. It was a sheltered, claustrophobic existence. I saw very few windows. I saw only four walls. Lettie was relieved that I was 'good enough' to accompany them to the Butchette. Until that point in time she had been forced to take time off work to stay with me at home everyday.

In order not to frighten away the customers, my adoptive mother stitched for me a cover, which was the shape of a large sock, with eyeholes through which I mischievously peeked. It had been made from clean men's underwear which had never been collected by its owners. Nobody asked why the baby was masked; tales of the creature that had mysteriously appeared on Lettie's doorstep were circulating at a spectacular rate of knots and everybody knew that I fell into the category of unmentionable things that lurked in the depths of the city's communal unconscious. I was the darkness that nobody wanted to acknowledge as theirs.

I learnt to walk on my own, simply picked myself up off the Butchette floor one day and put one foot in front of the other as if I had been doing so all my life. Nobody saw my first steps. Barry was hacking meat and Lettie was chatting with a customer. Arms outstretched, I toddled towards my adoptive mother, who did not notice that I was moving until I was right beside her, loving infant arms wrapped around her leg. She looked down and screamed. My cover had come loose and half my face was hanging out. The customer turned away in shock while Lettie hurriedly bent over and pulled my cover down properly. It was as if I had committed an indecent act, like a flasher exposing his willy to a gaggle of giggling schoolgirls. It was the revelation of all that they wanted me to hide. I learnt early the power of my freakishness.

*

Sometime after my third birthday, when I was five foot in height and weighed seventy-five kilos, Lettie decided that it was time for me to be taken to the hospital for a check-up. She didn't bother making an appointment; she shoved me in the back of the car and whipped me down to A&E, knowing that the sight of me would be enough to secure some instant attention. At the hospital they stared and stared. I was given priority treatment. Forget the stabbed men with punctured lungs, the old codgers in the grip of heart attacks, the women who were miscarrying. I was Number One, I came first; me and my big body and my black and white eyes and my fangs and my shock of colourless hair were whipped straight to the front of the queue. Barry and Lettie were left to sit in the waiting-room and I was led into a stark white room, told to strip naked and lay down on the table. Three humans in white coats stared down at me; I was a lab specimen, an etherised bug. They did not talk to me; they spoke about me, in whispers. They did not speak my name; they referred to me first as 'It' and then, after I lashed out and bit one of them on the leg, as 'The Vicious It.'

They probed orifices that I had not known existed. They examined every inch of me, they took skin and hair and mucus samples. They placed these parts of me in plastic containers which they neatly labelled. A nurse entered the room and took the pieces of me away for examination and later storage. They took photos of me as I lay there; turned me into nothing more than an image on a piece of paper. They did not tell me that I could rise to my feet and walk away from the table; it was they who walked away from me, left me lying there for three hours until Lettie began to wonder what had happened and peered through the glass panel set into the door.

"She's just lying there," she hissed to her husband. "Do you think they've put her down?"

She rapped on the glass pane and I sat upright with a start, empty eyes staring straight ahead. She pushed open the door and, muttering under her breath about the standards of health care in this damned country, took me by the hand (I was far too heavy to carry) and pulled me up off the bed. Hand in hand, Lettie and I marched down the hospital corridors, in search of the medics who had abandoned me. They were found in a spare room in the left wing of the hospital. They had microscopes and slides and chemicals. They were looking at pieces of me.

"What the hell's going on?" asked Lettie. "Who do you think you are to leave my little girl lying naked in the examining room?"

A clinical silence rang around the room. One of the white coats cleared his throat nervously and then bowed solemnly to the woman whom he assumed was my mother.

"I'm afraid I've some unusual news to tell you, madam. Your little girl has Progeria."

Progeria! An horrendous word. It rhymed with hysteria, malaria and diphtheria. Not only was I oversized, it had been discovered by these medical men and women, but I was also ageing at an unnatural rate, triple the rate, in fact, of your average human being. By the age of five, I would look fifteen, at ten, I would look thirty, by twenty, my bones would be arthritic, my vision failing, my hair thinning, and by thirty it would be all over. So they predicted.

Progeria, they had said, sometimes known as Werner Syndrome. It had never before been known to occur in a giantess; normally it occurred in dwarfs. There had been a sporadic gene mutation, they said, at the time of my conception. Lettie tried hard not to breathe a sigh of relief at the news that I was going to age fast and die early. I was devoid of reaction. The words were lost on me, meaningless. (My mind was developing only twice as fast as normal, therefore body and mind would be forever out of synch with each other, and also out of whack with the world. Though I was larger than your average nine-year-old girl, I had the cognition, said the doctors, of a six-year-old child. I was just a little advanced. I was no great genius.)

They never should have taken me to the hospital. I should have been their shameful secret, the thing they never declared to the world. Now they were on to me; I was tagged, I had a number. It was burnt into my left shoulder: 373603 11 333. I was branded. There were dark mutterings about my thyroid. Over the years, they took numerous samples; each piece was contained and marked with these digits. They wanted a record of my growth, my progression. They wanted to put me in a box and keep me there, pack of little Mengeles that they were. Are. Don't think this process of bodily documentation has stopped just because I'm on my last legs.

Weekly check-ups at the hospital were an integral part of my life as a 'child.' As I lay upon their table, as they peered down at me, objectifying me, I learned to detach myself from my body, to float up and away, to put myself elsewhere. From this place, high up near the ceiling, I would look back down upon my prone form and be thankful for this ability, this knack I had of absenting myself, of being present in body, but not in spirit.

And for the rest of my natural life, the terrible fact hung over me like a black shadow. My time was not the same as yours. Mine was life on fast-forward. I moved at triple your speed. I was dying at three times the rate of everybody else.

I was growing so fast that the only fabric worth encasing me in was stretch fabric. Lettie invested in some super-stretch fleecy knit casuals, tracksuit bottoms and matching tops, in black, always black. She knew that I would stain any other colour. It was a dress code, a uniform that I was to stick to my entire life. To this day I still dress as Lettie dressed me. Always in stretch-knit. Always in black.

Lettie avoided announcing my arrival to the matriarchs, Grandma Lolly and Grandma Stuff, for as many years as she could conceivably manage, five years, in fact. The two old biddies were practically housebound, which made Lettie's secret easier to keep. But this was Provencia after all, word was bound to get around eventually, and when the young woman who took Grandma Lolly and Grandma Stuff their meals on wheels hinted about the presence of a child in the lives of Barry and Lettie, both grandmas got on the blower and called up their offspring to find out what had been going on.

"What's this I hear about a child?" Grandma Lolly barked at Lettie.

"Barry," honked Grandma Stuff to Barry. "Have you been breeding on the sly?"

An explanation was called for.

"Couldn't we just *tell* them about her, rather than actually *showing* her to them?" asked Barry.

"Best to just bite the bullet," said Lettie. "Before Chinese whispers set in and they start hearing we're housing a fire-breathing cannibalistic demon girl. Best she meet them face to face."

*

We did Grandma Stuff first. Until this point in time, my world had been comprised solely of the Butchette and the family home; this was to be my first real experience of life beyond my familiar walls. This was to be my first time in the 'world outside'. Lettie planned the excursion for weeks beforehand, but to me it seemed as if it had come out of the blue. She leaned down over my Butchette pen one day, took me by the hand and pulled me to my feet.

"Time to meet the relatives," she said, guiding me to the passenger seat of the car, mushing my flesh into position and cramming the door shut behind me.

A number of firsts occurred that day; my first time meeting the relatives, my first time venturing outside the comfort zone that my 'world inside' had become, the first time my adoptive mother and I had engaged in any kind of outing together. And, perhaps most importantly, this was the first time I crossed over any of Provencia's three bridges; for that day, we drove straight over the Opal, with me eventually summoning the guts to sit up straight in my seat and peer over the edge at the black oily gloop that constituted our city's best known landmark.

Grandma Stuff, a.k.a. Dawn Doom, lived just across the river, on the South side, in the old brick cottage in which Barry had been raised. Lettie had warned her that we were soon to descend, and as my adoptive mother and I were driving across one of the city's three bridges, Grandma Stuff was busy preparing what she called 'a light luncheon', spreading her kitchen table with various hams, cheeses, pickles and breads. Lettie and I were both a little nervous.

"You'll be meeting two mothers today," Lettie had said to me that morning. "So be on your best behaviour. No howling, no tantrums, no grubbing round for insects in the back garden. You'll speak only when spoken to. Remember; little girls should be seen and not heard."

I nodded compliantly

"Now," said Lettie, as we pulled into Grandma Stuff's driveway. "You're about to meet Barry's mother, so remember what I told you. Be a good girl for Lettie."

She opened her handbag and revealed a little glass jar full of bugs and a couple of cans of my favourite orange beverage.

"Rewards," she said. "If you behave."

She always knew my weak spots, Lettie, and how to play on them.

I followed Lettie down the driveway to the cottage and stood beside her as she rang the buzzer. The front door was made of glass, with a picture of a deer sandblasted onto it. Rustling noises came from inside the house and, behind the deer, a blurred human shape came drifting into view.

"Stand up straight," said Lettie, prodding me in the back. "Shoulders back."

I was developing a nasty slouch as a result of my gargantuan size and the hunch that bloomed upon my right shoulder.

The door opened and there stood Barry's mother. She was no wizened old biddy, she was big, Grandma Stuff, with thick arms, a broad behind and a large monobossom across which her arms were folded. She wore a large blue floral dress made of stretch fabric.

"Hello there, love," she said, beaming at Lettie. "Come on in. I've been expecting you."

Lettie pushed me forwards.

"This is Celia," she said. "The orphan."

"Ah," said the elderly Mrs Doom, squinting at me. "So this is what you've been keeping secret, eh? Oh my goodness. She is a *big* girl, isn't she. How old did you say she was?"

"Five years old," said Lettie. "Going on fifteen."

"And what's that ridiculous thing on her head, Lettie?" asked Stuff, gesturing towards my cover.

"It's to keep her hid, Dawn."

Mrs Doom made tut-tutting noises and waved us into the house.

"Well, don't stand out there getting cold."

I hung back a little, shy. Lettie gave me a prod and I stepped across the threshold.

"She's deaf in her left ear," whispered Lettie, as we followed Grandma Stuff down the corridor, "so I'll stay on the right side of her and you stay on the left and that way if you say something silly she won't be able to hear it."

Grandma Stuff's living-room was a shrine to her husband's former profession. Taxidermied specimens greeted the eye whichever way you looked; Dawn had positioned bookshelves side by side around the room and on these the animals sat, glaring at you with their inanimate stares. Snowy owls and barn owls peered down from the top shelves, there were rabbits in human costume and kittens striking poses that kittens did not naturally strike. A frog shaved another frog with a cut-throat razor. A couple of Grandpa Doom's war medals hung about the neck of a stuffed cat which stood upright in one corner. The fire-screen was a gigantic, slightly moth-eaten vulture, with its wings outstretched. I felt quite unsettled, standing there, surrounded by so many glass eyes. Hung upon the far wall were numerous pictures of her deceased husband, Thomas Doom, always with a proud grin on his face, always holding one or other of his works in the air, like a trophy.

We moved through to the kitchen, where Stuff had laid out her spread.

"This looks lovely," said Lettie, motioning me towards a chair to the left of my grandmother. "You didn't need to go to all that trouble, Dawn. A cup of tea would have been fine."

"Gotta keep the tucker-box stacked," said Stuff, patting her stomach.

I did what was expected of me and ate my lunch, even though the insects in Lettie's handbag appealed far more to my culinary sensibilities. Lettie and Dawn kept up a pleasant chit-chat throughout the lunch; I was on the deaf side of the grandma and knew that talking would be futile. After lunch, the three of us retired to the living-room, Lettie and Dawn with cups of tea and me with the can of Fanta Lettie had handed me as a reward for being silent throughout the meal. We sat side by side on the sofa, surrounded by the terrible dead animals that stared.

"Bit dark out today," declared Stuff, peering out of the window at the thick storm clouds which gathered beyond the pane; and she reached down beside her, pulled up an electric cord and felt along it for the switch, which she pressed.

A blowfish which had been sitting on the shelf opposite lit up blue.

"My favourite lamp," she muttered, slurping again at her tea.

There were other goodies also, treasures which were kept out of sight. When Lettie excused herself to go to the toilet, Dawn Doom took my hand and pulled me into the bedroom. On the dresser sat a fine array of jars containing pickled newts, preserved frogs, a sheep foetus and her pièce de resistance, a pickled platypus. She tipped the jar that contained the platypus up at one corner, and the liquid in which the animal sat sloshed from side to side.

"Spirit of wine," she said. "From the early days, before taxidermy. It used to belong to my husband's great-great-grandfather, old man Doom."

She patted me on the shoulder in a congenial manner.

"You're alright, aren't you love," she said. "Bet you've got a great personality."

That old platitude. Still, her heart was in the right place.

I nodded, my little black and white eyes gawking at the platypus.

"Girl like you's gonna need a profession," she said. "That's for sure."

She tapped my head with one wrinkled finger.

"I hope you've got some brains in there girly, 'cause Lord knows you ain't gonna get by on your looks."

*

A similar verdict on yours truly was uttered by Grandma Lolly, to whose house we ventured after the lunch with Stuff. Dawn Doom had kissed us both goodbye and sent us on our way.

"Lovely to meet you, Celia," she said, not insincerely.

She, like Grandma Lolly, was to turn out to be an accepting old girl.

"When you've seen all I have," Dawn Doom would say. "You learn to take life as it comes and if life has given you to us, Celia, then we just have to accept you."

"That went well," said Lettie, on the drive to the home of the next grandma. "Keep that up and you'll be given every last one of these bugs."

She patted her handbag.

"Beatrice is deaf in her right ear," she said. "So just reverse the rule we applied to Dawn and stay on the right side of her and all will be fine."

Ten minutes' drive away, on the same side of the river, the South, was Grandma Lolly. On the drive over, Lettie informed me that her mother had suffered a severe stroke several years previously and was now confined to a wheelchair, in which she whizzed about at top speeds, often crashing into doors and walls and furniture. Also, said Lettie, although her old Mum wouldn't admit it in a month of Sundays, she suffered dreadfully from incontinence and a permanent scent of urine lingered about her person and her home.

"Just warning you, Celia," she said. "So as to spare you any nasty surprises."

Grandma Lolly's house was identical to Grandma Stuff's in every regard except one; it was wooden rather than brick. We pulled up outside, parked the car and stood on Lolly's doorstep. Lettie raised the brass knocker and tapped three times. From inside the house we heard *crash, bang, crash*, the sound of Lolly bouncing off the walls as she wheel-chaired her way towards us. There was a final thud as she slammed into the other side of the door, and then we saw the handle turning, the door swung open and there she was, as tiny as Stuff was large, a wrinkled old lady in a brown polyester skirt and beige twin set.

"Hello, sweetheart," she greeted her daughter. "Gizza kiss then, love."

She held her cheek out for a peck. An unlit fag hung from her lip. Lettie obliged with a short kiss and then took a hanky from her handbag and wiped off her lips. Lolly reached out and clasped hold of my arm. I looked down at her hand. There was a thick layer of dirt under her fingernails. The stench of wee hung about her like a cloud.

"So this is what you've been hiding from us eh?" she said to Lettie. She smiled up at me. Her teeth were short, brown stumps. She stared at the undie-cover which hid my face.

"What's that for Lettie?" she said, pointing.

"Don't even ask," came my adoptive mother's reply.

"Well you're not gonna stand on the doorstep all day, are ya?" asked Lolly, taking a box of matches from her pocket and lighting up her cigarette. "Come on in out of the cold."

Crash, bang, crash.

She led us haphazardly to the living-room.

"Fancy a cuppa?"

"I'll make it Mum," said Lettie. "You stay right where you are."

Which left me *alone* with her.

On Lolly's mantelpiece sat all the sweeties which had remained unsold after the stroke had forced her to close down Major's Sweet

Shop. The old hag had been too stingy to give them away to the many kids who could be found outside the store on closing day, empty hands outstretched in anticipation of a free sugar rush, as the newly wheelchair-bound Beatrice had shouted clearing-out and cleaning-up instructions to her daughter to whom the honours of shutting down the store had been allocated. The doctor had warned Lolly off the sugar, but she wasn't having any of it; she kept a jar full of assorted sweeties stashed down beside her in her wheelchair at all times, next to the bottle of gin which she was also never without.

"Here, dear," she said, taking her lolly jar out from under her skirt, unscrewing the lid and extending it towards me. "Have a sweetie."

I had been spoken to, and so I was allowed to speak.

"No thanks," I said. "I'll hold off for now."

No such holding off for Lolly; she pushed her right hand into the jar, pulled out a handful of candy and shoved it in her mouth. Down the corridor, I could hear the kettle boiling. I felt uncomfortable here, alone with this woman, and when Lettie returned with a tray upon which were placed two cups of tea and the obligatory can of Fanta, relief swept through me.

"Nice and sweet, Mum," said Lettie, handing her mother one of the cups.

"Oh lovely," said the old bird, then reached into her lolly jar and added a few sweets into the mix. "Just like little flavoured sugar lumps," she said.

She sat slurping at her tea and sucking at her lips.

"Not quite right," she declared, and added a splash from her gin bottle, with the comment, "Liqueur tea".

"You've not heard from that wayward brother of yours, have you dear?" she asked Lettie, after a spell.

Lettie shook her head and emitted a sigh.

"No doubt he'll pop up one day," she said. "When we're least expecting him."

Her mother nodded.

"Send him round to see me," she said. "Needs his old Mum to sort him out, that one does."

She was not as loquacious as Stuff, and I noted that Lettie was forced to make a good deal of the conversation, while her mother grumbled and fished out sweets from her little glass jar. I did what had been asked of me and kept my big trap shut. Lettie chatted away to her mother about progress in the Butchette, about Barry, about me, Celia, about Dawn Doom. I noticed Lolly stiffen at the mention of Stuff's name. When she'd finished her tea, Lolly wheeled herself across to the mantelpiece, took down a jar of brightly coloured sweets and gave them to me. It was a gesture of acceptance and also a gesture of farewell. Until next time. Lolly's parting words echoed those that Stuff had spoken earlier.

"I hope you've got some hidden talents, dearie," she muttered darkly, as we were leaving. "You're gonna need 'em."

*

Neither grandma had seemed upset that the first five years of my existence had been hidden from them; no doubt Lettie had told them of the temper tantrums that had once held me so firmly in their grasp, the tantrums which were, luckily for Lettie, subsiding with age. I was an oversized angel now, or at least able to act like one; I had control of the storms which had once controlled me. I was the closest thing to a grandchild the two old women had ever had; if there'd been other children, other options, they might not have been so accepting of me. I was all they had. It was Celia or nothing.

Sunday became Grandma Day, a weekly outing for Lettie and me. Into the car and across the river we would go, knocking on the two front doors of the family matriarchs, one with her rows of stuffed animals and the other with her jars of lollies. I came to enjoy the outing, it was a good chance to see something beyond my little Butchette pen and the cellar; I liked my two grandmas, I liked the drive.

You'd have thought these two old bats would've got on like a house on fire, but they hated each other with a passion. They were deadly rivals. The crux of the animosity, as I came to understand it, was that each thought their own offspring too good to marry the other's. They'd first met at Barry and Lettie's wedding; their initial meeting had been a tense occasion, as frosty as the icing on the wedding cake. Lolly had called Stuff a fat old cow and Stuff had told Lolly she was a grubby, smelly old witch. The recently wheelchair-bound Lolly had then run over Stuff's foot with one of her wheels, to which Stuff had responded by clouting Lolly on the head with one of her sizeable fists. Lolly had promptly leant over and bitten Stuff on the bum and Stuff had picked up a porcelain plate which she had been about to bring cracking down on Lolly's head when Barry had intervened and broken up the fight, ordering Lolly to sit at one end of the hall in which the reception was being held and Stuff to stand at the other. The two had not seen eye to eye ever since; and I came to be something of a pawn between them. They vied for my affections; Stuff by trying to press some of her dead animals into my arms and Lolly by giving me handfuls of sticky lollies. I was impartial; I liked both my grandmothers, appreciated the way they seemed to accept me without judging me. In their eyes, I was big old Celia, who wouldn't harm a fly.

*

The only time Lolly and Stuff agreed to be in the same room as each other was at Christmas, when they would sit, one at each end of the dining table, flashing daggers at each other with their eyes. They used to have farting competitions, two old matriarchs, letting rip over the turkey and cranberry sauce. They made Barry adjudicate, gave him a set of score cards marked from one to ten, like an Olympics gymnastic judge.

"Don't encourage them, Barry," Lettie would scold, but Barry thought it was a great game and his silent mood would fall away in keeping with the spirit of the occasion.

"Come on girls," he'd holler. "Give it your best. Oh, for God's sake, that was pathetic. Surely you can do better than that."

My first Christmas spent with the grandmas took place at the end of my fifth year on earth, after they and I had been formally introduced. At previous Christmases, Lolly and Stuff had sat upstairs, oblivious to my presence in the house; while I was locked down in the cellar, too dangerous to be let above ground. It was an historic moment, that first Christmas I spent with the four of them. I was on my best behaviour; I put a dampener on my insect cravings and I didn't howl once, the result of which self-discipline was that I was permitted to attend each subsequent Christmas and was sometimes even allowed to help Lettie wrap the gifts beforehand. I was crawling up out of the darkness. It was soon after my first successful Christmas that the goat wire was put out in the backyard. Lettie fashioned me a harness and would hook me onto the wire, in order that I might, every now and then, be put outside to catch whatever rays of sunshine sloped down into the backyard. Sometimes a piece of sun would burn like a coin in my hand.

It was at the second of these Christmas dinners that the dubious issue of my future was raised. It was Stuff who mentioned the topic. The farting competition had been held (won, on this occasion, by Lolly), the meal had been consumed and everybody was sitting back in their chairs, Barry with a port, the ladies each with a glass of sherry, and me with my Fanta.

"So," said Stuff, raising one eyebrow at her daughter-in-law. "How exactly are you intending to *educate* young Celia?"

Barry choked on his port and looked across at his wife.

Lettie sat up straight, looked Dawn Doom in the eye and replied with a firm and decisive, "We're not."

Her face said the case was closed.

*

Education was, for me, out of the question. My presence would surely have disturbed the other children; I would have induced nightmares. I was self-taught. In much the same manner as I mastered the art of walking, I taught myself to read on my own. Whenever she felt the societal pressure to be a 'good mother', whenever a rash of guilt came over her, Lettie would come and lean over the edge of my pen and read to me, holding the book out so that I could see the black print and it wasn't long before I was pre-empting her, snatching the words right out of her mouth. The first time this phenomenon occurred, she thought that I had simply memorised the story, and as an experiment she bought me a book I had never laid eyes on before. To her surprise and delight, I merrily rattled off the first three pages, as if it was a tale I had been told many times before. She was unburdened from the task of teaching me to read; she simply borrowed several books a week from the local library and tossed them into my pen. I tore through them like a caged tiger chomping through its daily ration of fresh meat.

What I remember most from this time is the expectation, the waiting, the sense that something was about to happen and the fear that nothing ever would. What I was waiting for was the arrival of the gift: my camera.

*

In my mind my life is divided and it is the gift that divides it. There are the years before and then there are the years after. It seems trite to say that nothing was ever the same after the camera was given, but, here, I'll say it anyway. *After the gift, nothing was*

65

ever the same. When I held that baby in my hands, I had my finger on some heavenly pulse; I could stop the flow of life. I was no longer a specimen; I was no longer captured and defined. I now held the power which had previously been used against me. I was no longer the named; I was now the giver of names. When I stared out at the world around me, it seemed that I looked only through the dark eye; I saw only blackness. But when I peered through the camera lens, I used the right eye, the white one and I saw a world bathed in light. The gift spun my world upside down, showed me the earth's inverse. And the giver? He seemed to me to be not human, but divine, a winged messenger who had delivered my salvation. It felt to me as if somebody had been watching, evaluating my life. It seemed that this person had judged that I had been dealt a rough hand, and was hoping to slide me an ace under the table. At this point in the story, however, I do not yet hold any aces and nor do I hold the Joker. I have not been saved. All that is around the corner. All that is the road not yet travelled, the unknown highway, the future. All that is yet to be.

VIII

I awake early, with the sun streaming in through the window. I must've forgotten to pull the curtains before falling asleep last night; now the sun's rays hit me full in the face, I squint up into it, as if into a searchlight. I lever myself upright, walk across to the window and examine the backyard. I note, with some surprise, that spring has arrived, the seasons are sneaking up on me again, the years are flicking by faster and faster, like one of those flip books that kids used to make; crude cartoon animation.

Time speeds up as you age; I used to believe that this is because time is relative to experience. When you are two years old a year is half your life, half of all you have experienced, when you are ninety, twelve months is a ninetieth of what you have known, a mere blip. Another theory is that, with age, the body's internal clock begins to deteriorate, the neurotransmitters don't function like they used to; your dopamine production, your serotonin levels, they're shafted. The hands of the clock are racing you to your grave.

And my own clock, set to overdrive, three hours to your hour, three ticks to your every tock? It's had it in for me from the start. It would bury me alive if it could. I am living on borrowed time.

But back to the seasons. We must reign in our minds; we must stop our thoughts from galloping off without us, like wild horses. The garden is in full bloom; geraniums, roses, carnations, little bursts of colour everywhere, like some kid has taken a set of felt tip pens to the backyard. Small green fruit which will soon be plums are taking shape upon one of the trees; tiny bunches of green grapes hang from the vine waiting to swell. Potential hangs in the air; everything is waiting to ripen. Then the birds'll be in there, greedy beaks taking a couple of vengeful pecks at every plum, every fig, as if they grow tired of any particular fruit after a couple of mouthfuls and feel compelled to move on, as if they're determined to puncture holes in as many pieces of fruit as possible.

Last time I looked it was winter, the city was covered in permafrost and I went slipping and sliding down every street, terrified of falling and breaking a hip. When you're carrying my kind of weight it pays not to go over, what with the other three hundred kilos of you coming crashing down on top of whatever poor old bone happens to have the misfortune to be the first part of you to hit the pavement. I should invest in a cane, or a gigantic Zimmerframe, better still, an enormous motorised wheelchair, scoot about the streets, wild white hair blown back behind me, young children scurrying, terrified, out of my way.

Soon it will be summer, long golden days, the smell of freshly-mown grass, the one ice-cream man that's left here will drive the streets in his Mr Whippy van, serving us dollops of creamy white mush. Good for the arteries; mine are clogged a little more every day, leaving the blood a little less room in which to pass through on its path to the heart, which beats in the centre of me like a giant red party-balloon. When I'm gone they'll snatch it from my body, exhibit it next to Phar Lap's in the National Museum of Australia, in a special curtained booth, charge the punters a buck – fifty each, just for a quick peek at it.

At the end of summer will come autumn, or fall, depending on which country you're from, with the coloured leaves dripping from the trees like candy wrappers, gusting about in gutters, blocking up the drains. After autumn, the winter, the snow, the blank landscape outside my window. And then the whole thing begins again, the circle. At the beginning, back to the end.

*

But there I go again, galloping. It's lucky I've got George here to provide me with his little reality checks, or I'd be adrift in Never Never Land with no hope of return.

Speak of the devil, he comes in through the front door carrying my morning paper under his arm, must have picked it up from the porch, where it is thrown every morning. On the front page is plastered a picture of the current mayor. George's right arm is behind his back as if he is hiding something.

"Election time again. Who you gonna vote for Celia?"

This question is a standing joke amongst Provencians. The national elections are not till next year, but coming up this weekend is the mayoral election, with its one candidate, Norman Lazarus. Norman's been mayor of Provencia for the last thirty years and would be more than happy to give up the post to an adversary could he find somebody willing to take over the job. Every three years his term expires; every three years he wins a race that nobody else wants to run. Only an idiot would want to lord it over this hell-hole. There have been efforts to lure in candidates from elsewhere (*we'll pay you good money to run*) but there have been no takers.

The election is, therefore, a farce. It's supposed to boost morale, but nobody bothers to vote. What's the point? They still print the voting forms, set up the little booths down at the local school. They give you a range of names to pick from on the form: Norman Lazarus, N.J. Lazarus, Norman James Lazarus, or Mr N. Lazarus. They want us to think we're spoilt for choice. Lazarus puts on a good show when he 'wins', dons his mayoral robes and his tacky bronze medallion and parades through the city streets, while his family act as if he has beaten off some fierce competition. He's the naked emperor in his brand new clothes. No chance of rebirth for this Lazarus; he refuses to die in the first place.

The city councillors consist of Norman's wife Beverly and their daughter Georgia. Various members of the extended Lazarus family take care of those civic duties normally attended to by employees of the city council; they tend to our two public parks, collect the garbage, sweep the streets, keep the books.

They're not short of wannabe mayors in the capital, of course, they've got mayors coming out of their ears. That's because they stole all of ours. It's hard to remember that it wasn't always this way; the war between Provencia and the capital often feels as old as the ongoing battle between God and the devil, but there was a time when the two were not enemies, but friends. This is a tale of two cities and the record of the relationship reads like this; we moved from friendship to friendly rivalry to swearing undying enmity.

When I was in my infancy, the two cities were entering the friendly rivalry period. The relationship between Provencia and the capital was a teasing big brother, little brother kind of affair, and you can guess who was forced to play the little brother. When it comes to sheer numbers, they've always had us licked; when we were three hundred thousand they were 2.2 million, but we gritty little Provencians still knew how to hold our own.

East and West met together for various sporting tournaments; we had our fair share of sporting heroes and took great delight in mopping the basketball court or football field with the opposition. As well as priding ourselves upon our superior sportsmanship, we also considered ourselves the cultured cousin; they had the Houses of Parliament, the corporate tycoons, the high-rise buildings, the cold hard kick-ass cash, but, per capita, we had ten times as many theatres, art galleries and fine restaurants. We thought of them as just a little crass, a little uncouth and they, in turn, thought of us Provencians as 'snooty' (their word, not ours). The comedy programmes they screened on nationwide telly often used to send us up; we'd be wearing berets and drinking lattes and trying to sound intellectual. We Provencians couldn't get funding for our comedy skits; we acted them out in local theatres, instead. We mocked their money-grubbing, 'Capitalism Is King' ways, their notoriously inefficient bureaucratic system, their society without a soul. In comparison, we considered ourselves highbrow.

All's different now, of course. Our artistes turned tail, fled to the city of the Golden Dollar, the more adventurous ones pay their tokenistic visits, they come sneaking round these parts writing about the desolation, or painting it, or filming it to show in their cinemas. I suppose they all have a good laugh at our expense. We are 'good material'.

*

"Celia?"

For how long has he been calling my name? I notice, not without alarm, that these temporal lapses of mine are occurring ever more frequently; I'll have to watch that. Keep my mind on the job.

He is extending his right hand towards me, he is holding a gift; a plate of leftover pork pies. Apparently his wife threw a bit of a party last night and over-catered, resulting in a glut of these stodgy goodies. She works, this wife of his, she's the receptionist out at the pulp and paper mill; he carries a photo of her in his wallet, I yanked it out one day when he left his wallet lying about by accident. Dark, glossy brown hair, thick red lipstick, nails like talons, painted up bright red to match the lips, no doubt she gossips on the telephone and reads trashy magazines all day. Living out the cliché. Still, nice of her to think of me vis-à-vis those pies.

"I want to talk to you," he says, as he pushes the plate into my hand.

"So that's it then," I think. "He's buttering me up."

He offers to take me out.

"You spend too much time sitting round this place," he says. He already has my coat in his hands, he's pushing it onto my shoulders, shoving me out the door. We're headed for *Tim's Diner*, which is the one café in Provencia that has not gone under. The place has been a favourite haunt of mine, during the later half of my life. I am fond of its red-leather booths, the rock-hard muffins, the dry scones, the thin watery coffee, the jukebox playing in the corner. The stale sweet odour; old ladies, old sweat.

The hippies next door are quiet today, heavy session on the ganja last night, no doubt. They're not really morning people. They've painted their letterbox with psychedelic swirls, their front yard is filled with stinging nettles which are more like stinging triffids, each day they creep a little closer towards my own front yard. Maybe I can convince George to get out there with the weed-killer and give the buggers a good blasting.

Progressing down Third Street, things deteriorate from there; burnt-out cars, half homes with missing roofs and doors and windows, houses inhabited by all kinds of unsavoury types. The hippies are not the worst, but the best of it.

When I walk the streets of Provencia, I sometimes feel as if I am stalking through a battleground, as if these vagrants squatting in other people's empty homes are snipers, aiming to send a bullet straight through my back whenever I turn my face away. At first, I wanted to win them over, I wanted them on my side, but I soon realised that their hearts are as hard as steel. Most of them eye me with cold contempt, knowing that I make money off their misery. They move through this city in packs, like wolves. They never have furniture; when the citizens who cleared out for the capital left Provencia they inevitably took all their possessions with them, ripped up the carpet, took all the pictures from the walls, cleared out every last vestige of humanity and left only the bare shell of a house behind them. These shells now provide shelter to these wanderers, who live without gas or electricity and go begging during the day, or rummage in garbage cans for edible scraps.

Where do they come from, these marginal drifters, these transients? They won't tell you. *I'm from nowhere, man*, they say, eyeing you through a crack-induced haze. *I fell from the sky.*

They seem to float in on one breeze and waft out on the next. I have learnt to snap them as soon as I see them; go back the next day in search of a shot and most likely as not your subject will simply have upped and left. *What happened to Jim?* You might ask somebody who had been left behind. *Where's Tommy?* Or, if they had refused to tell you their names, you would describe them as best you could. *You know, the one with the beard and the blue top.* Blank looks from the comrades, empty stares. Many gave false names, which were of no use to me the next day. *Who?*

I learnt that there was no point in returning; I took what I could while it was there for the taking, I seized the moment. I did not take without giving; in return for letting me capture them on film, I would hand each down-and-outer a tea and bickies voucher, which was an invite to join me for a chat. Most thought I was just being patronising; they knew who I was. *That Celia*, they'd say. *Who does she think she is? She can stick her charity up her enormous ass.*

But some were interested in visiting, or wanted the free biscuits, or both. And I liked these visits, I was polite; I wore my friendly face, good old bumbling, kindly, Celia, such a good listener. They would hand over their vouchers and I would sit them down at my table, let them talk about anything and everything they chose, and sometimes, admittedly, I would pick up my Leica and take a few timely shots. Some were reticent, saying nothing, simply reaching grubby fingers towards the packet of biscuits; others gave me their entire life story, or their version of it. I often suspected that the stories they told were fictional.

The only family still living in Third Street are the Whitsons; he's a foreman out at the mill and she's a dress-maker specialising in industrial uniforms. She does all the gear for the mill and also ships some of her other produce, boiler suits and overalls and such like off to the capital. They must be one of the few double-income families left in town. There are no schools left open in Provencia; the Whitson's two sons receive their education via correspondence. Mrs Whitson is convinced of the virtues of such educational methods.

Don't want my young 'uns at a disadvantage just 'cause we refuse to pack up and head West. They'll be the brightest sparks in the country, these two, you mark my words.

I am the official Whitson family photographer; I reneged on the vow I once made never to do portraiture and took pics of the Whitsons which they have now hung up on the wall behind their stairwell; a testament to endurance and inner strength. The picture

I took of Mrs Whitson clutching her youngest child makes Dorothea Lange's *Migrant Mother* look like a woman who's just hit the lottery jackpot. Both Whitson and child have a look of suppressed panic in their eyes, as if they are about to be mown down by a large truck. What will it take to make them leave? The closing of the mill, I suppose, for that will truly signify 'game over' for this half-town of ours. Till then, we hang on to the shreds of what we like to believe was once this country's finest city. Till then, we are as stubborn as the proverbial mule.

*

Tim's Diner is located three streets over from Third Street; there used to be a whole cluster of shops here, small delicatessens selling ham and cheese and olives, classy little Italian joints, a bakery, a vegetarian restaurant which was once considered vaguely radical. 'Tim' if there is one, is obviously made from pretty stern stuff; whoever owns the place must have gritted the teeth, hung on in there, as if for dear life. His asparagus rolls are legendary, though many of them look like they've been sitting in the plastic display cabinet since the diner opened, in 1973. We enter, pick a booth. George, obviously a novice, sits and waits for a waiter. I know better, and make my way to the counter, where I order us two black coffees, a dry old scone for me and one of those fossilised asparagus rolls for George. I carry the snack back to the table on a little wooden tray, but by then my bladder is bursting, and so whatever he wants to talk to me about will have to wait while I relieve myself.

The Gentleman's Room at Tim's has provided me with hours of literary entertainment. I don't often use the Ladies, not here, nor anywhere. The queues for the men's room are always shorter, their urinating is quick and communal, just a swift slash, up with the zipper and out, they don't loiter like the women do, they're not touching up lipstick and gossiping. The men stare a little less. Their judgment of me is less harsh, less damning. I'm not always feeling up to braving female scrutiny. And I like to spy. On their conversations, and also on their writing, on the words that have been scribbled on their walls. Lots of gay boys leaving their numbers.

For a good time call Jim – your wish is my desire.

There are also females advertising their services, either they walked right on in here, just as I do, or else they got a male friend to come in and write their words for them: *Asian beauty available, 18 years. Norwegian goddess; legs 11, performance 10/10.*

And who amongst the gents I stumble across, as I plod past the urinal and squeeze myself into the solo cubicle, would speak up and accuse me of *not* being one of them and thereby risk being on the receiving end of a thump from one of my big mitts? Not even the very stupid would risk a comment; they know it's me, Celia. They know of my violent reputation. They fear me. They nod briskly as I pass.

I know what the Ladies write, next door; I've been in there, too, upon occasion. Theirs is a different style of graffiti comprised mostly of declarations of adoration never seen by the beloved: *Karen loves Jason, Janine 4 Daniel, Kylie + Paul.* If the adored never sees it, why do they bother? Perhaps that is exactly the point; these are little confessional booths, someplace to get the unspoken off your chest. Nobody can pin you to your name, here. *That was another Karen, another Jason.* You can confess without nailing yourself to anything definite.

Today I take out my marker pen and write, not my phone number, but the other number, the one stamped onto my left shoulder, as if I am cattle that has been branded. *373603 11 333* I write. *Who needs to be a name, when you can be a number?* Then I push the lid back onto my pen and exit.

George has eaten his roll and is picking at my scone. I give his hand a sharp smack, snatch back my scone, which takes a good deal of washing down, thankful for the coffee.

"So," I say, through a mouthful of doughy slop, "what was it you wanted to say."

There is terror in his eyes.

"Well," he ventures. "You know how this is an exhibition and everything."

"Of course."

"Well, exhibitions are about pictures, not words."

"So?"

"So I know you've been asked to pen a few words for the brochure, but it just seems to me that you might be getting a little bit..."

"A little bit what?"

"Carried away."

Unsure of how to deal with this, I opt for a restrained politeness.

"I appreciate your concern, George," I say, sitting up and looking as prim as my size will allow. "But really these words of mine are, quite simply, none of your business."

"I just don't want you to become overly involved, and then face disappointment at some later date."

"Disappointment?" I say. "What kind of disappointment did you have in mind?"

"They asked for three thousand words, Celia. Any fool could see you've already exceeded that. They're not going to be happy."

"Well maybe it's not for 'Them' whoever 'They' might be," I reply.

"Who's it for then?"

"It's not for anyone," I say. "It's just something to do."

"Well then, I've said my piece," he says. "Continue at your peril."

On that ominous note, we leave our booth at Tim's and walk back home, me five strides ahead of him, feeling a little disgruntled. This process of remembering is perilous enough without his voice of doom ringing in my ears. I am scared that the memories will hook me, drag me down into their depths. I am afraid that I will never resurface.

Back at home, we slide back into our old roles; he plays the snoop and I play the misanthropic ink-stained hunchback. I have caused no disruption to him, but I must confess that he has thrown me a little. I pick up my pen, put it down, make a few marks on the paper, scribble them out.

Words that he spoke in the diner return to haunt me. *It won't work, it won't wash, nobody will believe you, quit now, stop wasting your time.* I stare through the big bay window set into the wall opposite, pick my nose, scratch my bum. Perhaps this story will fight its way out anyway, I think, flooding into my spare hours as if it were molten gold, filling in the gaps in me, filling in the blanks.

IX

Good behaviour did not come naturally to me. My mind was crying out for insects and Fanta, my heart wanted to howl and my soul desired only to tear and destroy, to reduce everything to dust and ashes and broken bits. Masquerading as a nice little girl was taking its toll; the tension built up behind my eyes like a swarm of angry bees that could not fly elsewhere, but were trapped here, in my mind. It was inevitable, I suppose, that what I tried to suppress would find its way to the surface eventually, come hell, high water or both. There were eruptions, terrible eruptions, when I lay in one corner of the Butchette and howled like a haunted wolf; horrible incidents where I bit the legs of young children carrying cans of Fanta; relapses where I was found scoffing insects; butterflies, spiders, moths. I always felt better afterwards. It was like lava overflowing from the mouth of a volcano; try to keep it in and sooner or later you were bound to blow.

For the most part, however, I managed to control my demons, and was, in fact, so well behaved that gossip had begun to circulate that Lettie kept me doped up on heavy quantities of Ritalin. This was a falsity; she didn't believe in chemicals. A customer had told her all about positive reinforcement and Lettie was keen to put what she had heard into practice. She bent down over me and she looked into my black and white eyes and she spoke.

"Celia," she said. "How would you like a trip to the theatre this Sunday?"

My little eyes lit up. My head nodded furiously. I was about to be let out.

"A keen bean, eh?"

More nods.

"And you promise to behave yourself."

I smiled my little smile.

*

It was a noonday excursion; a dreary grey day, the sun hidden behind thick clouds, the distant threat of rain. Lettie spent the morning in the Butchette and at midday shut up shop. Barry went home to watch the football. Lettie pushed me into the passenger seat of the family car and slammed the door behind me. Something must've been on her mind that day, for she drove like a demon, speeding down the main road with her neck craned forward and her foot pressed hard upon the accelerator pedal. A bird hit the windowpane with a dull thud. Lettie did not bat an eyelid. A cat was squished beneath the tyres. No response. Looking back now, I can see that it was probably sheer nervousness about taking her daughter out in public, coupled with anxiety over seeing a man she'd not laid eyes on for ten years, that made her so reckless, but at the time her behaviour mystified me.

Theatres were scattered across the city in those days; most of them were small, cold, ramshackle buildings with hard seats covered in black vinyl and wooden stages with scuffed floorboards and green-rooms out the back. This particular theatre was located upon the banks of the beautiful Opal and was a rather sad imitation of Shakespeare's Globe and was called the Sphere. The Sphere was circular and, in true Shakespearean tradition, theatregoers were required to stand. The place was normally reserved solely for those works that had been penned by the great bard himself. The theatre manager had been known to consent to the staging of some weird adaptations: a group of school kids had done *King Lear* as a pantomime, an amateur theatrical society had done a musical version of *Anthony and Cleopatra* which featured a singing asp, there had been an overly ambitious one-woman show barely discernible as *Macbeth,* which featured a frazzled female lunatic scurrying about the stage attempting to play every part.

However, there had never been another Ed on stage, nor anything like him. Our Edward was very much one of a kind. My speculation is that, in order to gain use of the theatre, he'd crossed the manager's palm with some cold hard cash.

Lettie pulled into the theatre parking-lot and the two of us walked indoors, me with my cover and my inverted eyes, she holding her head up high, daring the world to stare at me as we stepped into the small foyer. Inside we found chaos. There were kids everywhere; screaming brats with runny noses, girls playing with toy trucks and boys playing with dolls, there were shy children dwindling in corners, there were bullies running about thumping the quieter children. There were mothers in various stages of panic and a couple of overwhelmed-looking Dads. I towered over the other children; I was taller than most of the parents. I had no idea about what was in store. I was ignorant. A bell rang and we were ushered through a red door into the main section of the theatre, as mothers smacked their children's bottoms and told them to be quiet. Inside, all was darkness and silence. We stood in a circle, waiting for the act to begin.

"What's going on?" asked a child's voice.

"Shhh," came the maternal reply. "Wait and see."

We waited. Somewhere, a dim light began to glow. I could not discern its source. Small restless feet shuffled impatiently, mothers coughed, fathers cleared their throats. Something which might have been described as music, had it any tonal variety, started up; it was not song, it was more like a slow deep steady hum, like somebody meditating. The sound was not emanating from one direction, it seemed to flow from the very walls, as if the building itself was creating this drone. The boy standing next to me started to cry.

The hum we had been hearing broke into voices. Sentences were broken into single words.

"Thank," said somebody to my left, without moving his lips.

"You," spoke a person behind me.

"All," said somebody from the other side of the room.

"For," said the boy who had been crying.

"Coming," said someone else.

"To."

"The."

"Show."

We audience members studied each others faces. Nobody amongst us had spoken. These words were coming from elsewhere; they were being thrown across the room. There was a bang and then we were staring at a white flame, which brightly burned in the centre of this circle we formed. The flame wavered, formed the shape of a person, solidified. The flame was Ed.

There was confused cheering, there were a few frightened cries.

"Ladies and gentlemen," hollered this man born of flame. "Let there be leporids!"

Rabbits began to rain down from the ceiling; not toy bunnies of the stuffed variety, but real animals, alive and hopping. Most sprang and bounced about the theatre, though one or two which appeared to have injured themselves in the fall lay struggling upon the floor. Ed whistled and the rabbits who had survived the fall intact went bounding across to where he stood. The injured were picked up by sympathetic mothers and taken to join the others. Ed picked up the animals one by one and shoved them into a sack, then put the sack down behind him, where it sat wriggling. Beneath my cover, I wriggled too. Most of the other kids were crying and clutching their mothers, but I was mesmerised. Right from the start, Ed had me captivated.

Ed reached into his sleeve and pulled out a puppet, pushed his hand up inside. The puppet began to talk, a high-pitched gabbling.

"Hi de hi de hi, kids."

"This guy's weird," I heard somebody next to me say.

"Who's this loser with his hand up my arse?" said the puppet.

Several offended mothers took their children by the hand and led them from the Sphere.

"Don't get your knickers in a twist, ladies. Or I'll have to come and help you untwist them."

Lettie was looking horrified. This was clearly not what she had been expecting from the afternoon's entertainment. The dummy ceased its speech. With his right hand, Ed snapped the head off the puppet he had been holding and threw it across the room. It laughed and laughed. Lettie shivered. She was reminded of other severed heads. Now words began bouncing off the walls again, reverberating like sonar. Those voices we had heard earlier had been his. He could throw his words for miles. Voice projection was one of those arts he had come damned close to mastering.

"And"
"Now"
"For"
"My"
"Next"
"Trick."

He was a walking, talking variety-show. He waved one hand at the bag of bunnies. They stopped their squirming.

A little girl next to me said, "Mummy, are the bunnies dead?"

Her mother replied, "No darling, they're just sleeping."

Ed untied the sack. A flock of doves flew out and flapped up to the rafters where they perched, cooing. There was polite applause from the audience.

I think that was when he noticed me. I felt his cold eyes upon my face. I hunched my shoulders up about my neck. I tried to hide.

"Ladies and gentlemen, boys and girls, at this stage of the show I usually ask for a volunteer to step forward from the audience. Today, however, I would ask you to allow me to choose."

He pretended to scan the audience. I moved backwards, behind Lettie. He raised his right arm, index finger extended; he moved it across the crowd. He paused, he wavered. Then he pointed that finger at me.

"Oh no," said Lettie. "Here we go."

She turned away, blended into the crowd. I took a tentative step forward.

"Are you adult or child?" he asked.

"I'm a child," I said.

"Well my little hefferlump," said Ed. "How do you fancy helping me out here today?"

I shrugged. The shrug was my answer to almost everything. I was five years old going on fifteen.

"Step forward, my sweet giantess, and we shall see what we can do with you."

The crowd parted as I moved through, like waves clearing before the prow of a ship. Ed clicked his finger and a box was lowered down from the ceiling on ropes. A couple of doves perched on the lid of it. I was in the centre of the circle now and Lettie was nowhere in sight. Ed held out his hand to me and I took it.

"Step up, step inside," he instructed and I did as I was told.

I could see that he was expecting me to fit into half a box. I stepped in, began to lose balance, groped for Ed's arm. He steadied me, lowered me inside. My knees were scrunched up to my chest. My toes were against a wall. I pushed my arms through the holes which were found to either side of me. I lay down and the lid closed over me. It was black in the box. It was a tight fit. There was somebody else in the other end of this contraption, with their feet poking out the end. Probably a dwarf. Why the hell had he picked me? He should have chosen somebody smaller. I could hear boos and jeers from the audience. This trick was old hat, they'd seen it all before. I could hear somebody scraping at the wood near my feet; Ed hacking at the box, pretending to sever me in two.

Something burst near my stomach, liquid was flooding across me. I was moving; my half of the box was being pulled away, then pushed back towards the other half. The lid was lifted. Ed took my hand and pulled me out. There were cries of repulsion from the crowd. I looked down and saw blood spreading across my stomach. Nobody was more horrified than I. And that was when I started up with my howl, a long, demented cry for I thought that this red stuff was real. My howl ran round the edges of the theatre, it filled the ears of the audience. Ed was facing away from me, bowing. Lettie came scurrying towards me with a placatory can of Fanta and a jar full of bugs. She dipped her finger in the blood, raised it to her mouth.

"Tomato sauce," she declared. "Just as I expected."

She understood that Ed had pushed a bag of sauce inside the box, and, in order to add a touch of authenticity to the act, had applied pressure to the outside of the box when sawing in order to cause the bag to burst. But I understood nothing. I hollered and I would not stop.

"Ladies and gentlemen, boys and girls," yelled this 'magician', "I say goodbye!"

There was a puff of smoke, an explosion of coloured lights and he was gone.

"And that," said Lettie, "was your Uncle Ed."

My howl fell silent.

*

Outside the theatre, a light rain had begun to fall. Doors were slamming shut, cars were pulling out from the parking lot; nobody seemed terribly impressed with the show they had seen. Looks of disappointment graced many a face. Down by the Opal a lone figure in a long black overcoat stood smoking a cigarette. Lettie took my hand and led me down to the river, to stand beside this man.

"Ed?"

He swung to face us. He was impossibly tall, impossibly thin. He looked stretched. He wore tight black trousers, a black shirt and a long black overcoat which billowed out around him like the cloak of a true magician. He had lank black hair which hung down over his eyes, which, when you caught a glimpse of them through the hair, were a brilliant and piercing sky-blue; the kind of eyes you cannot hide your secrets from. On his nose were now perched a pair of small gold-rimmed glasses, through which he peered with magnified eyes, like a hawk seeking its prey. Ed suffered chronic myopia but felt the spectacles would ruin the illusion were he to don them during the shows; he performed without any real sight at all. To him, the dummies, the rabbits and the crowd were one big blur.

"Lettie?"

There was a brief, restrained hug.

"I suppose you saw the ad in the paper," he said glumly and Lettie nodded her head. "I would have telephoned but...."

"But what?"

"I wasn't sure you'd want to hear from me."

"Now Ed," said Lettie primly. "No need for hard feelings between you and me."

Her tone implied the opposite. She was used to this kind of thing; hearing nothing from her brother for over a decade and then seeing his name in the daily rag. I saw the ad later; it was a picture of Ed in a long black cloak, holding a ventriloquist's dummy with the words *Motor-Mouth McGee* printed across the bottom, with a list of dates and venues. Motor-Mouth McGee was one of the many names he was known to assume. Our Edward was a master of self-invention, an illusionist whose greatest illusion was himself.

"Have you been to visit Mum?" asked Lettie.

"Later," said Ed, in a dismissive tone.

"Well make sure you do," said Lettie. "She's always asking after you. You've been quite a disappointment to her, Ed."

Ed's mouth drooped at the corners and Lettie lightened her tone.

"Come on then," she said. "Let's go get ourselves a drink."

I had the feeling she was speaking the words she felt she ought to say.

Ed became immediately jubilant, as if somebody had hit a button in his chest which infused him with sudden happiness. He stubbed out his cigarette, danced a small jig and looked across at me, as if seeing me for the first time since the show.

"And might I inquire as to the name of my delightful assistant?" he asked, pressing his eyes up close to mine.

"This is Celia," said Lettie.

Ed smiled at me.

"That's quite a howl you've got there, Celia. Do you think you could teach me how to howl like that?"

"You're a strange one," said Lettie, as she led him to the car.

*

The three of us hunched over a table in The Muddy Duck, a traditional English pub which had been a regular haunt for Barry and Lettie back in the days when their lives had run side by side on parallel tracks, never overlapping. She'd sat with her friends at one table, he'd conferred with his cronies at another, each sneaking furtive looks at the other. My arrival on the scene had put paid to such shyness, such romanticism. They'd not been back to the Duck since the day of my delivery. On this occasion, Ed nursed a whisky, Lettie a red wine, and I had been given a glass of Fanta. Lettie had a napkin in her hand and was dabbing at the tomato sauce which had exploded across my stomach.

"So what did you think of the show?" enquired Ed, who was every bit as self-centred as he was fascinating.

"I thought that bit with the bunnies was a bit cruel," said Lettie, in response to his enquiry.

"Cruel? That's nothing. Least I wasn't biting the heads off bats or throwing live chickens into the crowd to be torn limb from limb."

"I'm not sure it's suitable for children, Ed. Perhaps you should advertise yourself as an *adult* magician."

"Ah, but the kids love it. Sure, the odd stuck-up parent takes offence, but it's a rough old world out there. The sooner the young 'uns learn that, the better. "

"I just wish you'd *stick* to something," said Lettie with a sigh. "It seems like every time I see you you've got a new profession."

"You only see me once a decade!"

"Wouldn't it make more sense to concentrate on perfecting one thing? One *decent* thing," she rephrased.

"You know me, Lettie. Jack of all trades."

"And master of none," finished his sister, sipping at her red wine.

"I just get so bored. Man's gotta try and entertain himself."

He slurped at his whisky, took a cigar from his pocket and lit it, then turned to me and smiled.

"You know who I am, don't you Celia. I'm the long lost brother. The boy that screwed up his life. Ruined everything for himself."

Lettie was looking at the floor, unsmiling.

"Oh, come on Lettie, I've made a living. I've survived. I'm here today to embrace you."

He reached across the table and took his sister's hand.

"You were booted out," said Lettie tightly, through clenched teeth. "You could have had a good solid career. And you were kicked out. You could have had everything, and you threw it all away. And now what have you got? This crazy magic show. Those ridiculous tricks. And worse, to make those disgusting blue..."

"Ah!" Ed held up his hand for silence. "Not in front of the children, Lettie," he said.

His sister frowned.

"Oh come on, Lets," said Ed congenially. "Once they kicked me out of med school, they'd not have taken me back, not in a month of Sundays, not even if I'd got down upon bended knee and begged. It was a simple mistake, that's all, human error, and they wanted to make me pay for it with my future. They thought it was the end of the road for me. They didn't think I would keep on trucking, but honey, I trucked alright, down my own little highway. I skipped trains, leapt off the one that had reached its final destination and jumped on board another that still had plenty of track. What I'm trying to say is, I kept going. Screw you, I said, screw you and your stupid medical elite. The faulty heart was not my fault. How was I to know? One minute everything's fine and then next time I turn around they're calling me a murderer."

I must have looked concerned, for Ed was suddenly reassuring.

"It's nothing, Celia, really."

Lettie interjected.

"Nothing? Pah!"

Ed was haughty now, filled with contempt for those who had wronged him. "Made medical history it did."

"Yes Ed," said Lettie. "But bad history. The kind you'd rather forget."

"Any history's good history, love. As long as it's you that's making it. Celia should hear this."

Lettie sighed and rolled her eyes.

"I was the boy who should have been golden," began Ed. "My name should have been writ large in the Great Hall, preferably in gilded lettering. Where my name should have been now rests blank space. I could have been first in everything, but I never made the grade. It was, quite simply, a harmless prank. I never intended to hurt nobody. It was just a little mechanical device, not much to write home about. Death had never repulsed me; in fact, on the contrary, I had always found it strangely attractive and often completely amusing. Others did not always share the joke."

"You can say that again," muttered Lettie.

"In the dissection room at the rear of the medical school sat 'the head box', into which the heads of cadavers were thrown after they had been severed from the bodies to which they had once belonged. My 'mechanical device' had been a toy laughing clown which emitted a cackling laugh and which my friend Larry, an engineering student, had hooked up to the lid of the head box, so that when this lid was opened in order that it might receive fresh bounty, the toy clown would let loose with its cackle, which sounded, in the circumstances, as sinister as sin itself. If the joke's victim had been other than Katherina Godwit, we might have got away with it, but unfortunately, as bad fate would have it, the first person to open the lid of the head box following the installation of the device was the only student at the school with a potentially fatal heart murmur."

Ed seemed to grow nervous. His knees jiggled constantly as he talked.

How was I meant to know it would be she who'd lift the lid?' I said repeatedly, to my friends, to the head of the medical school, to Lettie, to the judge who presided over my manslaughter trial. 'She never told nobody about her dicky ticker, how was I meant to know she didn't beat like the rest of us, but was marching to a different drum? Can't you see', I said, *it's not my fault.'* They didn't listen, of course. In their minds I was every bit as guilty as if I'd crept up behind her and bludgeoned her to death, like Maxwell with his silver hammer. The judge declared that I should have foreseen that my actions might possibly cause death, and although she, Judge Pliar, had been somewhat lenient on the sentencing, she had sentenced nonetheless. *Five years*, she said, slamming the hammer down upon the bench and her words reverberated around and around in my brain as if my mind was an echo-chamber.

'This is my dark past, my skeleton lurking in the closet, ready to leap out, all white bone and rattling skull. I have done hard time. I have spent years behind prison walls. My prison years are a black hole that is now behind me, but which I still feel has the power, the potency, to suck me irrevocably backwards, back and down, into the abyss. Sometimes I imagine that I can still feel the edge of it, the event horizon, beyond which nothing escapes, not even light. I carry the darkness with me everywhere, like a lead weight or an open wound. Like Eleanor Rigby, I keep my face in a jar by the door and this face that I wear is all you will ever see."

He had finished talking and he'd finished his whisky also. Lettie was staring at the floor. Ed reached out and tugged at my cover.

"They don't much like the sight of your face, do they lass?"

I shook my head and my Uncle turned to face his sister.

"What's so terrible about it, Lettie, that it cannot see the light of day?"

Lettie's lips were pursed shut tightly.

"That bad, huh? Well I'm no rose myself. Perhaps I could catch just a glimpse of her, just a tiny peek?"

"You don't know what you're in for," said Lettie. "If you did, you wouldn't be asking."

Ed peeled another twenty from the wad of cash he kept in his pocket and pushed it towards me.

"Go get us another round, would you love?" he asked and I toddled off to do as he said.

From the bar, I looked back to see brother and sister engaged in heated argument. I heard my name; I was the hot topic of conversation. But when I returned to the table with the drinks, they were no longer speaking of me. Ed appeared to have forgotten about my face and was off in his own La La Land again, staring into the middle distance, as if listening to some holy angel's trumpet.

"Tell you something for nothing," he said. "A man's gotta make a buck in this world, come hell or high water. He must use his time to his best advantage and during those long jailbird years I had nothing but time, a great, empty ocean of it. I had to fill it in or drown in the emptiness. I have always had a slightly obsessive streak and when I discovered the book of magic tricks in the prison library, my mind latched on, like a hook into a fish. I was not the kind of man to do anything by halves. For me, it was all or nothing. I threw myself into my magic, forgot about everything else. It engulfed me. It owned me. When magic and I started out, I was its servant and it was my master, but this hierarchy was soon reversed. "

Lettie scoffed.

"You mastered nothing," she said. "You're a two-bit smutmeister with a few hack magic tricks up your sleeve."

Ed stared hard at his sister. His eyes burnt fiercely in his head.

"I also perfected," he said, "the simple art of the disappearing act. I could vanish a bird cage, I could vanish a cane, I could vanish a radio, I could vanish a wand. And I could also," he looked at me and winked, "vanish myself."

And he did. No smoke or coloured lights this time. One minute he was there and the next he was not. Simple as that. I looked for him. I checked under that table. I peered under his chair. I went to the Gentlemen's toilets and I looked in there. Vanished without trace. I was suitably impressed. I didn't want to stay here, with Lettie, I wanted to go on the road with Ed and be the girl cut in half every night. I wanted him to teach me his tricks, train me up to be just like him. But Ed was a light moving through a station. He had appeared, worked his magic and left.

Had his words been fact or fiction? I didn't care. We drove back home. Barry was watching the telly. Lettie cooked up some bangers and mash but I wasn't hungry. I wanted Ed back. I wanted his magical world of bunnies and fire and doves. I didn't want this terrible mediocrity, days at the Butchette and nights in front of the telly. I wanted to be fabulous. Like him.

*

I sulked for a week, sat moping in my Butchette corner, refusing to read the many books with which Lettie tried to entice me, refusing to eat anything other than the odd irresistible insect, refusing any liquid except Fanta. *You'll be hearing from me*, I thought I had heard him whisper as he vanished. But what did that mean? I jumped every time the telephone rang, I snatched the mail from the letterbox each evening, I dusted off an old radio which I found in the cellar and ran the dial through a number of stations, tuning in, praying I would hear his voice, hoping for some message, some sign. Nothing. I was bereft, betrayed.

But I had not been forgotten. It arrived when I turned to look the other way, when I had given up on the radio and the phone and the mail, when I was thinking, *Right then, that's fine, that flakey bastard can go his own way and I'll go mine.* It arrived just as my trust in the innate goodness of humankind had been shattered once and for all. It sat in a box upon our front porch, a box with my name on it.

"Never look a gift-horse in the mouth," said Lettie.

My heart skipped seven beats. I fell to my knees; I tore open the box. My future clicked before my eyes. Laid out neatly was the instrument I would cling to for the rest of my days; a LeicaFlex SL reflex camera, with my initials scratched into the back. *C.D.* Next to that, an enlarger, and, strapped to the side of the box in a separate package, the chemicals that I would need to get me started; solutions for fixing and developing, a stack of paper and a couple of rolls of film, and at the very bottom of the box, a book, *Photography for Beginners* with a note taped to the front cover, "Happy Snappin', Tiger". I was filled to overflowing.

Click.

My first photo was a self-portrait; I simply held the thing at arms length, pointed the lens at my face and snapped. I loved everything about it; it was compensation, it would make up for everything.

Click.

That was Barry and Lettie, inside the house, unaware that I stood on the other side of the pane, snapping them.

Click.

That was a tired old woman wheeling her shopping cart down Third Street.

Click.

That was a stray dog in the park across the road.

Click, click, click.

That was me in the Butchette, snatching images, taking pics. I made these people my subjects; I objectified them. I imposed my sight upon the world. The present became instantly past.

My gift was greeted with enthusiasm by Barry and Lettie. They were happy that I had stopped sulking. Barry went out of his way to build me a little darkroom in one rear corner of the Butchette, in the space where my pen had been, complete with red light bulb, workbench and sink. Lettie bought me ten films at a time. In my hands, the camera was not a living thing. I had not yet hit adolescence, but I had found my great passion, my niche. I was unexposed, sensitised material. The world would imprint itself upon me.

*

The rules about keeping Celia in the cellar relaxed a little. Every other evening I would be allowed to sit upstairs, in the living-room, as Barry watched the telly and Lettie folded laundry or read a book. I was not allowed to speak or howl or eat insects while the TV was on. Silence was the golden rule. I obeyed. I liked the TV. I was allowed to take photos of it; I was a soft background *click, click, clicking* as Barry watched all his favourite programmes and Lettie turned the pages of her book. I would sneak photos of the two of them as well; Barry with beer can in hand, and Lettie with the look of studied concentration she wore when reading. Sometimes her lips moved.

And every time I took a photo I thought of Ed. I know it sounds foolish to say that I pined for him, but I was an impressionable young person. In those days I was easily dazzled.

"I'm glad he didn't hang about," I overheard Lettie saying to her husband one evening.

"Who?"

"Ed. Not only is he a compulsive liar, but he's also just a little bit...*unstable.*"

Barry emitted one of this standard grunts and changed the channel on the telly.

The word that Lettie had used made me think of war-torn countries, of volcanoes, of a row of porcelain plates perched precariously upon a shelf. The word carried an implicit threat; it was an accident waiting to happen. It was a word that was waiting to fall. But what did I care if Ed was not balanced? He had delivered my salvation.

Never did I feel more alive than when I was behind the camera. Only when I looked through the lens did I truly see; the rest of the time I felt blind, half-dead. Put that puppy in my hands and I swelled with excitement and enthusiasm, it was as close as I ever got to happiness. I ploughed through great rolls of film; I was an incessant taker of snaps, I was unstoppable, a photography machine. I devoured *Photography For Beginners* in a single gulp and persuaded Lettie to pick me up some more advanced reading material from the city library. I experimented. I produced many failures. I made many pictures that were too dark and many that were too light. I overdeveloped and I underdeveloped. I took pictures with too much shadow and pictures with too much light. But once in a blue moon I would hit it, slam, like a bullet between the eyes, I would capture something, some essence; the clock would stop and the moment would hang suspended in time, frozen. It was the slam that I was addicted to; the split second that split time. I was not just a freak with a camera.

I was the red right hand of fate.

X

Tonight I can't sleep. My eyes are wide open, like two saucers, my mind is working overtime. I rise from my bed, walk to the window and pull the curtains. It's a cold clear night; the moon hangs like a cardboard cut-out in the sky, the stars are hot white diamonds. I stand that way for some time, with the light from the moon shining down upon my face, my hair wild, my nightgown clinging to my body. The trees in the backyard appear almost magical; I fancy for an instant that they bear heavenly fruit that has not yet been tasted upon this earth, then shake my head and pull myself out of my little reverie. The plum tree bears only plums, the fig tree only figs.

Once I am up I don't want to go back to bed, I am restless, I pace from my bedroom to the living-room, wandering the hallways of my own home like a distressed ghost. The aluminium ladder that George climbs to hoist himself up into the attic has not been removed; he must have forgotten about it, usually he carries it back out to the garage, so I don't trip on it, sprain an ankle, break a leg. My bones are enormous but brittle, osteoporosis is setting in with a vengeance; I'd have to drink thirty litres of milk a day to combat it.

I put one foot upon the bottom rung of the ladder, test it, to see if it will take my weight. It holds. I look upwards, sizing up the gap that leads into the attic. I have never been in the attic before; it is not my territory. I belonged 'down below'; after all my years spent dwelling in cellars, even living on ground level makes me feel a little uneasy, let alone getting up into the roof cavity. Getting through the attic hatch will be a tight squeeze, I can see. Dangerous possibilities run through my mind; Celia, stuck halfway, like a cork somebody has tried to push back into a bottle, her head in the attic, her body dangling down below.

Perhaps the insomnia has affected me, but I am curious to see what George sees every day, curious to know what really is stored up there. When I had the house restructured the builders cleared everything out of the attic, stored it in one of the spare rooms and then carried it all back up into the new expanded space. When they took all Barry and Lettie's old junk back up, they carried up boxes of my photos to be stored amidst the other debris. Piles of stuff had lain down here for at least a week, but I had not bothered to look through the mounds; back then I had not been interested, but now I am.

Praying that I can squeeze through the gap, I begin my ascent, foot after heavy foot, poke my head through the space. Blackness. I should have brought a torch. I heave myself up, hold my breath, suck in my chest and wriggle my way upwards. I make it; I fit. My right hand gropes for the light switch, crawling along the wall, searching. I find it, flick the switch. Illumination.

The attic is criss-crossed with beams, like latticework, and in between the beams is the thin plywood of the ceiling, plain brown on this side, white plaster on the other. Nothing out of the ordinary greets my vision; just dust, dozens of boxes, an old rusting bike, a couple of kettles. I rise, my head scraping the attic roof, and with one foot in front of the other, like an oafish high-wire artist, I make my way along one beam to where the first stack of boxes sits. Does George do this every day, this tentative edging towards the goodies? Perhaps he has more courage than I give him credit for, although he's a good deal lighter than I am, there's a chance that the plywood would hold him should he slip and misplace his feet. No such chance for old Celia. *She doesn't know her own strength*, they used to say of me, but they were wrong. When you're as heavy as I am, you're always highly aware of the damage your weight could do, should you choose to throw it around.

The boxes that contain the photographs are open, with snaps spilling out every which way. It looks like a stray dog has been ferreting in there, in search of tasty treats. Other open boxes sit nearby, filled with clothes and old toys and crockery. Two windows are set into the wall above the boxes and one of these has been left open; the cold night breeze wafts in, a chill runs across my skin. Something caught my eye, a white shape, fluttering in the breeze like the wings of a dove. I edge myself over in that direction; it is fabric, silk. I lift it from its box. It's a wedding dress, it looks too old to have been Lettie's; possibly it belonged to her mother. Perhaps Lettie borrowed it for her own wedding. It's beautiful; a row of feathers runs along the hem, and above that, several thin lines of silver beads, dripping down, like rain. It's nothing that I would ever fit into. I hold it to my chest, imagining all the waltzes, all the dances my hideous self will never perform. There is a sudden noise behind me, like breaking glass, I turn and look over my shoulder, expecting to see Jacob. There is nobody there. My left foot slips and my right foot shoots forward. The roof gives way beneath me; there is a crack, a splintering and then I am falling through the ceiling, the wedding dress floating down behind me, a drifting swan, while pieces of plaster raining down all around.

Which was how George finds me, when he comes knocking this morning; in the middle of the living-room floor, with my left ankle twisted around behind me and with an aching 'wing' from my fall.

"You're lucky you didn't break your spine," is his comment, as he hauls me to my feet and telephones for a doctor, whom I know will charge me a fortune for being called out to pay a house visit.

Dr James arrives, with his shock of red hair and his freckles. I shoot him a look that says I know he's one of those who come to examine and document me. This is his alter-ego, this kindly, somewhat bumbling doctor, who patiently examines the large lump upon my right shoulder. ("Does this hurt? How about that? Feel that?") and then turns his attentions to my ankle, which has swollen up to the size of a rugby ball. He's running through the doctor act, doing what he thinks he should do, saying what he thinks he should say.

All he recommends in the end is a couple of icepacks and a lie-down. I could've diagnosed myself and saved the fifty bucks he's charging. I could've refused to pay, but I didn't have the heart. He has children, this Dr James, I've seen him playing ball with them in the park on a Sunday. He's struggling to survive, like every other Provencian. I am one of the few exceptions to this city's rule of poverty. They all know it; they whisper behind my back. I am sitting on a gold mine. I prise open the wallet and cough up the cash, which he shoves into his pocket, before departing with a grateful nod.

George is looking up at the ceiling, shaking his head in dismay. "What the hell did you think you were doing? The builders will have to be called, I suppose, to come and fix it."

He picks up the wedding dress from the floor, turns it over in his hands, as if it is some dirty dishrag covered in crumbs and cleaning fluid. "Planning on tying the knot, are we," he says sarcastically. "Who's the lucky bloke?"

"Nobody," I say. "But don't bother calling the builders. We'll just leave it as it is. You'll just have to be more careful walking about up there. Wouldn't want you falling down and hurting yourself as well."

"We can't just *leave* it," he protests. "The edges will only crumble away more. Soon there won't be anything left at all of the attic."

"It'll outlast me," I say. "Bet your bottom dollar."

I am nearing the end of my life sentence, my last sentence. He makes a few more feeble protests, whimpers a little, like a puppy deprived of its dinner, and then resigns himself to the fact that this is my house and what I say goes; I am using what little clout I have, making a few sad last assertions before curling up my toes, before laying down to die like a tired old elephant.

"Come on, George," I say. "Give us a hand up."

He hauls me to my feet, giving me one of his, *you're a batty old bird* looks, but I shoot him a smile, and convince him to help me over to my table so I can get on with the day's work. No time to waste, just because it's been an uncomfortable night on the floor doesn't mean I can take a day off.

I sit at my old table, looking up, 'cause now the roof's got a hole in it, a hole to match the gap at the city's centre, and the nothingness in the middle of me. A hole for the eye of God to peek through, spying on me, as my hand goes scrawling across this page leaving its spidery thread behind it, reeling out the words, like fishing line, like rope, too much of it, enough of it to hang yourself.

I imagine the Big Guy up there in the attic, various greater and lesser angels hanging on to his robes, their smaller wings overshadowed by his large feathered appendages, while his eye looks down upon me, evaluating, judging, as if this is the last day of the world and these words I write will admit me to heaven to sing beautiful hymns in His praise or send me shooting down to infernal realms where I'll burn eternally. A small delusion; no household god lingers in my attic. Just George, clattering about, searching for something he'll never manage to find; ploughing through my shots of yesteryear as I myself slip out of the present and back into the past.

XI

In the beginning, my subject matter was somewhat limited. My terrible howling at the Sphere was still sharp in Lettie's mind and she would not let me into the outside world unaccompanied. My early photographs were of those many varied folk who traipsed through the Butchette. The customers didn't suspect a thing. Barry had poked two holes at different places along the byobu and set up two screened enclosures, one on either side of the screen. I would stand on one side, hidden, and take photos of those on the other side, and then swap around and snap customers in the other half of the Butchette. I operated on both sides of the divide. All that was ever seen of me during these days was a brief scuttling shape scurrying furtively from one side of the screen to the other. All that was ever heard of me was *click*.

I did my developing at night, after hours, when Barry and Lettie had made their way home. It took a lot of fast talking on my part to convince them to allow me to stay behind unattended; it took getting down on bended knee and begging. It took promising never to walk home alone; they weren't scared that I would fall into the depths of the earth, they were scared of what would happen if I were let loose on my own, at night. I swore always to take a taxi, said that I would be fine picking my way across all the makeshift bridges to the next street over; I would catch a cab from there. I convinced them to pay. They wanted me out of the way and I played on it.

Some said I was too young for photography (*five years old!*), but my ages were not ordinary. I refused to listen. I loved being alone, late at night, just me and the photographic paper and the negatives and that gorgeous chemical scent to which I became so addicted. Lettie picked up an old tape recorder and a box of dubbed tapes for me from a garage sale and I would listen to my favourite, *Who's Next*, time and time again and watch as the images shimmered in the trays. I loved to witness the formation of the figures, like a disappearing act in reverse. The appearance of these people was as magical as the appearance of Ed himself; unlike Ed, these were people whom I could keep. I hung them up to dry on a wire which ran across my small darkroom. When they were finished, I graded them from one to ten and placed them in neat stacks according to how they were rated. I indulged in some amateur touch-up work. I added gold glitter and bright pink paint to my finished photos, I glued sequins and feathers to humans whose pictures I had taken; I made them greater than they had been. I made them greater than myself. In red ink, I wrote my name at the back of every picture I took, small print in the right hand corner. *Celia Doom.* And the date. And then the tiny, trademark tear, the rip in the right hand corner. *By their rips ye shall know them.*

*

They wanted me back in my box. I was still tagged and tracked by the medical men. I was still filed and compartmentalised. My hunch had begun to show itself; at this stage of the game it was a small but rather prominent lump on my right shoulder, about the size of a golf ball; my grannies used to run their hands over it, wondering if perhaps it were some kind of cancerous growth. But the medical men said no, it was not cancerous, it was benign. Their word was gospel. Their truth was absolute.

I continued to expand unnaturally; by the age of six I was six foot three and weighed one hundred and fifty kilos. Despite my size, I seemed non-existent. I had been written out, written off. My name had been erased from the Good Book. There were no snapshots of me on the wall behind the stairwell in the family home, no photo album to display baby shots, first day at school shots, first ride of bike shots, Celia and chums shots.

Photography would fill the blank space where I should have been.

And all the time I snapped, I prayed for Ed's return. He was the guy that I was always expecting to see, but he never showed up. I had him in mind each time I took a picture. There was a high, keening sound, a buzzing in my eardrums, a continuous note, and the note was Ed. All attempts to forget him were futile. He had spun gold in my mind, and the gilded web is not easy to forget.

My art failed to cure me of my former vices. There were numerous lapses on the insect front, many incidents when I was discovered in the back yard or in the basement, munching ants and crickets and snails. Barry said it made the bile rise in his throat just to think of it and Lettie had taken a leaf out of her husband's book and now ignored everything I did, as if she were attempting to will me into non-existence. No soul who entered the Butchette clutching a can of Fanta left intact.

It wasn't long before I grew tired of Butchette customers and longed to snap something else. How old was I then, when I convinced Lettie to set me free with my camera? I had been living with Lettie for nearly six years, but that tells you nothing. My ages were all over the place. I felt as old as Methusula. I nagged and nagged until she gave in and told me that I might as well just do as I pleased.

"Just stay out of my hair," she said, as if I were something annoying, a twig or a leaf, which had become entwined in her long curly locks.

My forays into the 'world outside' provided me with plenty of photographic fodder. I felt possibilities expanding before my eyes. The world was my oyster; I would capture and define it, I would make it my own. I stole a bike from some kid who'd left it outside the Butchette and I pedalled all over the city, an enormous clown on a tiny two-wheeler, weaving in and out of the traffic, dicing with death. I waited outside the hospital and I snapped the white coats who ventured out at lunchtime to sit on the patch of grass that ran down the side of the hospital driveway. *Click*, I impaled them upon the blazing sword that was my vision. I had the velvet hand; the hawk's eye. In my Butchette darkroom I made them into monsters; they stretched and expanded until they were great white ghosts, they peered out at the world through oversized eyes, their hands like clumps of sausages, their hair thick and matted. I painted boxes around them. They became mine.

I cycled to the houses of my two grandmothers and took pictures of Grandma Lolly and her many jars of sweeties and Grandma Doom and her dead stuffed animals. The two old birds struck poses, Stuff with her pickled platypus or one of her two hyenas and Lolly in her wheelchair, her cheeks filled with sweets, so that she resembled Marlon Brando in *The Godfather*. The two old dears were delighted that I had found a constructive way to occupy my time and took my new hobby as evidence that I did, after all, possess the 'brains' and 'hidden talents' they had declared I would need in order to survive.

"Bit of a dark horse, our Celia," said Stuff to Lettie, on a subsequent visit.

I stood outside women's clothing stores and shot the women strolling in and out, while behind their plates of clear glass, the mannequins provided interesting backdrops. I liked these clothes-horse dummies; the wigs without so much as a hair out of place, the vacant glass eyes, the way the clothes hung so neatly from the plastic bodies. What was up for sale was everything I would never be.

I shot kids pouring through school gates and families on Sunday picnics and early morning joggers in their Adidas tracksuits and hot dog vendors and jugglers and old men out walking their dogs. I shot nuns and construction workers and kids dressed up for Halloween. I took numerous pictures of Barry and Lettie. I shot secretaries and receptionists and businessmen. All these people, hiding behind their masks, sliding in and out of the roles that had been defined for them, never thinking of what might lie outside the act, never thinking of what they might become should they shuck off the shackles and risk becoming something other. Mug shots were my speciality. You can forget *Man With A Movie Camera*, this was *Woman With A Leica*. This was load, aim and fire. I could no longer tell where I left off and the camera began. The whole world squinted with me through my lens.

Sometimes it struck me as almost inhuman, the way I reduced my subjects to objects, reduced them in size, made them nothing more than an image on a piece of silver paper. There was something cruel and militaristic about it. A certain arrogance was necessary, to impose one's vision upon the world in such a way. Portraits were never my thing; fiddling about with lights and silly props while restless clients fidgeted and tried to 'act natural' while artificially posing, whinging that they'd turned out ugly when they saw the finished product. (*Do I really look like that?*) No, I did not wish to catch you when you were looking. I wanted you unaware.

There was a camera in my hands and there was also a camera in my mind. On those rare occasions when I would find myself out and about without my Leica, I would take mental photographs, in preparation for the real event.

I haunted the human race. I was the covered creep, lurking in alleyways, ready to spring out and snap you. I spied. You did not know that I was watching you, but my haunted eyes stared through the holes in my cover, one negative, one positive, the left eye the inverse of the right and I took in everything. I altered it. I spat it back at you. And in the end you loved me for it, because you thought I was talking about somebody else. You saw these pictures of checkout chicks and bankers and lawyers and clerks and thought you recognised your neighbour or your second cousin or the guy who lived across the road. Your laugh was a little uneasy; the recognition was a little too strong perhaps, a little too close for comfort. You felt a little queasy in your gut. And the reason for this was simple. You were the person you recognised.

I was talking about you.

XII

George's tap upon the front door each morning was making my big old heart skip several beats, each time thinking that it might be Death come to fetch me. Having grown so tired of his knocking and my reaction, I relented and have now given him a key. Today he lets himself in, comes up behind me as I sit at my table. He has brought somebody else to the house; this is strictly against the rules and he knows it. His guest is female, small, with short red hair and more than a whiff of the pit-bull about her. She has the brisk, overly efficient mannerisms of a born organiser; I pray only that this woman will not try to organise me. Lilith, she says her name is, as I sit before my telly, every bit the inert slob. My pen and paper are hidden away; these are not for her eager eyes.

"Lilith's in charge of your retrospective," says George. "She's driven all this way to meet you."

Implying that I should sit up and behave like a good girl or there'll be trouble.

Lilith hovers, her eyes darting about the room, taking it all in, as if formulating sentences she will later tell her friends. *And her house was an absolute _mess_. Coffee cups everywhere.* She wants to take away an anecdote. Something to dine out on afterwards. Worst of all, she gushes; she covers me in her sycophantic slobber, as if she thinks this would endear her to me, when, of course, it just drives me away. After years of being hated, it is not easy to be liked.

I don't differentiate between humans, I lump you all in together; long ago I decided that you were merely 'the race' and that I was going to win you. And now this woman is here, and I stare at the telly, which is switched off, and she babbles inanities.

"So much for Delarouche, lamenting 'from this day, painting is dead,'" she says. "Photography did not kill painting. Instead, it freed it from its former constrains, set it loose, while photography was left screeching about its desire to be accepted as a valid art form."

George is nodding wisely.

"Of course, when you started off," she continues, seemingly under the illusion that I have actually lived through the ninety years I look, rather than a mere thirty, "Photography was the perfect art for a woman. It was free space, not yet fossilised, not yet commandeered. Plenty of gals had walked the road before you: Julia Margaret Cameron, Clementina Hawarden, Gertrude Kasebier, the first woman to be elected to the prestigious Linked Ring. Also Immogen Cunningham, Dorothea Lange, Helen Lent, Margaret Bourke, Ellen Auerbach. You could extend the road you walked upon, but you did not have to lay the first stone. It was not as much of a male domain, as, say, was painting. You didn't feel all those dead geniuses hanging over you. It was what you made of it. The camera could be brought round to your way of thinking. Photography was a wide open space you felt you could fill."

I belch loudly and George shoots me a filthy look. How she thinks she knows what I felt is beyond me.

"What about Steichen?" I ask. "What about Man Ray and Stieglitz and Will McBride? How about the social import of Hine? How about Niépce, Daguerre and Talbot? It was men that got the ball rolling. "

That should stump her, but it doesn't.

"They were different," she says, then flails, lost for words.

"Right," I say. "You're the expert."

George lays out before this 'Lilith', as she calls herself, a sample from my oeuvre, a few of what he thinks are 'the best' but which are actually fairly standard shots; could have been done by a five-year-old with your average point and shoot device. And now she is drooling all over the photos and spurting superlatives; she is ejaculating.

"Amazing," she says. "You have captured a world that no longer exists."

What does she mean by that? Is she implying that I am past my use-by date? Does she think I am all washed-up, like a rotting fish on the beach and that I will never be relevant again? My white right eye impales her. Jacob gives a derisive snort.

"You had a heart," she says earnestly. "It was photography. You conjured up with the camera that which had never before been perceived," she says. "You created a new world."

I reach for the remote and switch on the TV, cranking up the volume to full.

"You were present everywhere and nowhere in your work. You stood back. You allowed your subject to speak."

Which is when I say, calmly and smoothly, "George, get this stupid tart out of here," and she flinches, as if I have struck her. I am not supposed to react like this; I am supposed to feel the bond of womanhood, to reach out and embrace her and feel the strength of her loving support.

George mumbles a few apologies to Lilith, "Don't take it personally, she always was a misanthropic old sod, come on up to the attic and let's go look through her work together," and Lilith leaves the room behind him, looking back over her shoulder and shooting me a wounded look as she does so. I don't know why they think I'm being cranky. This is me in a good mood, sprightly. Most days I feel like the living dead.

Just as I think I am finally going to be left alone to do some work, a car pulls up outside, a red station wagon. They are here for their tests and I must oblige. Wouldn't want them to miss out on any vital scientific information. Three of them drive down together from the capital, and I suspect them of collecting another doctor, Dr James, the only GP left in Provencia. They still wear the white coats, they still wear the masks, but Dr James' red hair gives him away. There is no use in protesting, I learnt that long ago, the best thing is to put your mind elsewhere and let them do what they will with your body. Think of England. Don't flinch. Today they lie me down upon the sofa and take a few snippets of hair and skin and toenail, pushing these into their little plastic vials. They weigh me, measure me, prod at my 'wing'. They feel my ankle, which has made a miraculous recovery. Write everything down to be filed away, not under my name, but under my number: 373603 11 333.

Why the hell did they bother stamping this number into me? It's not as if they could mistake me for anybody else. It was an act of appropriation; it was a way to try to make me theirs. When they've had their way with me, they silently make their exit; the chore is over for another month. Thankfully these check-ups are no longer weekly; I still find them traumatic despite having been through it all hundreds of times before. It wasn't my ease they had in mind, when they ceased their weekly visits and decided to arrive once a month, like menstruation. It was their own comfort that helped them make the decision. It's too much of a hike to drive across from the capital every week, three hours of winding mountainous terrain. Provencia's airport has been closed for over two decades, so flying is out of the question. There is no longer any medical or scientific team in Provencia, only Dr James. He's what we have left.

As soon as they have gone I heave myself up and over to my desk, where the story beckons, praying that today there will be words.

XIII

I was triple the size of a normal girl and adolescence hit me with three times the force. Lettie had been panicking that it would strike when I was five years old, when my body thought that I was fifteen, but it waited, thank God, till I was seven. The growth spurts were horrendous. All of my body suffered. My bones creaked with the impact of such rapid expansion, my big red heart beat hard in my chest; it strained just to keep me alive. My joints ached. Enormous stretch marks raked across my skin; its natural elasticity could not keep up with my unnatural rate of expansion.

Nobody had explained the wonderful ways of puberty to me; nobody had told me about the birds and the bees. Menstruation was just the first of the shocks that adolescence had in store for monstrous me. I had only just recovered from the first blow, in fact, I was still reeling, when sharp jabbing pains began to strike on either side of my chest. My bosoms were beginning to sprout. And these, bear in mind, were no ordinary titties; these were whoppers, gargantuan mammary glands that blubbered on either side of me. No way to fit them into a G-cup, these babies demanded that their bras be tailor-made. As my bosom blossomed, my fangs began to recede, lifted back up into my gums like a stage curtain rising, and there they stayed. Lettie breathed a heavy sigh of relief and I, also, was thankful. I did not wish to be known as the town werewoman.

Eyes followed me everywhere. I could never be free from the gaze. It was hard for a girl like me to go unnoticed and so there was nothing I fantasised about more. I wished for a Cloak of Invisibility which would hide me as I drifted about the city like a lost cloud, but this wish was never granted. I was out in the open and beginning to make a name for myself. I was the Secret Snapper, who hid behind trees, and sprang out to capture chosen images on film. Sometimes the world 'out there' was too much for me; the images would come rushing in, as if my mind was a camera with the shutter always open, as if the pictures were being burnt into my brain. On these occasions I would scurry back to my darkroom and switch the red bulb off, just lie there in the darkness, upon the Butchette floor, feeling the steady in-out of my breathing, feeling the two-four beat of my heart. Pulling myself together.

Ed remained always on my mind. I took pictures of tall, thin men and then altered them afterwards so that they looked more like Ed. What I wound up with was a whole stack of almost-Ed's; if you squinted right and practised a little self-deception you could convince yourself that his image was there, on the paper. For months my obsession continued and in the darkroom the pictures piled up. I was not aware of time passing. To me, this small corner with its dull red light hung suspended spinning in space, high above the earth. It transcended the temporal. Back on earth I grew rapidly older; up here, I was one of the immortals.

Try as I might, however, I could not deny my earthly existence. I had developed. It was inevitable that my knockers would begin to attract unwanted attention from males. They couldn't seem to help themselves; their eyes would stray, despite their best intentions, to my chest and there the gaze would stay. Everything else seemed to fade away, as if I were nothing more than a giant bosom, floating in space. I never spoke to these men; I had learned not to open my mouth. My voice was harsh, deep, rasping; it frightened people and I no longer derived joy from invoking fear in others. I wanted to be left alone; I wanted to be the unseen spectator, witnessing everything but never taking part, skulking in my darkroom, manufacturing. And then Jacob came along, and all my illusions were shattered.

*

If there was one piece of footage that was always playing in Jacob Lang's mind, it was this; a car, a blue Ford Cortina, smashing through a white barricade, sailing out over the edge of a cliff and falling to land in a flaming heap as both driver and passenger were flung through the front window like crash test dummies. Although Jacob had never seen this car, that cliff, those flames, he had created in his mind an imaginary film so vivid, that it seemed to him more real than any event he ever actually *had* witnessed. During daylight hours, the film nagged at the corner of his consciousness; at night, he did not dream, he watched this movie playing time and time again, as if on loop tape. At times he could not tell whether the dream was real and this world was an illusion, or whether the world was solid fact and the dream was a fiction his mind had created.

The remainder of Jacob's memories were clogged with wax and dough. The wax flowed and solidified in his mind; the scent of it, the solid white blocks, the big melting vats of it, the rolls of yellow beeswax. Heaven would smell like that, he thought, like honey, like divine nectar. He remembered too, the long white pieces of string his mother called wicks, the bottles of scent with which she would perfume the produce; he recalled the boxes of finished candles, lying in the garage, like thin sedated snakes, ready for collection. He remembered the feel of wax hardening on his skin, the exciting hours spent with nothing better to do than to drip the molten substance onto his hands, watch it harden and then pick it off in flakes. His mother always smelt of it; he would wrap himself up in her skirts and inhale deeply, the scent of perfume and wax soothing him like a bedtime story, like a caress.

Every alternate week was spent at his father's Provencian bakery and Jacob loved this routine, loved this environment almost as much as he adored the wax; the four in the morning rising, stumbling out of bed while the world still slept, into his father's truck, then off to the deserted world of the bakery, backstage, watching while his father mixed flour, water, yeast and produced loaf upon beautiful loaf of bread, row upon row of perfect white rolls, and out front, onstage, the bread would fill the plastic display counters, each little loaf an actor, Jacob would think, each roll an actress, hiding their origins, hiding the work that had gone into constructing themselves. The yeast smelt like home, like safety. He adored the thick piles of dough, he wanted to roll in it, he wanted his father to bake him in a pie, like Mickey in *Mickey In The Night Kitchen*. He wanted to make himself a bread-suit to wear everywhere.

He had no security-blanket. Instead, during his first socially awkward two years at primary school, Jacob was never without his loaf of white bread and his beeswax candle, both of which he would intermittently sniff, comfort spreading through him in warm waves. He stayed away from the other children. They scared him; he didn't understand the games they played, their rough physicality, the shifting and treacherous sands beneath the relationships they formed with one another. He would sit in one corner of the schoolyard, taking intermittent mouse-sized nibbles at one of his father's loaves, lighting and then snuffing out one of his mother's candles, waiting for the bell which signaled home time, the end of this torture posing as education, time to get back to the warmth, the womb that was the spare room in which the candles were made. He was the boy who was always running home to mother.

Sometimes, if his mother, Jane, was exceptionally busy, he would swing by the bakery instead. As he grew older, his father tried to encourage him to stand out the front and serve, but, when pushed 'on stage' Jacob would ruin things on purpose; he would deliberately short change the customers, he would hand them egg rolls when they asked for ham and cheese, he misheard their requests for baguettes and gave them bagels instead, so that his father became exasperated and consented to allow his only son to nestle back behind the scenes, toying with a piece of raw dough like an infant, cowering from the world. Jerry Lang feared that his son was becoming a pansy. The boy had even been seen with a Sally Lunn bun wrapped in a blanket, like it was some kind of *baby* or something. But when he tried to raise the issue of his son's inherent wimpiness with his wife, he hit a brick wall.

"Leave him alone," she would say. "He'll come out of his shell in his own good time. There's no point in trying to force the issue."

His father, Jerry, had his hands full running the bakery and did not have a good deal of spare time in which to encourage the lad towards activities which he considered more suitable for a young boy, so instead he showered his son with gifts intended to bring out the tiger in him, presents which he hoped would make the kid stand tall and be a man. Model trains, tin soldiers, a toy gun; these were items that any normal boy would've been proud to call his own, but Jacob Lang turned up his nose at all his father's gifts and once a week would steal a new loaf of bread from the bakery, to cuddle to his chest and nibble, and whenever his 'pet candle' had been burnt down to a short waxy stub, he would take another from the garage, light it and put it out, light it and put it out, until there was almost nothing left of it, whereupon he would pinch another. There was no point in attempting to deprive the boy of his comforters; if his candle and his loaf were snatched from him, Jacob would simply curl up in the foetal position and refuse to move, speak or eat until what had been taken was returned.

If there ever was a boy who needed a sanctuary, it was Jacob. It was not the bread and the candle themselves he adored, it was the associations each triggered in his mind, the connotations of safety, of warmth, of a magical realm in which he could not be harmed, a paradise. His heaven was soon to become a hell.

On Jacob's seventh birthday the Lang family awoke early. The sky was a clear blue overhead, the birds sang in the trees outside, the flowers in the garden were beginning to bloom. All was right with the world. The gifts were given; from his father, a toy sword, a pirate's patch and a football. From his mother, a kit for kiddies who liked to play scientist, comprised of several neat little bottles of chemicals, a few small test tubes, a present which, had she lived to see what it inspired, Jane Lang would've regretted to her dying day. There were whispers about the cake. His parents spoke in low voices.

"I need you to help," Jacob overheard his father hissing at his mother. "I can't carry it on my own."

The boy was taken by the hand, led across to the neighbour's house, a loaf of bread under one arm, a candle in his right hand, his new gifts left behind at the house. The bakery was being manned by Mr. Lang's understudy, a formidable woman named Martha, with arms like great, unformed slabs of dough. She was a worker, that Martha; she had six kids and no husband and great black bags permanently under her eyes.

As Jacob sat quietly on the floor of the neighbour's living-room, gnawing thoughtfully at one end of his loaf, which, on this particular occasion, was poppy seed, as he silently dripped wax onto the neighbour's carpet, his parents drove to his father's bakery, greeted Martha, who was rushed off her feet trying to get the day's orders ready, and took, from the large steel bench at the very rear of the building, an enormous mandarin sponge which Mr. Lang had baked the previous evening.

"What a whopper."

Jerry Lang had been gripped by the crazy idea that if he could get his son hooked on cake, rather than bread, the boy might kick that cursed loaf-cuddling habit of his and start out on the road towards becoming a nice, normal schoolboy. The birthday had been a perfect excuse for it; he might even allow the lad to carry a small piece of sponge cake about, in place of the loaf, then gradually reduce the slice in size until the kid carried nothing at all.

The Langs slid the sponge onto a large platter Jerry had borrowed from a nearby caterer, a dish which was normally used to display an entire roasted pig as part of a carvery. Jane stood at one end, Jerry at the other and the two of them carried the platter out to their Ford Cortina and positioned it somewhat precariously between the rear parcel tray and the tops of the front seats. It was then that Jane Lang remembered the other gift she'd intended for her son; a time piece, a hand-crafted watch designed by Jens Hansen, a watchmaker of Swiss descent who refused to live in the city, and resided instead in a small wooden cottage reachable only by an old gravel road which sloped up into the mountains.

"I don't believe I clean forgot to pick up the most expensive gift of all," lamented Jane, slapping her hand to her forehead.

"No problem," said Jerry. "The boy'll be fine where he is. Let's drive up there now."

"But the sponge..." began his wife.

"Stop worrying," said Jerry, exasperated. "It'll all be fine."

*

Life was about to become a good deal more cruel for young Jacob Lang. His parents reached the cottage, paid the watchmaker, a stooped old wizard of a man who assured the Langs that the day this watch stopped dead was the day the world would come to an end.

"That ain't no mortal battery I've put in there," he had crooned. "That old thing will tick until the stars fall from the heavens and the moon weeps blood. That clock'll keep on tocking until the sun turns black in the sky."

Jane had nodded wisely at his words. Jerry had given a sceptical sneer. And on the homeward journey, tragedy struck. On their son's seventh birthday, these parents went over the edge. Jerry took one of the many corners a little too sharply, the wheels of the Cortina lost their grip on the gravel and the mandarin sponge slipped forward from its resting place. The edge of the platter shunted into the back of the driver's head and knocked him out cold. Over they went, sailing out like a bird, till the flight became a fall became a plummet. Flames and wreckage, dead bodies, split bones, and all coated in the deadly sponge which had spelt their demise.

The only thing to survive the fall was the watch that the old wizard had made. It was picked from the wreckage still ticking like the old man had promised and was pushed into Jacob's hand by some well-wisher, shortly before he was shunted off to live with mean old Aunty May of the terrifying blue rinse and alcoholic Uncle Gerald who owned a semi-detached house in one of the capital's less desirable locales. Goodbye Provencia, sayonara Ma and Pa, adios to the bakery, see you later wicks and wax. No longer did these things comfort him; now they reminded him of everything that had been taken. He clung now to his chemistry kit and to the watch, which he did not wear on his wrist, but instead, strung about his neck on a chain made from fool's gold. The bakery was sold to Martha for a song; the home was claimed by the bank.

They weren't good to him, these relatives. Aunty May screeched orders at him like she thought he was some kind of servant (*put out the garbage, do those dishes, vacuum the house, cook me some eggs*) and Gerald was always sending him down to the shop to purchase booze and fags, then taking to the back of his legs with the jug cord when he didn't make it back in time, which he never did, no matter how fast he sprinted. He fantasised about putting rat poison in their dinner; he fantasised about leaving.

It was with the aid of the chemistry kit his mother had given him that Jacob Lang first discovered explosions. He borrowed chemistry books from the library and pored over them for hours. The kit, he soon found, was lame. He took to sneaking into the local high school after hours, when the place was deserted but for the cleaners doing their rounds, and pinching what he needed from the labs. His first experiment involved running six inches of water in the bathroom basin, adding some solid sodium and watching it explode. He kept notes in a textbook which he stashed down beside his bed: Aim, Method, Results, Conclusion.

This was better than bread, better than candles. He mixed nitrate and magnesium, he added sodium peroxide to carbon. The results were okay, small explosions, but he wanted more. At first he only exploded empty space; a bang without destruction. Then it occurred to him that he might turn his hands and his mind to *things*.

The first object he exploded was Uncle Gerald's pet gopher, a motley-coloured little thing called Fifi which was always crawling about in the old boozer's collar and pissing down his neck, spraying him with its unique perfume. Jacob strapped a homemade skyrocket to the creature's back and watched it fly off into space. He thought he was doing the old guy a favour in knocking off the animal, but Uncle Gerald did not take his pet's death lightly. There were beatings, there was cruelty. Other neighbourhood animals were detonated at random and every time somebody's moggy or mutt was blown to bits Jacob was beaten and every time he was beaten some other animal was subsequently exploded.

He ran away from his new home shortly after his tenth birthday. The mean streets of the capital did not swallow him. He was no longer the boy he had been; now he was somebody new. From the root of his spinelessness had sprung a new backbone and this one was made of steel. He was as hard as nails, as cold as ice. Nothing could touch him. He slept under bridges, in doorways, in dirty back alleys. For a time he survived by picking pockets and hanging around outside restaurant kitchens at the end of the night, begging the scraps which would otherwise go to waste. There was a period of child prostitution he preferred not to think about. He was small for his age, and soon discovered that he was a talented thief; he made a good cat burglar, sneaking into homes in the dead of night and making off with the telly or the stereo, pocketing the money, sometimes treating himself to a hot steak pie or a newspaper packet of greasy fries to complement his restaurant fare. There was a Dickensian gang of boys like him, a ring which was master-minded by a spry criminal the kids had disrespectfully nick-named the Fartful Codger. Jacob wanted no part of the circle. Nobody was going to take a cut of his cash; what he made was his and his alone. He was his own man. He was off to the side.

With the money he made he bought dynamite. He knew the factory where they made the stuff, but the place was far too much of a fortress for him to be able to burgle it; instead he made a pact with Dirty Al, who was known as the guy who could get you anything you wanted, anytime at all, ask me no questions and I'll tell you no lies. Jacob stole so he could destroy. Cars, animals, buildings. This little apple was rotten to the core.

*

This was the cloth from which Jacob claimed to have created himself; how much truth there was to be found in the stories he told me is another matter. He was my little surrogate Ed, he was somebody I could follow around, a person who extended a promise of something better than the here and the now, a touch of excitement, a magical glimmer. He offered me the chance to dabble on the wrong side of the tracks. He was the big city boy, now in his early teens, come to wreak havoc on Provencia.

But no matter how hardened he became, some things remained the same. He still dreamt of cliffs and cars. He still dreamt of fire.

It's so clear, this memory, it's a photo in my mind. Years had passed me by; it was my eighth birthday. I was twenty-four years old, bored, restless. This day I had, as usual, been ignored at home and so I had left, looking for material to shoot. There I was, out and about, camera strap slung across my shoulder, Leica hanging down under my arm. It felt like a rifle. I was headed for one of my usual haunts, a park near a stretch of riverbank just outside the city centre, frequented by fitness freaks and the elderly. There was a psychiatric home right next door; if you craned your neck right you could see over the fence to the garden filled with dead rose bushes and dry flower beds, amongst which the inmates roamed like ghosts, as if forever searching for something unnameable that they had misplaced. I had taken numerous shots of these peripheral people, hauling myself up so I could lean over the fence and photograph them as they meandered, capture the looks of stunned confusion upon their faces, the haunted looks, the emptiness. Turning to face the other way, I would snap the yoga freaks and the joggers, the women doing Tai Chi and the men doing press-ups. Then I would do the elderly, strolling along in their pastel-coloured jogging suits, some with small dogs, and at the end of the day I would go home happy, knowing that I had captured a good cross-section of the human race on film. This was what I had been hoping for; to return home with a nice set of images, to be developed by me the following day. But what I got was Jacob, who could never be photographed; when you took his picture, he was never there. You would swear that you had clicked and pointed, you had held him in the tiny square of the viewfinder, but when you looked at the negative it was always blank. I took whole rolls of film, attempting to snap him. Nada, zip, nothing.

I never saw him on film and I did not see him, that first day, until it was too late. I was unaware of his presence. I was hiding behind an oak tree, with my white eye trained on an old man out walking his Rottweiler. Just as I was about to press the shutter, there came an almighty sound from the river, as if God himself had ordered a special boom of thunder just for the occasion. The old guy squawked, the Rottweiler went apeshit, the health freaks froze and I dropped my camera in fright. The lens cracked. (From that point on, every photo I took had a hairline fissure arching across it and I would look at that fine line and think of Jacob.)

When I bent down to pick up the Leica, I heard a loud cackling and looked up to see a crazy-eyed young freak walking towards me, grinning, holding a stunned salmon in his right hand.

"Spawning upstream," he beamed, looking directly at me.

The hunch on my shoulder twitched. Why me? Surely there were other females there he would've preferred. I guess I stood out. My cover had slipped a little. Part of my face was showing, the lower left corner, where sags of skin hung down like the wattle of a turkey. He didn't seem to notice. He was looking at his catch of the day.

"There's a feed in this one, alright," he said, holding up the fish.

I was gobsmacked. I think this was the first time anybody outside my immediate 'family' had spoken directly to me.

"Best way to fish," he declared loudly. "Blast 'em right out of the water. Little buggers don't stand a chance."

Down by the river, you could see the mess that he'd made. The riverbank was a disaster; pieces of broken driftwood were draped in the slimy green algae that the explosion had blasted from the bottom of the river, a couple of black eels lay stunned upon the rocks, a few stones had been broken apart. And here was Jacob, seen for the first time through the cracked camera lens, traipsing off down the road with his salmon, and here is Celia, following him, clicking as if her life depended upon it, but capturing nothing.

I followed him all the way to his home, an old abandoned trailer parked a short way down river, and I said nothing, I simply watched as he sliced his catch down the backbone, then gutted it, tossing the entrails to the gulls that swooped and screeched overhead. He lopped off the head and put it to one side to use in fish head soup. He was left with a pale skeleton and two neat fillets. He ignored me as he worked, and I felt for an instant that my wish for invisibility had come true. But after he had lit the coals and fried the fish on the barbeque which sat nearby he brought me one of the fillets on a paper plate and I knew that he could see me. We ate in silence. When we had finished we tossed our plates onto the dim flames that still sparked beneath the blackened hotplate of the barbeque and then he asked me if I wanted to see some more explosions. I nodded eagerly. He walked across to the trailer that was his home. Through the open door I saw him rustling in a large paper sack and when he came back outside he carried a small red package in one hand and a box of matches in the other.

"Homemade fireworks," he said evenly. "Knock the store bought ones into a cocked hat."

He placed the package he carried a distance away from the trailer, leant down and lit the wick which poked out one side, then ran back to stand beside me. There was a hush; a tense moment of waiting and then a soft shrieking, like the wind whistling through powerlines. A mighty crack sounded out, as if the heavens were splitting in two; golden sparks shot out in all directions, and rained down upon us where we stood.

"Jacob Lang," he said, turning to me and shaking my hand. "Self-taught explosives expert at your service."

He clicked his heels and saluted.

"Come inside the trailer," he said. "I'll show you a few secrets."

Inside his trailer, all was immaculate. Everything was ordered.

"Ever see someone make napalm?" he asked me.

I shook my head.

"It's simple," he said. "That's something most people don't realise. Just how damned simple all this stuff really is. One part gasoline and one part soap. Gotta be either soap flakes or shredded bar soap. Detergents won't do the trick. Okay, this is how you do it."

He took a double boiler out from a cupboard under the sink.

"Right. First you have to heat the gasoline. But you don't want to do this anywhere near a flame. For obvious reasons."

He grinned at me then filled the bottom half of the double boiler with water and began to heat it on his gas stove. When it reached boiling point he removed it from the flame and carried it to the small table which folded out from the wall.

He completed the mixture with petrol and soap flakes from the small cupboard under the kitchen sink. I noted his lack of measuring equipment. When the mess had congealed, he scraped it out into a couple of glass jars. It had a thick consistency, like jam.

"Voila," he said. "Basic napalm. Dead simple. Not very exciting."

I had been speechless the whole time he was showing me this.

"Tomorrow's lesson," he said. "Your first explosion."

I held up my camera, ready to take a picture of the napalm.

"Uh, uh," he said, shaking his head.

"No pics of the product, love. Save your film for later."

He tugged at one edge of the undie-cover I wore over my face.

"And what's this thing?" he asked.

"It's to keep me hid," I said. "I'm as ugly as sin."

He made no comment. He accepted me without question. I was his fait accompli. He was lonely; he needed a sidekick.

*

The next day found me back at his trailer for my second lesson.

"Okay. You will need the following," he said, taking his items one by one from a cardboard box. "Now, watch carefully."

I was all eyes.

"Take a light-bulb. Drill a hole large enough to fit a small funnel into, being careful not to break the filament inside. Mix up your ingredients like so. Using your handy funnel, carefully pour the liquid through the hole and into your bulb, then glue the hole you made. Screw the bulb back into the fitting and wait for some lucky solider to switch on the lights."

He winked at me. Just filling you in on a few of the basics love. Before working you up to the big stuff."

He handed me the bulb.

"You wanna take this home and try it out on your family?"

"I don't have a family," I said.

He pouted.

"Oh, no family? Who do you live with then?"

"Barry and Lettie," I said. "They own the Butchette."

"Oh *them*. But you're not their daughter?"

"No."

"So who's daughter are you then?"

"I have no idea."

"So you wanna take this lightbulb away then?"

I considered it.

"Okay," I said.

"If you want you could just try it somewhere safe. Like the cellar."

"Maybe," I said.

"Okay. You give it a go. Come back next Monday. Next week's lesson is another easy one. Molotov cocktails."

That night, I tried out Jacob's bulb. I screwed the bulb he had given me into place in the stead of that which usually lit up the cellar. While Barry and Lettie slept safe in their beds upstairs, I flicked the light switch. There was a flash of sudden light, a bang and fragments of glass everywhere. Lettie came running down the cellar stairs.

"What happened?"

I shrugged.

"I dunno. I just got up to get a glass of water and when I switched on the light. Kaboom."

She look at me in disbelief.

"Must be faulty wiring, I guess," she said, in a tone that implied she thought the house's wiring was just fine.

She sighed and shook her head and headed back to bed.

*

"How'd it go?" Jacob asked me excitedly, next Monday, at his trailer. "Did it blow?"

"It blew alright," I said. "Lettie's blaming it on the wiring."

He laughed.

"They always believe what they want to," he said. "But let's get down to business. Right then. Another easy one. Your basic Molotov number. Find yourself one glass bottle."

He had an old glass soda bottle already sitting upon his table. He worked as he talked.

"Fill your bottle with two-thirds gasoline and one-third oil. Make yourself a fuse from an old gasoline-soaked rag, and stuff it into the mouth of the bottle, with a large portion of it sticking out. The bottle is then corked tightly. To use, simply light the rag and throw it at the enemy. The cocktail will explode upon breakage, and the enemy will not be able to extinguish the fire with water."

He plonked the cocktail firmly down upon the table.

"But we're not going to test this today. Today we'll take one of my finished products and give it a go. Whaddayasay? I promise you it will be fun."

I shrugged. "Okay."

He walked across to one of the bunks, lifted the mattress and the boards beneath, reached into the storage space and produced a square metal gadget, of which I caught only a glimpse before he wrapped it in an old pair of trousers and tucked it up under his arm.

"It's time to have some fun," he said. "Be sure to bring your camera."

"Never go anywhere without it," I replied.

*

We stood on one side of the oldest of the three bridges which spanned the Opal. Solemnly, we walked out to the mid-way point, knowing ours would be the last feet to tread the old wooden boards of this bridge that was over one hundred and fifty years old. We stood gazing downstream and then Jacob leant over and placed the explosive device he had been carrying upon the bridge. He hadn't shared with me the secrets of how he had made this one; though he'd muttered something about homemade TNT on the way here and seemed to know a thing or two about exploding caps and timers. His expertise obviously extended beyond the simple tricks he had shown me.

We walked on to the other side, me with my Leica slung over my shoulder, he with empty hands. Jacob checked the watch that hung about his neck. I set my focus to infinity. From the far shore we stood and we waited with baited breath, both of us savouring the moment before the big bang, the instant of anticipation. Silence, and then sound. Another of those sky splitting instants to which we both were to become so addicted and then splinters of wood flying in all directions as this city landmark was blown apart. I captured the moment. I was snapping for all I was worth. At times like this it was as if I were moving through a mirror to snap some fundamental essence of the way things were; the moment was condensed, crystalline. Later, when the photos were developed, I put them down side by side, in order, and we stared at the entire sequence; I had documented the fragmentation of the whole.

*

We made the national news; they did not have the footage I had, of course, for they'd had nobody on site filming. On the telly, they showed the gap where the bridge had once been; a divide which could no longer be crossed. In the papers, the same thing, photos of the emptiness, the absence. A write-up about the bridge's origins, its cultural importance, its status as a landmark. It was Jacob who encouraged me to send in what I had; snaps of the actual event. Late one Sunday he showed his face at the Butchette, pressed his nose up against the glass panes of the outer wall. I unlocked the door and let him in. He came back to the darkroom, where I had laid the photos out and he ran his critical eye across my work. He was the first; nobody, not even Lettie, had ever seen the snaps I took. I had not considered them fit for human consumption. But now here was Jacob, and he was nodding in appreciation.

"You know what you should do," he said. "Make another set of prints and send them, anonymously, to *The Provencian Daily Times*. Create a bit of a scandal. Get them wondering who shot 'em."

I hesitated. I was not sure that I wanted my private realm exposed to the eyes of others.

"You've got nothing to lose," he said. "They'll never know it's you."

And, lost as I was in my wishful fantasies that I remained invisible to the human eye, it did not occur to me that I was known about town as The Oversized Shutterbug and that suspicion would inevitably fall upon me. I smiled and nodded. I did as he said. Come Monday I had made the front page; or my photos had anyway. They had reversed the order; first took the place of last and last had been positioned where the first should have gone. Instead of falling apart, the city bridge appeared to be flying back together. Each shot had the same line running across it; a faint trace, like a fine blonde hair, a result of my cracked lens. This was not commented upon. This line was ignored. And I had experienced my first taste of notoriety. My first taste of being both creator and destroyer. My first taste of fame and anonymity. Nobody knew it was me. Yet.

"Nice one," said Jacob. "What's our next target gonna be, then?"

*

There are some people who cannot be found against their will. There are people who cannot be traced. There are some people who appear, briefly, to light up our lives for a short while before hiding from us for years. Then they re-appear, they come waltzing casually back into our little world as if they have never been away, a nonchalant look upon their face, whistling to themselves. It is as if they are attempting to teach us a lesson. *You don't own me*, they are saying. *You don't control me. I come and go just as I please.* Ed was one of those.

I was walking to Jacob's trailer one afternoon, when I heard somebody calling my name. I turned to the left, saw nobody, turned to the right.

"Celia."

Perhaps I was hearing things. I picked some wax from my ears.

"Celia."

There it was again. The voice.

"Psst. Over here."

A shadow was moving in a doorway.

"Surprise!"

I nearly leapt out of my skin. He stood before me in his long black

overcoat; a toy wand in one hand.

"What the hell are you doing here?"

"Just checkin' up on you, kid. Seein' how you're getting on."

He produced a glass eyeball from out of nowhere and rested it in the crook of my arm.

"I've been keeping my eye on you."

I didn't know whether to be happy or angry that he had finally decided to reappear after all this time. I decided to play it cool, slightly inquisitive. I didn't want him to know what he meant to me, didn't want to give him the power of knowing that the gift he had given me had become my reason for living. I had fantasised about him for so long that his actual presence now came as something of a disappointment. The real Ed did not live up to the Ed I had created in my mind. He seemed more haggard, more droopy. He looked tired.

"You like the camera?"

"I *love* the camera."

"Thought you would."

"So," I said. "What are you doing for a living these days?"

"Oh, you know. A little bit of this and a little bit of that. I get by."

He pulled a long string of flags from his left ear, then hit the side of his head till milk came streaming out of his nostrils, spilling down the front of his coat.

"No use crying over that," he said and waved his right hand up and down the length of his body three times.

The milk evaporated without leaving a trace.

He pulled at the leg of his trousers and three rabbits ran out and went bounding down the street.

I eyeballed him. "What did you come here for, Ed? What do you want from me?"

"Just a routine check-up. To make sure you're okay. To provide a bit of light entertainment, perhaps. Were you entertained?"

"Kind of."

He pulled a macaw from the front of my tracksuit top. He was starting to get on my nerves.

"Ed," I said. "I'm not in the mood for macaws."

"Oh, sweetie." He pouted, then pulled at his bottom lip with his forefinger. "Did naughty Uncle Ed desert you when you wanted him? He's sorry."

He sidled up to me and put one arm around my shoulders, produced three angelfish from his mouth, pushed them in his left ear, then pulled them out of his right. A pack of cards was now in his right hand. He flipped the pack over. The Joker was on the bottom. He shuffled, fanned the pack and extended it towards me.

"Pick a card, any card."

"No, Ed. I'm on my way to see somebody."

"Ohhhh," he said and whistled low through his teeth. "Male or female."

"Male."

"I get the picture."

He pretended to sulk. "I have been *usurped* by another."

"That's not true Ed. I just have certain....commitments, that's all."

"Fine. Your old Uncle Ed shall watch from a distance, making only the odd appearance, when he thinks it might be called for. So I say adios, sweet Celia, hasta manana, baby, till we two meet again."

There was a whirl of cloak, a puff of black smoke and he was gone. There was no point in attempting to cling to a being like Ed.

He was ephemeral, transitory. His very being reeked of impermanence. Fabrication was his essence.

That night I asked Lettie if she'd seen Ed recently and she shook her head.

"I expect nothing from that no good brother of mine," she said. "He's old enough and ugly enough to look after himself. He's turned his back on his home town. Born and bred here, we were, but he doesn't want to stick around for good, he just pops up from time to time, whenever he feels like it, full of crazy stories and twisted dreams. He's about as consistent as the bloody weather."

Provencia has always been known for its schizophrenic weather patterns; one day clear blue skies, the next, thunderstorms, or sleet rain or hail. We've been known to experience snowfalls in mid-summer and searing heat in the middle of the winter.

"And as for that other smut he's into...," said Lettie, then checked herself and went back to the pile of laundry she'd brought home to fold, as Barry gave a grunt and turned the telly up another notch.

XIV

Tick, tock. The grandfather clock with the smashed glass beats two-four time and I am waiting, once again, for his arrival. He is late. The air is heavy with anticipation. You'd think I was expecting some exciting guest, not just tiresome George with his nosey ways and his clumsiness. At ten o'clock he arrives, he steps through the door, promising that this afternoon he will drive me to the capital to see the National Modern, where the retrospective will hang. I will be expected to meet and greet various curatorial types; I will be expected to behave.

I know the gallery he means, I've seen it on the telly, it's a great big ugly construction near the centre of the capital, a brick monolith where budding artistes display their piles of garbage and their pickled cows. I do not belong in such a place; I am too close to death, though I am younger in real years than many of those who exhibit there. Personally, I would've rather held my last exhibition in the gallery that used to be *Crème de la Crème*, it's still up and running; a little moustachioed guy they call The Weasel bought it years ago, and it must be one of God's own miracles that the place hasn't gone under, like so many of the other institutions around this old town. It must be struggling, I think, it must be holding on for dear life. It receives government funding, of course, that always helps. Guilt got the money out of them. They're trying to pretend they're not enjoying watching us drown. The Weasel also runs the daily rag, the *Provencian Daily Times,* a sad little newspaper now just eight pages thick, its print extra large, taking up space, in a sorry attempt to hide the absence of articles and the lack of staff to write them. The PDT's filled with irrelevant tripe; just watered down news and tragic attempts to boost town morale. The Weasel, like our good mayor Norman Lazarus, only got the job because no-one else wanted it. He pens, each morning, his little editorial, filled with hearty good cheer. "Better Times Ahead. Provencia's Glory Days Soon To Return". His words sound hollow, as if he himself is struggling to believe in them.

However, it must be noted; despite or perhaps *because* of the absence in the heart of our city, Provencia has recently become a little more popular with cultural types in the capital, we're so far out we're almost in again, a sort of cult town, if you will. When all's said and done I'd rather have remained doggedly loyal and held my last exhibition in the same building in which I held my first, but George twisted my arm, "*They're dying to put your pics up, Celia*", and I simply shrugged my shoulders and went along with his plans. Sometimes I enjoy letting myself be bullied. They don't expect me to be passive; they expect aggression, anger, a charging bull with dangerous horns, and it's always fun to wear a different face than the one they anticipate that they will see. Also, secretly, I am flattered that they have finally opened up the door to me; they have let me in just as death is about to open up that other door, the exit that leads from this world to the next.

The morning passes with George thudding about above, and me, down below, scratching away with my old black pen and it is not until eleven that disaster strikes and it's him that causes it. He thought it would be amusing, I suppose, to sneak up on me as I sit at this old oak desk; he wanted to catch me in the act. He crept down the ladder like a panther and, the very image of stealth, he snuck up behind me and peered over my shoulder. I did not hear him, but I sensed his presence and the presence I sensed made me jump in my seat, jabbing my pen hard into the paper and breaking the nib. You can imagine the mess; ink from here to kingdom come, flooding across my pages like a stain. He fumbled and apologised. I bit my tongue, chomping down hard on my fury. Hours of work, ruined. I glared at him silently, crumpled the marred pages and tossed them into the bin.

"That's that then," I said. "No point in sitting here now. You've broken my train of thought and spoilt the thoughts of the last few days."

A mild reprimand; I could've been and should've been a lot more nasty. I pretended to shrug it off.

It was my suggestion to go to the gallery earlier than we had planned ('since the morning's gone down the drain', I said) though I regretted forwarding the idea the instant we left the house. As soon as I stepped out onto the pavement, I felt suddenly dizzy, overwhelmed. There was too much world out there for my liking, too much ground, too much sky.

I am forced to clutch onto George's arm for support, despising myself for this weakness as I did so. George looked worried, 'What if she falls over?' he was thinking. 'She'll drag me down with her. Or worse, she might land on top of me. Squash me like a bug. Snap my limbs like brittle twigs.'

But I do not fall down. I remained resolutely upright and the two of us walked together, down the street to where his station wagon was parked. The neighbours' eyes were not upon me; nobody stares these days, they're used to me. *Good old Celia*, they say to themselves. *Out and about. Doing her thing.* They're not scared of me anymore, more's the pity, they speak of me as if I am a small child that must be humoured, something harmless, benign. I am the town pet.

In keeping with this, George opened up the rear door of his station wagon and I clambered inside, like a dog, too meaty for the passenger seat.

I sit hunched there, the hump on my right shoulder pushed up against the car ceiling, my eyes to the pane, watching the scenery whip by as we drove towards the outermost ring road, past the pulp and paper mill, circling the city, before hitting the main road out, the road that runs like a vein from here to the capital. There is no corresponding artery; all the blood is carried from here to there, they are the heart, the hub, we are just some useless appendage, something you could function without, an appendix, maybe, or a little toe.

It's a three hour drive from my beloved Provencia to the capital, a scenic, winding road, across the mountain range which runs like a mohawk down the centre of our country. This is a road I have driven before. The view is, as always, magnificent. As we climb higher into the hills, I turn my head to look back over my shoulder; Provencia falls away behind me like a shed garment. Ahead are the mountains and that dreaded 'Other Place', the thought of which fills me with both apprehension and excitement. I am not a capital virgin; this will not be my first time in the big smoke. I have spent time in the capital before; I sometimes think of myself as the dilapidated bridge that spans both worlds. Hate one, love the other. One is my hell, the other is a strange and deserted sort of heaven.

Still, for the last ten years, I have stayed in just the one place; the capital has been the great big stain on the other side of the country, and now I am finally venturing west, across the twisted road once more. These mountains are the in-between place; no man's land. We are neither here nor there. George slots *Country*

Classics into the stereo and starts tapping his foot in time to *Rhinestone Cowboy.* I take a few good pictures of him as he drives.

"Probably a good thing we left early," he says. "Wouldn't want to be stuck in the big city after dark, would you Celia?"

I shake my head. Daylight hours will be bad enough; night time would be too much to bear. We drive on, winding higher, passing few cars, for this is a road not often travelled these days. Once settled on either side of this divide, people tend to stay put; it's a rare soul who ventures from East to West more than once in a lifetime.

When we reach the summit, George pulls into a parking bay.

"Must be time to stretch the legs," he says, and the two of us climb out and walk the short distance to the lookout point.

From here we can see both ways; Provencia to the east, the hole at its centre clearly visible, a scar on the landscape; to the west, the capital, the root of all evil, a sprawling mass of little matchbox houses, factories and high rises, spreading like a virus. I shiver though it isn't cold.

We head back to the car and start the winding drive downwards. George cranks up the stereo.

Soon we are there. As we pass through the outskirts, I keep my eyes shut, occasionally opening the right one for a little peek, a glimpse of a factory, a flash of a warehouse. Why did I agree to come here, after all this time? Strange demons roam these streets; I should have stayed at home, where at least the monsters are familiar, better the devil you know, as they say. I am here partly from boredom, partly from vanity, partly because I fancy I am facing up to something unnameable. I wish I could say what it was.

"Wake me up when we're at the gallery," I say to George, then tuck my head under my arm and pretend to sleep.

Shortly, the car pulls to a halt and he taps me on the shoulder. "We're here."

He leaves the driver's seat and comes round to the rear of the vehicle to let me out. I rise to my feet, peer wearily about. There it is, the building in which I shall hang; a condemned woman. This is enemy territory; I have strayed past the front line. I am out in the open, in the line of fire. I am dicing with death. I pull the hood of my sweatshirt up over my head and try to diminish myself, shrinking inwards like a gigantic violet, scuttling across the car park behind George, to the door of the gallery, where we are greeted by the little pit bull who came to my house some weeks ago.

"You remember Lilith, don't you, Celia," says George and I grunt a brief affirmative and pull my hood a little further down over my face.

Lilith ushers us inside, through the doorway, into the stark minimalist foyer. No pot plants or art works here; just a white space with a ticketing booth at one end of it, and two green signs against the left hand wall, one pointing to the fire exit and one pointing the way to the toilets.

"So glad you could make it, Celia," says the pit-bull. "I'll give you the royal tour of the place and then I've got a few folks here who are just *dying* to meet you."

These art gallery types are always dying to do something or other. We walk through the door cut into the far wall, into a cavernous room currently displaying an exhibition of contemporary furniture; a glass chair, a table made from orange perspex, a polystyrene bed. It's all far too small for me, of course. I'd need the size of everything tripled before I could even contemplate the use of such household items.

"This is where your first hundred photos will hang," says our guide. "We're spreading your work over three rooms."

I stare at the walls; I find it hard to imagine my early shots hanging here; the Butchette customers, the explosions, pics of Lolly and Stuff, but this is where they will go. Crowds will file past, comment, move on. Bored kids will be tugging at their mother's hands and asking to go to the toilet; somebody will say, *a five year old with a camera could've done that* and maybe, if I'm lucky, somebody will try to steal something.

Lilith is every bit as irritating as before; the same enthusiasm, same terrible phrases: *power of subversion, view of the underbelly, sights from the margins,* words which should mean something to me, but which slide meaninglessly from her mouth and fall to the floor. Is she even talking about me? She walks us through the other two rooms which have been allocated to the Doom exhibition; one currently containing thirty video screens all playing the same footage, a film of a woman in a black overcoat, standing on a bridge, with her hair blowing out behind her, and the other containing nothing at all, just a few gallery goers standing around staring at the walls.

"This is one of our most popular exhibits," says Lilith. "It's entitled "The Empty Room" and is by an anonymous artist."

Pretentious little twat, I think to myself, smiling at George and Lilith from underneath my hood.

"So these three rooms constitute your allocated space," says Lilith, as she leads us away, through the remainder of the gallery, through rooms filled with other works: stacks of broken glassware glued together, vicious, jagged edges poking out everywhere; a pile of tinsel spiralling upwards to create what appears to be a gigantic phallus; a pine forest made completely of paper.

Lilith talks nineteen to the dozen the entire time and I am thankful for this. Even if there were a small gap in her speech in which I might slot a sideways word, I don't think I would fancy speaking. Perhaps it is just my imagination, but there seems to be danger everywhere here; seeping out of the walls, oozing up through the floorboards. The sooner I can get out of this gallery, out of the capital and back to Provencia, the better.

When she raises the question of the narration I have been asked to pen, I open my mouth and hear myself fobbing her off with a trite comment. "It's coming along nicely, thanks." My voice sounds strange to my ears, as if it is coming from far away. The hunch on my right shoulder aches.

George coughs uncomfortably at the mention of the brochure; I wonder if he's told her that it's getting a little out of control.

She chats away to George about other 'projects' he has worked on in the past. It seems that he does this kind of thing all the time, ringing up artists who are tapping at death's door, insinuating himself into their lives, burrowing round in their old work and pulling together a show. He's an old hand at it; for him I am just one in a long line of humans with whom he will work, to him I am nothing special and the thought depresses me. I was born, I lived, I am soon to die. The mark that I used to think was important, this mark my work made, will disappear like a line drawn in the sand; the tide will simply come in and wash me away.

"Why so glum?" asks Lilith. "This will be your big moment."

My last big moment, I think to myself. *My last chance.*

"Let's go get her a cuppa," says George. "That normally cheers her up."

The three of us wander down to the gallery café, where a young woman with pink hair and three nose studs serves us each a lukewarm pot of tea and a piece of watery quiche. I stab dispiritedly at the quiche and finally hand it to George, who looks at me with worry; unlike me to turn up my nose at tucker, when you're my size you need all the energy you can get.

George and Lilith, it seems, go way back. Before he took to nosing around in old biddies' attics, George spent some time in the capital, did a Fine Arts degree at the local university, apparently, while working part time as a curator here at the 'Nat Mod', as he and Lilith call it. Upon completion of his degree, he moved back to his home town, Provencia, with dreams of buying up some cheap exhibition space and waiting for our city's economic and cultural upturn. The upturn never arrived, but while in the process of renovating his 'gallery' he met his lovely Wife down at The Muddy Duck on karaoke night. George eventually realised that Provencia's recovery was a dream, but The Wife, who was Provencian to the core, refused to leave the area and so in order to pay the bills, George continued to work for the National Modern as a sort of roving collector, roaming the countryside buying art works at auctions, searching second hand shops for quirky bargains, organising exhibitions of work by the nearly dead and the unknown. His 'gallery' is now inhabited by the ubiquitous Provencian crackheads.

George and Lilith run through the customary gossip; who's been fired, who promoted, who's been screwing who in the broom closet during the lunch hour. I remain silent, as silent as the grave, occasionally signalling to the studded girl to bring over some more tea, praying for the hour when I will be allowed to leave and return to the safety of my own home.

I am not to be let off lightly; there are still the introductions to make. When they finally appear to have run out of gossip, they lead me through to meet a couple of gallery big-wigs who look me up and down, scan me from top to toe, dismissive. So much for dying to meet me; they look bored to death after ten seconds of my strange, silent company.

George and Lilith exchange perfunctory pecks upon the cheek and agree to meet again, before the exhibition opens.

Outside the gallery windows, it grows dark; night is drawing in around this city. George and I step through the gallery door, and he reaches for my arm, but I don't need him now, I am being defiantly independent, walking upright on my own two feet. All around me, the buildings rise up into sky, cold, concrete, unforgiving.

"Do you want to go for dinner in a local restaurant?" he asks politely.

But I shake my head and hunch my shoulders up about my ears. I don't want to see any more of this city; this little slice has been perfectly adequate. I want to go home.

*

During the drive back I say nothing, just stare out of the window at the endless blanket of night, with the dark shape of the mountains like a stage set, and, high above me, the wheeling stars, pinned like metal badges to this blanket of sky, like cold eyes staring down at me, merciless.

He drops me on my front step, but I am not sleepy. I wash my broken pen in the kitchen sink and then return to the living-room and open the desk drawer in order to search for a replacement cartridge. I am all out of black and blue; I have only red left. I push this cartridge into the end of the pen, replace the broken nib with a new one and run it across a sheet of scrap paper until it begins to bleed.

Now I write in this bright red ink; it spills across the page like blood and the pages fall away from me and flutter to the floor, where they lie like torn petals or fallen angels. Soon I will sweep them together and attempt to create a coherent whole, like an architect structuring a building. An open airy construction; something that will let in the light.

XV

I pushed Ed from my mind. He took a back seat. I began spending increasing amounts of time away from home, always in the company of Jacob, my new-found friend. He was older than I was, but I made him look like a midget; I towered a good five inches above him and my broad shoulders were half as wide again as his. My arms were as thick as his legs and my thighs were as wide as his chest. I dwarfed him. I never told him my real age. Nor did I show him my face. I did not remove my cover.

He thought I could be easily led, and I was. I followed him around, like a duck trailing after its mother. He took to calling by the house first thing in the morning. Barry and Lettie were happy that I had found a human whose company I could tolerate and who would tolerate me; it was the first sign of normality in a life defined by the abnormal. It did not cross their minds that the strange explosions that were taking place citywide were engineered and executed by us, or if this thought did show its face at the periphery of consciousness, they quickly pushed it aside.

I accompanied Jacob to, and took photos of, a sum total of ten different constructions across the city. After the bridge, we did a branch of the National Bank, we did a Woolworths, a McDonalds, we did a menswear store, a shoe shop and a button factory. We did not do any homes. We did a sweatshop where ladies' lingerie was made and a printworks. We kept deaths to a minimum. We planted the bombs in broad daylight, but detonated them in the dead of night. We were one step ahead of the law; they couldn't touch us. They always arrived too late, the cops in their cars. I took pictures of them too, as they investigated the scene of the crime, failing to come up with any leads. I snapped the bomb squads and forensic experts who came along afterwards to try to make sense of these disasters. I read in the papers that they'd flown a couple of criminal psychologists down from the capital to try to understand how the mind of this bomber was working, to try to find a pattern, a reason, a rhyme.

There was no reason. We were bombing just to bomb. For the sheer hell of it. Just because we could. There was a routine though; sometime during the early afternoon hours, Jacob would walk into the targeted building with a backpack on, make his way to the men's toilets, lift the lid of the cistern and place the bomb inside.

Then we would leave, amuse ourselves for the rest of the day and return at midnight, Jake to hit the trigger and me to hit the button on my camera. By the time that they cottoned on to our modus operandi, by the time they figured out the method in our madness, the game was over. The final damage had been done.

I always took photos and the photos were always published. Nobody knew my name, but I had become a small-time celebrity. The Phantom Photographer, they called me. They thought that the bomber was also the one who took pictures; they did not realise that there were two of us. They thought I was singular, but we were plural. Jacob and I wreaked havoc right across the city. We always celebrated with homemade fireworks afterwards; we stood back and we watched the coloured sparks fly.

It never occurred to me to question this young man's sanity, never crossed my mind that he might be somewhat unhinged. When he came up with his next idea, I nodded eagerly. I was his follower, his disciple. If he told me to jump into the fire, I would have. I craved his approval; until he came along I had not realised that I had been lonely, but now that he was here, I wondered how I had functioned without him.

"I've got a good idea," he said.

Famous last words.

"I say we do the Butchette."

"Eh?"

"It's in the heart of everything. To take that out would be...I don't know. Spectacular."

"What about Barry and Lettie?"

"Oh come on. How good have they been to you?"

"They took me in."

"Only out of guilt. I promise not to kill them. It'll be another dead of night job. They'll be tucked up at home, safe in their little beds."

"But my darkroom..."

"Surely you can set that up in the cellar of their house."

"So we blow it up," I said. "And then what?"

"This one is unable to be photographed. An explosion too dangerous to document. So instead we make a model and you snap that. And we don't give the photos to the papers. We make them pay. Anonymous blackmail."

How easily led I was! I did not see the web he wove around me; I was naive, juvenile, a great big baby. I was a sucker. Hindsight; they call it a gift but I think it's a curse. It makes us feel our idiocy all the more strongly; if only I knew then what I know now, we say to ourselves as we stumble along in the darkness.

I made excuses to Barry and Lettie; I relocated my darkroom to the family cellar, where I still slept, set up my enlarger right next to my mattress, got my mitts upon an old table that had been kept in the garage and dragged that down the stairs, to place upon it my solutions, my touch-up paints, my glitter, my plastic trays.

I saw nothing of Jacob Lang for two days; when I called in at his trailer he was never there and I began to think that perhaps he had merely been a figment of my overactive imagination, part of a dream. The anxiety I felt at his absence resulted in a total relapse on the insect front and when he finally reappeared in my life, I was out in the backyard, clutching half a cricket between two fingers, while the other half of the creature hung dangling from my lips. Barry and Lettie were at work. The front door had been locked, Jacob must have picked the lock and walked quietly through the house and was now standing, looking at me with this insect. It was ten o'clock in the morning. I blushed and looked down at the dirt. In his hands he held a model of the Butchette, a perfect miniature, built of wood, a simulacra so real that had it been built to scale it could've been placed down on our old cracked road in place of the Butchette and nobody would've suspected a thing.

"I hope you've moved your stuff out of the darkroom," he said.

I nodded. In the family cellar I had been doctoring up some of the blow-up snaps, sharpening edges and fading away smudges. I had been practising this part of my art.

"Let's go down there now," he said. "And snap this baby exploding."

We headed down the stairs, to where I had set myself up. Jacob's coat swayed from side to side as he walked, as if lead weights were stashed in its lining. Below ground, Jacob placed his wooden model upon the hard dirt floor and took from one pocket a tiny replica of the explosives which had been used to blow up larger constructions across the city. Tentatively, with one index finger, he lifted the lid of his miniature and placed the tiny bomb inside. I held the Leica up to my eye; the fissure split my vision.

"Got your finger on the trigger?" he asked me.

I nodded.

"On your marks. Get set. Go."

He hit some button inside his coat. The thing exploded, pieces flying every which way and I was taking six pictures per second. Looking back with this fabulous 'gift' of hindsight, I can see what we were doing. We were, quite literally, making history, manufacturing it, bringing it into line with our own designs. We were shaping the way that people saw. We were changing thought. Our pictures of this miniature would be mistaken for shots of the real thing; they would believe that this was the way that it had happened. There was nobody to bring our story into disrepute.

When that tiny explosion was over, I turned around to look for Jacob, but he had gone. The heaviness of his coat had not slowed down his exit; he weighed a tonne, but he moved as if he were as light as a feather and could simply float out on the next breeze. I stood amongst splinters of wood.

If I'd known what he'd had in mind I would have stood inside the building he was about to explode; I would have used my physical presence to stop him, I would've thrown myself in between him and his own destruction.

He did not wait till midnight. He chose midday instead. He left me in the cellar and he made his way directly to the Butchette and the next thing I knew the sound was tearing through the bricks of our house as if it were made of paper, ignoring its solid four walls; the sound of catastrophe, disaster, as if God's wrath was being enacted, here on earth. I felt my mind split in three.

Overhead, all hell was breaking loose. I could picture the wreckage; the fat businessmen flying through the air like broken dolls, thoughts of the next day's golf session rushing from their minds, their briefcases splitting open and spilling precious documents across the CBD; the street-sweepers' brooms swept from their hands and flung into the air like enchanted broomsticks. I imagined the prostitutes who hung about the streets just to the south of the central city, their wigs torn from their heads to expose their true colours, their flimsy garments ripped from their used and abused bodies. I pictured powerlines falling to the ground and lying, sparking, upon the ground. I visualised buildings which had stood for hundreds of years, falling. It was if we were tearing back the city's skin to reveal the veins, the muscle tissue, the raw red heart that pulsed beneath.

And Jacob was dancing with death. He walked into the Butchette wearing the same overcoat I'd seen him in just minutes before. He was a walking explosion. The last in this long line of things that he blew up was himself. I imagine him flying, like a skyrocket, into the air, falling to pieces as he did so, body parts landing in different locales; his torso ten metres away, a foot in the next street, a hand in one of the surrounding suburbs and his head, I imagine, would have fallen down one of the many cracks in our street which had been caused by that other disaster, as natural as this was unnatural, the Great Quake that had occurred exactly one year before the day of my delivery.

In the cellar, I felt the world settle. I ran up the stairs, down the hallway and poked my head around the front door. Nothing. The street showed no visible signs of damage. Inside the house, the only thing broken was the face of the grandfather clock which sat in the family room. Shards of glass lay in a jagged pool upon the carpet. I did not bother to sweep them up, but left them where they lay.

I was horrified and distraught. Still, I did what I had always done; I photographed the aftermath. I took my camera and I headed for the centre of town, hearing the sound of sirens ringing out all around me, listening to the wailing of police cars and fire engines. And when I got close I could see that this had been as enormous as I was; the movie I had seen in my mind had been real. This was destruction on a massive scale.

I took photos of the faces around me; I captured shock, devastation and horror. These were faces who had seen their city caught in an apocalypse. Whole streets had been torn up, the asphalt peeled back like liquorice, the lampposts plucked from the road as if they were as light as lollipops, the cars flipped on their backs as if they were no more than matchbox toys. The pieces that I imagined landing in various locales were never found; it was as if he had turned into gold dust and floated away into the ether. The only thing they did find was the watch that had been made by Hansen, still ticking, lying in a pile of debris. It was placed in a plastic bag and taken away as evidence. It was this watch that led them to Jacob and Jacob that led them to me.

The other evidence they found, which was to be used against me, was discovered, later, at his trailer home. This was Super 8 footage of himself, filmed just before he set off for the Butchette, holding open his coat to show the arsenal that was hidden there, Jacob spinning around and saying *this one's for you, Celia* and cackling that same tortured laugh he had given the day I had first seen him 'fishing' for salmon.

I photographed others and I photographed myself, turned my camera around to face me. They showed this to me later, after they had snatched all recent films from me and developed them themselves. I never got the chance to send my last pictures to the paper. In this photo I took of myself, my haunted eyes stare out, nothing behind them, witness to this terrible loss. For it felt as if everything was gone, as if everything had been taken. Jacob had demolished Barry and Lettie and himself in one fell swoop. For my adoptive parents had not been safe at home, after all, they had been hard at work when Jacob had walked in through the Butchette door. I can picture it; Lettie at the steam press, Barry with his meat cleaver raised high. Perhaps one of them had walked across to serve this stranger who had just walked in; perhaps Lettie had looked at him and smiled and asked *what can I do for you?* Or maybe he had crept in unseen through the side door and had simply stood watching them for a minute, before taking it upon himself to play God and detonate. One thing's for certain; he spelt the end of them, he wrote their demise into the script of my life.

And my two grandmas? They were on the other side of the river, the South side and though they had not seen the blast, they'd certainly heard it, Stuff with her right ear and Lolly with her left, and they saw the news on the telly later and great tears ran down their wrinkled old cheeks when they heard that the bomb blast had originated in the Butchette. They did not yet know that Celia was in any way linked with the disaster and the first thought both of them had was to telephone to see if their only granddaughter was alright.

In the empty corridor of the family home, the black telephone rang and rang.

*

And Celia? All night I stayed out, documenting what I saw, fighting back the waves of grief, finishing one roll of film only to slot another into the camera and when I returned home in the morning, what I found was a couple of stern looking coppers, knocking on the front door, demanding to know the whereabouts of Celia Doom.

"I am she," I said.

And I fixed these men with my inverted vision. They stared as if their eyes were about to pop out of their heads, but I was used to this kind of treatment by then. No skin off my nose, that people liked to oggle me and risk damaging their vision. I was not exactly easy on the eyes.

"Is there anybody else home, Ms Doom?"

"No," I said. "I am alone."

God only knows what they made of me, these coppers, as I stood facing them.

"We must step inside," they said. "Just to ask you a few questions."

I let them in. I sat them down at the kitchen table, spreading my large hams across two chairs, one for each thigh.

"You must tell us the truth," they said, and I laughed.

"Do you now know or have you ever known, a Mr Jacob Lang?" they asked.

"Who?" I replied.

"Mr Lang. Do you know him?"

"Never heard of him."

"Go get the projector from the car," one of them said to the other, and his subordinate did as he was told.

"You have been named," they said as they played me what Jacob had filmed, his terrible last dance, as he spun around and around inside his trailer, coat flying out around him, exposing what he had hidden from me, speaking my name, implicating me. I felt my mask crack like my camera lens.

"We have reason to believe," they said. "That you and this young man have been in cahoots. We have reason to believe that you are the one to blame."

I shifted uncomfortably on the two chairs, which creaked beneath my weight. I had not been blessed with the looks of an innocent. My guilt was written all over me.

"How do you know that I'm the Celia he's talking about?" I asked and they produced a fistful of the snaps I had sent to the *Provencia Daily Times* and asked to see the makeshift darkroom I had set up in the cellar and I knew that I was doomed. I was following in Ed's footsteps.

They marched into my sanctuary and began searching through the many developed prints I had brought over from the Butchette in boxes. Every shot I had sent to the Mail had a double. Every double could be found in one of those boxes. They pulled my most recent role of film from my camera and took the other undeveloped films from my pockets.

They got their hands on everything; there would be no escape for me.

"But I did not do it," I said. "I was not there."

"We'll see what the law has to say about that," they replied and they bundled me into the back of the paddy-wagon and dragged me away.

Jacob had blasted himself sky high and left me holding the baby. This was the price we paid for our notoriety; his death and my incarceration.

I was framed. The shots of the model I had snapped were developed. Guilt piled upon guilt.

"So you knew nothing, eh?"

"That was a model! That was not the real thing."

Though the words I spoke were the truth, they sounded false, even to my own ears.

Nobody knew how old I was. They searched for my name in the official birth records of the city, but my name had been erased, or else had never been recorded. There was no record of my age. They had only my word, *I think I am eight years old.* I fit no category; was I even human? I was like a piece of misplaced baggage, shunted into lost property, waiting to be claimed. I was in limbo, hanging about, rotting on remand, sitting in my cell down at the local cop shop, my arms grasping the bars, rattling my cage, a zoo animal. My keeper, a jovial doughnut-eating cliché of a cop named Clint fed me bread and water and told me he would pay me sixty cents to remove my cover and give him a glimpse of my face. I refused point-blank.

There was talk of an adult trial, judge and jury and me in the witness box desperately trying to plead my innocence and that might well have come to pass, had not one of my medical friends heard of my predicament, and come down to the station, bringing reports which tracked the progress of my disease. I did not see him, I heard his voice through the wall.

"Eight years old," went the whisper. "We can't pass sentence on a child."

"We'll take her," said the doctor. "We want her for our research. We promise we will be kind."

A shiver ran over me. I knew what they needed me for; they wanted me to be their lab rat, their experiment. To them, I would never be human. They had stamped my shoulder; staked their territory, made their claim. My eyes were wide open in alarm.

There was a battle, medicine versus law.

"You have no right to her," said the police. "She's dangerous. She must be put away. She shows a distinct lack of remorse. Her own adoptive parents are now dead, and she's shed not a single tear."

They had read me wrong. It was not that I didn't want to feel, it was simply that I couldn't. Some vital part of me was frozen, numb.

"We'll take good care of her," said the doctor. "With Celia at our disposal we could make a very valuable contribution to medical science."

Not sure I liked the sound of that.

"You have no right," said the coppers, as I peered through the bars of my confines, "to reduce this human to an animal."

And while they fought, I waited, my fate hanging in the balance between them.

My fate was out of my own hands and so was my camera. They had taken my Leica from me, locked it away in some dark cupboard somewhere. My weapon was out of my reach.

*

The law won. Provencia's Centre for Juvenile Delinquents of the Female Variety went by the name of Sacred Heart Home. It was filled with little ladies whom Lettie would have called 'nasty pieces of work' and was run by vicious wardens who wore dark green smocks and had iron batons dangling from their belts.

Most of the girls slept in dormitories; matching sheets, matching pillowcases and blankets, all a uniform shade of regulation grey. Six to a room, nine rooms to a building, three small buildings comprising the grand institution at which I was to now reside. Each building was called a 'House', though personally

I felt this was stretching the term a little: Lunar, Solar and Stella were the names given to these three buildings, as if they were hoping that these celestial names would bring out the latent divinity in all of us. There were one hundred and sixty-two of us in total, all wayward and all female, ranging in age from six to seventeen, with nine wardens to control us. Or attempt to.

Regimentation was all. First bell at six am to let you know that you would soon be rising, second bell at six-thirty to tell you to get your sorry ass out of bed and your feet upon the floor, third bell by seven, by now you should be, must be, would be, in the exercise yard for the daily calisthenics, and then, by seven-thirty am, inside for thick, cold porridge and a glass of thin, warm milk. Lessons from eight-thirty till four, each hour carefully divided into minutes, scheduled and controlled, the library from four till six, dinner from six till seven, reading then lights out and shush no talking girls or I will be forced to amputate your tongues.

I was not placed with the other girls. I was shunted into the maximum security section, with the gals who'd murdered their mothers, set their brothers on fire, or done some other ridiculous thing, like bombing the city centre. Nobody was listening to my words of protest (*it was not me, it was Jacob*); as far as they were concerned, I was responsible for the bomb and should be punished accordingly. In the eyes of the wardens, I was up there with the worst of them. We had our own little wing, we dangerous ones, to the west of Solar House. We did not have a dormitory. We had cells. We had no education; they had deemed us too disruptive to be taught. We had been written off before we'd even begun. We were outside their scheme of things; this was solitary confinement. We were let out briefly, between the hours of six-thirty and eight-thirty for breakfast and exercise, but while the other ladies took their lessons we were locked back inside and told to brood on our crimes. At dinnertime, we were again released, led into the main hall and sat down beneath the eagle eyes of three wardens allocated especially to keep an eye on us. We never had fresh meals; we always ate the leftovers from the night before, like pigs cleaning up the slops. Then back to the cells again, but no books for us, we could not be trusted; we might tear out the pages, break the spines, eat the words.

The boredom drilled holes into my skull. My hunch ached constantly. My cell was minute; the bed was half my size, the chair broke the first time I sat on it and the tiny table was good for nothing. There was no camera, nor was there pen or paper for me to scribble upon. There were six of us in this dreaded West Wing; at night you could hear your fellow inmates bashing at the bars of their cells, while the warden on duty would shout *Quiet, girls,* switch on the lights and parade back and forth past the cells with a baseball bat swung up over one shoulder. The wing would fall silent at the sight of that bat; we had seen the damage it could do. The bruises that didn't fade.

I was grateful for my gargantuan size; I wore my body like a weapon. They were vicious, these West Wing girls, they would turn on you at the drop of a hat; bash your head against the wall, boot you in the shins so hard you couldn't stand upright for a week, punch you in the chest with a fist like steel. Somebody had once had an eye put out. But they could not tackle me; I was as strong as an ox, I would shake them off like ants, send them flying against the walls. I only had to do this once, in the corridor, when I was attacked by Terrible Tina and her sidekick Big Betty on the way to the dinner hall, when the warden's back was turned, and we were all marching along single file, like ants. Tina had grabbed my hair and Betty was pulling at my cover. One wallop and the two of them were sent spinning, arms and legs akimbo while the rest of the gals looked on, mouths slack, eyes wide, and I was never bothered again. After that one incident I had a reputation for having a ferocious temper and this reputation suited me just fine. I did nothing to contradict their beliefs.

By the end of my first week inside, all the girls had heard the news about the city centre; gone, exploded. The centre had not held; it was now a vacancy. It was common knowledge, of course, that I had done it, they did not realise that I had not even witnessed that final catastrophe and that at the time of the explosion I had been underground. I gained undeserved notoriety as the one who had actually planted the bomb. Jacob had skipped out and the load he should've shared fell upon my shoulders. In the mind of the nation, I was more than merely a shutterbug who found herself in the wrong place at the wrong time; rather, each and every explosion had been my fault. I was a sick and sorry legend. I was The Murderer.

*

There was a private funeral for Barry and Lettie but I was not let out to attend. They said that Lettie's coffin levitated, briefly, as it was being lowered into the grave. No doubt Our Ed was at work. There was also a city memorial service; the mayor giving a speech, the kids in black arm bands, the women weeping, the men with their jaws set square. I was not allowed to watch it on the old TV set which sat in the main hall, somebody else told me about it. I heard everything secondhand. I had not been mentioned at the service; I was the unnamed blamed. The finger had been pointed straight at me. My name was mud.

Sacred Heart fancied itself as a god-fearing institution. God was a fearful old man with a beard, vengeful. God was out to get you. God was an angry father, impossible to please. He *wanted* you to burn in hell. On the far wall of the dining hall hung a gigantic picture of Jesus, his chest ripped open to reveal a gigantic stylised bleeding heart, thorns pricking his head, blood dripping from his stigmata. My life so far having been completely devoid of religious influence, it did not occur to me that this Jesus guy had anything to do with the name of this God person which was bandied about with such abandon. I thought he was there to decorate the wall. Mass was held every Sunday in a small chapel to the east of the building. The West Wing girls were never in attendance. We were beyond redemption.

Time hung heavy on my hands. The four walls, the cell, I did not so much mind. What I minded was the absence of my art, for my camera had been taken from me, held, until the day when they would set me free. Inside my cage, I paced relentlessly, like a tiger, longing for the day when I would be set free in the concrete jungle I loved to prowl. On the wall of my cell I counted off the days, red marks all in a line, with a strike through six to make seven, a week. My ninth birthday came and went; the hands of the dining hall clock seemed to move at a snail's pace, creeping round the clock face one heavy tick at a time, marching inevitably onwards, like a soldier towards his death.

There were outings for the other girls, but not for us. They were tame; we were the savages. We used to hear about these journeys afterwards and pretend that we didn't mind that we had not been included.

So? We would say, lips curled in a sneer. *I don't care.*

We were feigning indifference. I would've killed to have been let out, camera or no camera, just to walk about, even if it was single file, forward march, behind one of the matrons, just to see something that wasn't this infernal institution. Something new to greet the eye.

Food fights were common; peas and mushy spud flung across the table, kippers flying through the air as if they thought it was the ocean, jellied eels landing with a smack on somebody's forehead, tomato sauce squirting into eyeballs, that sort of thing. Our keepers would go crazy, but they could never prevent the fights from occurring; the threat of punishment wasn't enough to stop us from having our fun.

There were other fights, too, brief scuffles in corridors, timely delivered thumps and more serious scraps, which were bragged about afterwards, when girls would appear wearing their cuts and bruises like some twisted badge of honour. Size was firmly on my side; if you were small you had to learn how to stick up for yourself, you had to stand your ground or you were dead. If they smelt the fear on you, you'd be history. I felt protective towards the smaller girls, but also powerless. I was the oddity here, the mutation. I hardly ever talked, all I ever seemed
to speak was the one lie, *I don't care.* I was emotionally retarded; I didn't know how to take somebody's side, felt incapable of it. Mine had been a selfish, solitary, solipsistic existence. I found myself wishing I had magical powers, the ability to cast a chalk circle for the defenceless to stand inside, but I was no white witch. Instead, I watched with a sick feeling in my stomach as the same girls showed up time and again with yellow and purple bruises on their faces and their bodies. Their only point of refuge seemed to be to take a sick pride in their wounds, to show off the damage that had been done, in order that they might receive some attention. When questioned by the matrons, they refused to tell who had done this to them, they would protect their oppressor, as to tell the truth would be to risk an even greater pummelling next time round. I suppose you could argue that they were complicit in their own victimisation. They would never name names.

The other inmates treated me with a sort of grudging respect which had its roots in fear. I was a landmine. I could blow. Voices fell silent when I walked into the dinner hall; chairs were cleared when I took my place at the table. Girls grabbed their meals and scarpered and I would find myself dining alone, at an empty table, with vacant chairs stretching out to either side of me. To the wardens I was some great lumbering beast that must be kept in line with the odd swift bash from the iron baton. Bruises blossomed on *my* body, also. I was held up as the living, breathing example of what would happen to you if you refused to reform.

You don't want to end up like Celia, the wardens would say, and the other girls would look at me, wide-eyed, and place obedient masks over their wayward faces. Ending up like Celia was touted as a fate worse than death. The idea of becoming me became so feared, that during the twelve months I spent at the detention centre, more girls were released for good behaviour than in the previous ten years combined and after I was released, a picture of me that had been taken just after I had received an undeserved beating from one of the wardens was pinned up in the main hall; I hovered there, like some deadly angel, my black and white eyes staring down at them, a reminder of all they would not ever wish to be. The wardens did not mention that I no longer resided at Sacred Heart, instead they concocted the rumour that 'the notorious Doom' was kept half-starved in a cell dug out especially for her, located somewhere underneath the exercise yard, and that those who refused to tow the line would be thrown kicking and screaming into my den, where I would eat them alive, bite off their heads and tear their meat from their bones, like a hungry lumberjack with a plate of spare ribs.

'She's down there now', the wardens would say, if someone was playing up, 'chewing on the old bones of other disobedient young ladies. Best you watch yourselves or you'll be following in the footsteps of all those other dead girls. You'll be Celia fodder'.

This murderous, carnivorous self, this bogey monster, was half a world removed from Celia the photographer. This was another girl entirely, a gigantic cardboard cut-out who had an existence all of her own. I had ceased to be fact; I was now invention. Thus it was that my legend lived on long after my departure from Sacred Heart.

I had no visitors. Lolly was housebound and Stuff was furious with me.

You mean all that time, she pretended to be a good little girl when she was actually a MURDERER?

God only knew where Ed was.

*

In the night I was crippled with Fanta cravings, in dreams I found myself adrift in an endless ocean of orange fizz, gulping great heavenly mouthfuls as I swam for my life. There was never a shoreline in sight. My cell was devoid of insect life; a couple of Daddy Long Legs who had been foolishly lingering in a corner up near the ceiling had been devoured within my first hour of incarceration and although I had scoured my confines for other such delicacies, I had not come up trumps. Although I prayed for my release, the freedom was also something I feared. There was safety in incarceration; life inside was an exercise in monotony, but at least it was a known quantity, a devil I was familiar with. Who could say what demons lay in wait for me in the big bad world beyond the detention centre gate? The future seemed unimaginable; what would become of me if I was set free? Jacob, Barry and Lettie were dead and gone, and the thought of returning alone to the family home terrified me. Beyond these iron bars, wolves waited to devour me.

Every week my medical friends would come and collect me from my cell and snip away a few more bits of me. I was something of a scientific phenomenon, they were not about to let me escape their clutches easily. They measured and weighed me, they charted my progress. They shone lights into my eyes and peered into my ears. They never spoke to me, they worked in silence, but for the odd observation.

Lot of leg growth.

Eyes aren't looking too healthy.

Nasty lesion on the lower back.

Bulge on right shoulder becoming increasingly pronounced.

You could almost hear them salivating as they spoke, they would've killed to make me finally theirs, to take me away and reduce me to a lab rat. But the large iron bell that sat in the centre of the exercise yard would toll, signifying the end of their time with me and they would slink reluctantly away, while the wardens came to reclaim me, to lock me back behind bars.

We West-Wingers had our own little bathroom, policed, of course, by the wardens. They would lead us in there one at a time, tell us to strip down and then shunt us into the cold shower, hollering at us which body part to wash, yelling at us to pick up and put down the soap, shouting that it was time to get out and quickly towel ourselves dry. I took my cover off to wash; the wardens would turn their eyes to the wall.

This bathroom contained the only mirror I saw during my time at Sacred Heart. I was a terrible sight to behold. All this ageing was taking its toll. My skin looked haggard; my epidermis was that of a thirty year-old, fine wrinkles, mysterious lines, scars that had never healed. The stretch marks incurred during 'adolescence' had refused to fade. Old age was descending like a ravenous vulture. I had the feeling that I had been shunted off to the side to reside here, in my cell, while my life, my real life, was continuing down some other road. There was a Celia who had been wrongfully imprisoned and there was a Celia for whom Justice had prevailed. This other version of myself was outside, camera raised to eye, unaware that her other self was incarcerated. One of us was free and one of us was not.

*

(There was a third Celia also. An all-seeing Celia, a fly on the wall of my life. This was the Celia who kept up a steady narration; she was elsewhere, looking on, watching the movie of my life, an impartial observer, snacking on popcorn, checking her watch, looking forward to half time.)

Back inside I waited and thought. Another birthday ticked by, unobserved.

And on the walls of my cell the small scratched marks gathered force, like an army planning an attack.

XVI

The hippies are out there again; bashing those damned drums like there's no tomorrow, singing their songs of protest, my bet is they'll be off down to the pulp and paper mill soon enough, hoping to succeed where so many others have failed. What with that ridiculous racket and the howling of Mutt, whom they adopted years ago, I often find it a little difficult to concentrate on my story. Still, good on them for taking our old dog in, somebody had to; when the bomb went off the poor thing was abandoned, forgotten. The neighbours fled before the city sank and drowned and when the hippies moved in and heard our poor canine half-starved and howling they opened their home to him. They refuse to feed him meat; bloody thing's a vegetarian now, lives on lentils and spinach.

Still in my night gown although it is three in the afternoon, I head out into the backyard. My head and chest loom over the fence, to where the six of them sit in a circle, like some witch's coven. My camera is in my hand.

"Hey, Celia!" shouts one of the males.

They all look up in unison, a sea of patchwork and paisley. They wave and give me a couple of peace signs. "What's goin' down, sister?"

These people are truly time-warped. "Having our own little Woodstock, are we?" I ask.

"Yea man. We're gonna *sing* Leechson's empire to death. Put an end to his pollution once and for all."

The Leechson they are referring to is Mr Leechson of Leechson and Co., owner of The Mill. The original Leechson is long gone, the place is run by his grandson. They've kept it in the family. The pulp and paper mill was the first factory to go up here, a hundred and twenty years ago, and has been the backbone of the economy ever since. Now that backbone supports not a thriving animal, but a withered, tired old beast that ought to be shipped off to the knacker's yard.

Not that Leechson would care, he doesn't live here anyway. Like all the rest he's headed west and has many other business interests elsewhere, both at home and abroad. He's probably all but forgotten about the existence of this mill, though it keeps churning over; the foremen continue barking orders, the workers do their impersonations of automata, the managing director spends most of his time playing golf with the finance director out on Provencia's overgrown golf course, which only the two of them use.

And the hippies cling to their sad illusions of conquering capitalism with song. (They say that I live in a dream world!) Tonight they'll come slinking home from the mill, world-weary. I won't say, 'I told you so', but, 'You think that Leechson and Co. care that our river is their dumping ground, you think they care about the sludge that snakes its way through the city, heading out to pollute the ocean, three hundred miles away? As long as there are workers to show up and clock in and play the robot and clock out at the end of the day, the place will continue to tick over, the sludge will continue to flow.' You can't tell the hippies that, though. Take away this thing that they fight against and they would be truly lost, they'd fall down flat on their faces, like a cardboard doll when you take away its prop.

Apparently they now have squatters' rights, my neighbours; I couldn't get them out of there even if I tried. I don't really mind them; at least they are a sign of life. This is a city where the living are outnumbered by the dead. There's nothing on the other side of my house but an empty dilapidated shack. Further on down Third Street, a few other unsavoury characters have made these abandoned homes their own; wet-your-pants Bill, Boozy Agnes, Karen the crack whore. Then there are those nameless ones who drift in and out like the ocean tides.

"What you up to today, Celia," asks a male hippy.

I make scribbling motions with my right hand. They turn to one another, nodding.

Oh, she's writing again, she's writing.

I have explained my recent attempts at literary activity to them. A girl needs somebody she can confide in; the hippies have been my sympathetic ear.

"What part of your life are you up to, Celia?"

"I am currently incarcerated," I reply.

"Oh, sister, we're sorry. Here, take one of these. Helps to dull the pain."

One of them passes me a plastic bag filled with those nice green cookies they're always munching.

"And get back to that tale you're telling. We're all dying to read it."

147

I feel a little uncomfortable at this; I'm not sure the hippies wouldn't think I was a fruit loop if they could see the words that are being laid down. I swiftly change the subject.

"So when are you off to the mill?" I ask.

"Five-thirty. We want the workers to see us when they walk through the gates. We want them to know that they've got a right to be angry."

"Well good luck," I say, though I know their efforts are even more doomed than I am. "Can I do before-and-after shots of you guys?"

"Sure."

They're always happy to oblige on this one; they're not without vanity. They indulge in a bit of frantic grooming; they position their headscarves and shawls, flick back their dreadlocks, adjust their striped long-johns. One holds the dog's face up near her own and smiles.

Click, click.

The positive attitude, the self-belief, captured.

"Well, back to it," I say, when I have my shots. "And, could you...." I make lowering motions with my hands, "...keep it down. Just a little?"

"What? A *quiet* protest?"

"It's only practice," I say. "Save your voices for later. Save your strength. You don't want to use up all your lung-power now."

That seems to convince them. They start up with a subdued chant and I stumble back inside and resume my tale. I start to snack on a few of the cookies they gave me, then push the remainder into the biscuit tin. I'll offer them to George in the morning; they'll make his day.

Back inside, I heave myself across to my desk, intending to make further progress with the 'brochure'. I get two sentences down before it all goes pear-shaped; a silly mistake to munch those cookies, for now I find it hard to write, the story won't seem to go straight, it sprouts false limbs, leads me in a strange direction, the lights seem all a little bit bright, the colours start to swirl till I fall into a restless and distracted sleep and do not awaken until several hours later. Dusk is drawing in.

I fix myself a cuppa and stumble out into the backyard. The hippies are sitting, cross-legged, in a circle. They are down but not defeated. I loom over the fence in order to get the report. They had stood outside the mill gates for two hours, apparently, and were paid not an ounce of attention. The factory workers simply walked through the gates, right past the hippies and got into their cars or onto their bikes and made their way home as usual. The night shift workers had arrived, ignored the hippies, gone inside to do their jobs. Somebody who thought they were buskers had tossed them some spare change.

I take a few photos; they are weary but not resigned. They'll be back there next week, singing the same songs, playing the same old tunes on the guitar. Hope springs eternal.

When I go back inside, there are humans in my living-room. There are two of them today; George has brought The Wife, she of the long red talons and the glossy red lipstick. It's a Saturday; they must have another receptionist down there at the weekends, because the mill never closes.

"Oh my," I say. "This is a nice surprise."

"Hello Celia," she says. "Lovely to meet you at last. And how did you enjoy those pork pies the other week?"

"Delicious," I reply. "But you must let me return the favour by sampling a few of my special cookies."

"Oh," she says. "Wonderful."

She walks inside, looks disdainfully about. The place is a mess, I'll admit. Cleanliness was never my strong suit; I live in harmony with the mould, the mildew, the crumbs, the dirt, the chaos. I should really get a cleaning lady in here, a bucket of bleach, a mop, someone to lug the vacuum cleaner about, get things into order; but then people like this Wife would have won. It's a quiet rebellion, this lack of order, a silent kind of a screech.

"George has asked me to come and help him clean some of your old stuff out of the attic," she says.

By 'old stuff' I suppose she means photos, as George is under strict instructions not to go fossicking in any of the other boxes. I have warned him against playing Pandora.

"Have a cookie first," I say. "Give you a bit of energy."

In the kitchen, I take down the tin, put a couple of the hippies' treats on a plate and take them out to her.

"Fantastic. Thanks Celia."

She sniffs it, takes a nibble, being careful not to smudge her lipstick, and then finishes it off. George grabs the other one, devours it in one bite. They head upstairs and I keep on with my story.

Half an hour later I hear a thump, a thud, a few swear words. Then silence. I scribble a few quick words while waiting for the prints to dry. Above my head, all is quiet. When the grandfather clock chimes twelve, I put down my pen, venture up the ladder for a look and see the two of them there, slumped in one corner, staring at the wall. George starts to speak but then thinks better of it.

I leave them there, head downstairs, slide the prints into a plain brown paper bag, swing my Leica over my shoulder and head outside for a bit of fresh air. I feel like a bit of a wander.

I pass the house inhabited by Jean and Bobby, who used to be Eugene and Bob till they had the chop. Theatrical types they are; used to act at the Sphere, back in its glory days, before it became the empty husk it is today. The house these two now live in was once owned by Dolly Jinxton who once ran three of city's hottest fashion boutiques and supplied Jean and Bobby with many fine gowns. Then times got tough and Dolly was forced to head elsewhere; she sold her home to her two best customers for a mere three hundred bucks. They kept all the mannequins that used to be on display in Dolly's boutiques; they set them up at the windows of their new home. Bobby changes the outfits and the poses of the dummies once a week. Wouldn't want things to get stale.

Jean and Bobby have been modelling for me for over a decade. Oh, they miss their theatrical days! They are never photographed as themselves; they have a remarkable talent for playing dress-ups, for becoming something other than what they are. Sometimes it seems that they can become almost anybody they choose, as if they have no real self at all, as if they are merely vacancies on top of which any mask at all can be placed. For the benefit of my camera and me, these two sometimes stage private *tableaux vivants* wherein they mimic women as they have been portrayed in masterpieces throughout the ages. It has been my unique privilege to capture these *tableaux* on film.

They are so splendid in their regalia that I conceded to shoot them in full colour, for the black and white film I had become so accustomed to did not do them justice. Before an audience of one, these two have made themselves into the Mona Lisa, an enigmatic smile upon their faces, Botticelli's Venus, donning long flowing locks and standing in a papier-mâché sea-shell they had made, and Picasso's fragmented, tear-stained woman. (Difficult; this took a lot of work on my part, altering the image after it had been taken, sharpening the curves of their soft faces, breaking them into segments. They couldn't cry at will, so I was forced to paint on the water which ran down their cheeks.) They have strapped on makeshift corsets, slapped on fake tan, glued nails to their skin and done spooky imitations of Kahlo's "The Broken Woman." When they pose, their stares are so alike to those of the painted women that you have to pinch yourself hard to remember who they really are; they are so still, so motionless, that you find yourself wondering if perhaps they have been sliced out of the painting and are not human at all, but oil colours hanging in the air.

For my eyes only, they performed a show entitled, "Great Women of History: The Imaginary and the Real", wherein they would both simultaneously become various 'great ladies', fictional and otherwise. Their range was startling; they did Cleopatra (straight, black, fringed wigs, long tight gowns, a plastic asp each); Lady Macbeth, with specks of blood on their hands, standing at the bathroom sink, condemned to be stained eternally, and Marie Antoinette, clutching pieces of cake as their heads were being put into a guillotine. They dressed as Joan of Arc (both of them strapped to stern wooden stakes as cardboard flames flickered threateningly upwards) and various queens from throughout the ages (crowns, gowns, tiaras and gilded sceptres). They did Venus de Milo; they strapped on wings and did the Winged Victory of Samothrace. All these I doctored up afterwards; lopped arms off their Aphrodites, beheaded their Victories, added gilt to the pictures of them playing royalty, mucked about with paints and different tints, took the airbrush to various parts of their bodies. I added and erased. I gave and I took away.

Today, all is quiet within the house of my gender-bending chums; the blinds are drawn, the house is sleeping. I scuttle past; I do not wander aimlessly. Today I have a specific destination in mind, I am headed inwards, towards the centre, on the edge of which sits the deserted Provencian Museum. They moved the more precious exhibits to the National Museum, but didn't bother shifting the less valuable items. They took the dinosaurs and the two mummified cats; they left behind a few tapestries that nobody had ever bothered to check the origins of, various semi-precious stones, and the collection of guns that had been piling up here for the last hundred years. Ridiculous, to leave so much of it behind, but everybody was in a hurry, everybody was heading West, the feeling in the air was that if you were the last one left you'd never make it out, you would be claimed. Besides which, the National Museum were being bastards. 'We don't have room for all of your trash, don't put your muck in our backyard.' This was their big chance to rub our noses in the dirt. 'We'll take all your precious stuff and leave the crap behind.' They came and took the best of it and left the rest of it for us. Many people were surprised they didn't take the guns; you'd have thought they'd be keen on such an arsenal. Maybe they thought if they left the weapons here we'd turn on each other, like cannibals. After the folks from the capital had taken what they wanted, the place was heavily looted by the locals, before being boarded up with quite a few goodies still left inside.

The building sits on a slight rise, overlooking the city's vacancy; stone columns run from its roof down to the ground, they were hoping for grandiose, but they wound up with grotesque. A couple of weary-looking stone soldiers stand, one to each side of the museum, they are nobody in particular, they are the Universal Soldier, at their feet are plaques which list the names of those who "willingly gave their lives to defend our fair shores" during the last war. I'm not so sure about that 'willingly'.

I make my way round to the rear exit and prise off the nailed planks, as if I were merely peeling off a loose fleck of paint, and toss the boards to one side. Once inside, there is little light; planks cover not only the doors, but also all of the windows. I am standing in a dusty hallway, above my head is the painted ceiling; angels cavort, blow trumpets, play harps, perch upon fluffy cotton wool clouds. I walk down the hallway; doors hang open to either side of me, and I peer inside these rooms. Glass display-cases stand empty, many of them smashed, the odd forgotten artefact lies upon the floor: a moth-eaten tapestry, a stuffed parrot with a nasty dose of the mange (one of Thomas Doom's works, no doubt), a small bronze Buddha looking beatific.

I am quite a regular at this Museum of Things Long Forgotten; every six weeks or so I make my little pilgrimage here, rip the boards away, steal inside, see what is there for the taking. Somebody from the council must come along afterwards to replace the planks I've torn away, one of those little Lazaruses. It's like a game we're playing, they nail them back up and I tear them down. I wonder if they resent their Sisyphean task. I've had some good raids on this place; I have quite a little stash at home, a fair few goodies hidden away in the wardrobe: a kimono, a selection of netsuke, a rusting Samurai sword, an old musket. I don't know what I am looking for today; I like the thrill of not knowing; the treasure hunt, flea market, garage sale feel of forcing my way in here and then scouting about for something of value, even if the value is only acknowledged by me. This is what they overlooked, our friends in the capital, this is what they have left behind. I root about in the treasures their eyes have missed, grabbing the unwanted.

Today I score. In one of the end rooms I get down upon my hands and knees, put my eye down to floor level and what I see, lying against one wall, beneath an empty display cabinet is something that looks like a gun. I rise, search the room for an implement with which to pry it out. In one corner I find a broom, poke about beneath the cabinet. It slides across the floor towards me, covered in dust, as if it has been nestling in a vacuum cleaner bag. It's a gem; a turn-of-the-century handgun, pearl-handled. Sharp-shooters in cowboy movies use this kind of weapon. I pick it up, turn it over, admire the way the thin shafts of light falling through the cracks glint off the handle. I put the gun in my pocket, turn on my heels, and walk back the way I came. No doubt one of the city councillors, one of the little Lazari, will return to nail the planks that I have torn away back into place before the week is out.

*

On the way home, I am feeling a little peckish, so I call in at Tim's Diner. The place is deserted but for two souls; a curly-haired woman eating a doughnut and drinking a coffee and The Weasel. I order the same as the curly lady and sit myself down at an empty booth. The Weasel is drinking a can of Coke and scribbling, no doubt penning the entire daily rag while sitting here. Beads of Coke drip from his moustache. Crumbs of some nondescript food item cling to his chin. His tongue hangs from the corner of his mouth in concentration. Beside him is a copy of the capital's major paper; the "Spectator" it's called, as if they over there, out west, consider themselves some kind of all-seeing eye.

He's copying out their articles and changing the words around a little, like some school kid trying to cheat on an essay without being busted for plagiarising. On the table in front of him rests his namesake, a stuffed weasel he carries everywhere, though he insists that the damned thing's a ferret. The stoat, ferret, weasel debate raged furious for a while; no final conclusions on the taxidermied creature were reached. But a name is a name is a name and a title such as 'The Weasel' tends to stick to the named like glue. If you ask him about his familiar, he'll tell you that it's of inestimable value, being the last thing that Thomas Doom, of the famed *Doom's Bird and Beast Preservers*, completed before his heart attack. It's hard to believe the scary little creep's considered by most to be a pillar of society.

The gun is burning a hole in my pocket; I want to take it out, not to show to The Weasel, but to the lady, whom I have never seen before. She must be from out of town. I want to tell somebody of my find, but I am afraid I will scare her. She might think it's a death threat, or she might think I'm some pathetic pervert; 'Come take a look at my gun, sugar. Come lay your eyes on this revolver'. I say nothing. I eat my doughnut, drink my drink. Nature calls. I make my way to the men's room. There are no queues at the Ladies today, but force of habit drives me to the Gents. I shut the cubicle door, lock it. A shock is in store for me. Somebody has replied to my graffiti. I freeze. A response was the last thing that I had expected. I had thought that my question was rhetorical, but now I have a reply. Or at least, another question. The handwriting is neat, meticulous. Each 'i' carefully dotted, each 't' precisely crossed, each letter neatly looping into the next. Attention to detail. In comparison, my own writing is a spiralling mess.

What do you add up to? reads the writing.

Not much, I think to myself. At the end of the day, when all's said and done, not a hell of a lot. Then my eyes travel a little further down the wall and I see that beneath the question, in the same handwriting, there is an answer.

Thirty-three.

I reach out and touch the writing. The ink is not yet dry; it smears beneath my index finger. Whoever did this left Tim's just before I did, or else is still in the building. What does it mean? And who is responsible? I walk back out into the diner. The woman is still there; I eye her, her face is a blank mask. It could not have been her; she would've used the Ladies; why would she venture into the Gents? The Weasel is still inventing the daily news. Could it have been him? The waitress is not a likely culprit. I've heard her speak; she struggles to string two words together, let alone an entire sentence. I poke my head around the door to the kitchen; a pimply-faced youth is scrubbing the pots and pans, up to his elbows in dirty water and soap suds. Must have been him, I think, zit boy. I test him out for a reaction.

"Hey you," I say. "What do you add up to?"

He stares at me. No sign of recognition. Perhaps this was a write and dash job; somebody sprinted in here, penned their question and answer as quick as they could and did a runner. Perhaps nobody present is responsible for these words. When I turn back around, intending to confront the doughnut lady, the diner is empty. She has gone. The Weasel picks up his papers and makes a hasty exit. The guilty party goes unnamed.

*

I head back through our streets, unlock the front door, climb the ladder which leads up to the attic, and poke my head up for a look around. The snoop and his Wife are gone. I shrug, sit back down at my desk. The phone rings. An irate George is on the other end of the line.

"Well, Celia," he says. "This explains a lot about these weird and twisted tales you have been telling. Whoever would have thought it?"

My voice is all innocence. "Excuse me?"

"I don't know what you put in those biscuits," he says. "But the wife and I don't think your sense of humour is very bloody funny."

"I have no idea what you're talking about," I say. "Really George. You ought to get out more. Being cooped up there in my attic day after day is no good for your mental health."

"The wife didn't know what'd hit her. She's *still* seeing things that aren't there. She's going to have to take time off work."

"Oh dear. Perhaps you kicked up some strange dust, poking about up there. Angel dust. You never know."

"You're lucky we're not pressing charges. You could be had up, you know. Forcing drugs upon the unsuspecting."

"I forced nothing upon no-one," I reply and hang up.

Poor George, they do have quite a kick those biscuits.

I take the revolver from my pocket, rest my finger on the trigger. All afternoon I sit dreaming of clocks and bullets, of dust and deserted rooms.

XVII

The Hartman household had been in a downwards spiral for some time. All of Arty's trousers had holes torn in the lower leg, he'd just been fired, and his wife, in the grip of one of her furious fits, had taken a pair of scissors to the photo album which contained the pictures of their wedding day and snipped every last photo in half, then thrown the pieces out into the street. Bride had been separated from groom, much to the amusement of the neighbourhood children, who had picked up these severed photos and passed them about amongst themselves, laughing, and yelling out, 'Wife's ripped your photos up, ha, ha, carrot top'. The old schoolyard nick-name still made him blush.

Arty, who had been naked when the Furies caught his wife in their savage grasp, had wanted to tell her to calm down, to ask her if it was that time of the month, but he knew from experience that it was best just to shut his mouth when she was in such a state, she would collapse eventually, exhausted, she would melt into a puddle of tears and apologies and all he would have to do would be to give her a kiss and a cuddle and say that all was forgiven. He had learnt long ago that there was no point in searching for an explanation for her rages, she didn't know the reason for them herself; they were as inexplicable as the weather. When such moods came over her it was best just to lay low and wait for the sunshine. When the sun shone she was an angel, a goddess, all smiles and love, buying her husband bunches of flowers, lavishing endless praise, cooking him elaborate gourmet dinners and giving him numerous blow jobs. When the storms came she was somebody else entirely; she smashed every piece of crockery in the house, she hurled abuse, she threatened to put arsenic in his evening meal and to bite off his penis. She was the devil incarnate.

She always said that she had married Arty for his even temper, his dependability, the way that he arrived on time where he had agreed to meet her, always phoned when he had promised to, always wrote her letters when he was away, but Arty often wondered if she hadn't just wanted an emotional punching bag, somebody who'd take the blows without fighting back.

After she had shredded the photos, he found himself out in the street, wearing a pair of his ripped trousers, his torso bare, grabbing their marriage back off the neighbourhood children, while his wife was in the front room, hurling paint at a blank canvass. His wife painted pictures which were exhibited in the largest of Provencia's many galleries, named (somewhat inappropriately, thought Arty), *Crème de la Crème*. *Skimmed milk is more bloody like it,* Arty would sometimes joke to himself, though he would never have dared voice these thoughts aloud to Angie.

In the back of Arty's mind was always a terrible sneaking suspicion, and the suspicion was this. *Angie's pictures were not actually any good.* He often felt that the artistic endeavour was just an excuse for the temperament; had she been in gainful employ as a filing clerk or a primary school teacher, her rages would have been completely unacceptable. As it was, her fits and tantrums were overlooked, that's just the way that painters *are*. He couldn't see the talent involved in randomly throwing globs of paint at a canvass, but then, what would he know? He was just the guy who delivered the post or he *had* been until Friday, when one of those very same brats who had just been outside laughing at his torn photos had discovered a pile of undelivered mail stashed beneath a holly bush and blown the whistle on him. Similar stashes were subsequently discovered and it was revealed that Arty had been poking a few letters into slots at random each day, ditching the rest of the mail and going off to the local R18 cinema to spend the day eating ice-cream and watching porn, returning home in the evening to greet his wife with a kiss and tell lies about how he had been spending his day.

When the piles of undelivered mail were found, Arty had tried to blame the vicious territorial canines he claimed inhabited the area.

"They terrorised me," he said. "I feared for my life. I had to drop the mail and run".

The boss wasn't having a word of it.

"The other postmen seem to manage," was all he had said. "You must have been doing something to provoke the animals."

The truth was, it had not been the dogs that had put him off at all. It had been the monotony, trudging the streets every day, heavy sack on his shoulder, slouching along through all kinds of weather. Only when he was threatened with unemployment did he realise how important it was for him to bring home the bacon. He was the only wage-earner in the house; Angie received small sums of cash that could not be relied upon, she expected him to come home with a tidy little pay packet each week. He hadn't thought about getting caught; he'd been concentrating on the titty-girls and the Haagen Dazs. He'd had his mind on the lovely Lucinda Fortune, she of the long golden thighs, the luscious blonde mane and the spectacular breasts, like two ripe melons. And that scar. He loved that scar, the way she flaunted it, no point in hiding a flaw like that. Only it wasn't a flaw on her. On her it became a feature.

When the boss put the hard word on him, he scuttled home, ripped holes in every pair of trousers he owned, and took them all back to work as evidence that he had been attacked by many a neighbourhood mutt. The boss remained unimpressed.

"I don't give a shit about the holes, Hartman, you freckle-faced git. Fired is fired. Here, let me spell it out for you, you little red-headed creep. F-I-R-E-D."

And Hartman had been out on his ass.

Angie was furious.

"What the hell did you think would happen," she hollered. "Did you think they'd never notice? Did you think that nobody would complain when the Christmas gifts and the birthday presents and the love letters they'd been expecting failed to arrive? What the hell are we gonna do for money now? Best you get your thinkin' cap on boyo and engineer some decent scheme to make us a bit of cash."

Arty was torn. He wanted to please his wife, but what he found was that he'd developed a bit of a taste for inertia; he liked the days doing nothing. What kind of job would he get anyway? He had no education, no viable skills. He'd find factory work or perhaps pick up a bit of labouring. He was sick of the mindless employ; if he couldn't find anything better, he wanted nothing at all.

*

He'd never stood in the dole queue before, and now he found himself lining up with refugees and other down-and-outers. He took a number, he took a seat. Six hours later he was still sitting in the hard plastic seat, waiting. When his number eventually came up on the red display screen (which was just like the one down at the local boozer that let you know when your pub meal was ready) he was asleep. The old man sitting next to him nudged him awake.

Arty's chin was wet; he had been dribbling. He approached the glass pane tentatively. The young woman sitting on the other side of the window looked like she'd seen and heard it all before.

"Can I help you?"

"I want to sign on," said Arty.

"Reason."

"Jobless."

"Were you fired?"

"Made redundant," he lied

"We'll need two types of photo ID, a letter from your employer stating why and when you were made redundant, your bank account details and your tax number."

He had all the documentation in his wallet; he'd forged the letter from his boss, he had known they wouldn't sign you on straight away if you'd been fired or if you had quit. Forgery, as it turned out, was one of Arty's few talents. She was resigned, this woman, he could see it, hated her job, just wanted to get these sad old unemployed gits back out through the door, just wanted the hands of the clock to tick round to five pm and go and have a drink with her mates. She didn't even look over his forms properly once he'd filled them out, just shoved them into a plastic tray to the right hand side of her and hit some button which made the display unit show a new number. He was in. Free money!

"There'll be a six week stand-down," said the woman.

He didn't mind, he had some measly dollars saved, enough to get by. He sat that night in the living-room, dreaming of the glorious days of freedom and nothingness ahead, planning the tangled web he would weave around himself, so that Angie would never know the truth.

Ready cash was reduced; he could only afford the R18 cinema once a week. He filled his days by walking; he came to know the city streets like the back of his hand, he mastered every side-street, every alleyway. He saw a Provencia he'd never seen before; he ventured far beyond his little postal circuit, he passed through suburbs he'd not even known existed, he wandered back and forth along the banks of the Opal. He'd never been so physically fit. At night, he collapsed wearily into bed beside his wife and listened to her moaning about a picture that wasn't going right; the handfuls of paint she threw never seemed to land where she wanted them to. They never seemed to make the right patterns.

He told her he'd taken a job at the pulp and paper mill; it seemed likely, hundreds of employees walked through the gates every morning, hundreds more entered at night. If he felt like having a day at home, he told her he was on night shift and did his wandering at night time, rather than during the day. The city by night was a slippery place; he wore his black anorak with the hood pulled up over his ears, he wore his steel-capped kicking-boots, in case he was messed with. He liked the violent parts of town, he found them exciting. It made his blood race to watch the organised fistfights held in abandoned warehouses back behind the CBD, to see the men with blood dripping down their faces and teeth falling out of their mouths. He bet small sums. He always won. He passed by doorways in which the homeless slept and felt how near he was to them, how close he was to the gutter. There were never stars above him. Thick clouds were always there. He was living a double life. His winnings were burning a hole in his pocket; he began frequenting peep-shows and whorehouses. He was quite the man about town.

Arty Hartman had never thought of himself as a duplicitous man, but now he found that deception came easily to him. He had always been a good honest bloke and so his wife trusted him, but now he was discovering what fun it was to lie, not about some small trivial thing, but about his whole existence. He liked the feeling that he might be exposed at any time; he liked knowing something that his wife didn't. He liked being a fraud. It gave him some weird kind of power over Angie. He could lie to her and she would believe him. He was discovering a whole new side to himself.

The hours he spent wandering were introspective ones, his powers of perception were becoming increasingly acute and he learnt how to read his wife's moods. He could sense one of her fits coming on, like a storm brewing on the far horizon and he would tailor his 'working week' accordingly. If he sensed discontent the night before he would tell her he had a day shift coming up, if she was anxious during the day he would tell her he had to be working that night. If he suspected she was about to be gripped by a major tantrum that would rage for more than eight hours, he'd say they'd put him on a double-shift. Thus, he engineered it so that he lived only with the goddess and never with the devil. He often came home to find that she'd trashed the entire house, and would patiently clean up the wreckage while his wife apologised and sobbed. The six week stand-down period passed in the blink of an eye and he received a lump-sum back-payment from the dole office. He bet larger amounts on the bare knuckle fights; won again. He forgot why he had ever taken a job in the first place. Life was good.

*

Arty Hartman had seen many strange things on the streets of Provencia, but the day a giantess wearing a mask made of men's underwear sailed past him on a bicycle which, in holding her weight, was surely denying the fundamental laws of physics, he thought he must be losing his mind. He blinked, pinched himself, rubbed his eyes with the back of his fist. There she was, receding into the distance, enormous legs pushing the pedals around and around, and was that, could that be, a *camera* she wore on a strap about her shoulder? She turned a bend in the road and was gone. He told himself he must be dreaming, he put Celia Doom down as a weird hallucination, chalked her up as a sick little fantasy. She was something that could not be.

*

It was inevitable that Arty's deceptions would be revealed. He was not as anonymous on the streets of Provencia as he liked to think he was. One fine Friday, one of Angie's friends saw him coming out of a theatre which screened only porn. The friend sat Angie down over a coffee in the diner and informed her that her husband had been seen emerging from an X-rated theatre at midday with a satisfied grin upon his face.

"Are you sure it was him?" Angie had asked.

"I'd know that red hair anywhere," came the reply.

Angie phoned the pulp and paper mill and learnt that Arty Hartman was not at that time, nor ever had been, in their employ.

Angie returned home that same morning and dragged her husband's sorry ass out of bed.

"Honey," he said. "Cut it out. I'm tired. I've just done a night shift."

"Night shift, my ass," said his wife. "I know exactly what your night shift involves. Skulking about these dirty streets and frequenting porn parlours, that's what."

"Sugar," Arty cooed. "I don't know what you mean."

"Don't *sugar* me," said Angie, and Arty flinched. "I can't believe you lied to me."

She was working herself up; he could feel the devil woman about to burst through. He decided to come clean; is honesty not the best policy? The hands on the clock read eleven forty-five.

"Okay honey, so I lied. I just couldn't face more monotonous labour. You don't know how life is for me. Boredom just kills me."

"How about money, Arty? How about cash? What about me? Did you pay my welfare more than a second's thought?"

"Now, now, darling. Don't you work yourself into a state."

But she was off, ripping pictures off the walls, then downstairs, into the crockery cupboard, hurling everything and anything breakable she could find to the floor, taking knives from the cutlery drawer, slashing the curtains, tearing up the linoleum with her bare hands.

Arty Hartman was the only soul in Provencia who was thankful for the bomb. It exploded just as he heard Angie starting in on their collection of fine crystal, of which not a good deal remained, thanks to various other of his wife's little episodes. It split their world; it froze his wife and stirred Arty to action. He leapt from his bed and ran down the stairs to where Angie stood, arm raised in the air, hand clutching a piece of crystal Arty had been intending to hide from her; a family heirloom, a vase that had once belonged to Angie's great-great-grandmother. Arty snatched the crystal from his wife's hand and shook her back to her senses. The blast appeared to have momentarily pushed his transgressions from her mind.

"What the hell was that?" she asked, shaken from the spell.

"Let's go see," said Arty, dragging her through the front door.

In the street outside, dazed housewives and the odd solo father stood gazing at each other, questioning looks upon their faces.

"Which direction?" Arty asked his neighbour, who pointed north.

"I think it was the centre," she said, and Arty started out in that direction, dragging his wife behind him.

They began the trek into the middle of the city. Everywhere it was the same; stunned confusion; bewildered, dishevelled, wandering women and distraught men, wondering who had died in the blast and what had caused it. Arty and Angie traipsed on; Arty with a look of grim determination on his face, Angie breaking into the odd bout of hysterical laughter. The closer they got, the worse it looked. When they reached what used to be the city centre, neither could believe their eyes. Disintegration and debris, remnants and rubble. A circle, three miles in radius, flattened. There were sirens and lights and confusion everywhere. There was horror written all over every face. Angie felt that this could not be real; she felt as if she was walking through a nightmare. Arty was speechless. And though he hated himself for the thought, he could not help but thinking to himself, *one good thing to come of this*; *she seems to have forgotten about my unemployed state.* Attention had been attracted away from his deceptions. The blast had upstaged him.

And that enormous girl, who had just walked past him, with a camera raised to her eye; where the hell had he seen her before? He shook his head, wiped his eyes. She was gone now; she must have been an apparition borne of shock. He put his arm around his wife and led her gently away from the scene, walked her home, up their street which remained unharmed. They went home to watch the disaster from a safe distance, on the telly.

*

When Arty Hartman found the fragments, he did not, at first, know what to think. He did not realise, instantly, that these had been left behind by that girl he believed was a hallucination. He was one of those scavengers who could be found for weeks afterwards, picking amongst the bombsite debris, in search of something of value. These foragers crept in there at night; during the day the area was policed, they had fenced off a circle three miles in radius and were still finding bits of bodies; pieces of bone, wrists severed from arms, stray feet. Skull fragments. This was disaster on an international scale; Jacob had really hit the big time and he had dragged a reluctant Celia with him. Late one Sunday, Arty was in there with his torch, kicking away rats and shining his torchlight into dark corners, when something colourful grabbed his eye. It was something I had forgotten; one of those family snaps that had been, unbeknownst to me, left in a box at the Butchette when I had cleared out the darkroom. The first fragment he found was a piece of me, my head, in fact, lit up like a light bulb. And on the back was part of my name, the last three letters, OOM. Another fragment; a glimpse of black tracksuit, a slice of unsightly flesh.

This was a piece of one of the few self-portraits in which I appeared as myself. As a subject, I was inordinately fond of costume. Hartman was intrigued and mystified. He scrabbled around a little further in the wreckage, picking up pieces of pictures; a slice of sky, a bit of the ground, something that might once have been part of a face.

Arty had seen me on TV – Celia Doom, notorious bomber, obsessive photographer. 'At her peak', they said, 'she fired over three hundred shots per day'. Hartman looked down at what he held in his hands. 'I'll bet my bottom dollar', he thought to himself, 'that this is one of hers'.

The next night found him back at the same spot, again with his torch, pulling aside rubble, as if in search of gold. He spent three hours finding torn shreds of my snapshots and then he heard sirens and ran from the scene; the cops were wising up to these marauders who pillaged the city centre at night. There had been reports of some very valuable finds: gems which had once been on display in the window of Jenkin's Jewellers and now lay scattered beneath the broken buildings, a couple of antique marble clocks and, miraculously, a Ming vase, which, it was purported, had somehow survived the blast intact. When those sirens came screeching towards where he stood, Hartman ran home with full pockets and spread his stash out on the kitchen table, as his wife hollered, 'What the hell are you doing?', from the bedroom.

Hartman had a tube of glue in one hand and some sheets of white paper in the other. What he was doing was of minor significance to him but of very major significance to me. From these broken pieces he was putting together my big break; he was making me. He worked in no particular order; he was tired, it was two in the morning and he felt like a sleepwalker. There was more to this than was meeting the eye. He was, in one way, attempting to piece together his marriage; he was working to please his wife. He was hoping to redeem himself in Angie's eyes.

A word in Arty's favour; he could've taken credit for all of this, he could've pretended that this was his. On the backs of other fragments he found further letters, a C and an E on one piece, LIA on another. He put it all together and it spelt Celia. He knew he could ride on the back of my notoriety; he knew he could market me. I would make a good commodity. Arty stayed up all night gluing slices of my shots to simple sheets of A4 and in the morning his wife came down the stairs to find him slumped over the table, head upon hands, snoring. She stared at these montages he had made then shook him awake.

"Arty?" she asked. "Whose photos are these?"

"Mine and Celia's," he replied. "Celia Doom. The bomber."

Angie gave a gasp of horror. I was the new Ned Kelly, I was Ted Bundy, I was the Una Bomber. My name carried the same power; it signified death and destruction, it struck terror into hearts. Angie, with her debatable 'artistic eye' looked at what her husband had put together, and saw potential. She could visualise these things hanging on walls; work by the jailbird, art by a cold-blooded killer, and just look at how jumbled it was; a reflection of my muddled mind. Criticism could be written on this, dissertations, even, notes on the relationship between art and murder, between creator and destroyer. No longer did it matter that her husband was a deceitful unemployed bum.

Before the week was out Angie was on the blower to the owner of *Crème de la Crème*. The gallery now sat right on the edge of what had once been the city centre. Now the gallery bordered nothingness; the gallery's owner liked to say that she lived next door to an apocalypse. Through the gallery windows you could see the ruined space stretching out like a scar, like the place where a comet has hit the earth, spreading out in a three-mile radius around the deep cracks which remained like a terrible reminder of that first catastrophe, the Great Quake. It was said by some, that the skeletons of those who had died that day had been shaken to the surface by this more recent blast; old bones, withered scraps of skin, white teeth, but that may have been just idle speculation, silly attempts to rouse the ghosts of the past.

The following week, husband and wife paid a visit to the owner of *Crème de la Crème*, who would go down in history as the first woman to hold a Doom exhibition. She was taking a risk, this was bound to be highly controversial, this might result in protests and riots. Somebody might take exception to the exhibition and burn her gallery to the ground. She was putting herself out on a limb and the tree was none too sturdy.

It was not my work which won her over and nor was it Arty's novel arrangement of the scraps that he had found. It was my gigantic and supposedly murderous self which sealed the deal in her mind; she knew, as did Arty and Angie, that my freak value alone would see the folks flocking. She was unsure as to what sort of reaction she might provoke; she would cross that bridge, she thought, when she came to it. She volunteered her walls.

"No need to pay me anything up-front," she said. "I don't even want a cut of the profits. Just link my name with hers if she's successful and erase me from her history if she's not."

"Done," said Arty and their verbal pact was sealed.

*

And Celia in her cell knew nothing.

*

It took them months to organise and arrange the exhibition, months in which I sat in my cell, wondering when they would set me free, wondering what would become of me. The doors to the gallery were eventually opened and on the walls hung the montages Arty had made. They were bright, apparently; colourful. I wouldn't know; I wasn't present. Angie had done her bit for the cause; she'd rung every journalist and reporter in the country and they were all there, flashbulbs popping, as the crowds rushed to the door and whispered about what might lie inside. Rumours flew about like dry leaves on a dusty autumn day; inside, they said, were sights too terrible to look upon, but they couldn't wait to get inside and look anyway. I paced the floor of my confines, ignorant. Their cameras continued to take it all in, 'the work of a killer', they said, and these montages of my photos were flung onto front pages everywhere, polarising the nation. There were interviews with Arty and Angie and the gallery owner.

"She didn't do it," said Arty. "She's innocent. For want of somebody else to blame, you made her your scapegoat. Jacob did it. Jacob's the one."

The petitions began. "Free Celia Doom!" and "Set Celia Free!" The fickle pendulum of public opinion swung back my way. New evidence was brought to light regarding Jacob; Angie herself went snooping about in his history and came back with the dirt. The boy was no good; he had a bad past, he was a rotten egg. She spoke to the kids on the streets of the capital; she bought their words, slipped them ten bucks and they spilt the beans. She got it all on tape. He was a hardened criminal, she said, a dirty dog. Justice shall prevail.

My case was brought before the Governor-General who looked at the evidence and declared that as long as a guardian could be found, I could be released. Art as redemption; art as excuse. Art to explain weirdness. That old blind tart they call fortune had spun her wheel and my world was about to be tilted back the other way. The cell gates flung open. My camera was handed back to me.

*

I was off the hook.

The world I had left was not the world that I returned to. When they let me out, I was an oafish celebrity. It was hideous. Everywhere I took my bulky form there were cameras shoved into my face; everywhere I looked my face graced the front of another magazine. My cover was on covers everywhere. There was no escaping myself. They wanted me to speak, to give them words that they could chop up and put in print, but my lips were sealed. I would say nothing.

They interviewed Butchette customers. *Celia and I were very close.*

They spoke to the medical men. *She's just a kid, she shouldn't have been in clink in the first place. We think she should come with us.*

The public were encouraged to come forward with stories about me, rewarded financially for anything they said, whether or not it was the truth. Nobody was interested in what had really happened. What they wanted was a good story. This was the paradox; it was destruction that made me.

And the city was struggling. I'd seen it on the news, but I'd not believed how bad things had become until I was out there, amongst it. The absence at the heart of the city had been conveniently neglected; there were no attempts to rebuild, it was left as it was, a gaping hole, which soon became infested with rats and cockroaches, with the odd hardy plant pushing its way up through the rubble. With the CBD gone, the whole place was falling apart, people were fleeing to the capital like rats leaving a sinking ship, nobody wanted to stick around, they were bailing out, selling up, and if nobody was buying, well, then they were cutting their losses and hitting the high road, there was no money to be made here anymore. The suburbs were not as self-sufficient as their inhabitants had liked to think they were; without the centre nothing held the city together anymore, centrifugal force was pulling it apart. A mass exodus was taking place; those left behind were either blind or stupid or both. I was one of those who did not leave.

They left me the family home. I was touched; I put the key on a chain and wore it round my neck. I could not bring myself to live there just yet. I was racked with guilt when I thought about the death of my adoptive parents, especially Lettie, who, it had to be said, had done her best when it came to me. Barry and Lettie had no savings; the profits from the Butchette had paid off the mortgage on the house, which was now entirely mine. The old home sat empty. Nobody wanted to rent homes in Provencia, and nobody wanted to buy. The Butchette had been uninsured; no company had been willing to take a risk on a building which sat upon a road so run through with cracks; so there was no lump-sum payment. There was nothing for me to fall back on.

*

Arty and Angie had put forward their names to the Governor-General and been declared my legal guardians. They graciously opened their home to me, or at least, their basement. I was used to cellars by now; I liked the darkness, the dinginess, the damp, the sense of confinement. I liked the insects. I refused to go out during the day, choosing instead to become a creature of the night. The shadowy side of existence became my subject. I loved all that shunned the sun. The world, which had once been coloured, was now black and white and matched my eyes.

My stint in the cell marked the end of my use of colour film; it no longer seemed appropriate, it was not how I saw. Each night I would creep up the basement stairs, and, while Angie and Arty snoozed in the master bedroom, I would stalk down the corridor, out through the front door, and take to the dark city streets; I did the hookers who hung around the edge of the city's hole, I did the derelicts who lay drunk in doorways. I did more than take pictures; I snatched souls. I was the ultimate voyeur. My gaze penetrated everything, it sliced through this world as if it were no more than flimsy diaphanous fabric; the surface did not hold me, I plummeted through to the depths and I snapped those. I knew that coincidence played a very big role; I did not find these photos, they found me. They hunted me down, thrust themselves into my consciousness. I was merely the vehicle that brought them into being. Sometimes I felt that they had always existed and always would; they had simply been waiting for me to come along and transport them from some other place to this world. I was merely the messenger. I could not be held responsible for how other people perceived the message. My work finished as soon as the picture was hung up to dry in the cellar.

That was when Arty's work began. Once a week he would venture down into my territory and look over the fresh batch I had snatched, casting his critical eye over these images. He was a ruthless judge and thought nothing of tearing shreds off me, ripping great holes in what I had produced.

"What's this shit," he would say, prodding with one pudgy finger at a shot. "That's just a shadow. I can't even make out a shape."

"It's a derelict," I'd say.

Or "It's a hooker."

Or "It's a shop window at night. Those women are dummies. Mannequins. They do not live. A sad diagnosis. I bet they wish they could walk and talk."

He never reacted to these comments of mine. To him I was a quirky seam of gold he intended to mine; he had very little interest in my personality, that was all by the by, he was only concerned about the shots. I was the hen that he hoped would lay the golden egg.

I stayed out of Angie's way. That woman had the shortest fuse I'd ever known, sometimes I heard her overhead, shouting at her husband, smashing whatever breakable objects were still left in the house. She was so highly strung she was stretched taut across the firmament. She admired my work, but she was jealous. I could see it in her eyes, I could hear it in her every sentence. She understood that I was a money-spinner, and that she would be cutting off her nose to spite her face if she tried to hinder my progress. But inside her grew a monster, a thing with glowing green eyes that fed upon the attention Arty paid me, a creature that whispered in her ear at night and fuelled her rage.

Arty pampered me. He brought me caseloads of Fanta and bagfuls of bugs. He bought me more paints and different tints, an airbrush and a knife with the sharpest edge I'd ever seen in my life.

"Don't cut yourself," he warned, whistling through his teeth as the light glinted off the blade.

He bought me a set of Lecia R Zoom lenses, allowing me to narrow in on my target, or pull back and bring a bigger picture into view. He bought me a flash.

Click, click and *double-click. Click, click* and *triple-click.* Always with the black and white film.

*

I missed my grandmothers. I wanted to rebuild whatever bridges I had destroyed. Stuff's house would be my first port of call.

Shuffle, shuffle, shuffle. Tap, tap, tap.

"Who is it?"

"It's Celia, granny."

"Celia? Is that you?"

"It's me, granny, it's me."

The door opened.

"Stuff!" I cried out, and gave the old lady a hug.

"Celia?"

Her eyes stared right through me. In her right hand she held a white cane. Her left hand reached up to feel my right shoulder, seeking out the lump which was, by now, the size of a small pumpkin.

"You'll have to forgive me," she said. "These old eyes of mine are now blind. But come on in, Celia. Come through to the sitting room."

The familiar, musky scent of Doom; old lavender water and stuffed animals.

"This is a surprise, Celia. I thought you'd forgotten all about your old Granny Stuff."

"Of course not, Gran," I replied. "I wasn't sure you'd want to see me, after…you know."

The bomb. She didn't speak the words, either.

Instead she said, "Let's put that behind us."

"Can I make you a drink?" I asked, thinking of tea or coffee.

"Oh go on then," she said. "Fix us a scotch from the cabinet, there's a dear."

She pointed directly at the wooden liquor cabinet on top of which sat two stuffed finches. I was unnerved by her sense of direction, which she seemed to have retained, despite her absence of vision. I poured Stuff a whisky, and though I had never touched liquor before that day, I thought what the hell, surely I was of age and poured myself one as well. We sat down side by side upon her old sofa, with its cover which she had often boasted was made from the pelts of Siberian tigers, though it had always looked and felt like fake-fur to me. Some of the colour seemed to have seeped from my granny's eyes; they had once been a dark shade of violet, now they were a pale, almost translucent blue.

"So the sight," I said. "It's...."

"EH?" she yelled.

"The sight, it's...."

"You'll have to come over on my right side dear. Can't hear a word you're saying."

I shifted my position on the sofa.

"The sight," I repeated. "It's..."

"Gone," she said. "Completely."

"Gradual?" I asked. "Or sudden?"

"Overnight," she said. "Woke up one morning and all was dark. It was soon after...."

The unmentionables: the bomb, the deaths of Barry and Lettie, my subsequent 'sentence'.

"Gave us a dreadful fright, of course."

I took a small sip of my whisky and grimaced. Fire water. Stuff downed hers in one.

"So you see nothing?" I asked. "Nothing at all?"

"Oh, I wouldn't say that, dear," Stuff replied. "At first, to be sure, there was only the unbroken blackness and nothing to relieve it. An overwhelming blanket of it, like the dark void before God made light. As dark as hell, you might say. Here, get us another one, love."

She handed me her empty glass and I rose to obey her wishes.

"Fix yourself another while you're at it," she said. "You're big enough to drink."

How had she known I'd made myself a first? The clink of the glass, maybe, or the sound of my sips. No doubt her other senses had become a good deal more acute in order to compensate for her loss of sight. I finished off what was left of my whisky and made us both a second glass.

"Where were we then?" asked Stuff, when I handed her the drink.

"The darkness," I said, noting that my second whisky was slipping down a lot more smoothly than the first.

"Ah yes. The dark, at first. But then colours that I had never seen before began to appear against the black. Just swirls, at first, then shapes, then distinct objects. Objects never seen in *this* world."

'So,' I thought. 'The poor dear's turned hallucinatory in her old age.' I passed her the requested scotch.

"I guess you could say that your old Gran's learnt how to see in the dark."

I didn't know what to say to that and there was an uncomfortable silence before Stuff changed the topic.

"And how about you?" she asked. "How're you getting on?"

"Okay," I said. "Living with some strangers. Still taking my pics."

She struck a pouting pose.

"Go on then," she said. "Shoot us. For old time's sake."

Clickety click click click. Gran on film. She changed position, stuck one foot forward, sunk her hip, lifted her skirt, just a little. Threw away her cane. That's it, Gran, ham it up for the camera. After a third whisky and a few more shots, I excused myself.

"Have to be getting along, Gran. Got the other one to visit."

"The other one!" she exclaimed, suddenly feisty. "What? You mean the old tart's not dead yet? You'd think the smell of her own wee would've killed her off by now!"

"Come on," I said. "Why don't you try to make friends with her? Surely you two could find some common ground."

"Common ground, my ass," said Stuff. "We're chalk and cheese us two. I just thank God I don't have to see her face at Christmas anymore. That's one woman I'm glad to make a stranger of. But *you* won't be a stranger to *me*, will you? Call by anytime, dear. It's always nice to have a bit of company."

Shuffle, tap, shuffle tap, tap shuffle shuffle, back down the hallway to her glass front door.

"Bye Granny, see you soon."

*

Down those old south of the river roads. They always did make me nervous, those streets. I am a Northerner through and through; coming south gives me shivers, I sometimes suffer the irrational fear that I will head back towards the Opal to find that our two remaining bridges have vamoosed. And then what would I do, to cross the divide? Swim, I guess. Fly.

Knock, knock, knocking upon Lolly's front door.

Down the hallway she came, her *crash bang crash* like a louder echo of Stuff's *tap-tapping*. But it wasn't she who opened the door this time; it was somebody else, a large, ferocious-looking woman with short dark hair and the persona of an army corporal. I could see Lolly behind her, looking even more wizened than she'd been the last time I'd seen her, a faded skeleton of a woman, though she still had that tenacious air about her, as if some infernal will kept her clinging on to life through thick and thin.

"Nurse Grout," said the woman who faced me, extending her right hand in greeting.

I almost saluted.

"And you are?" she enquired.

"Celia," I said. "A granddaughter of sorts."

Lolly's head peeked out from behind her guardian.

"Hullo love. Come to visit your old Gran?"

"Sure have, Lolly," I said. "You got a bit of time for me?"

"'Course, I have. Always. Come inside."

The nurse had obviously done nothing to rid Lolly of her reek; I held my nose as we proceeded to the living-room.

"Fix us a cuppa would you, Grout," said Lolly.

"What do you think I am?" said Grout. "A bloody servant?"

"An employee, Nursie," retorted Lolly. "I *pay* you. Remember?"

Grout huffed off to the kitchen as Lolly shot me a smile and dug in her little jar of sweets for a sugar rush.

"You've got to keep old Grout in line," said Lolly. "Mind you, even though I pull the strings, you've got to let her think she's got the upper hand, at least some of the time, or she gets in a bad mood. However, I always put my foot down when she tries to talk me into wearing those silly incontinence knickers. Your old Gran's never had a problem with her bladder."

I held my tongue.

When Grout returned with the tea, Lolly reached down beside her in the wheelchair, grasping for her gin bottle.

"Oh no you don't," said Grout, shaking her head.

"Piss off, Nursie," said Lolly, and added a splash of her favourite beverage to her tea, before dropping a handful of the customary sweets into her drink to doctor it up further.

"Have you seen Ed?" I asked.

"EH?" she said. "Have I been dead?"

"HAVE YOU SEEN ED?'

"You'll have to come on the left side of me, Dear. Can't hear a word that you're saying."

I shifted to the right hand side of Lolly and repeated my question.

"Oh," she said. "Edward. Well, not in the flesh. He wasn't seen at the funeral, although when Lettie's coffin began to levitate, I wondered if he wasn't in the vicinity."

I was surprised.

"So you know about his bad magic then?"

"Oh yes, dear. He pops by occasionally and does all kind of silly tricks. Pulls frogs out of my ears and bursts my lolly jars telekinetically and other such shenanigans. Boys will be boys, I suppose."

"I suppose," I said.

Lolly took a packet of fags out of her pocket, shoved one in her mouth and made to light it. Grout pre-empted her by snatching the cigarette from her lips. Lolly was left lighting the empty air.

"Oi!" she said. "Give us that back."

"You know what the doctor said," reprimanded the nurse. "You've already got emphysema. You'll have lung cancer too, if you don't watch out."

"And you'll get the bloody sack, if you don't watch out."

"Where did you get those anyway? You know I won't take you to the shop to buy them."

"I have my means," said Lolly, slyly. "Now give us back that fag, Grout, and piss off out of here. Leave me and my Celia in peace."

Grout snapped the cigarette she held in two, made a dive into Lolly's pocket for the rest of the packet, shredded those, and then exited the room, slamming the door behind her.

"All fun and games round here then," I said.

"Bloody bitch," said Lolly. "I'd fire her if I thought I could find another nurse. Most of them have upped and left, haven't they. Gone to the *capital.*"

She pronounced the word with a sneer.

"Here," she said. "Be a dear and pick me up a few of those fags she's torn in half. Your old Gran's not that easily deterred."

I scouted about on the floor for a few of the cigarettes that Grout had shredded and passed her a handful of the bigger pieces.

"That's my girl. Pay off my newspaper boy for these, I do. Give him the money for the fags and a bit extra for his pocket. Delivers them with me morning news, before that old cow arrives."

She chuffed away, slurping at her tea.

"And I heard they put you in that Sacred Heart place, Celia. Oh, my! Never thought one of the Major girls would end up there."

That's what I had always liked about the grandmas. They thought of me as one of the family. Lolly cackled.

"So young," she said. "And such a reputation. You're shaping up to be quite a gal."

"Thanks, Lolly."

Lolly summoned Grout to make another couple of cups of tea, which she again 'liqueured' and the two of us gasbagged for another hour till the clock struck ten.

"I'd better be getting home, Gran."

"Time you were going too, ain't it Grout," said Lolly to her nurse.

"What, and leave you to get into bed on your own and fall and break your hip like last time?" snapped Grout. "Not bloody likely."

Lolly raised her eyebrows at me in weary resignation.

"Come on then, Celia. I'll show you to the door."

I did a few pictures of her before I left, and a few of Grout looking as sour as vinegar, we'll see what Arty will make of those.

Crash, bang, crash heading down the hallway.

Till next time, Lolly.

*

I was weaving a little, as I made my way back over the bridge, my skin felt numb and my head light and happy. Back at the Hartman household, Arty greeted me with a searching look and a sniff of my breath before declaring, "You're drunk."

"Just been visiting the grandmas, Art," I said, before heading down to the cellar to collapse. "Surely Celia's entitled to have her fun."

I passed out on the cellar floor with my head spinning.

He reprimanded me in the morning, as if I was his child rather than his money-making scheme, but I paid him no mind.

"I don't want you visiting those grandmothers of yours again," he said, "if that's the kind of influence they have. We don't want you turning into a souse."

I pretended to obey his wishes, but no Arty Hartman was going to come between C.D. and her grannies.

*

Arty was trying to keep me exclusive. He had a few select customers whom he assured me were dedicated fans; he was not going to sell these slices of me to just anybody.

"You don't want to be hanging on everybody's living-room wall," he would say to me. "Your price will plummet. To have value, you must keep yourself rare."

Like a steak, I would think. *Bloody.*

I still divided the nation; half the country believed I should never have been pardoned and the other half thought I never should've been put away. Debate continued to rage, even while I was hiding out in the basement and skulking round the city streets at night. There were death threats; many Provencians had not taken well to having the centre of their city reduced to rats and rubble, many had lost friends and relatives, many were not listening to Arty and Angie who insisted that I was not the one to blame. To these people I was a terrorist; I should pay the price that others had paid. To others, the controversy only made my work more desirable. To many wealthy Provencians, I was like a scandalous treat, a juicy dinner-party conversation topic. *Did we tell you we just bought a Doom? It's going to hang above the fireplace. A little bit macabre, but rather striking. It's bound to rise in value. We can always sell it if it gets too much.*

Owning one of my works was, for the rich, like procuring some twisted trophy; even people who thought I should never have been let out of my cell bought pictures; I exercised a hold over them that nobody could quite explain. To the poor, I was out of range, something they couldn't touch. Although I was one of them, I had been shunted out of their reach. I sometimes felt that I had been appropriated by the enemy. The major galleries in the capital weren't having any of it; their belief was that I had made my name on sensationalism rather than talent, I was a fly-by-night, next year

I would be forgotten. Today's news, tomorrow's fish and chips.
They turned up their noses, shut their doors.
    Before, they'd locked me in, and now they locked me out.

XVIII

There was always the question of cash. After some time of residing with Arty and Angie, after a few months of night-snapping, of Arty coming downstairs and picking out what he called 'the cream of the crop' it occurred to me that I had seen not a penny of my earnings.

They had sold shots to magazines; *Photography Today*, *Shoot*, *Century Art*. Some larger sums had changed hands, nothing earth-shattering, but it was still money which should have been, at least partially, mine. A shot of a jaded hooker had gone for a grand, a snap of a mongrel roaming a dirty alleyway had sold for fifteen hundred and a picture of an old alcoholic lying in a shop doorway had gone for two and a half. The biggest sale had been a series entitled *Dummies of the Dark*, in which various shop-window mannequins, lit from behind by white lights, posed for the camera. They looked almost human; I had been convinced, when snapping them, that they had a secret life unknown to this world, convinced that when I turned my back on them, to change a roll of film, they had moved, shifted position, maybe spoken to each other. I had been trying to capture this sense of secrecy, this hidden life. One of the Leechsons had shelled out five grand for the series; I wasn't supposed to know this, I had overheard Arty talking on the telephone.

When I confronted my keeper, I was told that the money was being put into a 'special account' with my name on it, they reassured me that they were taking only what was due, ten percent, and I was too naive to suspect otherwise. I was so busy concentrating on the next snap I took that I couldn't find space in my mind to think about the money, my eyes were so focused on the next picture that I failed to see the greedy hands that were dipping into my pockets until it was much too late.

Just sign the back of these pictures, Arty would say. *So as people will know they're genuine.*

I would sign boldly, sign my life away, sign in large flowing script, putting the date neatly beneath my name. And then I would add, unnoticed, the tiny tell-tale tear in the upper right hand corner.

*

It was in hospital, recovering from a nasty bout of pneumonia that I had contracted while out shooting in the rain, when I first learnt of my adversary, Ms Claudia Dean, who was being touted as the Next Big Thing. The girl in the bed next door to me handed me some trashy women's magazine which featured a full page spread on the woman, which I noted focused on Ms Dean herself, rather than her work. Ms Dean, it had to be said, was a stunner, albeit in a Barbie-doll kind of way. Blonde hair cascaded to her shoulders, her eyes were azure blue, her long legs rose to meet a slender waist which blossomed into a gloriously rounded chest. She was a blow-up doll, a living wet-dream. Her hobbies were listed as aerobics and shopping.

Through sheer coincidence, Arty bought me some of Dean's work the same day. *This is what they're lapping up in the capital, Celia.* Flowers, babies, cute kids smiling and clutching teddy-bears, a couple of fashion shots, dolly-birds made up to the nines, a couple of coy self-portraits that looked like they'd been taken to send to some modelling agency. The article mentioned that the Lite Gallery, in the capital, was holding an exhibition of her work the following month.

My documenters were delighted; they had me right where they wanted me. My check-ups were no longer weekly, now they showed up every day, to snip and prod and probe. They were especially mystified by the lump on my right shoulder, which seemed to be expanding a little more every day, like a gigantic cyst.

Why just the one shoulder? they wondered aloud. *Surely if this bulge is the result of her constant stoop then she'd have growths on both shoulders, or in the middle of her back.*

And they would insert their long, fine needles into my hunch and prod about, a little disappointed when their implements were drawn out covered only in red blood, as if they secretly expected some otherworldly fluid to be brewing and bubbling inside this protrusion of mine.

Two days before I was due to be discharged from hospital, I saw the notice on the board which sat behind the receptionist's desk.

Adam Abrakazam invites you to join his wonderful world of magic. See the dream become a reality.

An Imitation of Life

Children's Ward (2A). 3pm Saturday, March 10.

"Big kids are allowed to attend too," said the receptionist, seeing me eyeing up the poster, and giving me a wink.

I didn't bother telling her that I was, technically, a child and was currently residing in the other kids' ward, 2B. (Or not 2B, as Arty would sometimes joke when he visited.)

I took the girl from the bed next door. She was just regaining use of her voice; the words that came out of her mouth sounded creaky, like a hinge in need of oil.

"This guy better be good," she croaked. "I'd hate to think that you'd dragged me out of bed for nothing."

"I have a sneaking suspicion that he'll be okay," I replied.

In Ward 2A sick kids sat up in their beds, propped up by numerous pillows. A couple of nurses stood against the far wall, a doctor poked his head around the door. My companion and I took a seat on the end of an empty bed. There was a sense of anticipation in the air; we were waiting for something to happen. Minutes passed; I saw the doctor check his watch. Nobody arrived.

"Hey, what happened to the magic man?" asked the kid in the bed next to us.

"Shh," said a nurse, "he'll be along shortly."

She shot the other nurse a worried look. The clock on the wall said twenty past three. There was a creaking noise overhead; all eyes looked up at the skylight overhead. Nothing and no-one.

"Who's for a game of charades," said the doctor, with forced merriment. "I'll go first." He laid his palms together then folded them outwards.

"Book," cried a kid from the other side of the room and the skylight shattered.

"What was that?" asked the doctor, looking a little peeved that his parlour games had been interrupted after such a short space of time.

A single white dove lay broken upon the hospital floor. A couple of kids started crying. A second dove followed the first through the gap in the skylight, falling like a rock to land with a solid *splat* upon the floor of the ward.

"Why don't their wings open?" asked the boy next to us.

"Hmm," said the doctor and made to walk across and examine the fallen birds.

181

"Don't touch the damned doves," screamed a voice from the roof and the doctor leapt back as if burnt.

One nurse said to another, "I knew we shouldn't have hired this guy."

"Show yourself, Abrakazam," said the doctor sternly, as if this magician were some kind of third-rate terrorist about to take a couple of hostages.

"Abrakazam answers to no man," came the reply.

It was a voice I recognised.

"Would one of you girls go call security?" asked the doctor, before turning to the two nurses.

Just as one of the nurses made to leave, a rope was flung down from one edge of the skylight and a pair of long, thin legs slid into view and slithered down the rope, to be followed by a lean torso and a head. It was, unmistakeably, Ed. His hair was a different colour and a thin black moustache sprouted upon his upper lip, but there was no mistaking the hook of that nose, the curve of that mouth, those bright blue eyes, like slices of sky. He was, as usual, dressed entirely in black, with a cloak which hung down to his knees hooked about his shoulders.

"The Indian rope-trick," he declared, "performed in reverse!"

In his right hand he held a gun. He pointed it at the doctor.

"Freeze! Hands in the air!"

The doctor, terrified, did as he was told. Ed pulled the trigger. A small red banner saying 'BANG!' in white writing flew out from the nozzle. Ed grinned broadly, as if in expectation of a hearty round of applause. There was a mystified silence. One of the doves gave a small, sad chirp.

"Arise my doves," declared Ed grandly. "And spread your little white wings."

The birds did not move, but Ed did not appear concerned. He walked across to the doves, picked them up one at a time, smoothed their feathers with his hands till they began to flutter and coo. He threw them into the air; they appeared to have made a full recovery and flapped across to perch on the bedstead of a young patient.

"The healing hands of Abrakazam!" said Ed.

Silence, till I heard a nurse ask the doctor, "How much did you say we were paying this guy?"

And the doctor's reply, "We're not giving the bastard a red cent. This is abysmal. Worse than pathetic."

"And now for my next trick," said Ed.

The same old lines, though devoid of voice projection. He'd obviously put the ventriloquism on the back burner. I whipped out my Leica and took a few quick pics.

From inside his cloak he took a small guillotine.

"Could I have a volunteer from the audience, please?" he asked, scanning the hospital beds.

There was a distinct lack of enthusiasm from the patients.

"Did somebody check this guy's credentials?" the doctor queried one of the nurses. "The last thing we want is a casualty on our hands."

"Oh come on," Ed was saying. "I'm not that frightening, am I?"

He leered at a small blonde girl who was trying to hide under her pillows.

"Come on out, sweetheart. Little girls cannot hide from Adam Abrakazam."

He grabbed her by the arm and pulled her out from under the bedding.

"Hey, hang on a minute," cried the doctor, but Ed silenced him with a wave of his arm.

"All will be made clear, Doc!" he said. "Just take a chill pill."

He waved his guillotine through the air like a miniature sword, before taking the hand of his captive and swiftly slicing off the tips of two of her fingers.

She screamed. Ed held the cut fingertips high in the air for all to see. He looked directly at me and winked. I buried my face in my hands.

"That's it," I heard the doctor hiss to a nurse. "Get security. *Now*."

"Don't worry, folks," yelled Ed. "The hands of Abrakazam will make her whole again."

He took the bloody hand of the blonde girl into his own large mitts, and then wrapped a cloth around his hands and hers. He muttered a few indecipherable words, and then whipped away the cloth. The hand was whole, clean, perfect. Ed took a bow, just as a couple of heavyweights came striding into the ward. He looked alarmed for an instant, then leapt onto the shoulder of the nearest heavy, flew from there to grab hold of his rope upon which he had descended, shimmied upwards to the ceiling and was gone. We heard his footsteps sprinting across the roof.

"What a bloody fiasco," said the doctor.

The blonde girl who'd had her fingers sliced off was examining her right hand, mystified. I slipped out through the door and out into the garden, where I suspected he would be waiting for me.

He was sitting out by the rose bushes with his head in his hands.

"Ed?"

"Celia!" he looked up in mock surprise. "Fancy seeing you here."

"What did you come here for, Ed?

"One of the nurses saw me performing in a shopping mall and asked me to do a show at the hospital," he said.

I strongly suspected that he was fibbing.

"Have you been spying on me again?"

"No."

His reply was quick, high-pitched, defensive. He clutched his chest, suddenly.

"What's wrong?" I asked, alarmed.

"Oh, it's nothing. Just the old ticker giving a bit of a flutter."

He smiled grimly.

"It's a bit too much of a coincidence, Ed. Why don't you just admit the truth? You wanted to check up on me."

"Oh, alright then. I wanted to see you. I thought this was the best way to make my presence felt."

"Why didn't you just come round during visiting hours, like a normal human?"

"I didn't think they'd let me in the door."

"Anyone can visit, Ed."

"Besides which, I wanted to...you know."

"What?"

"*Impress* you."

"I don't need impressing Ed. I just want to know what *it is* with these weird guest appearances of yours. You don't want to be properly involved in my life, yet you aren't content to just let me be. Instead, you linger on the periphery, occasionally slamming yourself onto centre stage before swiftly disappearing again."

My uncle never was a big one for confrontation. He sighed and changed the subject.

"I just don't know where I go wrong with these tricks," he said.

"Gee, I dunno, Ed. But I guess that if you wanna please the kids, then maiming and cruelty shouldn't really be part of the act. Even if they *are* only illusion. You want people to believe in your magic and they do. Can't you just go with tying balloons into the shapes of animals and a couple of nice, harmless card tricks?"

He looked bereft.

"Well," he said. "I know when I'm not appreciated."

He rose to his feet and began spinning on the spot, his black cape flying out around him. He seemed to grow even taller, even thinner, as if stretching up to the sky. He stopped, suddenly reverted to normal size, waved a quick goodbye, vaulted over the rose bushes behind us and was gone. Never had Lettie spoken truer words than when she had declared our Ed to be a strange one.

*

When they released me from the hospital, I went into hiding. I refused to come out of the cellar. I lurked down there like some sea monster, waiting for a time when I thought it might be safe to resurface. I was getting old. I had wrinkles and a few grey hairs. I was beginning to sag. A new kind of anxiety was gnawing at my gut; I jumped at every tiny sound, I was a bundle of frayed nerves and faulty synapses.

Relations between Angie and me were strained at first, but she apologised and I let it slide. What else could I do? She was no more in control of her temper than a storm is in control of its thunder and lightning.

Locked away in the darkness, I began to experiment with 'alternative photography.' My silver paper was pushed to one side. I tackled the platinum-palladium print method, obtaining a range of tones I had not dreamt possible. A whole new world seemed to open up before me; from blue-blacks through neutral greys to rich sepia browns. I was not back in the world of colour but I was a little beyond my black-and-white; I dwelt comfortably in the gap between the two worlds. I convinced Arty to buy me a contact frame, an ultra-violet light, which was needed for exposure, and the chemicals I needed. I hand-coated my paper in light-sensitive chemicals I had prepared myself, I made enlarged inter-negatives,

negatives of negatives, and used these for sandwiching in my contact frame. Before, I had been interested only in the image captured; now I was also concerned with the processing of that image, the method by which I could bring something out of nothing, not in just one way, but in a variety of ways. It was like choosing a different key in a musical composition.

Arty remained unimpressed.

"What do you want to go mucking about with all that artsy crap for?" he asked. "Just concentrate on taking a good shot. Nobody cares how you process it. It's the picture itself that's important."

I ignored him and went about my business, continuing to experiment. This was not his side of the operation. His job was to find the buyers. My job was to come up with something interesting to sell. I began mucking about with the cyanotype process, which was used for the first photographically illustrated book and also for architectural blueprints until the invention of the photocopier shunted it out of the picture. This cyanotype process was 150 odd years old by the time I got my hands onto it. I liked the effect, the way the photos came out tinted blue, the way the Prussian Blue would sometimes bleed across the paper, leaving uneven stains. It was nice to have a little colour back in my life. Arty hated it.

"Looks tacky," he declared. "Looks like royalty's bled all over it."

Months were spent down there, perfecting my technique. Months during which I took nothing new, but simply reworked old negatives, much to Arty's disgust.

"Go out there and take something new," he kept saying. "Stop revisiting old territory you've been over before. Go get me something I haven't seen. Go hunt and gather."

*

My medical friends came out to check on me on a regular basis; they went through their little routine. There were other visitors, not a huge mob, normally just one or two a day, banging on the cellar door, hoping for a chat. Some ran when they saw me in the flesh, sprinted away as fast as their tiny legs would carry them, and so I made time for those who stayed. I was not unfriendly. I ventured upstairs and made cups of tea and listened to them talk to me about their lives. I tended to attract desperados who would spill their guts upon the kitchen table while I politely sipped my tea and wondered what the hell I was going to do next. I felt damned myself, so I had no idea why they came to me looking for help. My silence, I think, was interpreted as sympathy. It now seemed that I had a new incarnation; I was the bumbling, friendly monster you turned to when you felt a bit low.

And this was the terrible thing; these people came to Arty's and yapped and babbled and I had not a clue which direction I myself was about to head in. Everything I could think of to do, I had already done. Oh, I had all the pretty techniques for developing negatives, I could produce some interesting results, but the absence of subject matter *mattered*, the knowledge that I could think of nothing good to shoot hung about my neck like a lead weight. I had stalled. I took up smoking cigarettes. One was not enough for me; I did three at a time, shoved the fags into my gob, and then lit them up, inhaling and exhaling, a regular chimney stack. Wealthy fans sent runners to try to buy a Doom work or three, but I had nothing new to put up for sale. I turned them away empty-handed.

Angie was as tough as a piece of old leather.

"We don't keep you here out of charity, you know," she said. "If you can't earn your keep, you'll be out that door quick smart. You've very nearly outstayed your welcome."

Her words filled me with terror. The world outside would chew me up and spit me out. Though my body was nearly forty, I was, in real time, still a young adolescent. I didn't feel I could face it alone. Her words spurred me to action.

I took to the streets again. I still shunned the day. I was still a creature of the night. When the sun began to sink over the far horizon, I would sling my trusty weapon of choice over my shoulder and head out into the darkness. Arty's only stipulation had been that I grab something new; no more scene of the crime shots, no more hookers and deros.

"It's all been done," he told me. "It's up to you to find the new subject. Don't disappoint us, tiger. Don't let the side down."

I strolled the streets, that first night, looking for something new to bring into existence. I walked through the suburbs which ringed the nothingness at the city centre, noted the empty homes, the struggling businesses. The mannequins in the windows seemed to laugh at me as I passed, *we've been done, we've been done*, the hookers flashed their suspender belts mockingly, *so have we, so have we* and it seemed to me that I would never find a new subject. I paced relentlessly, up streets and down side-alleys and along main roads, always searching, seeking. A light rain began to fall, no more than a mist and, as I turned down yet another side road, I heard footsteps behind me, perfectly in time with my own. I paused and so did they. I stopped, and looked back over my shoulder and saw nobody there. I resumed my steady gait, clip-clopping along and I could hear the steps of this other person, just behind me. Again, I turned. Again, nothing. I stopped outside a store with a Christmas display in the window; three reindeer and a tree strung with tinsel and angels and stars, and I studied the glass for the reflection of somebody other than myself. I was the only person there. So when the whispering began, it sent shivers straight down my spine.

"Hey, kid."

The empty air was talking to me. I put my fingers in my ears, attempting to block out the sound.

"Psst, buddy."

Perhaps the voice was in my head.

"Over here."

He was standing in front of Marty's Shoe Shop, right across the road. He was nothing but a faint shimmer in the air.

"Well aren't you glad to see me?"

All words were snatched from my mouth. He was not in such great condition; many pieces of him were missing. He had a hole in his left side the size of a football, his right leg was just a fleshy stump, and he held his head under his right arm, like a rugby ball. He was none too clean, neither. He was coated in some sort of unearthly slime he'd picked up while journeying through the Great Beyond. He'd definitely seen better days. My face remained a blank. I didn't want him to think he could just come waltzing back into my life any time he felt like it. I didn't want him to think that he had my number.

"What do you want," I asked him, staring him dead in the face.

He shrugged. "Life gets boring in the after-world, baby. Thought I'd come to keep you company."

Ed was not the only man determined to fade in and out of my life like a bad radio transmission.

"Well thanks a bloody lot for framing me," I said. "I really appreciated that stint in the jail cell."

"Ah, it's all good for you," he said. "Toughens you up."

"I'm not sure I needed toughening," I replied.

"Sure you did. The world would have eaten you alive as you were. Sacred Heart gave you that extra hardened surface. Another layer of shellac."

"You had the whole thing planned from the start."

"That's not true. Believe me, Celia. Jakey knows best."

"Jakey knows nothing."

"I've had your welfare in mind at all times," he replied.

"I highly doubt that," I said. 'If it wasn't for you I'd still be contentedly snapping my pictures, working in my darkroom at the Butchette. Now you've destroyed all of that and made me dependent upon the first person who opens up their home to let me in."

"But you can't see the whole picture, Celia," he said. 'You have no overview. You're too close to the details."

"So you're trying to tell me you can see the end already?"

"I have an inkling," he replied, "about the way things might turn out."

"Might!" I said, "might! You took my solid ground and replaced it with a might, a maybe!"

I swung round, so that my back faced towards him.

"Don't worry, Celia," he said. "You'll make your mark."

I turned to reply, but found only empty air.

*

I went home that night empty-handed. And the next night, and the next. Nothing I could find on the streets of Provencia seemed like it was worth doing. The world seemed stale, flat, weary and unprofitable and Arty was becoming increasingly agitated at my lack of 'new material'. It was in a despondent state that I called round to see Stuff one evening; nothing personal against Lolly, but I wasn't up to her *eau d'urine* on that particular evening.

Knock knock, granny, open up.

Tap shuffle tap.

"Hiya, Granny."

"Celia? That you?"

"Sure is, Stuff. Long time no see."

I regretted the thoughtless words as soon as I'd said them, but Stuff just laughed.

"Say that again," she said. "Where've you been, young Celia?"

"Here and there, Gran. Into hospital. Out of hospital. Trying to find something that excites me photography wise."

"Well, don't stand outside in the cold and the dark. Come on inside and chat to your old Granny Stuff. Let her know what's been on your mind."

In Stuff's lounge, I fixed us the customary glasses of scotch.

"There's pressure on me to find something new, Gran. And it just feels like everything's been done. I walk the same streets, see the same sights, and I know that I will take the same old photos."

Stuff sat back in her chair, her blind eyes fixed on her fire-screen vulture, nodding like a wise old crone.

"What you need is a change. I hate to be the one to say it, but Provencia these days is a bit of a dead-end street. You need to get right out of it, girl. Go west."

I couldn't believe she was suggesting that I desert our dying city, like all the rest, head for enemy ground.

"Not for good, Celia," she clarified. "Never for good. But simply for the sake of your photography. A fresh perspective, dear. The capital."

The capital! Was granny out of her mind?

"But the capital's evil," I said. "Concrete jungles ain't my thing."

"You never know till you try."

She rose to her feet and shuffled across to one of her many bookcases, lifted the wing of a pheasant and took out a small stack of snapshots.

"Although I cannot see these," she said, "I do remember them well."

I looked down at what she held. The top shot was of two men, one of whom I recognised from the photos on the wall as my 'grandfather' Thomas Doom. The other man was somebody whom I'd never laid eyes on before; physically small, nearly a head shorter than Thomas, with tiny squinting eyes, and black, greasy-looking hair. Both men were dressed in army uniform, standing proudly to attention.

"Best mates, these two were," said Stuff. "Friends from boyhood, then went through the war together. Same battalion. Fighters, both of them. Gritty. Thomas Doom and Donald Vitra. Wild horses couldn't have torn them apart in those days.'"

She turned to the next photo; the boys, home from the war, larking about in a park somewhere, Doom with the other man in a headlock and in the shot after that, the stranger pretending to wring my grandfather's neck.

"Oh they used to have some laughs," said Stuff. "My Thomas was always the looker, of course. Vitra wasn't much to write home about. And after the war, Thomas returned to his taxidermy, whereas Vitra displayed a talent for…" She paused. "…the darker arts."

Darker arts?

"What? You mean he was a warlock?"

"Don't be silly, dear. He became an embalmer. Left for the capital, said business was better there. The two remained firm friends. We all used to holiday together, out on the coast. Donald had his Michael at around the same time we had our Barry, so the boys were basically the same age, but they never really hit it off. Michael, the son, was one of those brainy types, a biology major, if I do recall rightly. Never married. He adopted a child who suffered something of a deformity, Celia."

The lump on my shoulder twitched.

"What kind of deformity?"

"He was webbed."

She spat out the word as if swearing.

"The thing is, Celia, that our two families are linked. And if you're in need of a room…"

"With whom?"

"Young Augustus Vitra. Donald's grandson. He's stayed here a few times, you know, when he's felt like a visit. The other two, the father and the grandfather, are dead now. Dead and gone. I'll give young Augustus a call tomorrow, dear. See if he'll put you up for a bit. Good idea for you to see something beyond this dying town. This Arty and this Angie that you've spoken of, I'm not sure they're good for you, Celia. You need to be your own woman."

These were revolutionary words coming from the mouth of my old Granny Stuff. Unheard of, for an old Provencian like her to suggest that a member of the younger generation go west; usually

An Imitation of Life

our senior citizens did all they could to keep us tied up here, where they could keep an eye on us. Keep us under lock and key. But Stuff was saying, get out, get out, at least for a little while and she was promising to give me the bus-fare and cash to keep myself in film and solutions, an allowance, of sorts. And as for this 'be your own woman' business, I'd not expected that from Stuff, who'd been her husband's right-hand woman, a Swiss Army wife, by the sounds of it, always prepared, like a good Boy Scout.

"It's different for girls of your generation," she said. "So many more options. Things weren't that easy in my day, dear. Getting married to a good man was the best I could hope for and believe you me, Thomas was considered quite a catch. My friends were frightfully jealous. His taxidermy had earned him quite a reputation, a lot of prestige. Word was that the Queen herself had asked him to do her a couple of pieces and both the Provencian and the National Museums were always phoning him up and commissioning works. But these days, a girl needs a good career. Especially a gal like you, Celia."

Tact had never been Stuff's strong suit.

"Just give me some time to try to arrange things, dear. Give us a call tomorrow night. Here," she said, handing me the photos. "Tuck those back under the pheasant's wing, would you?"

*

The next evening, I rang Stuff on the phone. If I stayed with Arty and Angie much longer I would rot.

"Hello? Hello?"

"Gran, it's Celia."

"Hello?"

There was no point in yelling; I simply waited for Stuff to remember to put the phone to her right ear.

"Hello? Hello?"

"It's Celia."

"Oh, hello, dear. Had the phone up to the wrong ear, didn't I? I can hear you now, love. Plain as day."

"Did you speak to Augustus?" I enquired.

"I did indeed, Celia, and he said he'd be delighted to have you."

I grew suddenly nervous. Leaving had been a distant dream; now it was becoming a reality.

"And you'll never guess what," continued Stuff.

"Try me."
"He dabbles in photography himself, dear."
*

I didn't tell Arty and Angie I was leaving, because I knew they would try to stop me. I simply packed up my equipment, shoved everything I owned into a suitcase and crept through the door one evening, heading for the bus which would take me West. Stuff was meeting me at the station with my ticket; Lolly and Grout were there as well, bickering. No chance of Stuff and Lolly seeing eye to eye as they aged; they stood, one at each end of the station, glaring at each other, hackles raised. I took my ticket from Stuff, kissed her on the cheek, thanked her for providing me with this 'wonderful opportunity' and promised that I would telephone on a regular basis, then walked to the other end of the station, bent down over Lolly (holding my breath), kissed her cheek and told her I'd be sure to keep in touch.

The bus was packed, as it always was travelling from here to there. I boarded, placed my suitcase on the rack overhead, and took my place in seats 3A and 3B, by the window, stared out at the brick wall opposite. My 'wing' poked up over the edge of the seat and was prodded, from time to time, by the little brats in the row behind. I was crowded in with adolescents getting out, with families too poor to afford cars, with the elderly who did not want to be left behind now that all their relatives had left.

The engine started, I waved out of the window to Stuff and Lolly and then the journey began; we headed out, past the cemetery, around the old ring road, till we were winding up and away, over the mountains, heading for that dreaded distant land, that Other Place, that terrible elsewhere we called the capital.

XIX

The cookies put George off for a week. Anybody would think I had poisoned him, like some wicked witch in a fairy tale. All I wanted was for him and his wife to relax and enjoy themselves. He came back eventually, however, knocking at the front door, ready to resume work. Opening Day looms ever closer. Time and tide wait for no man, as he is fond of saying.

He is making headway through the sediment; today's shots are of exploding buildings, detonating landmarks. The shot he showed me earlier, of the bridge, belongs with these photos; it must have strayed from the pack, gone wandering off on its own. My blood remembers these pictures. It remembers them now and it remembered them at the time. Sometimes, with the camera to my eye, I would be gripped by a feeling of inevitability, as if I was stumbling through something I had dreamed before. A hand was guiding me, a voice was whispering in my ear *now's your chance*, somebody else's finger was pressing mine down upon the shutter.

I am sipping my tea and giving names to the explosions when he suddenly notices something which has been there all along. He points to the mark which runs like a fault line, from the upper right hand corner, down to the lower left hand side of the picture, reaching downwards, like a lightning bolt, like the wrathful hand of God. At first he thinks that it splits just the one photo, but then he sees that it runs across another, and then another and then he sees that it marks the vast majority.

"What the hell *is* this?" he asks.

"Cracked lens," I say. "I would've thought you'd have read all about that when you were nosing through my pages."

"Oh, Celia. Why didn't you just get another camera? Or at least another lens."

"I was fond of that one," I said. "I liked the line. It set me apart. Till I began to attract imitators."

"I can't believe I never noticed it till now," he says.

"It's not on the early ones," I said. "It was Jacob's fault."

Jacob snorts. *Jacob's fault*, he mimics. He is divided today; his body is perched on top of the grandfather clock, and his head is on the other side of the room, sitting on the window-sill, catching a bit of fresh air.

George is laying out other shots, photos which seem inexplicably banal. An empty road, a dying tree, a patch of mud. These were my attempts at Jacob; look through the lens and he was present. Develop the film and he had mysteriously absented himself from the shot. Even when he was alive he was a ghost. The ghost in the machine, the unseen guest that causes disruption, destruction, a collapse in the system. Nothing's changed. He still likes to throw things about, especially if somebody else is there to witness it. Plates fall to the floor, books fly across the room, the CD player flicks on and off by itself. The usual spook tricks. Nothing too fancy.

If it's just me here he doesn't bother, he knows I am not fazed. Don't even bat an eyelid. After I moved back into the family home, I used to be keen on lone dining; I would sit in the corner of some quiet restaurant, spreading my bulk across two or three chairs, enjoying my evening. And at first Jacob would behave, he would sit quietly in his own chair, plaiting the hair on his head, watching the other diners. Later, he became bored, frisky, what with just the two of us, him and me, cooped up in the house all day. He started to get his kicks in irritating ways; garlic snails would leave their plates and go snaking across the table top, a candle would be blown out, relit, then snuffed out again, a piece of steak would levitate from its plate and go flapping through the air like some ugly, exotic, lumpish bird. There are some people you just can't take *anywhere*.

You couldn't do anything about it, of course. God forbid that you tell somebody the truth about what was going on. *Sorry, that's just my pet poltergeist, my other-worldly sidekick. I do apologise.* The only solution was to stop going out, no point in trying to leave without him, there was no locking Jacob up in the house; walls and doors could not hold him. So instead he and I took to sitting at home, dining on cans of beans and noodles, watching the mould grow on the walls, with me occasionally staggering out into the street to take a few shots of whoever happened to be passing by. A grim débacle.

"Celia?"

George is snapping his fingers in front of my face.

"Sorry. Miles away."

He has noticed something else; he is pointing to the rips, which have been torn in the corner of each shot. He has picked up on my mark.

"Cracks and rips," he's saying. "Anyone would think you had a destructive streak."

"That's my little mark," I tell him. "That's how you tell the real thing from an imitation."

"Hmm," he says. "So they all have the rip but only some have the line."

"Correct."

"Hmm. So what does that mean?"

"It doesn't *mean* anything," I say. "There is no meaning. It's just what is."

"What *was,* you mean."

"*Is.* I'm still right here and so are those photos. You can call me 'was', once I'm gone but those shots will be 'is', forever. As will my words."

"Right. I'll go hunt for a few more of your is's then, shall I? Leave you to it."

"Good idea."

And he's off, back up the ladder to lumber about overhead.

*

When he's gone I sit at my desk, chewing the end of my pen. Ink stains the sides of my mouth. I start, scratch a few sentences, stop. I read back over my words, they don't sound right, so I put a red line through what I have written and start again. It still sounds wrong, it sounds as if I am hitting false notes. I am out of key. The paper is scrunched into a ball, thrown against the wall. Restless, I pace the rooms of the house.

I can't sit still, it is as if my legs have a mind of their own, they carry me out through the front door, along our old street, down other roads to the river. I don't tell George that I am leaving; he'll be occupied upstairs for a good hour or two yet. He won't even notice I am gone.

Nothing new today, just my stock in trade, the bums and the vagrants who have appropriated the many abandoned houses and a few pictures of the families sitting warm within their homes, hanging on for a brighter day, convincing themselves that Provencia's economic boom is just around the corner, the bad days will pass, she will soon return to her former glory. You never know, the quirky little artistic types who come here to paint the deserted streets and the scarred centre might soon decide to move here, one by one at first, and then in groups, the housing's certainly cheap enough. They'll set up the usual small bohemian-style enclaves. A couple of bars and cafes will open, the city will become trendy, professionals will move back into the area, things will swing full circle. But then I would have to move somewhere else. This town is a ghost town and that's why I like it. *To Provencia*, I think, raising an imaginary glass, long may she remain as spooky as she is now.

It pays to have a destination in mind during these walks, else you end up circling aimlessly, like an aeroplane waiting to land at a congested airport. Today we shall pay our respects to the dead. The cemetery first, a bit of a hike from my place, but it pays to keep fit in your old age, it stops them snatching you and locking you away in one of those retirement homes, where they crank the heating up to keep everybody dopey and speak to you as if you're an infant. When you're this close to death you constantly have to prove that you can still fend for yourself; they want to body-snatch me, put me away and charge me an exorbitant sum to keep me when I am perfectly capable of keeping myself.

I lumber along, it's the weekend, I think, though I tend to lose track; Sunday morning is every day as far as I am concerned, especially round these parts. All the streets look the same, lined up as if part of a grid, lined up as designed by our founding fathers who sat round their table long ago, deciding how this city of ours would look. The houses are quiet, their blank windows like eyes, watching Celia as she scuttles along, head down into the wind, lifelong companion over her shoulder.

The cemetery sits out towards the innermost ring road, if you're driving in from the west it's one of the first city sites that greets you; a fitting introduction. I enter through the main iron gate; out of control ivy creeps insidiously across the ground, tangles of overgrown shrubbery lie to each side of the main path, which snakes its way through the graveyard. Upkeep of public places is not a Provencian forte. There has been recent rain, mud clings to the sole of my shoes, I tread carefully, don't fancy sliding around in this muck.

This is where they wound up, all those who lost their lives at the hands of Jacob. Or bits of them anyway. Many of the graves are empty; others contain a token thigh bone, or a hand, or a set of teeth, though these body parts never necessarily belonged to the individual whose name is engraved upon the headstone. The tombstones are to remember them by, to mark the existence they once led here on earth. Never mind that fragments of somebody else are buried here, bearing your name. What else could be done, under the circumstances?

The tombstones poke up out of the ground like stone tongues; they have devoured their victims. I'll be heading the same way soon enough. The graves of Barry and Lettie are positioned to the rear of the cemetery. One grave for the two of them; they share. *In Loving Memory of Barry and Lettie Doom* reads the headstone, followed by the dates. Short and sweet, no mention of the cause of death. If you want to be reminded of that you have to visit the town memorial, where I am headed later. I have brought no flowers, so I walk a short distance away and pinch some blooms from somebody else's grave. Carnations and babies' breath, more like what you'd give a love interest than what you'd leave for the dead. To the right lie a couple of flashy tombstones boasting stone angels with chipped wings, to the left lies Grandpa Doom and the space where Stuff will go, and a few metres behind lies Grandpa Major, and next to him, a place for Lolly. In front of Lettie and Barry is the space where my headstone will stand, a plot I have already purchased. No burial for me, I don't much fancy being a snack for the worms, though Lord knows I would provide enough sustenance to keep a good many of the critters going throughout the long cold winters ahead. I intend to go up in a blaze of smoke. For now, this plot is my marked place. This is where you will come to remember me even though no part of me will be there.

I turn on my heels, head inwards again, back towards the centre. There used to be buses running along this route, but that's all gone out of the window now. I pass the old stops, the old signs. This was route 37, it used to run right into the heart of the city; now I skulk along, partaking of this annual ritual of mine, this tokenistic tribute to the dead. The memorial they erected is hideous, but this is where I go to pray for forgiveness. I should have stopped him, I should have shown a bit of spine. I will never get over the guilt. I'm here now, standing before that great tacky bronze monolith, a thin single spire, topped with a sphere of black marble. *To those who died in the bomb of 1983* says the plaque at the bottom. No mention of my name, for I am the Great Unmentionable. My name is synonymous with death. I walk away, wishing this was something that I could leave behind. But this hole at the centre of Provencia is something that never leaves.

I don't want to go home just yet, I'm still restless. I take the track that leads down to the river. There's a path that runs along beside the Opal. Upkeep of this path has fallen by the way in recent years; fallen trees lie across the dirt track, the grass is wild and overgrown on either side and in places the path is completely missing due to past floods which have washed it away. It's more of a nature hike than a leisurely stroll, but today I feel like pitting myself against something, even if it's only this very tame wilderness. Life in old age is too easy; I have money, I have a home. The temptation is to do nothing at all, but simply to sit and rot, to wait patiently to die.

The usual oily stench comes off the Opal, the surface of it shines like its namesake, a treacherous gleam; this is one river you'd never fancy taking a dip in, not if you wanted to live through the experience. The gulls are quiet today; their beaks are stuck together with muck. The river runs its sluggish course from west to east, trickling down from the mountains, curving south once it has passed through Provencia, by-passing the desert and making its slow path towards the ocean, a determined stream of sludge. Downstream from here, our treated sewerage joins the flow; the entire city's discharge is taken by this river. I make my way upstream, heading for the factory, camera in hand. To the left of me is the river, unchanging, but for slight fluctuations in toxicity, to the right of me is an ever-changing landscape; riverside homes, tangled patches of trees and vines, a paved concrete lot which might once have been used as a car-park, a deserted warehouse; smashed windows, broken doors.

From time to time, I see the odd riverboat parked up against the bank, I keep my eye out for occupants, but see nobody; only the very bravest of sailors would ferry up and down this stretch of current. I am approaching what used to be the Sphere; deserted now, a circular husk with missing planks. I press my right eye to a gap in the wall, peer inside. That was where he stood; that was where I first saw him, doing those shoddy magic tricks, insulting the crowd. That was where I stepped inside the box to be hacked in half. This is where my fate was sealed. It seems like it happened yesterday and it seems like a million years ago. Sometimes I can't tell the difference.

Inside the theatre I can see something moving, a dark shadow; some hobo, I think, some vagrant, another of the homeless, jobless sifters who drift about this city. My eye is still adjusting to the absence of light. The shape shifts, shuffles towards me. It looks too small to be human, too low to the ground, unless it is the offspring of two of our homeless ones, our untouchables. Second generation vagrants; they'll own the city soon, stake a final claim, make it theirs, overrun the few of us who still have houses, take what is ours. The shadow shifts closer, raises its muzzle, gives a small bark. Not a human after all, but a stray dog hiding out here, it must have squeezed in through one of the gaps close to the ground. God knows what it lives off; rats probably, they're all over this city, whole packs of them, fleets of rats, with their little gnawing teeth nibbling away at anything and everything they can find. Most likely it's not the dog that's living off them, but they who are living off the dog, chewing on him at night, as he tries to sleep. Ah, things have come to a pretty pass.

I leave the dog and the theatre behind and progress upstream. The pulp and paper mill looms on the far horizon, looking like something out of Seuss' "The Lorax;" black smoke chuffs from its seven chimneys; the usual sludge comes gushing out of the steel pipe that pokes out into the river. There is nobody here to speak for our trees; then again, we don't have a lot of trees left to speak for. They've been chopped down, logged, strapped to the back of a lorry and driven to this mill to be mulched and refined and spat out as wood chips and paper. Sold to guess who? Our rivals on the West coast. Not much paper is purchased round these parts.

I am right alongside now, this great brick monolith looms overhead; it dwarfs even me. Next door to the factory is a small, dingy office block filled with workers, battery hens; shuffling pieces of paper back and forth, logging invoice numbers, keeping tabs, keeping records, building up files. George's wife will be in there, sitting at the reception desk, filing her nails and reading trashy magazines. Today I walk right up to the factory door, poke my nose inside. It's all forklifts and assembly lines, little ants doing their jobs, serving this giant inanimate queen.

Click, click.

They're caught before they even realise what's happening.

Click.

Caught again. Somebody yells out to me, waves. I have been recognised. I shouldn't be here; I am trespassing. They don't want us to see what goes on in here within these walls; they probably think I'm doing a documentary on exploitation in the workplace. Any ideas these people once harboured of forming a union have been firmly quashed; if you want to stay in Provencia, working here is the only real option you have; it's either here or one of the two supermarkets, or the gas station or our one bank. Or The Muddy Duck which is one of your two alternatives for fine dining, the other being to head on down to Tim's. Even our post office has been closed; a sure sign that a town is headed for certain death. There are other small shops, but these are all family run. They can barely afford to keep their own employed, let alone take on any outsiders.

A stocky man in a hard hat is heading my way, waving his arms in the air and yelling. I turn tail and flee, scuttling back the way I came, feet thumping down upon the dirt track, past the Sphere with its resident mongrel, slipping through the streets in the direction of my home.

*

Back at my table, I notice that he has been snooping again. My pages are out of order; first is in the place of last and last in the place of first, like the bridge when it was rearranged. He looks scared of me now; he eyes me warily, as if suspecting that I am becoming a little unhinged, like a door about to fall from its frame. No doubt he has been reading about the ghost of Jacob, which was to haunt me for the rest of my life on earth. Mental imbalance has always been an illusion I have been fond of fostering. When he ventures downstairs in the afternoon, I roll my white eye about in its socket, like a searchlight, while the black pupil stares straight ahead, like the eye of a dead fish. He shivers, as if some unseen spirit has run dripping hands along his spine.

"So, George", I inquire, polite and smiling. "What have you been up to while I've been away?"

I let one hand flick idly through my manuscript. He doesn't bother lying.

"Okay Celia. I had a little look through your notes. And I just have to say," he said, "that if this was your life then it was damned fast. One minute you were incarcerated, the next you're in the cellar, the next you're talking to some dead guy in the street. Bam, bam, bam. One event after another. Where's the sense of flow? Where's the continuity?"

"It's montage," I said. "I've edited out the boring bits. So shoot me. This ain't no "War and Peace." Who wants to hear all the details; meals consumed, people observed, sheets changed on the bed, teeth cleaned, faces washed, etc. There's too much monotony in the average life as it is. They don't need my daily rituals to add to it. They don't want to spend four years reading about my four years with Arty. This is my life, sure. But it's the condensed version. Nobody will ever know the extended, uncut story except me. Life is short and art is long and my life has been shorter than it should've been, but long enough to bore any reader if I draw the whole thing out."

"It just seems a little....jumpy."

The impudence of it.

"It was jumpy," I say, aware that I am using the past tense, as if I am already a ghost, narrating from beyond the grave. "It leapt. It was a leaping kind of a life."

"I just think some transitions would help. That's all. These characters just pop up and then disappear. Nothing is ever fully developed."

"Picky, picky, picky."

"Further, you describe episodes you could not possibly have witnessed. You switch from first person narration to 'eye of God' narration. Well, sorry to break the harsh news to you, Celia, but you're not God, so how could you possibly know all this Lucinda, Arty, Angie stuff."

"I have extrapolated," I said. "Hypothesised."

"There are also problems of pace. Time does not tick evenly through your pages. Sometimes a day seems to drag on forever, and sometimes a year is gone within a paragraph."

Anyone would think he owned the damned story.

"My temporal scale is out of whack," I reply. "I'm out of time."

"You're half-way through your life and this thing is far too long."

"How can you say I'm halfway? You don't know when the end's gonna come."

"Well you've still got at least fifteen years to go. In the book, that is."

"Most of those years don't count," I said. "Things ground to a halt after I moved back to Provencia. I lived the same old existence, day in and day out. Bore the reader to tears to describe the last ten years I've spent on earth. The first twenty will be tedious enough. I'll take it to age twenty, give you the main events of the ten years following and leave it at that."

He shakes his head.

"Also, what's with these wild variations in chapter length? Can't we have a bit of consistency?"

"Variety is the spice, George."

"Further," he says, "it seems to me as if some pieces are missing. It's like an incomplete jigsaw."

"Of course it's bloody well *incomplete*," I say. "That's because it's not finished."

"What I meant was, even the pieces that are finished are somehow...lacking. As if you're leaving things out. It's kind of uneven. Sometimes you're zooming way in on some tiny detail and at other times you're too far out, just blithely skipping over episodes that perhaps the reader would like to know a little bit more about."

"Why don't you just take up the pen and write the whole bloody thing, then?" I ask. "Since you seem to know so much about this sort of thing."

"I was just trying to help," he says.

"Go help someone else," I say and that gets rid of him, he's gone and I am back with my white pages, my red ink, my black-and-white vision.

I can't get his words out of my head. Doubts nag me, pulling at my mind like tiny whispering demons, *they'll never buy it, it can't have happened the way that you tell it, it's all a little too unreal*, but realism was never the point.

I want to leave the story alone, I want to quit, but the whole house is humming with something I cannot define, it is as if the words which want to be written have wings, they flap about this house like bats, not content to nest in the belfry, they fly through these rooms, tangling themselves in my hair. I would never admit this to George, but sometimes the house is easier to handle when he's here; sometimes the space is too much too deal with, even for a lady like me, even with the ghost of Jacob lingering like a trace of bad perfume. Sometimes we need these little reality checks, these people who will call us back when we are too far out at sea.

*

I stand in the doorway now, one foot in this world and one foot in the next. In one room, George, the exhibition, all that I have been and done in this life, on this planet. And in the other, life after death, all that I will be after I have shuffled off this mortal coil, shed this skin, finally, once and for all, ascended into the ether like a hot-air balloon.

*

Emptiness, pure spirit, a glittering cloud of gold.

XX

Although he was a great lover of the photographic art, there was nothing Augustus Vitra fancied quite so much as a fresh cadaver. He'd spent his whole life surrounded by corpses, death was in his blood; his old man had been an embalmer and so had his father before him. It ran in the family. Some of the very best had passed through the hands of the Vitra empire over the years: actors, writers, painters, musicians. Trusting relatives had brought forth the corpses of the famous, wishing that they be made as beautiful in death as they had been in life, praying that the thick waxy make-up might render the dead resplendent.

Only the best for the best. Augustus Vitra, it was widely known, was not just one of the capital's finest, not just one of the country's best, but one of the world's greatest embalmers and he charged accordingly. He was a clever, solitary man whose passion for photography had begun with the pictures he took of a corpse each time it was finished. He did not take pictures of the living. He only photographed the dead.

He lived alone, above the family business he had inherited from his father. He had few friends and no close relatives. His Dad was dead now; Augustus' first corpse had been his own father's, an emotional challenge which had not yet been surpassed throughout the remainder of his career. His father, who had been a chain-smoker, had croaked at fifty-five, leaving Augustus fairly much alone in the world. He had strange hands, they said, hands which could work miracles upon the dead, making even the ugliest of humans into a thing of beauty. They said that between his fingers and between his toes grew thick, dark webbing, which contracted and expanded whenever he flexed his digits. Nobody ever actually saw his hands, which only served to enhance their reputation. They were the boogey-man's hands, children were threatened with being given over to them when they misbehaved, they had a life of their own, those hands, a life which sometimes seemed separate from the existence of Augustus himself. Even in mid-summer, Augustus Vitra always wore mittens. On his feet were the shoes of a clown.

Still, when you saw the finished product you couldn't complain. For all his creepiness, it had to be said, Augustus definitely had a way with a corpse.

Augustus Vitra's life had been decidedly devoid of maternal influence; he had known neither his mother nor his grandmother. He'd grown up surrounded by men. He had been conceived and grown for nine months to the point of 'birth' (if you could call it that in his case) not in utero, but 'in vitro', literally, 'in the glass.' Egg had met sperm, but not in the usual manner. He was one of his old man's experiments.

His father, Michael, in a fit of post-adolescent rebellion, had completed a Master's degree in biology before consenting to turn his mind back to the family profession and pretending to embrace the art of embalming with all his little heart. It was a false enthusiasm; his father, Grandpa Donald, who had always disapproved of higher education, had threatened to cut his son out of his will if he didn't give up that stupid biology lark and come and settle down and learn how to dress a decent corpse. Michael had caved in under the pressure; he rented a place just down the road from his father's house, put in the nine to five shifts at the funeral parlour, as they were required of him and succeeded in feigning sufficient interest in the whole procedure; the draining of the blood, the filling of the body with embalming fluid, the application of the make-up, then dressing the body in its previous owner's Sunday best and closing the eyes, before laying the corpse in the coffin all in order to make it look as if the soul which had once inhabited this body was now at peace. Michael Vitra was a reluctant dresser of the dead.

His education had opened new doors in his mind. As fascinated as Donald Vitra was with death, with the end of the life cycle, so his son was intrigued by birth, with life's rich beginnings. He wanted to unlock the secrets of the miracle that was human creation. Michael had been popular with his professors, a straight A student whose aptitude for biology was surpassed only by his enthusiasm for the subject, a tidy, meticulous learner, always with his nose in a book, a bit of a know-it-all, the kind who was always three steps ahead of the rest of the class. One professor in particular, Professor Higgins, had been especially fond of the boy, and when Michael had telephoned and made an appointment to come to see him, three months after the completion of his Master's, Higgins, a specialist in embryology, had assumed the boy wanted to discuss further studies, a PhD. Higgins would've been more than happy to shoulder the responsibilities of supervisor, it would have been a pleasure, in fact, to work more closely with a young man so dedicated and so gifted.

But as soon as Michael had taken a seat in the Professor's office, it became obvious that a PhD was not on his mind. He looked anxious, thought Higgins, not a personality trait that he remembered Michael possessing. He fidgeted and would not meet the professor's eye. Higgins tried to put him at ease with a joke, but Michael did not laugh.

"What's up, son?" Higgins asked, praying the lad was not about to saddle him with a whole host of personal and emotional problems.

Michael pulled himself together, summoned his courage, and looked his old professor in the eyes.

"I want to make a baby," he said, and Higgins nearly choked on the glass of water he had been sipping.

What did he want? Advice? Instructions? Had nobody informed this twenty-five year old about the birds and the bees, had he not stumbled across these home truths himself? Could it be possible that the lad had completed an entire Master's degree in biology while remaining sexually ignorant?

"Outside the womb," added Michael, provoking another coughing fit.

That was it then. The lad was simply off his rocker. Making a baby outside the womb? It was January 1966. The Western world was filled with peace and love and tuning in and dropping out and The Beatles. The times they were a changin', but not that fast.

"Don't be ridiculous," said Higgins. "It's not possible."

"Never say never," said Michael, a little too confidently, thought Higgins. "We live in a world where anything is possible. We two can do what has never been done."

Bullshit, thought Higgins, smiling amiably at his ex-student.

"Listen," said Michael, leaning forward in his seat. "We still need the womb for incubation. We still need a placenta for nourishment. But the conception itself can be done artificially. Outside the womb. We take a small number of eggs from a healthy female, inseminate them, and then plant the best back into the uterus."

He sat back in his chair. There was a revolutionary gleam in his eye.

"But what's the point?" asked Higgins.

"To prove that we can," replied Michael. "Think of the possibilities for infertile couples. We can fertilise a number of eggs, wait to see who's gonna make it and who isn't, then place a nice lookin' little survivor snugly back inside. Think of what this could mean."

Higgins remained sceptical. He suspected that Michael was bored, and was merely filling his mind with fanciful notions as a way to help pass the many mundane hours at the funeral parlour, for Higgins knew that the work in which his finest student currently partook could not have been providing anything remotely resembling sufficient intellectual stimulation.

"It's not just your scientific expertise I need," explained Michael. "I also need your wife."

He talked for three hours solid, talked till he was blue, talked till he'd brought his old prof round to his way of thinking. Higgins could finally see where the kid was coming from, thought it might be worth taking a punt on the bright spark. But he would not volunteer his wife as guinea pig. He adored the woman; he wasn't about to offer up her body for any purpose, experimental or otherwise. He could, however, offer an alternative.

*

It was all very hush-hush. There were no notices pinned to departmental notice-boards. Instead, Higgins wrote 'see me' in red ink on the essays of several of his female first-year students whom he thought might be willing to provide the necessary ovum in return for a discreet, hefty, one-off payment, put forward by the two scientists. Three of the students laughed in his face and one started bawling, but the fifth girl, a lass who went by the name of Carrie Carton, agreed to donate her eggs to the cause and also to act as incubator. She needed the cash. She'd been considering prostitution. This seemed a preferable option.

Michael did the honours sperm-wise. Higgins came up with the bright idea of giving the girl hormone tablets in the hope that she'd 'ripen' more than one egg at a time. It worked. Twelve were ready at once. They removed the eggs and examined them for viability. Six were perfect, four were marginal and two were dead. They injected a single wriggling sperm into each 'good egg'. They waited, watching the process of mitosis take place, wondering who would make it and who would not. Three of the fertilised eggs faded and died. Three kept healthily dividing, replicating themselves, on their way to becoming embryos.

"Now then," said Michael, looking through a microscope, "which one of you little fellas is gonna be a fighter."

"We can't just pick one," said Higgins.

"Why not?"

"It'll never take. Why don't we put all three into the womb?"

"Three! What if they all make it? She'll have a litter."

"They won't all survive. Bet you. We'll be lucky if one hangs on."

"You're the professor, I guess," said Michael.

They implanted all three back into Carrie's uterus.

Ultrasound had not yet been invented, so they were unable to check on the progress of the embryos. Carrie's menstrual cycle would be their first clue. They waited with baited breath. She was a good, fertile lass. She skipped her first period. They cheered and held a small party; the boys on the whisky and Carrie on the orange juice. Higgins gave her a pregnancy test when she hit the seven week mark. It came back positive. Spirits were jubilant. Carrie prayed there was just the one baby inside her; she couldn't think of anything worse than giving birth to twins or triplets.

The two scientists held their hands to Carrie's belly when it kicked. They bought diapers and stretch-suits and baby food galore. They were preparing. Michael and Higgins spent many a night at Carrie's cold student flat, drinking cheap red wine and fantasising about the scientific glory in which they anticipated they were soon to bask. Michael's enthusiasm for the project was infectious. Higgins found himself more excited about the impending birth then he had been about anything since his student days; Carrie glowed with her pregnancy.

All that was left was the question of who was actually going to raise the kid. Higgins declared that he personally was not averse to taking a little bubba home, but his wife would not approve and he dared not go against the missus' wishes. Carrie said she'd been paid to be an incubator, not a Mum. There was talk of adoption, but something in Michael Vitra would not allow him to let this child go. It carried his genes; half of him had gone into making the whole of it. Who cared about the absence of wife, of a woman who would be mother to this child? He could raise the kid alone.

*

All this, Michael Vitra kept secret from his father.

And on 18 October 1966, Augustus Vitra made his first appearance in this world. He was a thing born and he was also a thing made. Higgins and Vitra were twelve years ahead of Bob Edwards and Patrick Steptoe, the UK embryologists who had been responsible for one Louise Brown, supposedly the world's first test-tube baby. And yet there was no glory. The circumstances surrounding the birth of young Augustus were kept secret, the girl was given hush money and Higgins and Michael swore a vow of eternal silence. And why was this miracle not shouted out to the world? Because something had gone wrong. The unexpected had happened. Those rumours about webbing were based on fact; Augustus' digits were not neatly separated, but joined with thick skin, like the feet of a duck. He might have been a miracle but he was also a mutation. Michael Vitra swore the webbing had nothing to do with the method of conception, but Higgins didn't want the professional shame of having created a child who was anything less than perfect. Michael cared enough for his old prof to respect his wishes. Carrie Carton wanted nothing more to do with the kid. She'd carried her burden. She'd received her cash. She was more than happy simply to shut her mouth and pretend the whole thing had never happened. Nobody wanted to repeat the experiment. Augustus Vitra's life was shrouded in secrecy and silence.

*

When Michael Vitra told his father he was intending to adopt a newborn baby, his Dad hit the proverbial roof.

"You'd better find yourself a wife first, hadn't you boy?" he'd bellowed. "Before you start up with this baby business. Who's gonna change the bloody nappies? Who's gonna rock it to sleep at night? How are you gonna feed it? Suppose you're gonna sprout titties, are you?"

"He's an unwanted child, Dad. Wait till you see him. Bet my bottom dollar you fall in love right away."

Michael fetched the newborn baby from the hospital, wrapped it up in a blanket so its deformities were not visible and presented the quiet child to his father. Augustus looked up at his grandfather with big brown eyes.

Uncanny, thought Grandpa Vitra. His eyes are just like those of my son. And that nose. That's the Vitra nose if ever I saw it.

He looked from the child to his son to the child. He put two and two together and made three. The conclusion that Grandpa Vitra reached was partially correct. He had deduced that some woman had given birth to his son's child out of wedlock, in which case this boy was a love child, a bastard. He shuddered at the word. But he couldn't abandon a Vitra kid; he reluctantly agreed that adopting the child was the right thing to do.

*

Augustus was a subdued child, content to sit in the front room of the funeral parlour, picking at the webbing between his toes, flapping his fingers at the receptionist. Michael was fond of him, but more as an experiment than a son. His grandfather begrudged him a smidgen of affection. The webbing had come as a terrible shock to the old man; he just about had a heart attack when he saw it. A member of the Vitra family, deformed? He could've killed his son for hiding the truth from him, but as Michael pointed out, 'It's too late now, Dad. It's best we just treat him as an ordinary kid.'

Augustus didn't seem to notice the absence of maternal influence in his life. His Grandmother had passed away a year before his birth. He'd never known a mother, so he never missed having one.

It wasn't until he started school that he learnt that the unusual skin which grew between his digits was something of which he ought to be ashamed. They called him all the names under the sun: Duck Boy, Paddle, Webby. The family profession didn't help matters; things might not've been so harsh for the boy if his father had been a plumber, or a doctor, or an engineer. But everybody knew what it was that the Vitras did and most people were vaguely spooked by it. Augustus' skin grew thick, tough, like the hide of a rhino. He eventually discovered his latent sporting prowess, which helped to win him a small amount of social acceptance. He won every swimming race he entered. He could play tennis, badminton and squash without a racket, albeit a graceless, clumsy game. He was a demon on the volleyball court. His serve was a thing to be reckoned with.

His father hid his origins from him until adolescence and then he sprung the news. The questions were starting to come thick and fast from his placid son.

So who was my mother then? And where is she now?

Michael was racked with nerves at the thought of the tale he had to tell, but when he told his son the truth, he found that Augustus didn't care. He was proud of his experimental origins. The story about the birth of Louise Brown hit the media shortly after Michael had told his son the nature of his conception. Augustus would look smugly at the telly and know that he was the one who had got there first. Grandpa Vitra remained ignorant of the truth to his dying day.

Michael often conducted scientific experiments down in the basement, and Augustus understood that these were to be kept secret from his grandfather, who disapproved immensely of such pursuits. The cellar was full of rats in cages, microscopes and slides, Petri dishes and little bottles of chemicals which Augustus had been warned were strictly off-limits. There was the world above ground and there was the world below. Above, Augustus understood, his father dressed up corpses to make them look pretty, he played the prodigal son; below, there were experiments and danger.

It was his father who had first encouraged young Augustus' interest in photography. Ever since he had been big enough to hold a camera steady, it had been Augustus' job to photograph the corpses when they were all laid out, to take a variety of shots, the best of which would be stored in his Grandfather's album, a thick black book which contained one picture of every corpse which had ever been embalmed by the Vitra empire. This book was a secret; Grandpa Vitra suspected there might be legal prohibitions designed to protect the rights and the dignity of the dead, prohibitions against snapping them all laid out. Michael sometimes tried to encourage his son to head outdoors and take pictures of something other than the dead bodies, but Augustus wasn't interested. He was fond of the funeral parlour, it was familiar, it was safe. He liked the smells and sounds and sights. He liked the sense of patriarchy, the linear progression, grandfather, father and son, all working together to keep the family empire up and running. But he wanted more. He wanted to learn the family art; the way of the embalmer. The webbing between his fingers and his toes made him clumsy; he stumbled about the parlour, pestering his father. Can I do the make-up, can I do the draining, can I dress up the dolly, please? They trusted him only with the camera.

He left school at fifteen to join the family gang full-time. Still they would not teach him their secrets. He watched instead. There was talk of bringing in an outsider to take over where they said that Augustus could not. When Grandfather Vitra kicked the bucket, Michael began looking about for an understudy to train up to take over the Vitra empire and allow him to spend more time down in the basement with his microscope.

Pick me, pick me was Augustus' silent cry, the words his father never heard.

Michael's death was sudden, unexpected, and it struck before an understudy had been found. Augustus leapt at the chance to put himself to the test. His first corpse was his father's. It wasn't magnificent, but it was okay. He'd made his old man look halfway decent and the mourners were forced to admit that perhaps this boy, despite his deformities, had been blessed with the Vitra touch after all.

He was the world's only webbed embalmer, he was determined to prove that he could do it. He wanted to prove himself to the ghosts. His photography fell temporarily by the wayside and he threw himself wholeheartedly into learning the profession that was rightly his. He was not content with being second-best. He overcame his webbing. He was a mouth artist; he would grip the various make-up brushes between his teeth and delicately apply the required coats; with skilled manipulation of teeth and tongue he could turn any face into a masterpiece. He knew exactly how to drain, fill, dress, make-up and lay out a corpse. He worked long, hard, unsociable hours, staying up right through the night, drinking endless cups of coffee. He never saw the sun; his skin became a whiter shade of pale. He was a perfectionist; when dissatisfied with the results, which he often was, he would force himself to start again from scratch; take the corpse from the coffin, remove the make-up and clothing, drain the formaldehyde from the body and begin from square one. His perspiration paid off. By the time that I came to make his acquaintance, Augustus Vitra, he of the webbed fingers and the webbed feet, was one of the best damned embalmers this world had ever seen.

There were social problems. He was a lonely guy. He had trouble pulling chicks. He couldn't go down his local pub, they all knew who he was, so instead, on Friday nights, he would take a taxi to the other side of the city, and try his luck there. He did his best to eye up birds whom he thought might be game. His big mittens and his clown-like shoes did not help the cause much, but he could usually get them chatting with little more than the offer of a drink or two. It would usually go okay until he mentioned what he actually did for a living and then they would stare at him, terrified, make some excuse, and leave. Sometimes he would try to lie, tell the women that he was actually a graphic designer or a journalist, but the truth would always out, he would let slip some comment about a cadaver, or the art of making up the dead and the same old looks of horror would flit across their faces, the same old excuses, Gosh, is that the time? I really must be going. He didn't know how to behave with women, they were foreign, an unknown quantity. He tried too hard; he scared them. He always returned home alone, back to his empty house, to face the funeral parlour in the morning, just the old receptionist and this new bloke, Clive Minor, whom Augustus was supposed to be training up, for company. Somewhere in the pit of his gut, Augustus knew that he was condemned to a wifeless existence.

Vitra had taken on just the one assistant. He was frightened that further expansion would result in the loss of that golden Vitra touch, the touch that had made the family name. Clive had originally been promised a full apprenticeship, but Augustus was having difficulty trusting him with the real work and had a tendency to allocate him the more mundane chores; washing down the cadavers when they first came in, making sure all was tidy out in the reception area, showing guests down the hallway when they came to view their dead friends and relatives, sweeping out the parlour at the end of the day. Augustus hardly ever even let him near the corpses.

*

And Celia was soon to arrive.

He met me at the bus station; he'd driven there in his hearse, the rear boot of which he opened in order that I might climb in. Stuff must have warned him about my size, for he did not blink twice when he saw me, simply smiled and extended one mittenned hand.

"Hello there, Celia," he said. "Augustus Vitra. Pleased to meet you."

"Lovely to meet you too," I said.

The Vitra embalming empire was situated in one of the suburbs on the edge of the capital. The entrance to the flat upstairs was located at the side of the building, and reached via a cracked sidewalk, down which Augustus led me. The sky was dark overhead.

He ushered me inside, led me up the stairs and offered me a choice of rooms. I turned up my nose.

"Can't you take me down to the cellar?" I asked.

I wanted something familiar, something dingy, something damp.

"A cellar-dweller, eh," he had chuckled and led me to the appropriate stairwell. We wound down to ground level, where the real work went on, where the funeral parlour itself was located and from there, to the cellar. Down I went, into the darkness, my hand groping for the light-switch, finding what it sought. The lights came on. I heard insects scurrying in all directions and my stomach gave a rumble. I saw slides and microscopes and a couple of rat skeletons in cages; evidence of his father's pseudo-scientific activities of the past. Augustus disappeared for a minute, and then returned with a tiny mattress, not much in the way of cushioning, more like something I would use as a pillow.

"It's all we've got I'm afraid," he said, handing me a moth-eaten blanket. "I guess we'll have to sort you out something else for next week."

I didn't get much sleep that first night; the lump on my shoulder was now the size of a basketball and prevented me from sleeping on either my back or my right hand side. When I finally did fall into a restless slumber, I was awoken soon after to the soft sound of a camera shutter clicking away. In the darkness, I could just make him out. The outline of his stumpy body, the shape of his mittens. My brother; my keeper.

This was what he expected of me; that I pose as his model. The morning after that first night, I responded to his call to come up and join him at the breakfast table. It did feel most strange, I must say, sitting there with a complete stranger, making polite chit-chat over the tea and toast, as if this were a perfectly normal situation, as if we had been living together for years. Let's not forget, I was getting on a bit; I was far from in my prime. My fifteenth birthday was just around the corner, I was no spring chicken. My knees were feeling a little arthritic; my vision was beginning to blur, as if somebody had hit soft focus. It never crossed my mind that I was the kind of girl somebody else might be interested in imprinting on film. 'Scuse my naiveté.

The funeral parlour gave me the creeps. All that oak panelling, all those arum lilies, the receptionist who looked like a living corpse himself and Augustus plodding on ahead of me in those big old shoes, his mittens out to either side of him, as if he needed to extend his arms for balance. And all as quiet as hell. You could've heard a pin drop in that place. It made me want to scream and holler and cry, to do something, *anything* to break the silence. But I made no noise; I simply waddled in behind Mr Vitra, bent nearly double, what with those dreadful low ceilings and my old bones giving cries of protest every inch of the way.

He showed me the finished product first: a corpse like a wax doll, a woman, large, dressed in a neat blue suit, tidy navy shoes upon her feet, her arms folded across her chest, a peaceful expression upon her face. This was the first time I had seen a body without a soul. I remember that first parlour tour as if it were yesterday. I kept staring at his mittens and his big clod-hopping shoes, wondering what he was trying to hide. He spilt the beans about his webbing eventually, when he was drunk one evening, drunk and crying about how they'd all thought he couldn't do it and now he'd really proven himself, but his victory felt hollow, he said, because he had nobody to share it with. Tears in the whiskey. Snot in the wine. I suppose he thought I might be something of a salve for his loneliness.

Eventually, he took me 'behind the scenes' to where the real work was actually done. I didn't like the feel of *that* room at all; it stank of chemicals and old blood, it had an understandably creepy feel, as if the ghosts of all those whose bodies had been dressed up here still lingered on.

"Oh you poor wee dear," said Augustus when he saw me shivering and took an old grey blanket from the end of the table upon which he laid out his corpses and threw it about my shoulders.

*

Click. This time he was blatant about it. He put me, literally on a pedestal, stood me on a block of wood and made me turn this way and that while he took pictures of various body parts from various interesting angles.

Raise the right arm little, would you. Tilt the head a little to the left. That's my girl.

I was his model and he was my photographer and these roles would never be reversed. I would never have the chance to turn my gaze upon him. I wasn't offended. For the first time in my life, my body was being looked upon with something other than horror. He said I was the angel of his life.

It was Augustus who removed my cover, simply reached out and peeled it off, as if it were a skin I was ready to shed. He winced when he saw me.

"No wonder you wore that cover everywhere," he murmured.

Then he leaned in close and whispered in my ear.

"I want to see you as you are. Naked."

Nervously, I nibbled a spider. He threw the filthy rag in the rubbish bin and no more was said about my face.

When he didn't want me to model for him I was free to roam wherever I chose. I took to prowling the streets. Stuff was right. Although pollution hung like fog about the buildings, the city felt like a breath of fresh air. The capital was growing so rapidly that large areas remained only partially made; cranes and scaffolding were everywhere you looked. Everything was under construction. The capital was as prosperous as Provencia was poor; as wrapped up in the throes of progression as we were caught in the downward spiral of disintegration and decay. I was almost anonymous; size prevented me from blending into the crowd in quite the manner I would have wished. Sometimes I played a little game entitled 'spot the Provencian', wherein I tried to pick who was and who wasn't a native of this thriving place. We were easy to spot; we were the ones trying a little too hard to fit in, the ones laughing a little too loud, the ones working harder than anybody else, always wearing the nicest clothes, appearance always immaculate, over-compensating. We were the ones screeching, *oh God, just don't make us go back from where we came. Oh God, please grant me asylum.*

My photographer's block had been beaten; I did a whole series dedicated to Provencians who had left for this terrible, prosperous elsewhere and I titled it, *Fish Out of Water.* The faces all wear the same ingratiating smile; the desire for camouflage, the compulsion to *fit in*, the need for acceptance. It was written all over them.

With my trusty Leica on my shoulder, I would wander for hours, round and round, spinning in aimless circles, with no particular place to go. I carved out weird, looping routes for myself, routes that took me through a variety of 'burbs, 'burbs which all looked the same; row upon row of brick two-storey houses, tiny front yards which were fenced off from the road and out the back, little patches of green, barely enough room to swing a cat and you had to walk for miles to find yourself a decent park to muck about in. They crammed them in here; not like Provencia with our mandatory quarter-acre sections and our public gardens (never mind that they're tangled and overgrown now); not like Provencia with our endless hectares of green parks which stretch on and on (never mind that these are now empty and neglected); not like Provencia where you can find greenery not just in the wealthy areas, but everywhere. This was a city where nature came with a very big price-tag.

*

Arty and Angie were doing alright for themselves. I saw articles in the papers, Doom exhibitions were popping up nationwide. I thought at first that they must have stolen rolls of my negatives; it wasn't until I saw one of the first reviews that came out, with close-ups of several of the pictures on exhibit, that I realised that somebody else was applying my name to their shots. These shots that were on display were nothing that I had ever snapped; my name had been appropriated. My name had become a commodity. These pictures could not have been taken by Angie or Arty, who knew a little about marketing, but nothing about photography, these had been done by somebody with a fair bit of photographic experience, and this person, this third party, was mimicking my style, signing my name and taking credit where credit was not due. My name was their fortune. They didn't need me in the flesh; they only needed the myth of me. It was the worst form of robbery; but worse than the theft was the feeling of impotence with which I was left, like a stale taste in my mouth. I could do nothing; even if I stormed into one of those shows and demanded that the truth be told, they would think that I was lying.

In a nice ironic twist, these were the exhibitions which received the rave reviews and so, inadvertently, I too was taking credit where it was not due. These were the shows that really made my name, and the name was made on the strength of work which was not even mine. These photos were printed on magazine covers, with my name writ large underneath, but none of this work belonged to me. I was unsure whether I should laugh or cry.

Arty was playing publicist, he was quoted as saying that I was safely back in Provencia, in the Hartman basement, doing what I did best, hiding from the world and developing pictures. It was said that I still stalked the streets at night and the papers declared that on any given night of the week you could find a small crew of people waiting outside Arty's home at dusk, hoping for a sighting of the bumbling giant. Part of me said that any publicity was good publicity and what the hell did it matter whether I was responsible for these photos or not. They were popular with Joe Public; it was fine for me to be linked to them. And if the truth ever came out then I could not be held responsible for what had happened, I could simply claim that the activities of Angie and Arty and this mystery third person, this other photographer, had been beyond my control. Another part of me felt wretched. It was as if I had striven for some great trophy all my life and had now won the grand prize, not through honesty, but by cheating.

*

Claudia's star was still in the ascent, still eclipsing mine. Her face could be found gracing many a tabloid page; during the course of my meandering, I would often call into a corner store and have a quick flick through the latest gossip columns which inevitably showed pics of Claudia at some exhibition or gallery opening, wearing low-cut evening dresses and looking glamorous, with some male accessory or other draped across her arm. They were lapping her up. Somebody was calling her the zeitgeist; she was a sign of the times.

*

It was a male world I now lived in; the receptionist was a stooped old geezer called Johnny, who'd been with the Vitra empire since the very beginning; he was a hundred and eight if he was a day. Deaf as a doorknob, God knows how he managed to use the telephone. Clive Minor, the so-called apprentice, eyed me with empathy. He knew what it was like to be caught in Vitra's web. He'd been taken on board with the promise of being trained up, sitting his exams, becoming a fully qualified embalmer, but all Vitra ever gave him was the dirty work, sweeping and cleaning, when all he really wanted was a chance to start learning the real stuff; draining the body, pumping it full of formaldehyde tinged with just a hint of safranine to bring back that rosy glow to the cheeks, pushing a needle through from lower lip to nostril to prevent the mouth from hanging open, suctioning the abdomen clean. All the fun stuff. He was growing increasingly tired of being Vitra's dogsbody. It was just as if Vitra was taking revenge for all the years *he* had not been permitted to practice the embalmer's art.

So where did I fit into the picture? I was Vitra's hobby, his plaything, his stress relief. I was something to fill in the empty hours. They were long hours, the ones I spend modelling for him. I was far too restless. *Keep still, Celia, stop fidgeting.* He wanted a statue but I had ants in my pants. He called me his Raphaelite dream, but I made *those* girls look like waifs. He never did the whole of me; he only ever did one piece of me at a time; a breast, a thigh, a foot. Close-ups of the number with which I had been marked. He was especially fond of my lumpish right shoulder; he called it my best curve, though I myself had always thought of it as an unsightly bulge. I wasn't allowed to leave my clothes on; he wanted me nude. He wasn't all bad, Augustus, but he had a nasty controlling streak. The head? Just the once. He wasn't big on the cerebral. He preferred the body shots. His bedroom used to make me shudder. Sometimes, if he was out of the house, I would poke my head around the door and see naked pieces of myself everywhere; an enormous right boob, a foot, complete with verruca, a hand. I was spreading rapidly across his walls. He made me feel both frightened and flattered.

*

I used to do the shopping malls. There was something about them that I found irresistible; the clean, bright light, the elevator music, the plastic plants, the packs of kids skipping off school; the housewives searching for that elusive item they felt their lives lacked: an egg slicer, a bread maker, that special pack of scented candles; the compulsive spenders, grabbing goods that they neither wanted nor needed from the shelves; and the thieves, the blank masks on their faces as they took what they desired and walked casually from the stores, as if defying the guards to nab them, as if daring the alarms to go off.

I took photos of the surveillance cameras that peered down from every wall, from every ceiling. In the shopping mall toilets I read not the writing on the wall, but the advertisements that were plastered on the backs of the cubicle doors. I found consumer culture reassuring; an antidote to the weird world of the funeral parlour, where Augustus shuffled about whistling dirges to himself and Clive was always whinging about never being given any extra responsibility, and his inability to net himself a girlfriend. He was finding out what Augustus had discovered earlier, that girls just did not fancy men who worked in funeral parlours; he was forever lamenting his lack of luck with the chicks. (Didn't they know a guy with career prospects when they saw one?)

The aged receptionist was encased within his own silent little world. If the funeral parlour was the dark side of the moon, then the malls were the side that saw the sun. I never bought anything of course. Poor as a church mouse. Not a cent to my name. And Arty and Angie were cashing in. In the larger bookstores I flicked through *Art Weekly* and *Photo Now*. So called 'Doom shots' often featured and if there was no photo, there'd usually be a write-up of an exhibition of what they were calling my photographs. They must have been making a mint.

My reputation was growing without me, spreading like fungus. Sometimes I would feel tempted to show my face at these shows; just walk in casually off the street, humming to myself and say, *This whole thing is a fraud. These shots are not mine. Somebody else has stolen my name.* But who would believe me? They'd think I was just talking crazy, *What do you mean you didn't take these pictures? Of course you did. See? Your name is on the back there.* Nobody knew about the identifying rip.

*

Jacob would often appear, at night. As I lay down in the cellar on my little single mattress, he would come gliding through the brick wall as if it were no more solid than a sheet of paper and sit himself down at my feet, sometimes laying his severed head on the pillow beside me.

"Getting some nice new pictures?" he'd inquire.

"I'm doing okay," I would reply. "Cured my block, anyway."

"You'll find that a change of scenery has that effect," he replied. "Come on then show us some of your latest snaps."

And he would run his critical eye across my work, picking flaws in everything; he would point out each and every tiny shadow which fell in the wrong place (*throws the whole thing off balance, Celia*), each instance of bad positioning, any sign of bleeding.

"I might as well just destroy them all then," I would say, grumpily.

My mouth would droop down at the corners. Then he would change his tune.

"Oh, stop your pouting. Don't you know it's all gonna be alright in the end? Here, I know what'll cheer you up. How about a game of headball."

And he would take his head and kick it about the cellar, bouncing it across the floor and off the walls.

"Come on, Celia," he'd cry. "Get into the spirit of the thing!"

But I could never seem to muster sufficient enthusiasm for the game.

*

On the mantelpiece in Augustus' living-room sat a collection of death masks he'd inherited from his Dad. He still made the odd cast of his own; I'd seen him laying the Plaster of Paris over the faces of the dead, waiting for the cast to dry, peeling it away, leaving the real face behind, adding this new cast to his collection as if it were some kind of trophy. It was his suggestion, of course, to do me in the same way.

"A life cast," he said. "I'd like to have some reminder, some memento if you ever should leave me."

His talk scared me; he spoke as if we were lovers, as if this were some grand affair we were conducting. Still, he had taken me in. I felt that I owed him something.

"Alright then," I said. "Get it over with."

He couldn't wait. He took me to the room in which I modelled for him, laid me down on the same table upon which he laid his cadavers and, rubbing his little hands in glee, he took his box of Plaster of Paris out from one of his cupboards, mixed a little in a bowl with some water and began spreading it over and under the rolls of my face. I panicked for an instant, wondering how I would breathe with that stuff covering my nostrils, my mouth, but he was careful to leave the appropriate orifices clear. I lay back and thought of Provencia, lay staring up at the ceiling, waiting for the stuff to harden and dry, while Augustus simply watched me, stood as still as stone while waiting for the plaster to set. When it was done, he pulled the cast away, satisfied. I felt unclean. I went upstairs to take a shower.

*

Christmas hit the shopping malls with a vengeance; tinsel everywhere, streamers and kids grabbing at presents they wanted their parents to buy them. I moved glumly from store to store. A fine Christmas this was going to be; just me and Augustus and a few dead folks. There were Santas in every mall; happy Santas, sad Santas, bored Santas, angry Santas, fat ones and skinny ones and Santas with their beards falling off. They were fantastic to photograph; I did a whole Santa montage. I had taken to developing my film upstairs, in Augustus' bathroom. The two of us never discussed our mutual passion for photography. We never discussed anything at all; I was simply a gigantic doll he took pleasure in capturing on film and I was merely 'paying my way' while trying to overcome the block I had experienced while remaining in Provencia.

Ho, ho, ho, boomed Father Christmases everywhere. *Come and get your picture taken with old Santa Claus.*

Kids would line up to sit on Santa's knee; clamber up into his lap, pull at his beard and jab at his stomach. The flash would explode in their faces like lightening. *Click.* The sound I loved. I would lurk just behind the many photographers of these many Santas, just to hear that sound, just to see that bright white light.

It was while standing directly behind one such photographer that I discovered a Santa who was not like the others.

"Ho, ho, ho," he was shouting. "Come and plonk yourself down on Santa's knee."

But when the kids climbed up to get their lollipop and have their photos taken, events would take a turn for the weird. Daisies would sprout spontaneously from their ears, frogs would leap from pockets that they had thought were empty, turtles would come tumbling out of their noses. A lot of the younger kids started crying and calling out for their mothers, but the older ones were fascinated and did not leave after they'd had pictures taken (complete with turtle or frog or daisy) but would hang about just behind Santa's big seat, hoping to figure out how he pulled off his tricks. I stood watching this particular Santa for a while, waiting for him to take a break.

He had seen me. At twelve noon he rose up from his chair, stretched and declared to the rapidly gathering crowds, "Well folks. It's time for this Santa to get himself some lunch."

He stepped down from his little podium and began heading in the direction of McDonalds, winking at me as he passed, gesturing that I follow him. I trailed on behind, as did a little, intrigued, group of children. He finally had some fans. At the counter, he ordered us both a burger, fries and Coke and we took a seat in the far corner. The kids hung back a little, staring. He nodded in their direction as he took a bite of his burger.

"Pretty cool, huh? I must finally be doing something right."

"It's great, Ed," I said. "A fan club."

"So what have you been up to, Celia? Since we last met."

"I'm living with Augustus Vitra," I said. "The embalmer guy."

"What? Augustus Vitra of the Vitra embalming empire?"

"The very same. He makes me pose for him," I confessed, before adding "naked" as an afterthought.

"Hmm," he said, looking a little disturbed at the thought of a nude Celia.

"How's Lolly," I said. "You been round to visit?"

He gulped and his hands flew to his chest.

"What?" I asked, alarmed.

"Nothing," he said. "Must have just been a chip going down the wrong way."

"Heart playing up again?"

"No, no. Nothing of the sort. Fit as a fiddle, me."

He jumped up and did a few quick callisthenics, as if to demonstrate the point, then sat back down, finished his meal, waved his hands over the burger wrapping and produced an origami crane. He threw it into the air and it flew away.

"Been practising," he said.

And then he reached across and took my hands in his. "Promise me something, Celia."

"What?"

"When you've got what you need here, promise me you'll go back to Provencia, back to your roots."

"Where would I live?"

"At Lettie's."

"*How* will I live?"

"Photos, dummy. I didn't give you that camera so you could live your life as somebody else's *model.*"

"Maybe," I said. "I can't tell you for certain where I'll go."

"Well then," he said solemnly, still holding onto my hands. "Can you promise me something else?"

"Depends what it is."

"When I die, Celia, please think fondly of me. Think of your old Ed with a smile and not a frown. Forgive him his transgressions. Celebrate his presence in your life and dwell not upon his absence. Can you do that for me?"

"I guess so. Why? You're not planning on croaking right now, are you?"

"Who can say when my hour will come," he dramatised. "Death could be right around the corner for any one of us. At any moment his icy finger could tap you on the shoulder and say, *Hey buddy, you're comin' with me.*"

His eyes held a febrile glimmer.

"Just remember me, Celia. Remember me fondly."

He rose to his feet, took his empty Coke cup in hand, squeezed, transformed it into an orange and tossed it to one of his fans.

"Nutrition is important, kids," he said. "Never eat this rubbish. Go get yourselves some vegetables for lunch."

He clipped his beard back on, walked slowly from McDonalds and resumed his role as Santa.

Ho, ho, ho.

I walked home to the parlour, erasing his words from my mind, marking him down as the man who cried wolf. Ed would long outlive me, I thought, my own death was descending at a frightening rate, each day took me three days in the direction of my demise.

*

A gloomy Christmas came and went. Augustus wasn't much into celebrating; on the big day he and I sat silently at his table, eating turkey with cranberry sauce. Never had I felt so glum. I wished I had Ed's confidence, his belief that I could eek out some kind of livelihood from photography if I tried. Instead I was stuck here, paying my way with that terrible nude modelling. There were no gifts exchanged between Augustus and me. Augustus declared,

"The greatest gift I've ever been given, my Celia, is your sweet presence."

After dinner, there was a sad attempt made at parlour games. After a spell, Augustus went out to walk off his dinner and I called up Lolly and Stuff on his telephone. The two old birds were over the moon to hear from me. Lolly had been celebrating with Grout, and our Christmas greetings to one another were interrupted by bickering and shouts, threats from Lolly (*I'll knock your bloody block off, you sour old trout*) and warnings from Grout (*I'll quit and leave you to die in your misery you evil old cow*). Stuff had just got home from The Muddy Duck, who'd put on their usual Christmas spread, providing an exciting variety of fare: turkey and chips, ham and chips, chicken and chips, chips and chips, or chip butty. Both grans sounded a bit sozzled and speaking to them sent a pang of homesickness shooting through the centre of my chest. I didn't have the heart to tell Stuff that her dreams of my becoming 'my own woman' had resulted in C.D. being reduced to nude modelling for Augustus; there was no point in worrying the old dear unnecessarily.

*

Life in the new year continued along the same track as it had in the old. Augustus and I rarely talked; in the morning, at breakfast, if he wanted to photograph me, he would make clicking noises with his tongue and I would be forced to follow him to the funeral parlour and stand dutifully naked while he snapped away. If breakfast passed without his tongue clicking I was free to spend the day as I chose, roaming the capital, snapping at random.

Another birthday passed me by, marked only by a phone call from Stuff and a second call, later in the day, from Lolly. I was getting older. I began to despair of ever being free of that place, despaired that I would never be able to pay my own way in this world.

*

All was not well between Clive and Augustus. I heard fights. I witnessed steely silences. I would come back from a hard day's perusing of the shopping malls to find the two of them at each other's throats, or else separated, Augustus locked away with one of his bodies and Clive sulking in the reception area. The tension between them was almost palpable; you could slice the air with a knife. Clive took to inviting me down to the local pub and sharing his troubles over a pint or three after work.

"If I'd known it was going to be like this," he would lament. "I'd have taken a plumbing apprenticeship instead. I thought I'd know everything there was to know about embalming by now. But knowledge is power and he's guarding his secrets like they're the crown bloody jewels. And as for your addition to this little family...."

He would pause and shake his head.

"It's not right, Celia. He's controlling you. I've seen what he's doing. And I just want you to know that I don't approve. Not one iota. If he insists on taking your photograph he should at least allow you to choose your own clothes and your own pose, instead of those silly nude pics. I've seen him bringing them back from the chemist in their neat little packets. Why do you allow it?"

I would shrug.

"What choice do I have? Girl's gotta pay the landlord."

He would nod.

"I've gotta say," Clive would lament. "Never thought I'd find myself caught up in this racket. Now I'm stuck aren't I? Who else is gonna employ me?"

"What did you think you were gonna do for a living?" I'd ask him.

"Well, I'm okay with oils," he'd say. "I thought I was gonna do the art thing, but it never worked out. You don't know how lucky you've been, Celia."

"*Lucky*?"

"I've seen your stuff in those magazines. Somebody's really on your side. To be honest with you, Celia, I don't really understand what you're doing here."

I shrugged.

"Just getting some new material," I said.

"Where's all your money gone?"

"Agent took it," I replied.

I did not let on about Arty and Angie and the mysterious third party. Didn't say that all these Doom shots that were going up on gallery walls and being printed in magazines had been taken by somebody else. My lips were sealed, my tongue was still. Mum was the word.

XXI

In a cold abandoned warehouse located somewhere in Provencia, Lucinda Fortune posed naked for the cameras. She was freezing.

"Can't we get some bloody heating in this place?" she called out to nobody in particular.

Nobody in particular responded. She shifted her position on the green vinyl sofa. There was something sticky under her left leg. *Ick*, obviously it'd not been cleaned after yesterday's action. The director was pacing up and down, hand moving thoughtfully over his chin like he thought this was some kind of *art* flick, obsessively reading and re-reading the script he had penned himself.

Holy hell, Lucinda thought to herself, adjusting the dark sunglasses that were her trademark, the glasses she never removed. *You'd think that after all these years he'd realise that the script is totally not the point? Let's just get today over and done with so I can go home.*

Home. Hardly. A grubby little motel run by a grubby little man whose eyes bulged out at her from behind his milk-bottle-thick glasses. She quickly pushed the thought of him out of her mind by focusing on the male lead who was, at this very moment, off set (if you could call this ridiculous makeshift 'room' a set) working himself into an appropriate state of frenzy with a tub of vaseline and a couple of porno mags.

At least he's a bit of alright, Lucinda mused to herself. *Compared to some of the mutants I've been asked to shag in the past. Terrifying.*

"I'm not sure about line twenty-three," the director called out, raising his right hand in the air. "Lucinda, do you think we could change that from, 'My, aren't you a *big* boy', to 'My, aren't *you* a big boy?'"

"What's the difference?" she asked.

"Emphasis, darling," he said. "Emphasis. Give it a go, now, before we begin. Try the old way and then the new way."

It was always the same with him; he was never satisfied. They all had to bear the brunt of his perfectionism. She ran through the lines, emphasising first one word and then the other.

"Right," said the director. "So we're definitely going with the second way. Stress on 'you'. And make sure we get plenty of footage of her scar? The guys love that. Everyone ready to roll?"

He looked around the warehouse. Nobody was paying him an ounce of attention.

"I said, 'Is everyone ready to roll?'"

Various mumbles and nods.

"Can we please have some *energy*, around here?"

He looked about.

"Yesterday's performances were as flat as a pancake."

He paused. They all knew what was coming.

"So, who's for a bit of pick-me-up?"

The lighting guy was keen, the sound guy wasn't, the camera guys were in, the male lead was otherwise occupied. Lucinda had made a vow to quit. The director took the daily dose of amphetamines from his pocket, one of the gophers ran over with a mirror and the lines were racked up. The usual rule applied. *Three for me and one for anybody else who's keen.* If he didn't watch out the insides of his nose would burst like a sausage splitting its skin, his septum would disappear completely.

He rolled the ten dollar bill, shoved it up the right nostril because the left one had been making some scary, damaged noises recently and snorted. Waited for the speed to hit. And then it was all action. The cameras were rolling, the male lead was called in, primed and ready, his leading lady put the emphasis on all the right words.

The director jiggled his legs, paced, anxious, then picked up pen and paper and began sketching out ideas for his next movie, while still yelling out instructions to cast and crew when it suited him, and intermittently stopping to do sets of fifty sit-ups just to keep in trim. He was struggling to keep his mind and body on one thing at once, but he liked that, liked skipping from thought to thought, from action to action, he'd come up with some of his best ideas in such a state, like that one with the horses, now *that* was unique.

He liked to think that his flicks ruled the high end of the porn market, they had style, they were leading the genre, really, they broke rules, invented new formulae, but then refused to stick to the formula they had invented, they were always pushing on, pushing outwards. He liked to think he was discovering new territory, like a telescope in outer space, filming what had never before been seen by the human eye. Or imagined by the human mind. Avant-garde porn. Cutting edge.

The only recurring theme you'd find in his movies was his star, Lucinda. He knew a good thing when he was onto it, and Lucinda was as good as they got. A professional. You'd never know she was faking it, she could fool even him, she could fool even *herself*. A natural, and without the baggage that some of the girls carried, the ones who'd been raped by their fathers or brothers, the junkies who were working to pay for their addictions, the hookers who'd stumbled into porn because they thought it was glamorous and soon found themselves forced to work longer hours for less money. Girls who were always complaining that they were being treated like dogs. Meat on the rack. Lucinda was here to pay the bills and everybody knew it, she was a tough girl, no nonsense, she knew how to use her assets to full advantage. If you've got it, flaunt it, and Lucinda Fortune had it in spades.

There had been, at one time, a *liaison* between them, but they had both vowed never to go down *that* particular track again. It had been a slip-up, shoddy on his part, to go for his leading lady, but certainly he was not the first director to do so, nor would he be the last. He thought of it as a sort of occupational hazard, she was there for the taking and so he took her, though he regretted it ever afterwards. Sorely. She swore to him she'd been taking the pill.

A fresh flutter of panic hit him and he quickly did another fifty sit-ups. No-one was looking. They were used to his obsessive-compulsive behaviour. He swung between crippling bouts of insecurity and delusions of grandeur where he believed he could conquer anything. In the grip of these delusions, he was king of the world, master of the universe. But the old insecurities would always come creeping back and then he would be, in his own eyes, a louse, a worm, a hissing, evil snake. The cast made excuses for him because they knew that he was the one holding this whole operation together.

Splat. What was that? He looked up from where he lay on the floor. Those damned pigeons again, rats with bloody wings. He thought of *Naked Lunch* and wondered if he could hire not a bug exterminator, but a *bird* exterminator to get rid of the buggers once and for all. *Splat.* Right in his fucking eye. On set, the male lead, whose name he could never remember, was still pumping away on top of Lucinda, who must have been bored to tears, though she never let it show. He wondered, vaguely, about incorporating the pigeons into the picture, somehow, and then thought better of it. You can't always trust your instinct on these things.

He reached up and wiped the pigeon crap from his eye, walked across to the props table, took the silly little cardboard crown he liked to wear and placed it upon his head. Speed King. King Expedite.

"Cut," he yelled.

This was Ed in his element.

*

They rolled through the day; her mind was elsewhere. She was a blow-up doll, a puppet, a thing. Lunch-time came and went, no such thing as catering round here, some were eating the sandwiches they'd brought with them, others were doing more lines. Then back into it, the same old poses and phrases and bullshit. Just waiting to hear the golden words.

"And that's a wrap."

Day's over.

"Well done, team. A good effort."

Occasionally he went in for that whole buddy-buddy team spirit directorial crap.

"Who's for another line?"

One of the extras untied Lucinda and she walked across to get her overcoat, the one with the big fur collar that she liked to nuzzle her face into. Warm. Comforting. She swapped the silly white stilettos she'd been wearing for a sensible pair of boots.

"Lucinda?"

He held out the rolled bill. He was trying to tempt her. Probably still hankering to get into her pants, even after all that had happened between them. She shook her head, made for the door.

"You're not walking home alone, are you?"

She nodded.

"Those are mean streets out there, darlin'. You take care. We should really buy you some mace."

He turned to one of the gophers. "Get Lucinda some mace, huh? Order it in if you have to. I want my star to be safe."

He winked at her. "See you tomorrow."

*

She stepped out into the darkness. It engulfed her like an ocean. She pulled the fur collar up about her face. It wasn't far from here back to the scungy little motel, ten minutes if she walked swiftly. She was not the kind of girl who dawdled. Her assertive stride carried her swiftly away from the warehouse, her boots thudding down confidently on the pavement. Head held high, shoulders back, exude confidence and they won't be able to get you. It's any sign of weakness that attracts them, they smell it, the fear, like sharks sniffing out blood. She was hardly in a desirable neighbourhood.

Then she heard them. The footsteps. Out of time with her own, behind her just a few paces, a tread she recognised, the same steps she'd heard before. She refused to quicken her pace or cross to the other side of the street. She kept on, same steady speed, same confident manner. At the motel door, she stopped, turned, looked back over her shoulder. There was no mistaking it. There was somebody there.

Lucinda Fortune refused to cower in fear. She would pull this bastard out of the shadows and drag him into the light. Make him reveal himself. Show his true colours.

"Come out, you coward," she shouted. "Come and face me like a man."

Silence. Just her voice echoing between the buildings.

"Come on you dumb bastard. You chicken."

She flapped her arms and made clucking noises. She heard a giggle, a laugh. She was aware that she looked ludicrous, but she wasn't as ridiculous as him, this total wimp who had been following her about.

"Come on then. Show us you've got balls."

He stepped out from the shadows. He was small, a tiny red-headed guy, with so many freckles you could hardly tell where one left off and another began. He was one big blotch.

She stood with one hand on her hip, took a cigarette from her bag and lit it. She had never been afraid of direct confrontation.

"So what's the deal, man? What is it you want from me?"

He was nervous, she could see. He probably had a stutter, she thought. He looked like the scared kind of guy who sometimes approached her for an autograph; single guys, lonely, without girlfriends or wives, coming up to her in restaurants, or in the street. Can you please sign my napkin? It's not for me. It's for my friend.

But when he spoke he was confident.

"Are you Lucinda Fortune?"

No point in denial.

"Sure am. What's it to you buddy?"

"It's just I wasn't sure. You look a lot...."

"A lot what?"

"A lot plainer, than I'd imagined."

"Thanks a lot."

She blew a thin stream of smoke at him. Pushed her sunglasses more firmly onto her face.

"So whadda you stalking me for? You not got anything better to do with your time?"

He said nothing. You've gotta watch the quiet ones, she thought. They're the ones who snap, grab machetes or machine guns, and go in for a bout of mass murder.

"Well?" She stubbed out her cigarette, searched his eyes for the tell-tale murderous gleam. "What do you have to say for yourself?"

A shrug. What the hell. He seemed harmless.

"Look," she said. "Why don't you come indoors and I'll fix you a coffee and then you can see that I'm just an ordinary gal and you'll bugger off and leave me alone."

He followed her into the motel, looked about with big eyes.

"Milk? Sugar?"

He shook his head.

She handed him a strong black coffee. He took tentative sips, as if he thought she might have slipped a bit of arsenic in there when he wasn't looking. He looked like he was trying to escape something.

"What are you running away from?" she asked.

There was a long, heavy silence, but when he finally replied, his voice seemed clear and confident, at odds with his mannerisms. "My wife."

Then he started talking and didn't seem able to stop, spilt his guts all over her tiny motel room table. She made him cup after cup of coffee. She liked listening to him talk. He was interesting. She didn't want to be rid of him. He was like a stray that latches onto you, a stray which, despite yourself, you become inordinately fond of. When he rose to leave, she felt disappointed. She invited him to return. He accepted the invitation.

They struck up an odd kind of friendship. She had to admit, it was nice to know somebody who was outside the whole porn circle, a fresh face, an outside viewpoint. A local. Theirs was a platonic relationship; he was open about his wife from the beginning, told her numerous entertaining Angie stories, so many that she almost felt sorry for this wife, who had become something of a subject of amusement between them. And she, being in her line of work, didn't much feel inclined towards fostering sexual relations with anybody. She was too shagged out to bother. She was grateful for his company. They met secretly, like lovers, took long walks, with the hoods of their coats pulled down over their faces so that nobody would recognise them, they drank red wine together, but there was absolutely nothing else between them.

He told her his name. Arty Hartman. She told him hers. Maude Blightman.

He started laughing and she punched him on the arm.

"No wonder you changed your name."

"Exactly. How could I go into porn with a name like that?"

"Who dreamt up Lucinda Fortune?"

"I did," she said, proudly.

"It's saucy," he replied.

"I know."

But she wasn't Lucinda Fortune when she was with him. Nor was she Maude. She was another person entirely, a third person, a woman who had been invented not by one or other of them, but by both. She wore plain clothes, like an undercover policewoman, a hat, sometimes, to cover her give-away long blonde hair, dark colours, sensible garments. She talked to him of all manner of things, from the ridiculous to the sublime. About what she'd really wanted to do with her life, before circumstances had driven her to smut.

"Photography," she said. "I was the best in my high school class. I really could have been someone. But..."

"But what?"

"Necessity drove me in another direction. Money. Cash. Paying the bills. It's still a hobby of mine. I guess."

"You still take pictures?"

"Sometimes. It's a bit of an antidote to the porn. Balances things out a little."

"Will you show me some?"

"Maybe."

A pause.

"Now?"

*

Back in her motel room, she reached under the mattress and pulled out what appeared to be a portfolio, laid it down upon the table. Lit a cigarette then plonked herself down on the sofa.

"Aren't you gonna talk me through it?"

She shook her head.

"Too shy," she said.

"Shy? How can a porn star be shy?"

"People are shy about different things. In different ways."

"That's true."

He opened the cover and it struck him immediately, like someone had just kicked him in the guts. Or knifed him. Raw talent. The kind of talent that can't be learnt, either you had it or you didn't. She had it. She was looking at the floor.

"Do you have any idea how torturous I find this?"

"Why?"

"I'm just embarrassed."

"Embarrassed. Never be embarrassed."

Her pictures made his wife's artistic efforts seem positively pathetic. Celia's pictures paled in comparison. These photos didn't just sit upon the page. They shone. They leapt out and grabbed you by the balls and twisted. You were putty in the hands of these pictures, they owned you, they mastered you, you felt as if you had seen them somewhere before, in some dream your memory had stored. None of them were pretty, but many of them were beautiful. They were of landscapes, mostly, but distorted land, ugly land, shots of the barren desert, nothing in sight for miles, shots of the Opal clogged with oil and muck, shots of plain red rock (where had she been? Mars?), shots of the sheer face of a cliff. Arty felt his heart lurch over it.

The last photograph was of her scar, a close up, so close you could see all the various little wrinkles and puckers where the skin had gathered as it healed. Lucinda got up to pour herself a gin.

"So," said Arty, eyeing his Porn Queen. "What are you like at imitations?"

What was she like at imitations? She was great at imitations. She could mimic almost any style you cared to name. Show her a picture, any picture, ask her to do something similar and she would, she could, she did. She could do you a Steiglitz, or a Weston or a Cartier-Bresson. She could develop them, as well, although she preferred not to. She'd rather just take them down to the local pharmacy, she said. It was quicker and easier. The motel was far too cramped, but there was always the bathroom, if she had to. If she was pushed.

When he told her his plan she just stared at him. A gleam appeared in her eye. She immediately agreed. She had followed Celia Doom's career with interest. And so they embarked together on Project Doom.

It was weekend work for Lucinda, and although Arty paid her, paid her well, she didn't do it for the money. She did it for the company, the friendship. Porn superstardom was a lonely game. She also had another, stronger motivation for playing along with his game. Lucinda always had her reasons.

*

Arty was torn. He desired Lucinda like he had desired no woman before her, nor ever would desire a woman again, but he didn't want to risk the slightly fragile, precarious friendship they had. A couple of wrong, sleazy moves and the whole thing might come crashing down round his ears, she'd shut him out, cut him off. Withdraw. He'd seen it, the blank look that came over her face, as if she was vacating her person, putting herself somewhere else, into a corner nobody else could reach. It was a black place, a corner in herself that the porn had made her excavate. Retreating into that place was a defence mechanism, a way of keeping herself safe. Put the wrong foot forward and she'd scoot into that part of herself never to emerge again. At least, not for you.

Softly, softly, catchee monkey, he said to himself, as he laid his arm down next to hers on the table, just a *little* too close, as he slid his chair across the floor, in her direction just an inch or two, so that their thighs touched, as he spoke into her eyes. He imagined himself removing her dark sunglasses; fantasized about being the first one ever to see her eyes. One of the things he loved about her; she never mentioned her scar. He dreamt about that scar; he wondered how she had got it. Had she lost something, some organ, had a transplant maybe?

He often imagined reaching out and touching it, lifting her top, just a little, pulling down her skirt, just a little, and running his index finger across the thick, damaged skin. She did not show her physical scar and nor did she flaunt any emotional ones at him, none of this *I was abused as a child so then I had to become a porn star bullshit.* She had no tragic tale to tell. Or if she did, he knew it was a story she would never speak. She was notoriously cagey about her past; all she'd let on was that she was a nice, normal middle-class girl doing her best to appear untainted by trauma, doing her best to appear psychologically sound; she had not been abused as a child, she'd never been a whore, she'd never been a junkie. It was as if her past had been erased the minute the star, Lucinda, had been born. Maude Blightman was somebody else, another woman entirely.

And every day, he made his subtle moves, dropped his quiet hints, tested the water. Nothing ever happened. It wasn't that she was *resisting* his advances, as such, she was just *oblivious.* She just didn't seem to notice. She wasn't putting up a wall, because she didn't feel there was anything to put up a wall *against.* His hand would brush against her breast as they sat gazing at her latest shots; no reaction. He would reach out and tuck a wisp of blonde hair that had strayed back behind her ear; no reaction. He didn't even get the feeling that her reaction was a *refusal* to react. It was just as if she'd never even considered the possibility of taking their relationship just that one step further, just that one little step across from the motel table in the direction of the bed. He had been hoping that the secret they shared would weave itself around them like a cocoon, draw them inevitably, finally, together. It did not.

Could she be frigid? He found himself wondering. *A frigid porn star? Not physically, obviously, but emotionally, maybe?*

He bought her flowers and chocolates and perfume. She scoffed the chocs, doused herself with the scent, shoved the pretty flowers in a vase. Said thanks. That was it.

His thoughts turned self-critical.

Could it be me? He wondered. *My dress sense, my hair? Do I smell?*

He splashed out on some designer threads, had a haircut, switched aftershave, made sure he plastered himself with deodorant. She complimented him on his hair, noted the fine cut of his clothing, said "Mm, you smell nice today," but there was absolutely nothing flirtatious in it. She was merely making a series of simple observations.

Probably best that nothing ever take place, Arty took to telling himself. *Let's not forget about Angie.*

He'd be better off dead if *she* ever found out he'd been carrying on behind her back. He settled upon the only sensible solution he could find; whenever he had sex with Angie, he would close his eyes and pretend it was Lucinda.

Angie was as angry as ever. She was trapped indoors with her fury, stuck inside with her frustration, her thwarted ambitions. Every now and then she would demand to know the identity of their mystery third party.

"So who is this hot-shot bloody photographer then? Why are you being so bloody secretive about this whole thing? I thought you were meant to be my husband? Spouses share things with one another, don't they? That's what being a spouse is all about."

Arty always gave her the party line.

"They've only agreed to take the shots if anonymity is guaranteed, he declared. If word gets out...

"You can tell me. I'm your wife!"

"Sorry, love. I'm sworn to secrecy. I promised I would tell nobody. Not another living soul."

*

Lucinda loved being anonymous. Loved hiding behind this gigantic Celia Doom, who floated about in public like a zeppelin drifting high about the country. She was far from precious about her work; didn't care what happened to the pictures once they'd been done, she didn't want to know in whose name she was doing what she did. She was a creature of self-invention, and like all such creations, her motto was *don't look back*. During the day her eyes faced firmly forwards, on the next Doom shot, on the future. But at night her head would swivel around on her shoulders, involuntarily. Memories she didn't want to face would flicker before her vision. She could feel the weight of them, dragging her backwards, dragging her down. She would awaken from dreams with a start, sit bolt upright in bed, her eyes wide open, staring straight ahead.

*

I was the ghost that stalked her in the darkness.

XXII

Embalming was no lifelong ambition of Clive's; it was simply something he'd fallen into, by accident, through lack of alternatives. His mother, having tired of her son lingering, jobless, about the house long after he should have left home, dragged him down to the employment centre one morning and told him he'd bloody well take whatever was on offer. It so happened that Vitra had called the centre two weeks earlier, for having concluded that he was destined to progress through life wifeless and childless, he had also been struck by the realisation that if he stubbornly refused to take on an apprentice, the golden Vitra skills might never be passed on to another and would die out with Augustus himself. Vitra's notice had been given pride of place upon the job centre notice board.

Wanted.
Intelligent youngster to learn art of embalming.
Strong stomach required.
Interpersonal skills not necessary.
Please enquire at desk quoting Job No. 369A.

Clive stared at the notice. His Mum, Ruby, gave him a nudge.

"That's you to a 'T', innit," she whispered in his ear. "Well, you might not have the intelligence bit, but you've got an iron gut and no social skills. That's your one, son."

"Just make stuff up," Clive's Mum had hissed at him as they walked across to the table to fill out the form. "Put a couple of your uncles down as referees and no-one will be any the wiser. The family'll back you up. Tell 'em you've been working down at the abattoir. That's near enough to embalming. Dead humans, dead animals. Same diff. And mind you don't mention that silly art course you did at the Polytechnic. Fat bloody lot of good that did you. What did you learn there? How to sit around all day getting stoned?"

Though he'd never done a day's work in his life, Clive's CV, as written down for Mr Vitra, declared that he had extensive experience in the fields of slaughter and cleaning.

"Make sure they know you're versatile," said his Mum.

The next day he had the job. His mother told him he was a big boy now and shunted him out of the front door with a suitcase in his hand.

"New job, new life, new home," she told him. "Find yer own place, son."

The last thing she did before she sent him on his way was to take him down to the barber to get his dreads shaved.

"Get rid of all those nits and things once and for all, Clive," she'd said.

Clive assumed residence in a cheap bedsit just down the road from the funeral parlour and lived off a steady diet of microwave dinners and baked beans, supplemented with the odd Sunday roast whenever his Mum felt guilty enough to invite him around for dinner.

First day at the funeral parlour, Clive had freaked. He thought he'd met some weirdos at the Polytech, but the guy who answered the doorbell when he rang looked like an extra from the Adams family, not just an old granddad, but a *great*-grandad, bent nearly double, bald but for a few wisps of white hair, leaning on a *walking stick*. "Mr Vitra?" Clive asked tentatively.

"Eh?" said the old geezer, craning forward.

"ARE YOU MR VITRA?" Clive repeated.

"Am I gonna bite you?"

"MR VITRA," Clive yelled.

He didn't know whether or not the words had found a way through the deafness, but the old guy stood back and motioned for him to enter. Inside, he hit a brass bell, and then sat down behind the reception desk, pursing his lips together.

There was a shuffling in the corridor. Clive leaned out expectantly. A middle-aged, dark-haired man entered the room and extended a mittenned hand towards him.

"You must be Clive."

Clive nodded. So *this* was Vitra. Check out the guy's shoes! Majourly Creepsville. Vitra took him on the grand tour of the place, a tour which ended in the smoko room, where he told Clive he could make himself busy by doing the dishes that had accumulated over the last month. When that job was completed, Vitra told him he could go and vacuum the reception area. When that was done he could polish the oak panelling that lined both sides of the corridor. And so it went on. At the end of his first week Clive was amazed at how exciting a prospect actually being let at a corpse had become.

Am I ever actually going to go near a dead body? He asked of his employer.

All in good time, my boy. All in good time.

He asked the same question at the end of every day, and always the reply was the same.

Inevitably, Clive was left wondering whether the good times would roll around at all.

And when Fatty showed up, it was a regular house of freaks. Here he was, following a so-called career path he'd never wanted, and not even *progressing* down that path, just stalled at one end of it, the start. Going nowhere fast.

The more Clive cleaned, the more Vitra found for him to clean. The miraculous day, the day when the apprentice would finally be allowed to get his hands on the bodies, receded one step away from him whenever he took one step in its direction; it was like the mythical pot of gold at the end of the rainbow, it would never materialise. Having employed a youngster to whom he had intended to impart his wisdom, Vitra was now struggling to share his track secrets. He couldn't let go. Clive grew increasingly restless. The pints we shared down at the boozer were indulged in with increasing frequency, until it came to the point where we were boozing more nights than we were not.

"I was thinking," he said to me one evening. "All that posing you do for Vitra. We could take a leaf out of his book, you know."

"Whaddaya mean?"

"Please don't take offence at this, but a body like yours and a face like yours, well, they lend themselves so well to parody."

"Of what?"

"Hollywood stars. I was thinking we could do a few Sherman style stills. If you'd let me."

"With *my* camera?"

"You could take them. We'll hook up a cable-release."

"But Sherman's work is already parody."

"So we'll parody the parody."

"What for?"

"In the name of independence," said Clive. "I can get you a list of places to send them away to, these photos of yourself. You can learn how to make a living."

I agreed out of sheer boredom. I agreed because I wanted to know how to get my work seen. It was decided that we would use Clive's bedsit as a studio. I'd not known that his room was so tiny; there was barely space for anybody else at all, once Celia had positioned her bulk inside. I didn't want to put my camera in somebody else's hands, so Clive, as he had suggested, secured me a cable-release and we hooked the Leica up to that. We did a whole series of Hollywood style stills. Clive had a mate called Sharon, who was majoring in fashion design, and consented to whip me up a number of enormous and glamorous dresses for free, as part of her final-year project. She made special allowances for the 'unsightly protrusion' on my shoulder and secured a number of wigs through a friend of a friend who ran a costume hire shop. I was nervous. I'd been dressing in those fleecy knit casuals for as long as I could remember and the thought of the fabulous frocks filled me with fear.

"It'll be superb," Clive and Sharon reassured me.

They brought in a friend, a make-up artist who went by the name of Mack, who had blue hair and thick silver eye-shadow and tight leather trousers and was of debatable gender. We all tried hard not to laugh when we saw what could be made of me. I did a gigantic Marilyn, bent forward, pouting, with Sharon standing under me with two hair-dryers so that my skirt would billow up. I did Rita Hayworth in a long evening gown; I did a feisty Mae West; I did Josephine Baker in a papier-mâché 'banana skin' skirt. In each photo, you can see the black release button I held in my right hand. We did them all in black and white. I ripped each photo, made my mark.

"We can't send them away torn," protested Clive.

"No rip, no photo," I replied.

I stuck to my guns.

Years later, I showed prints of these photos to my transvestite friends. How they laughed! "We thought this was our idea, Celia," they said. "Looks like you beat us to it."

Clive printed me up a list of magazines and galleries we could send the shots away to.

"Who normally handles this stuff for you, Celia?"

"An agent," I said.

"The same one who took your cash?"

I nodded.

"Well, it's always good to know how to do all this for yourself. I've marked those people who have accepted your work before with an 'x'. They're the first port of call. Then we try the others."

*

There were two Dooms in action now; myself and the phantom. The phantom met with greater success than I did; many of these shots of myself were sent back marked 'inappropriate material' or 'there is no mistaking the fact that you possess photographic talent, but we are afraid to say that we are currently unable to find a place for your work' or 'I am afraid that our exhibition space is fully booked until next July' or, in one instance 'tremendous potential, but unsure as to the choice of subject matter.' All these responses came from magazines in the capital. They had never heard of me; they had never heard of my double.

We had two hits in amongst these misses: the Marilyn shot was printed in *Limited Edition*, a small magazine with a circulation of around two thousand, and another picture, me as a naked and pregnant Demi Moore (strap-on stomach on top of my usual bulge) graced the inside back cover of *Aim and Fire*, which was run by an art cinema located in one of the capital's less prosperous suburbs. There were no exhibitions of genuine Dooms, though we read, in many of the mags who rejected my shots, that the work of my impersonator was hanging on many a wall. It was a life apart for all of us; it didn't seem quite real, getting together in that bed-sit and taking those shots. It was the flipside of life, the underbelly. Back on the right side, the three of us had other commitments; Clive had his cleaning, Sharon had her course to complete and I had the poses I continued to strike for Vitra.

Sharon used the shots of me as part of her end-of-year project; displayed them on a sheet of cardboard and submitted them along with the costumes in the original. She received an 'A' for the project and was over the moon.

On Sundays, when he felt so inclined, Clive would take Sharon and me to exhibitions held by the other me; I would walk about amongst the pictures my shadow had taken, admiring his or her handiwork. These Dooms were better than mine. There was sometimes a photograph of me in the exhibition brochure, or on some leaflet blowing about; a snap Arty or Angie must have taken while I had been residing in their basement. Often there'd be a quote that somebody had made up; *these pictures mark a real shift in direction for me. Lately I've been moving away from my usual themes of fragmentation and disjunction and trying to achieve a sense of unity in my work.* I would cringe; sometimes I would tear up the words. On the walls of these galleries there usually hung a sign, a black camera with a red line through it, a sign which I would ignore. I would lift up my Leica and take photos of these fraudulent Dooms, then develop them in Augustus' bathroom in order to try to learn from this master in the guise of an imitator.

It was hard for me to hide on these Sunday outings. My size was a dead giveaway; I used to get the odd punter scurrying up to me and asking *are you Celia Doom?* And I would simply glare at them, stare them down, black-and-white eyeball them and say, *No I'm not. You must have mistaken me for somebody else.* This usually reduced them to silence. What could you say to that?

We attended Dean exhibitions, too; Clive thought we should. Claudia appeared to be going through a phase of shooting buffed male models in black and white film, or young couples kissing, or, in full colour, beaches at sunset, or mountain tops, or other such devastatingly original delights. She liked her self-portraits, too, did our Claudia. There was a full-size colour photo of her on every wall; her fully made-up face beamed down at me, framed by those locks of golden hair. Her mouth was smiling but her eyes looked dead.

Clive often used to take us round to his Mum's for a Sunday roast after these little jaunts of ours. The old girl got a right fright the first time she saw me, but she soon warmed to old C.D.

"Oh, I do like a girl with an appetite," she'd say, as I put away three plates of meat with three vegetables and a triple helping of pudding to boot.

She wasn't so keen on Sharon, whom she described as a cheap-looking little hussy.

"I hope you're not dipping your fingers into *that* honeypot, Clive," she'd hiss behind Sharon's back, the minute she left the room.

But Sharon was full of bright ideas; it was she who had the next artistic brainwave; a way for us all to beat the tedium of our little existences.

"Fairy tales," she said. "Let's do Celia as Cinderella, Snow White, Rose Red, Sleeping Beauty; she can be a parodic Beauty and a literal Beast, she can be a joke 'dwarf,' she can be the giant at the top of Jack's beanstalk, she can be an ugly sister and an evil stepmother. Our Celia's a versatile kind of gal."

"I can do Hood and I can do the wolf," I added, thinking of my visits to my two grannies.

We went to a considerable amount of trouble. Sharon, now in her final year of fashion design, sewed me a number of costumes: a variety of flowing fairy-tale-style gowns; a furry ape-suit for my role as the Beast; spotted knickerbockers, a white shirt and a red cap for my performance as 'dwarf'; a huge pair of oafish brown trousers and a black corduroy jerkin for my role as giant; an enormous red cloak for my Big Red Riding Hood; a wolfish mask and grey fur suit for my debut as wolf. Sharon's efforts were first class, and were again submitted to the Polytech; she looked set to receive another couple of As for her course-work. Mack did my make-up; he or she would bend down over me and I would stare up with my mismatched eyes as each stroke of colour was applied, the layers of it, around my eyes and upon my mouth, the circles of rouge, the black coating of mascara upon my lashes, that other gloop they call foundation, as if it is the building block upon which you lay the rest of your face. I took every picture myself; they were responsible for arranging me, but it was my job to capture myself.

They talked me into using colour film.

"We haven't put all this effort into the costumes and backdrops just to have you shoot in black and white," they said. "Full colour or nothing."

I could see their point. I swapped my black and white for full colour.

Clive was responsible for the mise-en-scène. He painted the backdrops: numerous castles; a ball scene (painted dancers for my glammed-up Cinderella to stand in front of); the cotton wool 'clouds' through which 'Jack' (in these tableaux played by Clive himself) would climb to reach me, the giant; a dirty kitchen for my Cinders, in tattered rags, to scrub; a forest for my Hood; a cottage bedroom for my wolf. Clive also helped Sharon with the larger props; a great cardboard axe for the nasty giant and a long green beanstalk made from scraps of velvet Sharon had found lying about the Polytech, a big bed complete with enormous patchwork quilt for my wolf to lurk under, a hearth for my Cinders to scrape.

Clive's bed-sit proved too small to house many of the backdrops, so Sharon organised for the three of us to use a spare room out the back of the Polytech.

When it came time to play Snow White, Clive and Sharon knocked us up a nice looking glass coffin, three metres long by two wide. They wrapped me in a clean white sheet, laid me inside, and then lowered the lid down over me. I stared up through the glass like a fish peering through the wall of an aquarium, my hand on the cable-release, the black cord of which snaked out through a tiny gap where lid did not quite meet coffin, down by my feet. I was their gigantic dress-up doll, their anti-Barbie, their oversized trinket.

We sent our pics away to various magazines and galleries, angling for a bite. Me as the Beast made the cover of *Sharp Shootin'*; the shot of Clive's 'Jack' climbing his beanstalk up through the fluffy clouds to reach my ferocious giant was printed in *Line of Fire*. Somebody at the Lite Gallery saw the photo of me as Snow White and wrote back to us saying they weren't interested in hanging the print, but they were keen on a live installation.

Like those people who live for a week in a shop window, they said. *A girl like that, she'll really draw the crowds. She doesn't even have to do anything. She just has to lie there.*

I wasn't so keen on being displayed in this gallery that had housed work by Claudia Dean; was far from certain that this was the right place for me, but Sharon and Clive twisted my arm till I agreed. Clive took Vitra aside for a little chat, told him that, for the next three weeks, he'd have to photograph his model after dark, because her daylight hours were taken up with other activities. The webbed man was a little peeved, but soon came round to our way of thinking, after Clive threatened to quit if our wishes were not granted.

Three weeks as a statue; three weeks playing dead. They dressed me in a long white flowing gown, Mack paled my skin with foundation, made my face as white as snow, and they laid me out for all to see. Day after day, I remained perfectly immobile, eyes closed, lips unmoving. On the other side of the glass, the people filed past, their eyes staring in at the zoo animal. I made a change from the usual Lite fare; I was a good deal heavier then the usual exhibits housed there. Lager louts would stand above me and I would hear them daring each other to kiss me, daring each other to lift the lid and place a kiss on the lips of this Sleeping Ugly. Nobody ever took his mates up on the dare. Each evening, at six pm, after the gallery doors had been closed, somebody would lift the lid of my coffin and I would be let out, back to Augustus' cellar, often to put in a few hours as his model before retiring for the night.

It was Sharon who came up with the back from the dead joke. It was the kind of stunt you can try to pull only once. On the final day of the exhibit, a Sunday, when the hands of the clock read three pm, I rose again. The usual crowd surrounded me, staring in through the glass. One minute I was lying supine, as still as death, and the next, I came crashing up through the glass, like some oversized Lazarus, splinters of my coffin flying out every which way, slicing me, embedding themselves in my skin. Women screamed, men ran. It took Sharon ages to pick the splinters out. Shards and fragments. Glass and blood. The coffin behind me, ruined.

*

Three weeks after I had given my little performance as Snow White, my scientist chums tracked me down. One of them had attended the exhibition I had made of myself and had contacted the gallery owner, who'd contacted Clive, who'd given away my address, not knowing I was in hiding from my medical mates. I was posing, nude, with a couple of corpses when they came knocking on the door of the funeral parlour, walked straight in past Johnny the aged receptionist and found me. Theirs was a clinical kind of anger.

"There are gaps in your history now," they said. "We're very disappointed. We wanted to track this disease from beginning to end."

Augustus watched with open mouth as they swooped down upon me, hooked their claws in. Pried and prodded and peered. I was carrion. I was back in their white-coated clutches. They made up for lost time; they snipped at my skin and my hair, took away pieces of me, told me these visits, this little ritual, would now be conducted daily.

"Every morning," they said, "Eight am, you'd better be ready for us".

*

"Let's do Celia as a man," said Sharon one weekend, with her usual infectious enthusiasm, and so we did me with a fake moustache, my shock of white hair pulled back from my face, me in an enormous pin-striped suit, carrying a cane and looking just dandy. Me in a great big white safari suit and a khaki-coloured hat, me in breeches and suspenders, me in a curly white wig and the robes of a high court judge, me in a long black cassock, clutching the Holy Bible tight in my right hand.

We did me as a fifties housewife, apron on, holding an apple pie in one hand and a rolling pin in the other, smiling a satisfied smile. My own camera took me every time.

Another birthday, another Christmas, this one celebrated with Clive and Sharon, at Clive's Mum's house, with his mother hissing, *I told you not to bring that hussy round here,* within earshot of Sharon, and talk of his no-good Dad who'd flown the coop when Clive was an infant.

"Oh, don't go dragging those skeletons out of the closet, Mum," said Clive. "This is neither the time nor the place."

"You're lucky, Celia," said his Mum. "Girl like you ain't never gonna have no man troubles, 'cause a girl like you ain't never gonna have no man."

I'm sure she wasn't being intentionally cruel.

"As for you Clive," his mother continued. "It's high time you got yourself a little lady and settled down."

She looked Sharon up and down.

"Someone with a bit of a future ahead of them," she said. "Someone sensible."

Her tone implied that sensible was something Sharon most definitely was not. She was a vegetarian, for one thing, wasn't she and God only knew *that* wasn't natural, for what purpose did the good Lord give us canine teeth, if not to chew up animals with, what did he put animals on the planet *for* if not for humans to eat them? Decoration? She carved huge big hunks off the Christmas ham and waved them in front of Sharon's nose. Sharon seemed impervious; the words spoken by Clive's mother fell upon deaf ears. She helped herself to roast vegetables and fruit mince pies and an open bottle of sherry.

After that, my second Christmas dinner in the capital, was over, Clive's Mum plonked herself in front of the telly in order to watch the Queen's Christmas message; Clive and Sharon went back to Clive's bed-si;t and I went 'home' to find Augustus and Johnny drowning their sorrows in a bottle of bourbon, Augustus' little webbed feet tapping along to "Heartbreak Hotel", his mittenned hands clapping together, keeping the beat, while Johnny's head nodded in time. I made my way down to the cellar, to spend the rest of my Christmas developing shots of myself in drag disguise; those photos we had taken of Celia as a man were hung up on the wire.

*

We were quite a team, the three of us, Sharon, Clive and I. We used to gather together in Clive's bed-sit and pore over the photos that I had developed, discussing what it was we were intending to do next.

The team were together one Sunday, at three in the afternoon, with Clive's little fourteen inch TV switched on behind us, when I heard the smooth voice of a female TV presenter smoothly declaring, *And now it's time for 'Merlin's Magical Hour.'* My head jerked upright, as if strings extending out from the top of my skull had suddenly been pulled. The theme music began, tinkling and child-like, carousel music, and, sure enough, when I looked at the screen, I saw all the pretty little horses, bobbing up and down on their candy-striped poles, saw the platform revolving and, superimposed on top of the carousel, a transparent outline of Ed's face, looming like an overhead projection. The words *Merlin's Magical Hour* scrolled across the screen in flowing pink script, then the intro finished and we cut to a shot of Ed, standing in a studio, donning the same black overcoat I had seen him wearing on the occasion of our first meeting, that fateful day, at the Sphere. His glasses hung about his neck on a chain; he looked even thinner than usual, gaunt, more like a walking skeleton than a man of flesh and blood.

"Good afternoon," he said, smiling, looking directly into the camera with his piercing gaze. "And welcome to 'Merlin's Magical Hour'. Today I'm going to demonstrate a few simple card tricks. What you will need..."

Just in case anybody hadn't heard him, the words 'WHAT YOU WILL NEED' flashed up on the screen in the same pink flowing script that had been used for the introduction.

"A full deck," said Ed, producing a pack of playing cards from inside his coat and holding them out to the camera.

The words 'A FULL DECK' appeared beneath the earlier message.

"And nothing else," said Ed, with a grin.

The script disappeared.

"Now," this presenter continued. "Remember. Magic is all about making the eyes of your audience look one way, while the trick takes place in the other direction. The trick always takes place elsewhere. Just a small tip from me. Could I have a volunteer from our live studio audience, please?"

The camera shifted to a shot of the audience, children, mostly, with the odd adult sprinkled in amongst them. A small boy with blonde hair raised his hand in the air.

"Come on down, son," said Ed. "Step forwards and help Merlin with his magic."

The kid climbed down from his seat and made his way to where 'Merlin' stood.

"Now," said Ed, fanning out the pack of cards and extending it towards the boy. "I want you to pick a card, any card."

The boy picked a card from the deck.

"I did not see that card, did I?" Ed questioned the audience. "There's no way I could have seen that card."

Shots of the audience, shaking their heads. *No, Merlin, there's no way you could have seen that card.* You got the feeling that their response was scripted.

"Hold onto that card, then," said Ed to his volunteer. "It's yours. Don't give it back to me. Just hold it in your head. Picture it in your head, and I will prove to you that Merlin the magician has the power to read minds."

The kid was looking a bit bored.

"You got it clear in your head?" asked Ed.

The boy nodded.

"And to prove to you, that I can read minds, your card is…"

Pause of a single heartbeat.

"The Queen of Hearts."

The kid turned his card over, held it up to the camera. It was just as 'Merlin' had said it would be; the queen. The boy looked less than impressed.

"It's a trick," yelled somebody from the audience. "He's got a whole pack full of those red queens."

Ed was not flustered.

"Of course it's a trick," he said calmly. "But I have not deceived you in the manner that you have imagined. The camera may inspect my pack."

He fanned his deck again and held the cards face up to the camera.

"Lay them on the table," the heckler yelled, though you got the sense that this, too, had been scripted.

Ed walked across to a table which stood nearby and laid down his cards, all fifty-one of them that remained, all different, you could see them all, including the Joker, grinning his clownish grin.

"Add the queen back to the pack, son," said Ed to his assistant and handed the kid a lollipop.

Clive and Sharon had shifted their eyes away from my photos, shifted their minds away from talk of our next move and were staring, transfixed, at the telly.

"Who *is* that guy?" asked Sharon.

"Uncle Ed," I said.

"You're related?"

"Not a blood relative," I replied. "He's the brother of my adoptive mother."

She nodded.

"Cool," she said. "Cool."

We watched for a few minutes longer.

"Hey man," said Clive. "Do you think we could get some photos of him?"

"If you can find him," I said. "He's difficult to track down."

Clive was already a dedicated fan; *Merlin's Magical Hour* became one of our Sunday afternoon favourites. Clive made various attempts to track Ed's whereabouts, in order that we might do a series he proposed calling *Mug Shot Magic*, but the studio would reveal no details about 'Merlin'. They said his identity was protected. Clive made me take shots of his image as it appeared on the TV instead, but the photos didn't come out very well; too much static.

It felt like I was leading two separate lives; one with Vitra and one with Clive and Sharon. The three of us never seemed to tire of playing dress-ups. Sharon was a never-ending well of ideas. Kids' books were her next theme, a variant on the fairy tales we'd acted out earlier. We did *Charlie and the Chocolate Factory*, with me as all five children *(the five lucky winners of the golden ticket!)* I was Charlie Bucket, I was a big fat Augustus Gloop, I was Mike Teavee, I was Veruca Salt, and, last but not least, I was Violet. I was also a couple of oompa-loompas. We did various tableaux from *Alice In Wonderland*: me as Alice and Clive as the White Rabbit, me as the Mad Hatter, me as the Cheshire Cat, outside, up an oak tree, perched out on a branch we thought would be strong enough to hold me, grinning and grinning. From the best Cheshire shot I made nine prints, then gradually airbrushed myself away, a little bit more of me vanishing out of each shot, so that if you look at the Cheshire series, you will see me disappearing, fading out, till I become invisible, nothing but the faint trace of a smile, hanging in the air.

Clive was fascinated with Merlin.

"That guy's crazy," he would say, in admiring tones, as the televised Ed spun his head three hundred and sixty degrees or turned water into wine or, harking back to his more sinister tricks of old, disappeared a couple of children.

Clive's bed-sit was lined with shots I had taken of the televised 'Merlin'; he didn't care about the poor quality. Ed's show was beginning to increase in popularity and spin-off merchandise had been generated. The first and second Merlin series (which we had missed) were put out on video; Merlin t-shirts hit the shops, as did plastic Merlin dolls, toy wands and little black cloaks for the kids. Clive collected all of it; he was a true aficionado. Sharon demonstrated a slight jealous streak, and began making snide comments about Ed whenever we watched the show; although her relationship with Clive was purely platonic, I suspected she was developing a soft spot for her friend. She was not the kind of girl to wear her heart on her sleeve.

Clive went out and bought Merlin's first and second series and we watched them on video. I was beginning to worry about my uncle's health. He was unwell; when you watched the first two series in order, there was no mistaking his steady deterioration, his decline. He was growing gradually thinner, ever more pale and emaciated. Whenever he took off his coat (which he rarely did) you could see that he was skin and bone, no trace of muscle, not much in the way of flesh. He remained as hyperactive as he had always been, twitchy, as if somebody had their finger permanently pressed down on his fast-forward button.

*

The grannies still telephoned upon occasion; it was always heart-warming to hear their voices coming down the line. They never had much news to impart, they'd not usually been up to anything too exciting; Stuff just tapping about her house, conversing with her many dead pets, Lolly fighting with Grout and keeping up her sugar intake.

"Just called to say hello, dear," they'd cackle and I would fill them in on life in the capital, tell them all about the fun I was having with Clive and Sharon, always glossing over the degenerate 'work' in which I partook in order to pay for my keep.

"When're you coming home, dear?" Lolly would question. "We miss you awfully."

Stuff, by comparison, was encouraging me to stay right where I was. "Don't you come back till you feel you've drunk your fill," she'd advise. "Get yourself all the images you need, Our Celia. Remember; we're counting on you to represent the family."

I did my best. Me in my various guises met with limited success; a few more magazines, the odd space allocated on some gallery wall. I used to wonder what my shadow made of these pictures done in my own name, the same name she operated under; I used to wonder what she made of our little tableaux. Although there were two of us, it sometimes seemed that we were not separate, but the same, two halves of one whole, a pair of hands, she the left and I the right, both of us with something to add to the Doom name. Both of us with something to detract. Both of us giving, both of us taking away.

*

Ruby Minor wasn't warming to Sharon; her demeanour remained decidedly frosty. Sharon did nothing to endear herself to her friend's mother; she didn't seem to need to be liked. She would shrug off Ruby's rude manner, chalked it up to jealousy.

"She just feels threatened," she would say. "She thinks I'm trying to steal her son."

I'd recently noticed her 'making eyes' at Clive, but he didn't appear to be taking any notice of his friend's advances. I wondered if all her good ideas weren't just ways to try to impress him. The next concept was Sharon's, too. The idea struck her when we had hired a car to take us out to Periphery, a gallery situated on the edge of the city. Positioned to either side of the highway upon which we drove were looming billboards, boards covered in lingerie-clad women, women in various poses, reclining, or sitting or standing, and the advertising slogans above or beneath them, the names in our faces: Berlei, Bendon, Calvin Klein.

"We gotta get you up there, gal," said Sharon, peering through her passenger seat window.

The suggestion gave Clive such a fright that he slammed his foot on the brake and nearly caused a crash.

"Keep driving," said Sharon, looking out at the space where she was envisaging I would go. "Our Celia's gonna be right up there, with only the sky as a backdrop. "

I was stretched out on the back seat, my right shoulder pressed to the ceiling of the car. I struggled to see myself in these places at which she was pointing, failed to envisage myself upon a billboard, but Sharon couldn't stop talking about our new plans.

"You'll go up on top of them," she said. "Think of the implications."

I didn't know what she was talking about, but I nodded anyway.

It kept us occupied for three weeks. Sharon stitched me three new bras; said my old ones were far too tattered, far too torn. She sewed me several pairs of enormous black lace knickers and a couple of garter belts, never mind that my legs would never fit women's stockings, my garters would just have to hang down unattached. She whipped me up a colossal corset. *They're coming back in, Celia. You want to keep up with the times, don't you?* We visited her friend at the costume hire shop and walked away with a number of fine glossy wigs. We purchased a whole stack of women's magazines, and my poses mimicked those of the ladies displayed therein; I pouted and preened and placed myself before the artificial eye of the Leica. The mags we bought always included some little juicy tit-bit about Claudia Dean; shots of her frolicking in the Bahamas with her latest flame, shots of her attending the premier of some new flick which had just been released, photos of her relaxing in her beautiful home. Did she ever do any work?

*

Our labour seemed endless. We did one piece of me at a time, I developed the shots and then we ran them into a place downtown that specialised in colour copying; we enlarged them onto sheets of A3. They weren't such great quality, but Sharon said it wouldn't matter once we had me up on the board. On the floor of Clive's bed-sit, we put me together; placed the segments down side by side; a variety of scantily clad Celias. Personally, I thought the whole thing was going to be a little bit obvious, a little bit naff, a little bit *in your face*, but I said nothing.

We hired the same car again, went back out on the highway at midnight, the sheets of paper upon which I was printed stashed in the boot of the car, along with a bucket, a bottle of water, and a few packets of paste. Up I went; plastered over the other women, C.D, in saucy lingerie, the great rolls of me hovering there, in the sky. An item about the billboard was on the news the following night; they chalked up the work to a feminist activist group known as *Servants of Sappho*. They interviewed the group's spokeswoman; she took credit for the billboard, said they were attempting to make some sort of statement, though she didn't specify exactly what it was they were trying to say. We three didn't mind. We were just having a laugh, happy to have gone undetected.

Merlin's Magical Hour was still the highlight of every week. The theme music would play, and Clive would press his eyes up to the TV, mesmerised. It appeared that Ed had lulled the producers into a false sense of security only to sock them with his innate wildness. His tricks were taking a turn for the macabre. No longer was he content to be simply Merlin; he had to be other men besides. He always introduced himself.

"And now it's time for Iron Gut Ivan," 'Merlin' would declare.

The camera would cut to a shot of the audience and next time we saw the stage, Ed would be standing there in a suit of chain mail, as if his outsides provided some indication as to what was inside. He would proceed to swallow anything and everything he was given by audience members and by his 'assistant', a blonde dwarf who went by the name of Oscar. 'Ivan' ate spoons and knives and a couple of glass ashtrays. He swallowed an entire bag of marbles and he ate burning hot stones. He swallowed three swords, pushed them deep down into his gut then drew them out again. He ate six pens and several razor blades.

"His insides are gonna be totally sliced," Clive would say, a look of awe on his face.

The following week, Ed came onstage as Merlin and showed X-rays of Ivan's stomach; the outlines of the various objects he'd swallowed stood out clear. He left the stage, came back on as Ivan and added to the collection that was gathering inside him; he devoured shards of porcelain, a packet of drawing pins and an entire coin collection that had been brought in by an audience member. He swallowed boiling oil and molten lead.

Iron Gut Ivan consumed his indigestibles for three weeks running, and the following week he was somebody new.

"Boys and girls, allow me to introduce Sid the Tamer of Snakes," he declared, before exiting the stage, and reappearing clad in cowboy boots, a pair of tight, imitation snakeskin pants and a frilled shirt, with three black mambas draped around his neck. The audience recoiled in horror. The mambas were milked for venom, and then placed into a sack held open by to a terrified looking Oscar, who quickly scurried offstage with his bounty. The next guest appearance was made by a boa constrictor that came slithering onstage, to be grabbed by 'Sid' who wound the creature round himself, as if daring it to choke him. Tighter and tighter the snake curled around the body of its intended victim, until, when it seemed as if the creature could not constrict him any further, 'Sid' reduced himself to a pencil-thin shape, and slid out from within the creature's grasp. The snake was left, confused, still curled in spirals. Then, as if performing some sort of strange finale, it chomped down hard on its own tail and Oscar tentatively came onstage and carried it away. There were more reptiles waiting in the wings; Sid hissed at a cobra that was hissing at him, he rattled castanets at a rattlesnake, as if trying to beat these slithering serpents at their own game.

Then snake week was over. Ed's next trick was to set himself on fire; he doused himself in gasoline and then he struck the match. He didn't burn; the flames flickered on the surface of his skin and then dissolved.

"Is this guy even human?"

Ratings were on the rise; it didn't matter whether or not the show's producers liked what Ed was doing, 'cause the kids were sold. You saw them all over the city, wearing Merlin t-shirts, waving little plastic wands, singing the theme music. A line of Merlin clothing stores was set up. Called 'Merl', the stores specialised in 'smart casuals'; tidy jeans and brightly coloured tops, with perky store assistants who were programmed to greet you with 'Hi, Welcome to the World of Merl' the minute you walked through the door. You almost expected them to ask 'Would you like fries with that?' with every purchase. The stores popped up in each and every one of the malls I was so fond of perusing popped up like zits. Merlin was contagious. Merl stores stocked nothing that I would ever fit into, but I took the time to take some shots of their insides; the rows of neat garments, the clothing laid out on tables, with assistants rushing over to straighten any item a customer may have rumpled into a state of disarray. There were spin-off stores as well; Baby Merl and Merl Sport.

"He's a phenomenon," Clive would whisper, in hushed tones.

In the final episode of the third series, 'Merl' hacked off his own legs with a chainsaw and then miraculously reattached them to his body. Clive shook his head in disbelief and went out to buy himself and Sharon another Merl T-shirt each.

*

During the eighteen month hiatus between the third and fourth series, the Merl merchandise was hit with something of a scandal. It was discovered that the goods were being manufactured in sweatshops throughout Asia and that the entire weekly wages of a worker in one of the Merl factories were equal to the price of one kids' cloak. Clive stuck up for his hero.

"Oh come on," he said. "What's he meant to do? If it's the cheapest form of labour, then it makes smart business sense. Truth be told he's probably doing those workers a favour in employing them at all. If it wasn't for Merl they'd be back in some decrepit village that lacks running water, out in the fields, labouring, mucking about in the dirt. "

"Exploitation's bloody exploitation," said Sharon. "How would you like it? Stuck in front of some machine, day after day, seventy hours a week, just to survive, the deafening racket from the other machines, away from your family and friends, thrust into some cold, hard city."

"If they don't like it they should leave," said Clive, matter of factly and Sharon scoffed.

"You complain enough about the funeral parlour," she said. "*You'd* never deal with a sweat shop, so why do you expect them to put up with it."

There were protests; picketing outside the Merlin stores, but the Merl empire did not seem to be relenting.

When the fourth Merl series started up, not only had ratings dropped considerably, but the response from the studio audience was decidedly lukewarm. No longer did they greet his entrance onstage with hearty cheers and cries of enthusiasm; now they booed and jeered and one or two threw mushy fruit. Merl tried to put a brave face on things, but it was a sad débacle. He must have known he was on the out.

*

His final show? He went out in grand style. Could he have known that this show was to be his last? Was it possible that Ed could have foreseen his own death? This we know; he was out to break world records. Three weeks after he set himself on fire, Ed played King of Bees. Onstage, a glass enclosure was filled with an angry swarm. The audience looked uneasy. When Ed walked into the shot, his entrance was not greeted with the jeers that had become customary, but with a cautious silence. He wore no protective clothing; he carried no placatory smoke.

"Ladies and gentlemen," he said, "I give you the King of the Bees."

Oscar scurried onstage and opened the door to the hothouse. A few rogue bees escaped and buzzed out into the audience, to be swatted by angry Mums and scared children. Ed stepped inside the cage; the door was slammed behind him.

How did he do it? They crawled all over him, they buzzed all around him, but they did not sting.

"It's like he's protected by some kind of invisible force field," said Clive.

Sharon scoffed in scorn.

For six full minutes we watched as Ed stood inside his glasshouse with the little winged demons all around. Outside the glasshouse, Oscar stood looking at his watch.

"Out to beat the world record. Will he make nine minutes in this glasshouse, swarmed by three hundred thousand bees?" Oscar boomed.

A giant clock hung on the wall behind the audience; we all watched the hands creep round, three minutes, four, time ticking steadily on. He made the full time. Nine whole minutes inside with the bees and then Oscar opened the door and the audience began to applaud loudly, a standing ovation, louder, applauding even when the king crumpled and fell to the floor, applauding as he clutched his chest. Applauding as he died.

Clive and Sharon started laughing. They thought he was clowning about. They had no idea that, for Ed, for Merlin, for Motor Mouth McGee, for Iron Gut Ivan, for all the other men he was, this was the end of the line. Not from any bee-sting, but from one of those faulty hearts that are so ubiquitous in this tale of my life on earth.

I knew the truth and was frozen. I had seen the life go out of him; seen his spirit leave earth, leaving his body behind.

His death was screened on a million TV sets. No private final moment for Our Ed, he made a show of his life and he made a show of his death.

His death was simulcast.

XXIII

Splat. A lump of red paint went flying past Arty's ear and landed in the middle of a canvass which was positioned against the far wall. Angie reached around behind her again and grabbed another handful of gloop from the tin. Arty ducked. *Splat.* This lot landed half on the canvass and half on the wall. Angie spoke one word with every handful of paint she hurled.

'*Just*'
'*Because*'
'*Celia's*'
She changed colour; from red paint to gold.
'*Everywhere*'
'*Doesn't*'
'*Mean*'
Another colour change, this time to a lurid shade of lime green.
'*I*'
'*Should*'
'*Be*'
Change to black paint.
'*Nowhere.*'
"Honey, calm down. She's not everywhere. Far from it."

Arty ventured across to rest his left hand on his wife's shoulder. Oh for the glory days of porn and ice cream and nothing to do but wallow. The days of deviance and deception. Ever since he'd been busted life had been a lot harder for Arty to handle, and, more and more frequently, he was beginning to think that the root of his troubles was his wife. Everything else was splendid. The cash was mounting up in the bank, he'd finally found meaningful employment as agent to the mythical Doom, and, of course, he got a very big kick out of the feeling that he was pulling the wool over the eyes of the public. But if she didn't learn to curb this tantrum throwing business, that silly wife of his was going to find herself up a certain creek without a certain paddle, for the woman doing the dirty work, the woman out there on the front line taking the actual imitation shots was a contact of his. Nobody knew her name except him, nobody else knew how to find her. Ultimately, he told himself, he was the mastermind behind this whole enterprise known informally as The Great Doom Scam; Angie was dispensable, she needed him, thought Arty, in a way that he didn't need her. He was the manipulator, he knew what photos to take and where to send them away to and when, he had all the right lines to give to the press. He was the manager and the publicity guy rolled into one. He was great at his job. He dreamed of having the courage to leave, to go it alone. But for now, he was stuck with Angie as partner in crime and all he wanted, for the moment, was to bring his wife down to a state of calm.

"Don't you understand, sugar? We are Celia Doom. Think of her as your alter ego."

There was a brief respite from the paint hurling.

"What, that fat ugly retard? An alter ego of mine? You've gotta be bloody kidding."

She turned to a tin of turquoise paint.

"Alright then. Think of her as a puppet we've made and now have the ability to manipulate. There is no real Celia Doom. She's just a gimmick to suck in the gullible public."

"There's a great big ugly freak somewhere who's gonna be mighty peeved when she realises what we've done."

"But that's the brilliant thing. She can't blow our cover. Without us, she's nothing. We made her."

To Angie, it seemed that there was a fault in her husband's reasoning somewhere, she just couldn't pinpoint where. All she knew was that ever since they'd started up with this imitation Doom lark her own work had been shunted offstage, into the wings, where it waited, flapping uselessly. Nobody wanted to exhibit her anymore; she couldn't find a wall to hang herself on.

And now she was reduced to this, yelling at her husband, throwing handfuls of paint, as the resentment she felt towards Celia bloomed and blossomed in her chest, and the frustration she felt at being ignored vented itself, as Angie's emotions usually did, through one of these childish tantrums.

Arty left her to it. He wandered off to the kitchen and made himself a coffee, walked out into the back garden. Later, when she'd worn herself down to a faded frazzle, he would tuck her into bed with a cup of hot soup and a few reassuring words, "There, there, darling, it's alright," and then he'd slip downstairs for a hot date with Lucinda Luscious Fortune. The hum of the video player, her face, her body upon the screen, the way she moaned and writhed that he found so exciting. Half a world away from the way she acted when off the screen. When she wasn't being filmed.

So different to the way she was in real life. In real life she was a Sensible Girl, she wore jeans and T-shirts, mostly, and tied her hair back in a pony-tail. It was another kind of disguise. You'd never know it was the same person. Except for the dark glasses, which he had never seen her without. They may as well have been glued to her face. She could switch the whole Porn Queen act on and off like a light; she could glow incandescent, or she could wear this dull librarian-style façade which served to keep the world at bay more effectively than any bodyguard ever could. Kind of like Wonder Woman, thought Arty to himself, sculling the dregs of his coffee, venturing back inside to see if the storm had passed.

In the house, Angie now lay collapsed upon the sofa, the odd, single tear streaking its way down her face. She held her arms up to him for a hug, like an infant. He obliged, putting on the baby voice he reserved for such occasions.

"Does muffin want some soup?"

She nodded, woefully, as he had known she would.

"Pumpkin or tomato?"

She shrugged. Either. I don't mind. I'm easy to please now. I'm sorry. He looked across at the far wall. Paint everywhere. Ridiculous. His wife wore the expression of a puppy that has just wet the carpet, but Arty knew better than to rub her nose in it. He moved back through into the kitchen, opened a can of Heinz tomato soup, plonked it into a saucepan and added milk. Poured it into her favourite mug, the one with her name written on the side. Strange how that had never been smashed. Strange how mostly it was his possessions, his belongings which she destroyed when in the grip of one of her fits. He tested the soup to check it wasn't too hot. Wouldn't want the little darling to burn her mouth. When he walked through with the soup she was feebly scraping up the paint with an old spatula, attempting to put it back in the tin, leaving streaks over everything; the furniture, the carpet, the walls.

"Don't worry love," he said. "It's only a silly old house. I'll do my best to clean it up after you've gone to bed."

She burst into tears. He handed her the soup.

Soon, he thought, she'll be out of my hair.

Soon, I'll keep my date with Lucinda.

Soon, I'll be with the goddess.

XXIV

Only two things are certain in this life. Death and taxes. Or death and change, depending on who you're talking to. Death is the constant. The other is the variable. Certain death. The one thing we can all count on facing, at some time or another.

It was Lolly who called to tell me to come home, said it was a matter of urgency.

"There's been a death, dear," she said.

She didn't say whose. She didn't need to speak the name.

"And there's a lovely lawyer here who needs a word with you."

Byson, that would be. Provencia's *only* lawyer.

"He wants you to call him, dear. To set up an appointment."

She gave me the number.

"And you will come stay with *me*, won't you. Instead of that *other* grandmother of yours."

I thought of Grout and of the stench of urine.

"Can't promise anything, Lolly," I said. "We'll see how things pan out."

I called up Byson as Lolly had instructed. He answered the phone on the second ring.

"Byson, Barrett, Hoggs and Willocks. Can I help you?"

Who was he trying to kid? He and I both knew that there was no Barrett, no Hoggs, and no Willocks. Nor was there a secretary or a receptionist. There was simply him, Byson, in an empty building; the lone lawyer.

"It's Celia Doom," I said. "You've been expecting my call?"

"Ah yes, Ms Doom," said the voice on the other end of the line.   "I've been in touch with your grandmother."

"I know."

"You'll need to make an appointment. I have some news for you, Ms Doom. Mixed news. I'm fairly busy but I may be able to squeeze you in later on in the week. Why don't I transfer you through to my secretary and she can book you in."

I hesitated, then decided to humour him.

"Sure," I said.

There was a pause, a click, and then Byson came on the line again, speaking in a terrible falsetto tone.

"Can I be of assistance?"

"Could I make an appointment for Thursday, please?"

"Name?"

"Celia Doom."

"Certainly, Ms Doom," squeaked Byson. "Just let me check Mr Byson's diary."

A rustling of paper.

"He's a very busy man, Ms Doom. But let me see...we might just be able to squeeze you in on Thursday at say...midday? Would that suit?"

"That's fine," I said. "Done."

I phoned up Stuff to ask if I could stay in her spare bedroom.

"Just for a bit, Gran," I said. "Just till we see what this lawyer has to say."

I let Lolly down easy.

"It's Grout, Lolly," I said. "I just don't think I could put up with her, day after day."

Little white lies never hurt anybody.

*

I took everything I owned with me, just in case I did not care to return. I thanked Augustus for his hospitality, and Clive and Sharon for their companionship. Clive, Sharon and Mack held a small farewell party in Clive's bedsit, though Clive was a little down at the mouth, having just witnessed the death of his idol on national TV. Nevertheless, they wished me well for the future; Clive copied out the list of potential 'targets' he had made and pressed it into my hands; galleries and magazines who might be interested in work by C.D. As a farewell present, Sharon gave me the wolf costume I had worn in one of our Big Red Riding Hood tableaux, and said I could keep the bras she had sewn. Augustus began to snivel as I was leaving.

"But Celia! We've left so much undone!"

"All good things must come to an end," I muttered, as I headed for the door, my suitcase in my hand.

I was the only passenger on the bus back to Provencia. It pulled out from the station at five in the morning, in order that it might be in my beloved city by eight, to pick up those who were still needing to get out. We drove through the dark, that driver and I, up and over the mountains; outside, blackness all around me like a blanket; inside, the dim lights of the bus, my only illumination. I did not know whether this return was to be permanent or temporary; all I knew was that I had been summoned. My reflection in the window loomed back at me; my large ugly mug, as round and as white as a full moon. As we snaked our way down on the other side of the mountains, the sky lit up with a dull glow; dawn was creeping in.

When we pulled into my old city I could see by the light of the flickering lamps that the process of decay which had begun the day Jacob bombed the Butchette was in its final throes. Disintegration had obviously been taking place at an exponential rate. The city was a shadow of its former self; everything had emptied out, leaving only a husk. Winter was upon us; there was an unearthly quiet pervading the once bustling streets, as if a bone-chilling wind had whipped through, sweeping up every living thing, and leaving behind only a carapace. Now and then I would catch glimpses of life; a face at a window, a body moving in a park. These figures seemed but flickering ghosts haunting some city of the dead.

The bus deposited me on the edge of the city's hole, leaving me to walk across the bridge, down Stuff's street to her home. *Tap, tap, tap.* Never had her tapping sounded so good, so welcoming.

Granny!

Darling!

Her blind eyes saved her from my terrible face. We embraced and she ushered me inside.

She'd made up the spare room for me, covered the bed in an elaborate patchwork quilt, sprinkled everything with lavender water, laid a moth-eaten stuffed squirrel and an old mouldy rabbit on my pillow.

In case you're wanting for company, love.

I lay down on the bed that she had made, lay down on my stomach, with my hunch rising up towards the ceiling. Stuff left the room and I was out like a light.

I awoke to a snowfall. I rose from my bed, pulled back the curtains, saw nothing but a blanket of blankness, stretching out before me like an unwritten page. As if sleepwalking, I moved to the sliding door that led to Stuff's back lawn, stepped out, walked across the snow to her back fence, the tracks behind me, words on a page. I didn't feel the cold; I felt numb myself, frozen.

"Celia? Celia?"

Stuff was calling my name from the house.

"You're awake, darling. Come on in and have some breakfast."

I made my way back to the house, sat down to a Stuff-style fry-up. Outside winter rapped at the panes with its icy fingers, like the big bad wolf trying to make his way inside.

*

It felt slightly awkward, living there with Stuff. I had a sense of non-belonging, as if I was drifting about, just waiting to take up residence in a home which I could call my own. The glass eyes of the animals stared down from every shelf; Stuff's blind eyes peered out from her head. She'd adapted remarkably well to her blindness and moved about her house like a woman with 20/20 vision, never knocking into doors or walls; it was as if she'd developed some special kind of sonar. I felt uncomfortable here; I didn't belong. I fingered the key which hung about my neck; any day now, I thought, I can return to that old family home, find a way to take care of myself. Clive had instilled confidence in me; genuine Dooms would find their rightful place.

Only shreds of our city remained. On my third day back in Provencia I began shooting the desolation; Stuff was right, I saw it with fresh eyes, having been away. The snow which had fallen had turned to ice, a thin sheet of it, across which I went slipping and sliding. It looked new to me now; I saw it as a foreigner would. I wandered down Third Street, number thirty-three was still there, paint peeling off its old weatherboard exterior, the grass in the yard three feet high, the shrubbery wild and overgrown, all our old fruit trees still standing, just the same as they had always stood. I could envisage myself living there now; I could see myself returning and casting out the old ghosts.

On the afternoon of that third day back, I called round to see Lolly and Grout, I knocked and knocked, but there was no reply. I took the path which led round to the rear of Lolly's house, let myself in through the rear door and found the two of them seated at Lolly's kitchen table engaged in a game of Scrabble. Neither woman looked up from the game. A roaring fire blazed in the hearth.

"It's me," I said. "I'm back."

"You'll have to excuse us for a minute, Celia," said Lolly. "Things are getting quite heated here. I'll be with you shortly."

The score sheet read: Lolly 103, Grout 105. I remained standing, from which vantage point I could see the letters each had at their disposal; each had helped herself to far more than the customary seven; Lolly appeared to have about fifteen, Grout had at least twenty.

"We make our own rules," hissed Grout, when she sensed me staring at her letters.

Neither woman had yet looked up at my face. Their eyes were on the board. Lolly laid down zygote. Grout laid down Quechua.

"What's that?" asked Lolly.

"Native South Americans," said Grout. "Live in the Andes."

Lolly grabbed the dictionary that sat by her right hand and looked up the word.

"No proper nouns," she said and booted Grout under the table. Grout booted her back, then snatched her letters back off the board and laid down queech instead.

"Queech," screeched Lolly. "What's a queech?"

"Exotic species of bird," said Grout. "Lives in the Andes with the Quechuas" and, before Lolly could check the truth, or otherwise, of her words, she snatched up the dictionary and threw it onto the flames that flickered in the hearth. In retribution, Lolly upended the scrabble board; the black letters on their little white plastic squares went flying across the room. Amongst the orange flames, the thin pages of the dictionary combusted, the words reaching heaven via Lolly's old brick chimney.

"I guess that's that, then," said Grout, and stomped off to another room.

Lolly looked directly at me for the first time since my arrival.

"Oh my Gawd," said Lolly, when she saw my face. "What happened to your cover, love?"

"Vitra took it," I replied.

"No wonder Lettie encouraged you to hide."

I nodded.

"I know," I said. "It's grim."

My grandmother averted her eyes.

"I'm very sorry about Ed, Lolly," I said, handing her an *In Sympathy* card I had picked up on the way over.

A morose expression fell across her face.

"Didn't amount to much in the end, did he," she said. "Despite the high hopes I once had for him."

"Oh, he did alright for himself," I said. "Had his own TV show."

"Silly lot of shite that it was," said Lolly. "Killed him in the end, too. Imagine. My son, dying in public like that. Shameful."

"I doubt it was the show that knocked him off," I said. "His health can't have been too good."

"Dunno what did him in," she said, chewing on a mouthful of sweeties. "But he didn't inherit his old Mum's tenacity, did he?"

She wheeled herself across to the fire to watch the last pages of her dictionary burning down to ash, burning down to cinders.

"Some of us live long, Celia," she said. "And some of us live short. You just gotta make the best of the time you got."

I left Granny Sage to her musings, went home to Stuff and her lavender water, Stuff and her many dead pets.

*

Thursday rolled around. I had a certain man to meet.

I was late. Byson was struggling along in a dilapidated old building, he's as run down as the rest of us. He didn't answer when I rang the doorbell, so I took it upon myself to open the door and squeeze my flesh through the doorframe. I called his name down the empty hallway.

"Mr Byson?"

No reply.

"Mr Byson?"

I walked down the hall to the first open door. There he was, behind an oak desk, his qualifications framed upon the wall, a name-plate perched upon his desk. He was a greying man in his mid-fifties, dressed in what appeared to be a smart navy blue suit, till you saw the patches on the elbows. He was on the telephone. Acting the part.

"My view is that the ECO will prefer not to be bothered with these names and forms as the QM community clearly stated that these names are not part of their target market anymore. In my opinion, it's the business that needs to sign off as we have the contacts with those clients and as per Mr Marker's earlier message, the business assumes the responsibility for them."

I walked across, took the phone from him gently, held the receiver to my ear. There was nobody on the other end of the line.

He looked a little sheepish. Ah, we cling to our old roles when the world around us falls. Byson grasped at his lawyer's mask.

"Ms Doom, I presume," he said, rising to his feet and extending his right hand. "I've been expecting you."

"The one and only."

He gestured towards one of his chairs and then hesitated when it became obvious I was not going to fit in either of them.

"It's okay," I said. "I'll stand."

I remained, stooped, in one corner of the room while he took a seat back behind his desk. Somewhere nearby, somebody was playing *The Great Pretender*; the song drifted in through the open window.

"It's regarding a Mr Edward Major, Ms Doom"

"Thought it would be," I muttered under my breath.

"To cut straight to the chase, Ms Doom, I have some good news and some bad news. The bad news is that Mr Major passed away last week."

"I know," I said, perhaps a little heartlessly. "Everyone knows. The only question is *why* did he die? He wasn't that old."

"Heart attack. I hate to be the one to tell you this, but your uncle had quite a soft spot for amphetamines, prolonged abuse of which can put quite a stress on the old ticker. The coroner's verdict was that it was Mr Major's addiction to the use of such drugs that was to blame for his untimely demise. His insides aged more quickly than his outside."

"Ed was a speed freak?"

"It appears so."

I attempted to take this in.

"And what's the good news," I asked, eventually.

"The good news is that you've come into a bit of a windfall."

"A windfall?"

"He's left you everything."

"Everything? What's everything?"

"The Merl stores. A percentage of sales of all Merl merchandise. Rights to the series. Need I go on? Let's just say you're set for life."

I steadied myself against the wall.

Byson cleared his throat.

"There is other *ahem* income. I am told by certain sources that Mr Major was involved in…"

He paused.

"In what?"

"The porn trade."

"The *porn trade?* My Uncle Ed?"

He coughed again, nervously.

"Your Uncle? Is that what he told you?"

I nodded.

"Oh no, Celia. Edward Major was your father."

He handed me an unopened envelope with my name penned on the outside.

"He left this for you, along with his fortune."

"Hang on," I said. "Just hang on a minute here, Mr Byson. Ed can't have been my father. Well he doesn't look anything like me, for a start."

"Does *anyone* look anything like you?"

He had a point there. My confusion was turning to anger.

"Why didn't he tell me?"

Byson pointed to the envelope. "Perhaps you'll find some answers in there. I'll leave you alone, for a minute, to have a read and collect your thoughts."

I ripped open the envelope and took out the note that was kept inside.

Dear Celia,

I don't know how I should begin. I know that I owe you an explanation, but it's hard for me to write one which doesn't sound like a soap opera. If I slide down through the register into melodramatic tones, please forgive me. Please don't think I never loved you Celia. It wasn't that I didn't want to raise you as my own. I hate to pass the blame, but it was your mother who wanted to be rid of you and I did not feel that I could raise you alone. I knew that Lettie had always wanted children and would be able to provide you with some stability. My sister knew nothing of your origins, did not recognise you as a blood relative. Lolly is also ignorant of the truth. Please forgive me my silly magician's ruse. It was a way I felt I could keep close to you without arousing your suspicions regarding your paternity. I hope the gift of the camera went some way towards assuaging the pain of being an orphan. Please do not think badly of your father. I hope that what I have

given you in death helps to make up for what I could not give you in life.
Blessed are the cracked for they shall let in the light.
Your loving Dad,
Ed.

*

I folded the note and slipped it into my pocket. Byson re-entered the room.

"Life sometimes throws us the strangest things, does it not, Ms Doom?"

"My life," I reply, "has mimicked a bad novel."

He gave a wry chuckle.

"Well, truth is stranger than fiction, as the old cliché goes. I must say," he added. "You're remarkably calm considering the knowledge which has just been imparted to you."

"It's a façade," I coolly replied. "I'm a hurricane on the inside. There's just one question, Mr Byson, remaining in my mind."

"What's that?"

"Who the hell was my mother?"

He shrugged. He knew nothing.

*

It was time to return to the family home. Enough time had passed that the majority of my ghosts had been laid to rest. I inserted the key into the lock of my old front door. It turned with a click. Inside, everything was covered in dust. It rose up from the carpet in small puffs as I walked, it lay in a thick coat upon every piece of furniture, it clogged my lungs, tickled my nose and irritated my eyes. I slept, that night, not down in the cellar, but in one of the spare rooms upstairs, though I doubt you could call it sleep, for I sneezed myself awake every five minutes. In the morning I vacuumed the whole place, dusted every surface, mopped every floor, a good spring clean, you might say, though outside my window, winter was setting in with a vengeance. I was alone in the home which belonged to me.

XXV

The last third of my life was a bit of a non-event. I had made it to the finishing line and now I was just hanging around, waiting to be told that it was time to make my big exit. I was a twenty-one year old recluse with a ghost at her elbow and a great pile of cash in the bank. Some wanted me to leave the country, go and take pictures of faraway places, bring them home like trophies, like the heads of hunted animals. Some said I was wasting away, back in that house, back in that city, but I was happy enough. It felt like home. I was something of a national institution; I was too old, I said, to go roaming about the planet like a restless spirit. Home is where the heart is, I said, my heart is right here, in this little suburban bungalow, on its quarter-acre section, in this half-dead city of ghosts. I'd had all the life experience I wanted; I was more than content to retire quietly in order to photograph the dying city, to chat to my ghost and to anybody else who happened to swing by the house.

My usual visitors began to pay homage; the same doctors who'd plagued me all my life started showing up at the door in their clinical coats, pale masks across their faces.

Genuine Doom works began to find slow acceptance in the capital, chiefly thanks to the success of the many fakes that Arty had sent into orbit, partially thanks to Clive, who had found a small niche for the shots of me playing dress-ups. I sent a few of the pics I had been taking on my citywide walks to one of the magazines that had previously printed a couple of photos snapped by my shadow; they did a spread entitled *Doomsday* and I was subsequently approached by one of the more decrepit galleries in the capital to send in more photos for an exhibition.

Miracles amaze me; this was a small island of acceptance in an island of disdain. I complied. For them, I did a special series entitled *Inhabiting Forgotten Spaces*, which concentrated on those who had moved into the areas everybody else had moved out of; the bums, the hippies, the vagrants; old men and women with no teeth clutching bottles of spirits with both hands, young men with their grey overcoats wrapped tightly around themselves, as if shutting out more than just the cold; skinny women, some of them holding babies or young children. The hippies next door obliged with a few provocative poses. Nobody seemed to realise that there were two of us; me and my shadow, my other and I.

Citizens of our enemy city devoured these pictures of down-and-out Provencia with hungry eyes, it made them feel better about their own lot, *Isn't it terrible*, they said, as they turned the pages of another magazine, as their eager eyes took in the walls of some gallery or other. *I don't know how they live like that.* And the thought behind it was, *Thank God it's them and not me.*

A couple of journalists turned up for an interview, with a photographer who got the hump when I refused to let him take my picture. They pried me for facts about my life, I gave them two-word answers and they took this as a license to fill in the blanks, to invent what I had not told them. *It Wasn't All Doom and Gloom*, said the article the next day, a write-up which tracked the ups and the downs of my life, with a liberal dose of exaggeration and a few creative liberties; 'a rollercoaster' they called it, which I suppose was a fair enough comment, although the swings were not as violent as they had chosen to depict. They called me 'Documenter of the Desolate,' 'Shooter of Suburban Slums,' 'Photographer of the Forgotten.'

*

Arty and Angie had cleared out of their old place; they bought a home in the capital, no doubt the cash that they earned selling imitations of my pictures had allowed them to do so. It was said that they had the largest collection of Dooms in the country and that the collection was growing every month. The cheeky bastards were claiming to have a collection of 'old Doom' a.k.a. 'early Doom'; they were taking new shots and back-dating them. Nothing they said was mine had been done by me. They were also claiming to have some of the newest work, from Doom's return to Provencia. This made me feel uneasy; the other photographer was still out there, attempting to do what I had done, taking my pictures, forging my name. This was my dark shadow, my double in a life filled with triples. I used to fantasize about catching this person in the act, in their darkroom, maybe, while Doom-like shots came shivering into view in the developer, or while they sat at a table, signing my name with their pen. They would not be expecting me; it would be dark outside and raining. I would enter without knocking. I would throw open the door, squeeze myself through the door frame and loom over them, an enormous avenging angel. I would not need to speak. The sight of me would be enough to make them squeal and cower. Fear would enter their heart (I was not sure what I would do if it didn't.) Their camera would be lying conveniently next to them on the table. I would grab it, smash it up, despite their feverish apologies that they would, by then, be muttering.

There can be only one Celia Doom, I would say. *There's not space here for two of us. So one of us has gotta go.*

I would take out my little pearl-handled revolver and wave it about a bit. And then I would exit, having instilled sufficient awe in my double that they would never dare take another Doom again.

Or else I would meet them one night upon some dark city street, like meeting your fate. I would turn a corner and there my shadow would stand, camera raised to eye, photographing exactly the same hobo I had photographed the week before.

Oi, I would shout, *take your own shots. Stop stealing.*

And the shadow would scarper, frightened, sufficiently deterred.

In these dreams, my shadow is genderless, faceless and nameless, just a dark presence in the shape of a person, like a cut-out made from black cardboard. And, of course, this goes without saying; my double is always smaller than me.

Please note: these dreams of instilling fear into the heart of the enemy were in direct contrast to my real actions. In real life I was a coward, a pussycat, too scared to blow the whistle in case my name went shooting down in flames, in case I dragged myself down into the mud along with my imitator. And frightened, also, that I would not be believed, that my claims would be dismissed as just another daft theory from that crackpot Celia. And in refusing to tell the truth, I was, I suppose, complicit in the lie that was being perpetrated.

I did meet my shadow eventually; she and I came face to face. But by then I was no longer angry. By then I was resigned.

*

I attended Ed's funeral. I thought I should, being his only beneficiary. It was held here in Provencia, Ed's home town. I wore a black tracksuit and a hat with a diaphanous veil. I had been asked to give a small speech, but I declined the offer. Never was much of a one for public speaking. I stood solemnly in the church aisle, too large to squeeze in and take a pew, hands clasped in front of me, eyes to the floor as the Reverend said his piece. No mention of the speed, no mention of the porn career, though the church was packed out with his X-rated buddies; I looked out across a veritable sea of buffed bodies, dyed hair and PVC clothing.

Lolly was there, with her nurse, a bewildered gaze upon her face as she took in the other mourners. Ed's profession had obviously been kept a lifelong secret from his Mum. She knew about the magic though.   There was a party afterwards, held on a stretch of lawn to the rear of the church, more like a University piss-up than a wake. Lolly's nurse wheeled her charge quickly away, shunted her into the back of a hatchback to drive her home. I ambled tentatively across to the gathering of porn kids, heard them whispering about me, *his daughter, sprung from his loins*. I loitered on the outskirts, near the snacks table, not daring to talk to anybody, feeling myself shrink inside my body, a deflating rubber doll.

A blonde woman caught my eye, stared at me. I could see her arguing with herself. Should she talk to me or leave me alone? With both hands, I grabbed at a plate of hors d'oeuvres. She headed in my direction.

"You're Celia?"

"The one and only," I replied.

"Daughter of the marvellous, frightening, Ed."

"So it would seem."

"Lucinda Fortune."

She held out her hand, and then lowered it again when she saw my own hands were full of party snacks.

"Oh Celia," she said "Sometimes your father was brilliant and sometimes he was as mad as a maggot. A wild imagination when it came to the porn. A porn genius, even, maybe. Oh, he often got it wrong. The bestiality scenes would go amuck or he would leave gaping holes in the plot (not that I suppose many of the viewers would actually have noticed and not that there ever was much of a plot to start with) or he would do foul things like drenching the actors in tomato sauce before the shoot, as if he thought this would somehow make the scenes more erotic. But when he got it right, Celia, oh, you just couldn't beat him at the game. He was King. He was wasted in the porn industry, he really was. A magical mind. Maybe that's why he did the magic tricks, Celia. A boredom buster. He always had to have something to do. And an antidote, I suppose, to what some call the impurity of the porn industry. A kind of cleansing. I don't know. I guess we can only speculate. The shows, the spin-offs. He had to sell the world. He was a true artist, your Dad."

"Yea," I scoffed. "A bullshit artist."

I was feeling resentful at having been deceived by my own father for so many years.

"And what about that TV show," I said. "Surely it was inappropriate for a porn king to be working around kids."

"You didn't know your Dad like I did, Celia. Half his heart was as pure as snow and the other half was as black as night. The pure half of him ran that show. Ed had one of those *rampant* minds, Celia. If he struggled to control it, it would just rebel all the more. I guess the excessive speed consumption didn't help matters."

"I guess not," I said wryly.

"He loved that Merl series," she said. "He drove across to the capital every week, just to do that show. Back the next day for filming."

She stopped, stared at me. Did she want to say something else?

"Celia?"

"What?"

"Nothing."

Pause.

"Celia?"

"What?"

"Nothing."

Pause.

"I guess I'll leave you to it then," she said, looking down at my hands which were still full of hors d'oeuvres. "Let you get on with your lunch."

*

And the years ticked slowly on, dragging me with them. I still took photos, as I always had, as I always would. But something had changed. I was not the girl that I had been before. I was wealthy. Ed's home was located in one of the more affluent parts of the capital and fetched quite a sum when I put it up for sale. My account balance had hit the six figure mark and was not far off the seven. Following Merl's death the show had been pulled off the air, but the videos of the three series he'd made were selling as well as ever, as was the spin-off merchandise. I closed the 'Merl' stores down; I wasn't going to have the exploitation of the sweatshop workers on my conscience. Merl merchandise has subsequently become something of a collector's item, and clothing bearing the Merl logo is now considered retro.

I had no real complaints, as I slid through my third decade on earth. I was living the kind of existence I'd always longed for. I was independent, I did not want for money and my pictures were still in demand. I finally had the money to create the kind of house I'd always dreamed of. These walls, these ceilings, these floors; I could do with them whatever I wanted. I chose expansion. I paid three local builders, who were eternally grateful for the employment, to come and work their magic with the old family home. I took out several inner walls and the entire second storey and made three gigantic Celia-sized rooms; a living-room, a bedroom and then the extra room out the front. We extended the rear of the house into the backyard, and tacked a kitchen and a bathroom on there. The attic was then extended upwards; extra storage space. For once I could move comfortably; I felt the hunch on my right shoulder stretch and expand in accordance with the new space it had been granted. It clicked and creaked, as if about to unfurl, finally, and become one glorious, brightly-coloured wing.

I employed a couple of local potters to make me a complete oversized dinner set, gave an enterprising electrician the job of knocking up a few enormous household appliances; a vacuum cleaner, a toaster, a kettle, three lamps. A local carpenter was allocated the chore of whipping up some Celia furniture: a bed, a chest of drawers, a wardrobe, a sofa, a few chairs and three tables. I paid them all well; I had cash to burn. For the first time in my life, I felt truly at home.

*

Two or three years after I had returned to Provencia, I noticed that other imitators were beginning to leap aboard the Doom bandwagon. Their crimes were a little different from those of my mysterious double. They signed their own name to their pictures, they only stole ideas. Many of them copied the Doom fissure, the hairline crack running across most of my photos. They drew it on afterwards or they threw their cameras to the ground and prayed their lenses would break in the right way. Shots of deros and hookers and mannequins were rife. A couple of galleries in the capital were holding exhibitions by 'hot new talent'; wall to wall pictures that looked much like those that I had done in my youth. I tried not to be angry; I wished them good luck. You couldn't accuse these little buggers of theft; they'd just say it was parody. Had I not done the same myself, stolen ideas from those who went before me? The cracked lens was cheeky though. The cracked lens was pushing it. Nobody knew enough to imitate the rip.

Dean was still reigning supreme. You couldn't escape the woman; I read in the papers that an exhibition of her work was touring the States; the normal headlines graced the tabloids; *Dean's Boozy Weekend Getaway, Dean's Boob Booster, Dean in Spicy Sex Scandal.* I didn't fantasise about meeting Dean; had no wish for a confrontation with the Barbie doll. When it came to Dean I wished for something different; I wished for a time travel machine, Dr Who's phone box, so that I might zap forward ninety-nine years to see which one of us would fade and which one of us would last.

*

I paid regular visits to Lolly and Stuff, who were always glad to see their 'favourite' (read: only) granddaughter. Every now and then Lolly would talk Grout into wheeling her round to my place for a cuppa and a chat; it was good for the old dear to get out of her usual environment. She liked what I'd done with the place.

"Immense," she commented, admiring my great wide rooms, my high ceilings which seemed to stretch infinitely upwards. "So spacious."

And she would take off in her wheelchair and grab a few doughnuts, leaving tyre marks burnt into my carpet, while Grout looked disdainfully on.

I brought Stuff round sometimes, too, when the old dear sounded too lonely. I would walk across the bridge to fetch her, take her arm, and lead her tap-tapping over to the north side. ("The north!" she would exclaim, "so foreign!") She would feel her way, blind, around my home, marvelling at the gigantic appliances, the great over-sized furniture, the enormous table at which I sat. Her hands felt through the stack of paper I penned my words upon.

"Where on earth did you get sheets this size Celia? Will you read me a bit of it dear, when it's done?"

I promised I would have a Braille brochure made especially for her.

Whom did I attract, as I headed headlong from middle age into old age towards death? The odd fidgety academic who wanted to do a PhD on yours truly; *Deconstructing Doom: The Woman and the Myth,* or *Who's Views: Self and Other and the Question of Representation in the Work of Celia Doom.*

I used to get a bit frisky when these folks called by, would fart and pick my nose and say, *'What does that mean?'* when they told me of the titles that they had dreamed up. No tea and biscuits for these folks, I made them take *me* out to lunch, they had the money, university grants, scholarships and such like. I'd drag them down to Tim's Diner and order several sausage rolls and a couple of pies, smother the lot in tomato sauce and sit there scoffing, while they jabbered on about French Feminist Theory or Postmodernity or Marxism.

They made good photo fodder, these twitching pseudo-intellectuals; they winced when I held up my camera, but did not want to risk offending me by disallowing the picture and so in every shot their faces are split by grimaces which they hoped would look like smiles, their eyes look panicked. They are rabbits caught in the headlight's glare. I never gave them photos of myself, I never volunteered any information; I was a closed book. I gave nothing away. I took down their addresses, promising to be in touch, and then I would send them these photos of themselves through the post. I could imagine them, tearing open the envelopes, hoping for some gem from me, some witty reminiscence, something nobody else knew, and finding, not Celia, but themselves.

These were the long slow years when my joints began to ache and creak, the years when I began to slow down like a clockwork toy grinding to a halt; I did not rage against the dying of the light, rather I felt myself fading into that good night, like a light bulb being gradually dimmed. My white hair faded to grey. Various delivery services still operated in our area; each morning I would open the front door and step out onto the porch to find that two newspapers and a pint of milk had materialised during the night, as if by magic. The thin little PDT lay beside the thick healthy newspaper produced by the enemy; the *Spectator.*

I would make my morning cuppa, spread the newspapers open upon the kitchen table, and pore over the black printed words. Nobody would be able to accuse me of being out of touch with current events; I kept a little scrapbook full of clippings, penned "News of the World" on the front in black ink, and sometimes brought it out to discuss the goings on of Planet Earth with my visitors. Silly, maybe, a time-filler. Perhaps I should have tried to find something better to do. As much as I hated to admit it, the "Spectator" was my link to the world outside Provencia's ring roads, the world beyond. The PDT was a bit of light comic relief.

As well as the desired deliveries which arrived on my front porch every morning, I also received mountains of junk mail, leaflets and pamphlets which piled up on the front porch and blew out onto the street. These were mostly advertising for various mail order joints that wanted to sell me egg-slicers, fairy-lights, exercise-bikes, aromatherapy oils, books on reflexology and Fung Shui, 'face massagers.' These brochures were scattered with happy men and women demonstrating use of the product and were often accompanied by quotes from satisfied customers, *Never felt better, so easy to use, saves me hours every day, don't know how I functioned without it, I feel like a whole new woman.* With most of its businesses having gone under years before, Provencia is a prime target for companies selling these items that we need to be convinced are fundamental to our well-being; those who have remained here, whether through choice or through necessity, like to pride themselves on being up with the times, they do not like to think that anybody living elsewhere has anything they don't have. When Provencia's revival arrives, they tell themselves, we do not want to be caught lacking; they fill their homes with these gadgets, I watch them through their windows, fiddling about with their electric toothbrushes, sitting before their heaters with the little fake flames and the fake hot coals, warming their hands, waiting for a brighter day.

I lashed out on a few goodies myself; I liked the feeling that presents were going to arrive on my doorstep any day. It gave me something to look forward to each morning.

Photography still occupied much of my time and attention. I forced myself to partake of certain duties every day, simply to keep myself ticking over, as thought I feared I might stop, finally, once and for all, like a clockwork toy with nobody to wind it up. I took a set number of photos every day, I developed a set number of shots. Sometimes I felt as if I was carrying the weight of the entire world on my back, like Atlas. There was no mistaking the fact that I was winding down; the curtains were drawing slowly across the stage of my life, the actors were preparing to leave via the nearest exist. I was waiting for my standing ovation. But the pageant wasn't over yet. The script had yet to deliver its last ludicrous twist.

XXVI

Arty was a man who had been on fire for years. Combusting slowly, torturously; a man trapped in his own hell. After he and Angie had relocated to the capital, he thought that he might forget Lucinda. She was living back in the capital too, in her old house, and he could have refused to see her again, he could have written her off entirely. But he still went around to visit her. He still sent her on photo missions, back to the old haunts, more Doom photos, get me more. Something inside compelled him helplessly in her direction, he still had to see her, still had to deal with her. He felt that there was unfinished business between them.

They'd made their money off Project Doom, they'd done quite nicely, thank you very much, and the project was little more than an excuse to be by her side. He went to her house almost every Sunday to discuss 'Doom direction'. She'd given up the porn, retired. She was no spring chicken. He liked that. He loved it. He loved the lines on her face, loved the odd grey hair that sprouted out through the blonde, loved the way her tits were beginning to sag. Just a little. Reassured her that there was no need for surgery or bleach.

The years had done nothing to diminish his ardour; if anything, they had only intensified it. At first he had loved the act but gradually he had come to love the woman behind it. In the beginning, the kick used to be knowing that he could spend all day with her, the goddess, in the flesh, and then go home and watch her perform on his little TV screen. Knowing that he could see both sides of her. Now the kick was anything, any small part of her, any tiny memento. He stole strands of long blonde hair from her hairbrush and slipped them inside his wallet, he picked up toenail clippings he found lying about on the floor, he took her soap from the shower because it had been against her body. Dead skin might have rubbed off on it. Detritus and dust. He collected these little pieces of her like a man intending to cast a spell. He had even (and here he blushed at the memory) stolen a pair of her knickers from her washing line, like a simple ordinary pervert. But an ordinary everyday pervert he was not. He didn't want only her body; he wanted her heart and her mind, her soul if she still had one, if it had not been sold to the porn industry.

He burned. He yearned. He pined. When he was with Lucinda, you could almost see it, the flames licking out the top of his head, dancing. The more he couldn't have her, the more he wanted her. Her presence in his life only seemed to make it worse. He had been hoping to grind her down over time, but the weeks had turned into months and the months had turned into years. He couldn't believe, didn't want to believe, that his love would go unrequited, that he would die unfulfilled. That he'd wasted the best part of a decade in futile longing.

*

And Angie?

The fury which had held Angie upright for years burst like a balloon and she deflated, the air hissing out of her in a thin stream. She went to bed one day and she refused to get up. At first Arty thought that she was kidding, she was only pretending to lie down and die in order to secure herself a bit of attention. He tried to chide her out of it.

"Come on, don't be so bloody pathetic. You can't just lie there for the rest of your life."

But his wife wasn't moving.

"Come on Angie. Stop being silly."

But she was done with the world. She'd had enough, given up the ghost. Her muscles atrophied; she wasted away. This was the flip-side of the fury, this inertia, this apathy.

"I know you never got what you wanted career-wise, but there's more to life than conquering the art world, Angie."

She was scaring him. Her eyes were dark, as if her lights had been put out, as if she was dead inside. When he spoke to her she didn't even move, didn't even speak. Not even so much as a shrug in acknowledgement of his words. He couldn't get through to her at all. Her bedridden days turned into bedridden weeks. He brought her cups of soup, and magazines which she did not read. He emptied her bedpan and rolled her over from side to side so she didn't get bedsores. She was only forty-five. Plenty of life ahead of her. She was acting like she was ninety odd, retirement home stuff, crank up the heating and sit about staring at the walls.

"It's enough to drive any man to adultery", thought Arty

*

Arty Hartman was not a man given to direct confrontation. He was a scuttler, a crab; he approached issues sideways, pincers ever ready to sharply nip anybody who threatened his often fragile ego.

He took a deep breath. He looked down at the floor.

"Lucinda," he said. "The wife's not up to much these days and…"

"And what?"

"Well you know all these years, you taking the pics, the Doom thing, in many ways it was just…."

"Just what?"

"You know."

"No. Know what?"

"An excuse."

"An *excuse*? An excuse for what?"

Did he have to spell it out? He swallowed the shreds of his pride.

"An excuse to be near you, Lucinda."

"*Near* me? What would you want to be near me for?"

"Because it started out as lust but now I love you Lucinda."

The ground did not swallow him, the sky did not fall.

"But Arty," she said, "why didn't you say this years ago?"

*

And as she lay in bed, Angie plotted. For she was only playing dead, lulling her husband into a false sense of security. Arty might have known a lot she didn't; but she knew a thing or two Arty had no inkling of. She'd been watching him for years. Had hired a Private Eye back in the good old Provencian days. She had pictures, hundreds of them, pictures of Arty and that big dumb chesty blonde with the dark glasses, whose name she knew, Lucinda Fortune, pictures of them huddling in that old motel room, pictures of the blonde taking pictures, pictures of Arty signing Celia's name. She had all the evidence. She'd been saving up. This lying in bed thing was just a way to make him think she'd given in; it had allowed her time to plan her comeback. And if they tried to implicate her? She'd say she knew nothing; sure, she'd helped Celia out when she'd actually been *staying* with them, but as for continuing the myth when that fat old giant disappeared? She'd had no hand in that. She still had a few journo friends who'd be only to happy to spill the beans. Exposure of this fraud was just a telephone call away.

She picked up the phone, she dialled.

*

Finally, utterly, completely satiated, Arty returned home to find his wife whistling to herself, watching TV and eating pizza from the box.

"Angie?"

She smiled at him. He smelt of sperm.

"You're up, darling. You're out of bed."

He couldn't help but feel a little disappointed.

"Couldn't stay there forever, could I?" She replied. "I had work to do."

"Wait till tomorrow," she thought.

The silly little bugger wouldn't know what'd hit him.

XXVII

I shuffled out onto my front porch in my nightgown and slippers, wondering what I might find to add to my little *News of the World* scrapbook today. I found myself.

Great Doom Fraud Exposed, screeched the "Spectator".

I felt as if I'd just been punched in the gut.

Sources today reveal that over a decade's worth of photos touted as being the work of this country's most notorious photographer, Celia Doom, are in fact forgeries. It has been proven that the vast majority of works supposedly taken by Ms Doom were in fact the work of porn star Maude Blightman, who goes by the stage name of 'Lucinda Fortune'. The scheme was said to be master-minded by Arty Hartman, one time manager of Ms Doom, who, following the disappearance of the real Celia Doom, encouraged Ms Blightman to take the photos to which the Doom name would be signed. Police are currently said to be debating whether to press charges against the pair.

The *Provencia Daily Times* was twenty-four hours behind; the same news, just a watered-down Weaslified version. So much for a peaceful old age. The quiet I had enjoyed for over a decade was shattered. The next morning my house was swarming with journalists trying to get the true story, from the mouth of Doom. I shut my windows, pulled my curtains across, locked my doors. I was a fortress under siege; I raised the drawbridge, added crocodiles and sharks to my salt water moat. But I couldn't shut out Lucinda. She came knocking in the middle of the night, when all the journalists had gone home. Groggy with sleep, I pulled back the door and saw her standing on my doorstep. She was tired from night-driving, she'd come across from the capital, to bring me a gift in gold paper, all tied up with a silver bow. She was all apologies.

"You've every right to be angry, Celia."

"What do I have to be angry about?" I asked. "You've thirty times the talent I have. I'm flattered that you thought to sign my name to the back of those photos."

"That was Arty," she said. "We were a team. *Are* a team."

"You're intending to continue then? Masquerading as me?"

"No," she said quietly. "My days as you are over. We're an *item*, I mean."

An Imitation of Life

"What about Angie?"

"Exhibiting," she said. "This 'exposure' resulted in positive publicity for Angie and she's holding a show consisting of a few of those splatter paint works of hers. Who does she think she is? Jackson Pollock?"

She shook her head. "I shouldn't criticise Angie," she said. "I'm sure she's very talented. But Celia..."

She handed me the gift she had been holding.

"This is for you."

I opened it in front of her. It was a jewellery box, covered in pink flowers and fairies. When I opened the lid it let loose with its tinkling music. A tiny ballerina rotated in time to the tune.

"Gee," I said. "Just what I've always wanted."

"My mother gave it to me," she said. "It's the next best thing to an heirloom. I thought you should have it."

And then she did the unthinkable. She removed her sunglasses. Her eyes peered out at me; one black one white. Just like mine. Then without another word, she turned on her heels and away walked my mother.

*

I did the noble thing. There was talk of an official criminal investigation. I got them off the hook by issuing a formal statement saying that I'd condoned the whole thing all along, sure they may have been taking the shots, but I *let* them use my name. There were two of us, I said. It was a double act. But I bow down to Lucinda. She was the one with all the talent. At the end of the day what does it matter who was behind the art? What's in a name? We were both responsible. Lucinda and me; me and Lucinda. Three of us, if you include Arty.

That was the night I sorted through all my boxes of photos, making three neat piles; the good, the bad and the atrocious. All these were soon to wind up in the attic. But when I had completed my task, I had something left over. I had shots which did not fit these categories; I did not know whether these were the best or the worst, all I knew is they were beyond my own system of classification. These are the shots which will never be put up for sale. They are beyond judgement. I opened the jewellery box and laid them inside. I pulled aside the grandfather clock. I picked up a hacksaw that had been left behind by one of the builders and I cut out a piece of the wall and I pushed that jewellery box inside. I shunted the clock back into place. It guards its secrets like a good sentinel; its blank face does not let on what it is hiding.

And the box lies in wait for whoever may come next.

*

It was shortly afterwards that George posted his letter, his seductive words. And a few days after the letter arrived he came knocking at my door in person.

"You're the good guy here. They want to see a selection of genuine articles. The National Modern, Celia. It's not to be sniffed at."

I was not convinced and I told him as much.

"Three hundred and thirty-three genuine Dooms, plus they've asked you to pen a brochure. Just a few short words."

"As opposed to long words?" I asked.

"Come on Celia. There'll be champagne and party snacks and you at the opening, looking as glamorous as ever in one of your old black tracksuits…"

"When you put it that way, George," I said. "How could a girl resist?"

It was the party snacks that convinced me, as much as anything.

I ordered in the supplies I thought I would need; a few oversized calligraphy pens from a gadget shop in the capital that specialised in such items (left-handed scissors, flowers that squirt you in the eye with a jet of water when you bend down to sniff them, blooms that danced in time to music.) From a reputable art supplier I ordered A1 paper; three hundred gigantic sheets of it, sheets across which my large right hand would go scrawling. I settled myself down at my old table, my old chair.

I picked up my pen and I began to write.

*

What am I now? And old woman sitting out on her front porch, watching the world go by. An old woman wrestling ghosts, wrestling words. An old woman waiting for the knock at the door; for the next word, for the next world, for the kindly release of death. Biding my time.

Today, I am still in bed when I hear George letting himself in. I think of all the things I could do with my day and none of them seem terribly appealing; the white pages, the blank space I have to fill seems as threatening as an executioner. I hide from the words, burying my head down under the blankets like a mole, blinking in the darkness. I must have snoozed off for a bit, for suddenly he is at the door, the harbinger of doom.

"Celia?"

Silence.

"You can't hide from me. I know you're listening."

He comes across to the bed and jabs me in the back repeatedly until I finally concede to poke my head out from under the covers.

"Whaddaya want," I snarl, somewhat unconvincingly.

"I'm done," he says. "I've taken everything I need. I just need you to say a little something about these last three."

He holds three photos in his hands.

"Some other time," I snap. "Later."

"Whenever you're ready," he says. "I'll just be waiting in the lounge."

I make him wait. I lie in bed for the entire day, curtains closed, ruminating over what a muddled old stew of a life it's been, tossed hither and thither on the storms until I learnt how to spread my... I halt; I check myself. I was no Winged Wonder. That hunch on my shoulder will never unfurl into a fine, multi-coloured plumage; I have made no pact with gravity. I never took to the sky; I was an earth-bound misfit, my legs firmly planted upon terra firma, and as much as my eyes might have gazed toward heaven from my various hells, I was always a gutter girl and never a star.

I don't rise for a cuppa at eleven, and I don't get out of bed for lunch; he stands in the doorway, holding a plate of bacon and eggs trying to lure the dragon from its lair, but this old fire-breather ain't goin' nowhere. His attempts to coax me out result only in my sliding further down under the bedclothes, wallowing in my enormous bed like a hippo in mud, snoozing the afternoon away until, when the old clock in the living-room strikes three, he enters the room and shouts my name repeatedly, until I concede to rise from my prone position, staggering to my feet, woozy from too much sleep and lack of fresh air and exercise. My polyester nightie crackles with static as I walk; at night it gives off tiny electric sparks, small crackles of light in the darkness. I am in the mood for obscenity; I dispose of whatever shreds of social nicety still cling to my person and do not bother to ask him to leave the room, I just whip off my nightgown and throw it to the floor.

"Did you have to?" asks George.

Solely for his benefit, I jiggle about as I reach into the wardrobe; my old flesh sags upon its bones. The floor shudders beneath me. George is looking a little unwell. I can't believe that it's really his last day. Then he springs me another surprise.

"Lilith's coming over soon, Celia. She wants to collect the photos to take them back to the gallery. And I thought you could give her your *a-hem* 'brochure' if you've finished it."

Eh?

" Couldn't you have given me a bit more warning?"

"I only just got the call," he says, holding out his mobile phone as if it is proof that he had no warning.

I leap into yesterday's clothes, which lie in a heap on the floor, beside the bed.

"I ain't finished my tale," I tell him.

"Best you get scribbling then," he says. "She'll be here in half an hour."

"Can't I just post it to her next week?"

"It's now or never, Celia. This'll be your only chance to convince her of the validity and worth of your story. Play your cards right and you could be in."

He needs tell me nothing more. I thunder down the corridor to the living-room with him behind me, saying, *hang on, you've got to give me some captions for these last three shots.* I pay him no heed; I have other matters in mind. I can't believe that after all my hours of fiddling about and arranging and re-arranging that my ending is going to be *rushed.* How can they expect me to find the right phrase on the spur of the moment?

In my old chair, at my old table, my pen scratches across the page, sounding like a mouse scampering across floorboards. George hovers behind me.

"Piss off," I hiss. "I can't concentrate with you looking over my shoulder" and he retires to the kitchen to raid the biscuit tin.

The self that I was draws ever closer to the self that I now am. Now I am a week away, now three days, now I write yesterday and then this hour. Now I have caught up with myself; the self that I was and the self that I am are one. It feels like gluing somebody's shadow back onto their body; it feels like finally jumping aboard the speeding train that you have been sprinting behind for years, it feels like catching up with all the other versions of yourself, the ones who are living the lives you did not. These other selves turned left when you turned right, headed east when you went west, stayed on at the job you quit, left the country that you refused to leave. All these versions of me are pulled together. Now all my selves are synthesised. Now all of us are whole.

I lay down my last word, sign my name.

I blow on my final words in order to dry the ink, then stack my pages neatly and push them to one corner of the table. I wait.

I am perfectly composed.

*

There comes a timely *yoo-hoo* from the doorway. It's Lilith, she who will judge my words. I don't believe my fate is in her hands; she'll wave her magic wand and the words will appear in print or she'll turn up her nose and this will be a story you'll never hear.

She enters my home, sniffs the air, like a dog. George follows her, playing servant to her Queen, taking her through the photos he's selected. He's neatly numbered them all, one through to three hundred and thirty. He still holds the final three in his hands. He shows her the little scraps of paper upon which he's written his captions, each corresponding to a shot. She won't let on whether she's pleased or not; she keeps him hanging on hooks.

When he's taken her through his selection he surprises me by speaking up on my behalf.

"There's another thing," he says.

"What's that?" she asks, eyebrows raised.

"That brochure you asked for," he says. "Well, she's finished it."

I look sheepishly down at the floor.

"Oh right," she says, as if the brochure is the last thing she cares about at this moment in time. "Let's have a look at it, then."

George nods at me. I walk across to the table, take the manuscript I have been working on these last six months and push it into her arms. She staggers beneath the weight of my words. The huge sheets of paper seem to dwarf her.

"What the hell is this? We asked for two thousand words, not an epic. This thing's a tome. Visitors to the exhibition will need a caddy just to wheel her narration around."

Her former sycophancy appears to have flown out of the window. She stumbles across to the sofa and plonks the manuscript down, then peels off the first page

"It's barely even legible. Half of it's red, half of it's black; it looks like a drunken spider dipped its legs in ink and sprawled across the page."

She reads a few sentences aloud. I cringe. Perhaps George was right, I think, perhaps the whole thing has been a big waste of time and I should have simply sat in my chair, waiting to die. George apologises on my behalf.

"It's not real life, of course. God knows where she gets her ideas! It's not this world she's living in. She's existing in some kind of fantasy realm. A parallel universe. She's on another planet."

Not real! I baulked. It was real enough to me.

"Nobody's claiming that this is autobiographical," continues George. "We'll sell it as Celia's novel."

Betrayed, betrayed.

"Still," George goes on. "I'll bet there are a couple of punters who'd find this stuff interesting. I guess we could edit out some of the longer passages."

"Over my dead body," I say, somewhat prophetically, for it was neither George nor me, ultimately, who swung Lilith's mind round to our way of thinking. Fate played the Joker and the Joker was death.

On my thirty-third birthday, I curled up my toes and I died.

*

When I heard the knock at the door, I was lying in bed with my eyes wide open. In the living-room, the grandfather clock with the smashed face uttered its last terrible tock.

He made no dramatic entrance. He crept into the room on slippered feet and tapped me on the shoulder. He held no sickle, although he wore a long black cloak, with the hood pulled up, hanging down, hiding his face.

Well Celia, I thought to myself. *It's time to meet your maker.*

I welcomed him with open arms.

*

There was nothing painful about dying, nothing untoward or graceless. It was easy. I simply began to leak out of my skin like vapour escaping a glass jar and I floated away, up high, near the ceiling and looked back down upon my old withered flesh, lying upon the bed like a shed cicada shell. The body that I left behind was just something I rented; it no more belonged to me than a house for which you must still pay the landlord. In the crematory,

292

it will burn and burn, it will give off energy as it combusts, it will spark with heat and light. Its game is over, but I am still right here. Never *did* get to receive that special letter from the Queen. And George's last three photos went without words. I never saw what they were.

*

One last detail. As death hovered over me, preparing to deliver that last final kiss, as he prepared to take me with him, I stared up, I saw beneath his hood. The shock of that alone was enough to finish me off. No skull, no skeleton, no black charred bones.

His face was a mirror of mine.

*

They embalmed me first. Wanted me looking good for the funeral. You can guess who did the honours. I was back in the hands of Mr Vitra again, much to his delight. He had me right where he wanted me, where I couldn't protest. I was the biggest challenge that had come his way since he'd done his old Dad; there was so much of me I took three times as long to do as his average corpse. They say he sobbed as he drained the blood from my body, said that the twisted old codger even held some small spark of affection for me in his body. Drove all the way over from the capital; brought all his equipment with him, and he bloody well embalmed me in the front room of my own damned house.

Posthumously, of course, my words were more valuable than gold dust. George didn't give them to Lilith, he *sold* them to her; cash enough for him to comfortably retire on. Lilith paid a private printing house to churn out three thousand copies and give the thing a gold cover upon which was printed, in bold black type, *Imitation of Life: A Novel* and beneath that the names, *By George Gregson* and underneath *that*, in tiny print *With Celia Doom*. The little prick! He'd turned me into a sort of *ghost-writer*. Jacob was laughing his head off.

"Always someone to steal your glory, eh Celia?"

"He'll be laughing on the other side of his face soon enough," I said. "Don't think he'll be getting any rest in that old house of his. He can expect a little more than creaky floorboards and rattling chains, believe you me."

They say that more Provencians crossed the divide the day of my exhibition opening than in any other day in history. They piled into their beat-up old vehicles and trailed across the mountains in order to pay homage and to check out this exhibition George had put together. I had to hand it to him, after all that farting about he'd come up with a nice cross section: lots of early work, some from my 'experimental' phase, a few Hollywood stills and a couple from my final decade on earth; the trannies, the vagrants, the deserted city streets. It reminded me of that horrid old programme they still run on the telly; Celia Doom, *This Is Your Life*. Was. I must face facts. I shall slide gently from the present into the past tense. My race has already been run.

Outside the gallery, a white banner blew about in the breeze, proclaiming in loud red ink: *Doom: From the Womb to the Tomb*. Only one thing was missing. The best shots, which I refuse to show, which I have left behind, hidden where only the right kind of minds may find them.

It was one of the few exhibitions in which the photos were exclusively mine. It was pure Doom. These snaps had come straight from my attic; there was no mistaking their authenticity. These were not fakes; these were the real thing, rips and all. This show was the silver lining; but there was also a cloud. Coinciding with this, my last show, was a major exhibition held at the Royal Gallery, one street over from the National Modern, and the title of the exhibition was this; *Masters of Photography*. We were outshone by *them* again. Their opening day coincided with mine. They drew all the crowds; they outnumbered us thirty to one. And how many of my pictures hung on their gallery walls? Answer: not a one. And the salt that was poured into the wound? That bloody Claudia Dean, the one mistress admitted to the rank of master. Six of her baby shots were placed on the wall, bubbas doing ridiculous things; perching in flower pots, bathing in custard, dressed up as bumble bees. Greeting card material. My final thoughts on the matter? If that's what makes you a master then I'd rather not be one.

*

And now it is time for the third and final funeral. Mine. It was a circus. George had gone overboard in the publicity stakes, *this whole death thing is gonna be just great for sales,* he said to Lilith, and to the TV cameras he said, *Celia was not only a great photographer, but also a very close friend. Her death has struck a blow to the heart of the country and nobody feels that blow more keenly than I. Her thorny exterior hid a heart of pure gold. Within that gigantic, lumbering body lay the gentlest of souls.*

What a crock! I was laughing before I was even in my grave. My coffin would not fit in our one Provencian church and so the service was held outside. My funeral was conducted in an empty field, out near the town cemetery. Helicopters were whirring overhead, securing footage of Doom's death from an aerial vantage point. Clive was there with Sharon and Mack; Arty and Lucinda were present, Angie stood on the other side of the field, wailing in true drama-queen style, blubbering, doing her best to upstage me at my own bloody funeral.

My tenacious old grandmothers were in attendance, Stuff with her cane, and Lolly with her nurse. They'd seen a few funerals in their time, those two old iron-willed witches had. They'd outlasted not only all of their friends but also all of their family, as if they'd drunk the elixir of eternal life or entered into some infernal pact with time. The hippies next door put in a show, as did a few of my vagrant friends and various other anonymous fans I'd never even known existed.

Ashes to ashes, dust to dust.

Stifled sobs, crocodile tears. Lolly and Stuff started up with the farting, still trying to outdo each other. Grout stood reluctantly by, arms folded across her chest. Then six grown men lugged my hefty coffin upon their shoulders, pushed me back into the hearse and drove me to the crematorium.

Wait! I must describe the events that took place in the sky at the time of my death. As the Reverend said his solemn piece, as Arty clutched onto Lucinda's hand, as Angie wailed, as George and Lilith thought of what my death would do for exhibition numbers and book sales, the skies overhead grew dark. The moon, on its slow, steady circumnavigation of the earth, passed in front of the sun; an eclipse. Sun, moon and earth lay in a straight line; syzygy.

The guests looked at one another and granted me a moment's respectful silence, as if I were somehow responsible for this celestial event. And then I was shunted into the back of the hearse and driven right around Provencia till the car hit the main road out; we'd got no crematorium, had we, so I had to be taken to combust in *theirs*. I had specified in my will that I must not be buried; I wanted to burn and burn.

You'd be best not to deny the dead their wishes.

*

But I don't need to tell you who got their hands on my body before my body got to the fire. No escaping them; before the hearse had pulled into its parking spot they were hauling me out of my coffin, *we'll take care of her, thank you very much*; my friends in white coats had my body in their clutches at last. They cut me open. They took my heart, yanked it out of my chest, like some primitive tribe intending to make a meal of it in order that they might digest my courage, my power. They sliced open my head to take a good look at the brain which lay, like broiled cauliflower within the cage of my skull. They noted that it was disproportionately small in comparison with the rest of my body. They lopped off limbs, tore out vital organs, ripped my hair out by the roots.

There was an element of frenzy about the whole thing; they were having their wicked way at last. They pillaged me. And then they burnt what was left over, which wasn't a hell of a lot, threw me onto the flames like a widowed Indian bride, like an effigy. The smoke from my remnants spiraled upwards, like steam from the funnel of a ship. The ashes were given to George, who had asked for them. Not that they're my ashes specifically, just a pile of anonymous ash scooped out of the crematorium, all that's left over of me mingling with all that's left over of all the others who were burnt before.

George tipped the ashes into a Perspex urn and put them on display at the gallery; they're in the final room, the last thing you see before you hit the gift shop selling tacky souvenirs: ceramic plates to hang on the wall, a hole in the middle, like a record, and pictures of our fine city all around the outside; snowdomes with a Provencian cityscape inside, again, the hole at the center; mugs with my face on them; Celia Doom calendars which display, on each page, one or other of the many third-rate photos I took during my lifetime. (These calendars were printed up shortly before I karked it. When I heard the word about them, I tried to convince the publishers responsible to place shots of me, personally, in negligee, bikini or evening dress upon each page, a Celia for every month of the year, a parodic page three girl. They showed no interest, the fools.)

My heart was never exhibited publicly; instead they pickled it, put it into a jar and donated it to the State hospital, where it sits in some dusty back room, all but forgotten. What with all the fuss they made ripping it out of me, you'd have thought they would have made something of a trophy of the thing, but there it sits, the heart of Doom, relegated to obscurity. The other pieces of me were used for 'research purposes' whatever the hell *that's* supposed to mean. I suppose some scientist got a hefty grant to examine my cells through a microscope, pick me apart, decode my DNA.

My headstone went up, just as I had wished it, in the space I marked long ago, lying next to Lettie. Upon the stone they engraved the immortal words:

Here lies the space where Celia Doom
Would have been buried if we'd had the room.

Life after death, what a hoot! Such fun we have, Jacob and I, such laughs, haunting George, retribution for his theft of my words. When he opens the fridge door the milk bottles spontaneously shatter and the eggs explode in their cartons. When he shaves, one of us bumps his elbow; he cuts himself every day. He never sleeps at night, what with the TV 'mysteriously' switching itself on, with the volume, of course, cranked up full bore. Jacob bounces his head off various surfaces, like a basketball, creating a diverse variety of thuds which are not unpleasant to the ear. And now we stomp up and down in *his* attic, and he's the one who sits down below listening to the thud of our footsteps. The Wife's going out of her mind. George knows it's me, of course, though he doesn't suspect that Jacob is also in on the act.

"Okay Celia," he says. "I'll admit that I've done you wrong. I took credit where credit was not due. I stole and I lied. But I can't turn back time. I can only try to make it up to you."

But how do you make it up to a ghost? He leaves silly offerings, hoping to make amends; plates of cookies and glasses of milk, plates of eggs and bacon. But we are pure spirit; we have no use for such gifts. I have not yet caught sight of Barry or Lettie or Ed, though no doubt they linger on somewhere. You think that we dead have lain down and died, but we're even livelier now than we were when we were living.

This haunting is one of my small compensations. The other is the knowledge that he'll never find the golden shots which still sit behind the grandfather clock. As specified in my will, my old home was put up for sale. The proceeds, along with the rest of my cash, were donated to the Royal Photographic Society.

*

There's a young woman living in my old place now. I do not know her name. When they put the family home up for sale she was the one who bought it; she used a sum of cash she'd inherited from her grandmother. She kept all my furniture, crockery, household appliances and home furnishings, even though it wasn't practical. She said she liked the thought that I'd used all this stuff before her, my hands had gripped the handles of those cups, my paper had rested upon that table, my bum had plonked down upon that chair. She even kept all my old clothes.

The house was going cheap, of course, like every other home in Provencia. It was worth next to nothing. This new inhabitant of my old home has something of a photographic flair herself; perhaps one day she will stumble across my shots, my hidden treasure. Perhaps she will know I left them there for her; for whoever should come next. Although she does not broadcast, I note that she appears most fond of Lettie's old record player, and often slips on one of the old black records and dances around the living-room like a mad thing. Switches the player to repeat. She's got my Leica too, by the way. It went up for sale at the same time as the house; auctioned. She placed the highest bid.

Sometimes I sneak quietly into my old home and watch over her, the one who will take the next shots. Although I make no noise when I enter the room, she always looks in my direction. She knows that I am there. I hover, watching, when she is working in the darkroom, down in the cellar. Sometimes the bulbs burst. And when the lights go out, I am always there.

There is no end to us, really, we great gals. We stretch back in a line to the dawn of time and onwards to the crack of doom. 'Scuse the pun. You think that you're the only one, but you are never alone.

XXVIII

In the end we are left with the name. The words were not our own; we stole them from the Greeks. Photography; light added to writing, writing with light. It was a way of capturing and manufacturing images; a way of freezing time and a method of achieving immortality, both for your pictures and yourself. My name became synonymous with this word. I was photography and it was me.

It wrote me with its right hand. I wrote my name in light.

In the front room there's a record playing, spinning ceaselessly around on the turntable. When it gets to the end of the song, the needle picks itself up and returns to the beginning. Outside the window, the stars go wheeling, hurtling, across the sky. The old song plays on, the record spins, the axis turns, the universe expands and recedes, terrible Father Time keeps ticking. The script is spoken true to every line that has been written.

*

We keep the date that fate has penned. As you started off with me, so too will you end.

*

The first word you heard came from my mouth. And the last word?

*

It was mine.

www.ingramcontent.com/pod-product-compliance
Lightning Source LLC
Chambersburg PA
CBHW021039030726
47496CB00006B/1608